Claudia,

Wife of

PONTIUS PILATE

Other books by Diana Wallis Taylor

Journey to the Well
Martha
Mary Magdalene

"Diana Wallis Taylor has written another stunning and powerful novel of controversy, romance, and rebellion, this time focusing on the life of Claudia. . . . Meticulous research, drama, and passion hold readers to the page in this exquisite tale of inspiration and intrigue. Buy a copy for yourself and for a friend."

—**Karen O'Connor**, author of *When God Answers Your Prayers: Stories of How God Comes Through in the Nick of Time*

"Expertly researched, Diana Wallis Taylor's *Claudia, Wife of Pontius Pilate* takes the reader into the very heart and soul of an obscure New Testament woman whose few but compelling words have captivated readers for centuries. Inspiring and imaginative."

—**Susan Meissner**, author of *The Girl in the Glass*

Past Praise for Diana Wallis Taylor

"Taylor has crafted an exquisite love story about Martha, sister to Mary and Lazarus, in this absorbing biblical drama. Readers will embrace Taylor's vision of Martha as a woman of imagination, dignity, and grace. This book will enhance and further every woman's spiritual journey."

—*RT Book Review*, 4½ stars TOP PICK

"Taylor pays great attention to detail in order to provide verdant descriptions of this world to create an eye-opening expedition into the past. Fans of increasingly popular biblical fiction centered around recognizable characters . . . may have found themselves another author who can write historical inspirational novels of strong, faithful women."

—*Booklist*

"Excellent historical detail and a respectful yet not cloying retelling of this story make *Martha* an outstanding choice for readers looking for inspirational biblical fiction."

—*Historical Novel Review*

"This imaginative retelling of the biblical story of the Samaritan woman who encountered Jesus at Jacob's Well traces her path to that fateful meeting. Set in a vividly depicted first century, this absorbing debut novel is populated with charming characters."

—*Library Journal*

Claudia,

Wife of
PONTIUS PILATE

a novel

Diana Wallis Taylor

Revell
a division of Baker Publishing Group
Grand Rapids, Michigan

© 2013 by Diana Wallis Taylor

Published by Revell
a division of Baker Publishing Group
P.O. Box 6287, Grand Rapids, MI 49516-6287
www.revellbooks.com

Printed in the United States of America

Library of Congress Cataloging-in-Publication Data is on file at the Library of Congress, Washington, DC.

ISBN 978-0-8007-2138-1

Scripture used in this book, whether quoted or paraphrased by the characters, is taken from the New King James Version. Copyright © 1982 by Thomas Nelson, Inc. Used by permission. All rights reserved.

This is a work of historical reconstruction; the appearances of certain historical figures are therefore inevitable. All other characters, however, are products of the author's imagination, and any resemblance to actual persons, living or dead, is coincidental.

The internet addresses, email addresses, and phone numbers in this book are accurate at the time of publication. They are provided as a resource. Baker Publishing Group does not endorse them or vouch for their content or permanence.

13   14   15   16   17   18   19   7   6   5   4   3   2

To the women who,
with love, finesse, and courage,
stand behind their man,
even in adverse circumstances.

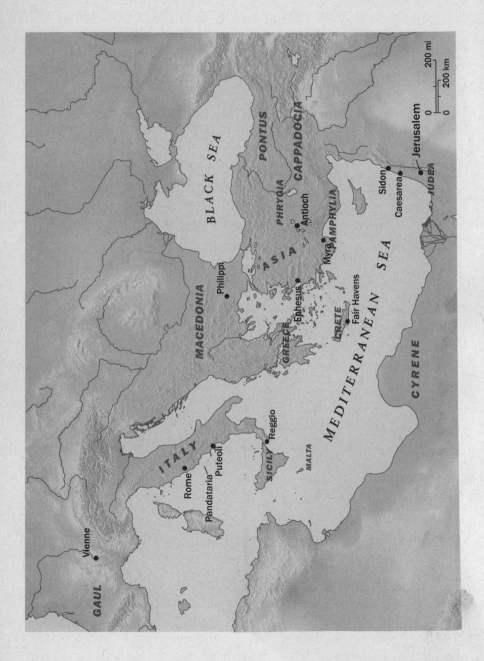

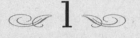

1

"Who is my father?"

Claudia was sitting with her grandmother on a stone bench in the garden reviewing her Latin. It wasn't the first time she had asked, but so far she had never received a satisfactory answer.

Scribonia sighed heavily. "You need to ask your mother that question."

"I have and she won't answer." Her mother, Julia, ordered her out of the room whenever she persisted.

Her grandmother rose, her mouth prim with impatience. "I have things to attend to. Practice your words on your tablet." Without a backward look, she hurried away.

Claudia frowned and put the wax tablet down on the bench. *Why don't they tell me who he is?* She knew it was not Tiberius, her mother's third husband. He had divorced her long before Claudia was born. She would find out somehow, she resolved, and reluctantly returned to her Latin.

With the question lingering in the back of her mind, it took little to distract her from her studies. A butterfly settled delicately on a leaf and fanned its wings, but the beautiful creature suddenly flew off into the blue sky before she could capture it. A small lizard caught her eye and she watched the creature's quick spurts of movement until it disappeared over the wall. The pear that Medina, their Syrian slave, had given her looked delicious, so she took a bite and savored its sweetness.

The garden in the center of their villa, which had been a refuge for her as a small child, now seemed confining as she grew older. Now, on her twelfth birthday, she longed to see something of the outside world. The faint sounds of the city could barely be heard, muffled by the thick walls of the villa. It was more a prison than a home, for only their two slaves were allowed out to go to the market for food.

Why are we not allowed to leave the villa?

She knew from her grandmother that the town was called Reggio and it was far from Rome.

Her grandmother told her their living situation had been ordered by the emperor, Caesar Augustus, Claudia's grandfather. A shadowy figure she'd never met but, from her grandmother's description, feared.

"Our lives depend on his favor," Grandmother had divulged to her one day. As the years ticked by, her mother and grandmother grew more apprehensive when speaking of him.

Julia's soft laughter came from the atrium. The latest soldier was leaving. Claudia was old enough to know why they came. Julia ignored her mother's admonishments, but when they argued, Claudia, who had learned to move quietly and listen unobtrusively from the shadows of the latticed pergola, learned many things.

"Augustus has eyes and ears everywhere, Julia. Sooner or later there will be a reckoning. The soldiers put their careers and perhaps even their lives in jeopardy. Do you not care, daughter, about the consequences? What of your daughter?"

Julia sighed impatiently and waved a languid hand. "They are probably transferred to another post. Don't be so gloomy, Mater."

Scribonia shook her head and walked away.

It didn't seem to matter how often or strongly her grandmother voiced her opinion, Claudia's mother brushed it off and did as she pleased.

Hearing voices, Claudia rose from the bench and slowly approached the atrium, her soft footsteps making no sound on the tile floor. They were arguing again.

"Julia, you are forbidden their company. Do you wish to be sent back to the island, or worse?"

"I should be allowed a little entertainment, Mater, seeing as we must spend day after boring day within this accursed villa."

"He could take his wrath out on the child. Only the gods know why he did not order her exposed to the elements when she was born. Obviously she is not the child of Tiberius. I'm asking again. Whose is she?"

Claudia held her breath, and stood in the shadows, watching them.

"Perhaps someone resourceful who bribed the soldiers guarding me."

"Sempronius Gracchus? He got himself exiled to the African coast for his efforts."

Julia shrugged and Scribonia pressed her case. "If you hadn't treated Tiberius the way you did, you wouldn't be here now."

"Tiberius was a harsh man, Mater." Julia nearly spat out the words. "All of Rome knew he and Vipsana were expecting their first child. Do you think he wanted to divorce her and marry me? Tiberius hated me and we were both miserable. When our infant son died, it was the end of any pretense of marriage."

Scribonia paused and regarded her daughter, her eyebrows raised. "It was your actions that caused your father to send the divorce papers in Tiberius's name. The letter Gracchus wrote to your father asking him to allow you to divorce Tiberius was his undoing. He was too ambitious and your father knew it. He had the choice of executing you for your adulteries or banishing you from Rome. Your father spared your life, but what kind of a life do you have?"

Julia waved a hand in frustration. "You didn't have to come, Mater."

"I petitioned Augustus because of the child, Julia, and I am your

11

mother. I felt you needed me after five years on Pandataria, that barren island. Be thankful he allowed you to come back to the mainland."

Julia's shoulders sagged. "That was lonely, but it is lonely here too." She turned to her mother. "I'm sorry. It was a sacrifice for you to come."

Scribonia reached out and put a hand on her daughter's shoulder, a rare sign of affection for the austere woman. "I worry about Claudia. What will become of her?"

Julia shook her head slowly. "I don't know. She is his grandchild, whoever the father."

"A common Roman soldier, not a man of nobility. Was it Gracchus?"

Julia didn't answer. Scribonia's gray eyes flashed. "Well, it is done and you have an illegitimate child."

"Why should it matter now? My father has not contacted us or acknowledged her."

"Julia, in three years Claudia will be old enough to be married. What then?"

"I don't know."

Scribonia gave a huff of exasperation, then noticed Claudia standing in the shadows, but didn't acknowledge her as she hurried away. "I must see to the weaving."

Claudia regarded her mother. Julia had dyed her hair a red-gold in the fashion of the day. The blue *stola* enhanced eyes that could twinkle like tiny stars when she was excited, yet brood darkly when she was angry. She was still beautiful. At meals her mother ate little, always priding herself on keeping her well-proportioned figure. As Claudia gazed at her now, she wondered if her mother was eating enough; her face had a gaunt look.

Julia turned and faced her daughter. "Spying on us again, Claudia?"

"I heard you and Grandmother from the garden."

"Your grandmother worries about too many things."

"Mater, it's my birthday. I was wondering . . ."

"Speak up, child, I am not one of the gods that I can read your mind."

"I would like a pet to keep me company. Please, Mater?"

Julia looked at her daughter thoughtfully. "A pet?"

"I'm too old for the other toys. I want something alive."

Julia tipped Claudia's chin up with her finger. "I don't know, child. I will speak with Medina. Perhaps when she goes to the marketplace she can find something."

They had been allowed two slaves when they came to the villa, a pauper's household to be sure, but the women were grateful Augustus allowed the help. Medina did the cooking, looked after the house, and helped with the weaving of cloth for their clothes. Cato, from the African coast, had to do everything from repairs on the villa to taking care of the small garden.

Medina had been Claudia's nurse since she was born. She would do anything for her. Claudia hurried to find their servant.

The slave listened and folded her arms. "Your mother does not consider costs. The allowance from your grandfather is small. It barely covers our needs. A pet would require food, *Dominilla*."

"But it is my birthday and that is the only thing I want. I have no one to play with. It would be company."

The servant's face softened. "This is no life for a child. If your mother did not tell you no, I will see what I can find."

Claudia hugged her. "You are so good, Medina."

The woman gave her a skeptical look. "Don't let your hopes rise too high."

Claudia returned to the garden. Medina was thrifty. She would bargain for day-old vegetables and fruit, and upon rare occasion, fish, then prepare them as only she could into tasty dishes. Claudia was sure Medina would find a bargain for her pet too.

She sat on the bench, swinging her feet, and let the name Sempronius Gracchus sift through her mind. She liked the sound of the name. Perhaps he was her father, but remembering that he'd been banished to a distant post, she wondered, Would she ever meet him?

2

Claudia's birthday dinner seemed their usual meager meal. She watched her mother and grandmother quietly eating pieces of goat cheese, and hoped for a word about her request for a pet. Then Medina brought in a stew with small chunks of goat's meat, cabbage, and garlic. She had bargained for something special for Claudia's birthday. To her surprise, her second treat was a slice of melon. She smiled up at Medina, who smiled back. Nothing had been said about the pet she requested, and when her mother and grandmother were not looking, she raised her eyebrows in question. Medina gave an imperceptible shake of her head. Claudia's shoulders slumped. She had been told not to set her heart on it, but she had hoped.

Julia broke off a piece of the coarse, dark bread. "Did the courier come today?"

Scribonia shook her head. "Not yet."

Julia sighed. "My father sends so little. Medina is thrifty in the *subura*, though it grieves me to have her shop in a poor man's market." She turned to Claudia. "I wish you a happy birthday. Enjoy it while you are young, for soon you will have no control over your life."

Claudia nodded. Her mother was in a strange mood.

After dinner her grandmother rose. "Let us go to the garden. It will be cooler there."

Claudia dragged her feet. She would spend another boring evening, sitting and practicing her embroidery.

They reached the garden, where Cato stood solemnly with a basket in his hands. He waited for the three women to be seated and then with a nod from Scribonia, set the basket at Claudia's feet. Small whimpers emanated from the container.

With trembling hands, she removed the woven lid and gasped. A tiny mongrel puppy lay on a bed of rags, so thin, its ribs were showing. It looked up at her with large, luminous brown eyes.

She carefully lifted the puppy and cradled it against her chest. The small creature quivered and she could feel its rapid heartbeat.

"It was abandoned, Mistress," said Cato. "The runt of the litter. It was all Medina could find. It will need much care."

"Oh, Cato, I will care for it!"

Her grandmother reached out and stroked the puppy with one finger. "He may not live, Claudia, he is very weak."

"Oh, thank you, Mother, Grandmother. He will live. I will tend him day and night."

Her mother merely exchanged glances with her grandmother and gave a slight shake of her head.

Claudia stroked the soft fur and spoke quietly to the puppy. "I will name you Felix—*lucky*—for I am lucky to have you."

Julia rose from the bench and looked at the puppy. "Take him to the kitchen and see if Medina has some goat's milk for him."

Claudia gently placed Felix in the basket and, with Cato following, hurried to find Medina.

His tummy full, the puppy promptly went to sleep and Claudia gently placed him in the basket. Claudia looked up into the slave's dark brown eyes. "Oh, thank you, Medina."

Cato's deep voice behind her answered. "Pray the gods will have mercy on the small creature."

Claudia gave one last look at her puppy and hurried to the *Tabilnum*, the alcove where the statue of their household god, Vesta, stood and prayed fervently for her puppy to live.

⸎

Felix began to fill out, and while his extended stomach seemed out of proportion to the rest of his body, Claudia thought him beautiful. She spent hours throwing a knotted rag for him and laughing as the puppy waddled after the toy and tentatively explored every inch of his limited surroundings. Claudia held him and talked softly as the puppy licked her cheek with his small wet tongue.

Felix made the long days bearable.

⸎

It was obvious that Julia was losing weight. One evening as she picked at her meal, Scribonia shook her head in exasperation.

"Daughter, we must call for a physician. You cannot go on like this."

"We cannot afford him, Mater. I am just tired. I need to rest."

"You rest most of the day, Julia. This is more than weariness. You are ill."

Seeing her mother's condition and her grandmother's anxious looks, Claudia felt a knot of fear form in her stomach. What was this illness that was draining her mother of her beauty and leaving her so weak?

Her mother walked the house now on Scribonia's arm, moving slowly as they talked together. Claudia continued to listen to their conversations every chance she had. She had to find out what was happening. Today her mother sounded so sad.

"My father must not know. It is best, Mater. I am dead to my children by Agrippa and to the rest of Rome. If my father thinks I am ill, he may take the child."

Scribonia nodded. "Who knows what he will do? He can be cruel."

Julia's tone was bitter. "I can still remember crying out to you as his soldiers carried me away to the palace."

"Such is the law of Rome, daughter. The children belong to the father. I had no say."

"I know, but what was my life, Mater? At least Agrippa gave me children to fill my life. Yet now they are forbidden to contact me."

"Were you happy at all with Agrippa?"

"Agrippa was kind to me. He didn't die a natural death, I'm sure of it, but I had no time to mourn, for Father ordered me to marry Tiberius. I was a mere pawn in his scheme of things."

Her grandmother sighed deeply. "That is our world, daughter."

Just then Medina returned from the marketplace and put down her bag of meager gleanings.

She faced Scribonia. "*Domina*, I met the courier. He brought a scroll along with the coins."

Scribonia took the scroll, and as she read the words, she put out a hand to brace herself against a chair. She handed the scroll to Julia who read aloud, "Agrippa Postumus murdered."

Julia clutched her throat as a cry of anguish wrenched itself from her mouth. "He was my only living son."

Scribonia put a hand on her daughter's shoulder. "This means trouble, Julia. Someone ordered this, but who would do such a thing?"

Julia turned to her, and Claudia could see agony in her mother's eyes. "It was not my father. It was one who fears for his succession to the throne. Who else hated anyone related to me?"

Scribonia's eyes widened. "I have contacts in Rome. Surely someone will send me further word." Her voice softened. "I am sorry for your loss, daughter, and in such a way."

Medina interrupted. "There is more news. It is whispered in the marketplace that the emperor is ill."

Julia wiped her eyes. "My father is ill?"

The slave nodded.

Julia gasped. "Mater, we must seek the favor of the gods for his recovery. If he dies . . ."

Claudia felt her mouth go dry. The fear in the room became almost palpable as her mother whispered, "Tiberius!"

Clutching the now squirming puppy tightly for comfort, Claudia tried to piece together what she'd heard. She knew Tiberius hated her mother and divorced her. She knew why her mother was banished from Rome, for she had seen with her own eyes over the years the men who had come and gone from the villa. Something terrible was coming, but what she didn't know.

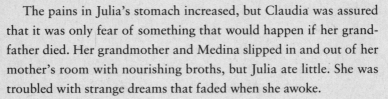

The pains in Julia's stomach increased, but Claudia was assured that it was only fear of something that would happen if her grandfather died. Her grandmother and Medina slipped in and out of her mother's room with nourishing broths, but Julia ate little. She was troubled with strange dreams that faded when she awoke.

Whatever her mother feared, Claudia sensed it would change her world forever.

3

The days moved with monotonous regularity as Julia faded before their eyes. Her once voluptuous figure wasted away and her skin seemed almost translucent. Medina brought herbs from another slave woman who practiced healing remedies, but they did little to dull the pain. Claudia sat by her mother's bedside for hours. Sometimes her mother would speak to her of her own childhood. Past and present wove themselves together as she rambled. Sometimes Claudia held her hand and watched her mother sleep, as unchecked tears ran down her cheeks.

One morning, as Claudia's thirteenth birthday approached, there was a loud knocking at the entry door of the villa. Claudia, hearing the commotion, slipped out to the atrium just as Medina went to open the door. The servant was brushed aside by a large Roman soldier.

Behind him, she could see a large company of soldiers on horseback.

The soldier was powerfully built, nearly six feet tall. His very presence filled Claudia with terror. His face was hard as his eyes rested briefly on Claudia.

"I am Captain Marcus Laurentius. Gather the household for an announcement from the emperor."

Claudia ran down the columned peristyle that surrounded the garden and found her grandmother in the doorway of her mother's room. Her eyes widened at Claudia's hasty approach. "What is happening?"

"Grandmother, a soldier is here with a message from the emperor. We are all to gather in the atrium. Come quickly."

Julia struggled to rise. Claudia and Scribonia helped her from her bed and pulled a stola over her head to cover her wrinkled tunic. Between them they supported her as she struggled to walk toward the atrium. She gathered what little strength she had, insisting she could stand alone. Finally, the three women faced the captain. Medina, who had taken the puppy from Claudia when the captain barked his order, stepped back into the shadows, her eyes wide with fear as she too listened.

Captain Laurentius opened a scroll and began to read—

"By order of the Emperor, from this moment, the woman, Julia, is to be confined to one room in this villa. She is to have no visitors, including family . . ."

Scribonia interrupted him. "Can you not see she is ill? She is already confined to her room . . ."

The captain gave her an angry look. "Be silent, woman." He continued reading.

"The woman, Scribonia, will accompany the child, Claudia Procula, to Rome where she will relinquish the child to be brought up in the palace as the granddaughter of an Emperor. Her grandmother is to return to her own villa in Rome. The servants will remain to care for the villa in Reggio, but they are not to contact the woman Julia in any way. Soldiers will be posted to make sure this edict is followed. By order of the Emperor, Tiberius Caesar."

He turned to Scribonia, his eyes narrowing. "The emperor requests that I inquire if the girl, Claudia, is a virgin."

Claudia leaned against her mother, who put a protecting arm around her.

Scribonia drew herself up and stated tersely. "The child is a virgin."

"You will swear to this?"

"I will swear by Vesta, the goddess of our household."

20

Claudia clung to her mother as her eyes pooled with tears. "Grandmother and I have to leave the villa? Why must you stay behind? Will I not ever see you again?"

"You will not see me again, child. But it is as the gods will it. Remember me as well as you can, and know that I have loved you." She held Claudia close and kissed the top of her head.

At that moment one of the soldiers wrenched Claudia away from her mother.

"Where is her room?" The captain asked tersely.

Taking Julia by the arms, two other soldiers began dragging her down the peristyle.

"Medina!" Scribonia cried out.

Medina thrust the squirming puppy back to Claudia and hurried ahead to show them the way to Julia's room.

Her grandmother held Claudia firmly as she cried out and tried to follow her mother. Scribonia's voice broke as she addressed the captain. "This is a monstrous thing to do to."

"Are you questioning the orders of the emperor, madam?" His face was like cold marble.

Scribonia, with a slight shake, bowed her head and remained silent.

He rolled up the scroll. "Gather your belongings. You have one hour before we leave. There is a covered coach outside. Have your servant prepare food and drink for your journey."

He stepped to the doorway of the villa and ordered his men to dismount and wait.

Medina returned with one of the soldiers and looked at Claudia with tears in her eyes. The other had been left behind to guard the door to her mother's room.

Scribonia grabbed Claudia's hand. "Come, Claudia, Medina, we have work to do, we must obey the captain."

Captain Laurentius stepped outside to wait.

Scribonia reviewed their storage room, but there was little food in the house to prepare or, for that matter, to leave for Medina and Cato.

"No messenger has come, Domina."

"With Augustus dead, our allowance has evidently been stopped by Tiberius. I pray to the gods that he will make provision for you and Cato."

Medina looked up at her mistress. "Domina, what will happen to the Lady Julia?"

With her back to her granddaughter, Scribonia answered sadly. "I don't know, Medina. I don't know."

A look of sudden understanding came across Medina's face. "Yes, of course. I will see to her mother so the child will not worry."

Claudia, her voice breaking, cried, "What will happen to my mother?"

Scribonia took her by the shoulders. "Listen to me and listen well, child. You must be brave. Your mother is dying. She wished to keep this from you as long as possible, but now you must know. You have seen how ill she is. It took her last ounce of energy to face the captain. She has but a few days to live. When the time comes, Medina and Cato will see to her burial. Perhaps we will bury her ashes in the garden by the roses she loved. You are of royal blood, the granddaughter of an emperor. You must learn early in life to endure what comes your way. We, as women, have no other choice."

Her grandmother's arms dropped to her side and she looked away. "This is the revenge of Tiberius. Your mother knew it would come someday. There is nothing we can do."

"And Medina? Will I never see you again?"

Medina moved closer and tilted Claudia's face with one finger. "When I have done what I must do, I will find a way to come to you."

Claudia could only nod before throwing her arms around her grandmother as great, wrenching sobs shook her body. For once Scribonia did not push her away.

※

Felix whimpered as if sensing the emotions of his mistress when Claudia placed him gently in his basket.

"The dog must stay," the captain said harshly as he saw Claudia standing in the atrium, holding the basket.

She felt panic rising and looked anxiously at her grandmother. Scribonia took a deep breath, then in a calm voice, asked the captain. "Do you have children, sir?"

The captain eyed her suspiciously. "I have a young son. Why do you ask?"

Scribonia's voice was soft and submissive. "Sir, we wish to be obedient to the emperor's command, but the child is the granddaughter of the Emperor Augustus. She has had no companions her entire life, save this small dog, and her mother has been wrenched from her. Would you be merciful to her and leave her this small comfort?"

The captain looked at Claudia's stricken face. His voice softened for a moment. "I suppose she can keep the dog, but she must be responsible for it." The hard look returned as he spoke to his men from the doorway. "Mount up. We must deliver our charges safely to Rome."

The large group of soldiers and their weapons would insure the women's safety as they traveled.

Claudia glanced around the only home she'd ever known for the last time. She turned longingly toward her mother's room, but a sharp look from the captain erased all thought of going that direction. Anger smoldered in her heart. How could Tiberius be so cruel? She would hate him until her last breath.

Medina had packed a little bread, some cheese, a couple of pears, some dried apricots, and a goatskin bag of diluted wine. It was all they had in the house. Captain Laurentius seemed surprised at the paltry bundle Medina handed her mistress.

Claudia gathered her courage and faced the captain. "Who will provide food for Medina and Cato?"

"The emperor has made provision for the slaves to care for the villa. You need not concern yourself with them."

Claudia, her emotions in turmoil, took her lead from her grandmother, gathered her courage, and held her head high as she carried

Felix to the coach. She stopped suddenly, staring at the large ornate wagon that had been pulled in front of her. There were carvings in wood on the side panels. Figures that Claudia felt must be gods and goddesses. The wagon was pulled by two huge mules that stood stamping their feet and snorting.

Scribonia put a hand on her shoulder. "It is a *carpentum*, child. Those of our praetorian class travel in these. It will protect us from the sun and make our journey more comfortable." She bent down and whispered, "I'm surprised Tiberius allowed us this extravagance."

Medina and Cato waved bravely from the doorway and Claudia struggled not to cry in front of the soldiers. She would be brave, as her mother and grandmother were.

As the coach pulled away and began the long journey to Rome, her heart felt constricted. Why did the emperor suddenly send for her and what did he have in store for her at the palace?

4

There were two small windows in the coach, and in spite of her anguish, Claudia found herself looking out at things she'd been unable to experience while confined in the villa. They passed through the marketplace, alive with the sounds of goats bleating, birds squawking, and merchants calling out for people to buy their wares. She smelled the bread, hung in long narrow loaves, and the tangy fragrance of onions and garlic. Baskets of crisp apples, juicy plums, and quinces lent their colors to the variety of foods. Claudia had never seen such bounty.

The coach stopped in the shade while the captain bought white bread, olive oil, some honey to mix with wine, hazelnuts, grapes, and two apples and brought them to the coach.

On the road, villagers stepped aside to let the coach and soldiers pass. Some glanced up, their eyes wary. Others gazed at the ornate wagon with open curiosity. They didn't know who was in the coach, but it was someone important.

Claudia wrinkled her nose. The heavy smell of fish filled the coach as they passed the fish market.

Her grandmother was keeping a close eye on her and, when Claudia was on the verge of tears again, would point out something for her granddaughter to observe.

"The sea is so vast, and so many shades of blue. It is calm now, but when the storms come up, it can be hard on a ship, for the waves are very large."

The wind drafts from the Tyrrhenian Sea wafted through the coach. Claudia lifted her chin, remembering the times she had smelled the sea from the window of her room. Once the road passed so close to the shore she could see the waves crashing on the beach.

"How far must we travel, Grandmother? It is so hot."

"As I recall, when I came from Rome to Reggio, it was around five hundred kilometers. It will take several days of travel." Scribonia sniffed. "We will get there tomorrow at this speed!"

The captain drove his men at a steady pace. The roads, the pride of Rome and succeeding emperors, were relatively smooth. The large stones that topped the clay and gravel bed had been fitted carefully, sloping down from the center so rain would run off.

They passed *mansios*, where fresh horses could be procured, but the captain did not stop. He kept up his pace until they reached a second mansio, offering food and lodging.

The next morning, after little sleep, Scribonia combed Claudia's hair and bound it up in a knot at the nape of her neck. After a very unsatisfying breakfast, they were glad to be on the road again.

Her grandmother took something on a chain out of her cloth bag and held it out to Claudia. It was a ring of bright silver in which two vines intertwined. Two small emeralds imbedded glittered in the sunlight.

"Your mother had a premonition and asked me to give this to you if anything happened to her."

Claudia looked down at the ring. "It is beautiful." Something to remember her mother by. "I've never seen her wear this."

"She had her own reasons." Her eyes held Claudia's. "It was given to her by your father."

Claudia's eyes widened. "My father? Who was he, Grandmother?" She leaned forward and waited.

"I truly don't know, child. There were other men besides Gracchus, Claudia, do not set your heart on one. Keep this to yourself. If anyone asks, say only it was a gift from your mother."

Claudia sighed and nodded her head, fingering the ring as she looked out the window of the coach. She would keep it forever.

When they stopped again to rest the horses, Claudia was grateful to be able to stretch her legs and let Felix sniff around in the grass. Some of the younger soldiers looked at her and whispered among themselves. Coarse laughter followed and she felt uncomfortable. Other than Cato, she had not been around men. Her mother made sure she was in her room or the garden when a Roman soldier was in the villa.

Scribonia took her arm and drew her away into a small copse of trees to relieve herself. As they approached the coach again, Claudia kept her eyes down and, picking Felix up, quickly climbed into the coach.

"Why do they look at me like that, Grandmother?"

"Because you no longer have the body of a child, Claudia. Have you not noticed?"

Claudia looked down. She had been aware she was no longer flat-chested but had no means to look at herself further.

"You have experienced the time of women. You are young, but your body is now capable of carrying a child. In two years you will be married." She gave a huff of irritation. "At least I hope Tiberius will see to that for you."

The next mansio where they stopped for the night had a little more to offer. When the innkeeper saw the ornate coach, he gave them his finest room and brought out his best meal—broiled fish and fresh fruit, along with the white bread Claudia enjoyed.

Scribonia looked carefully around their room for any signs of the unwanted creatures she'd seen in the last mansio and couldn't find even a spiderweb. She nodded with satisfaction, and this time they got a good night's sleep.

Before they left, her grandmother spoke to the captain about the men staring at Claudia. He listened and walked over and ordered his men to look the other way when the girl was out of the coach. The threat of the emperor's displeasure was enough to deter them.

After two days of being shaken by the rapid pace of the coach, Scribonia finally approached the captain.

"We travel with great haste. Is it to deliver us in as short a time as possible or do you fear we are in danger somewhere along the road?"

She waited while he regarded her for a moment, his face bland. Scribonia had given him no trouble and had not complained, but when the captain looked away, Claudia thought for a moment he would not answer.

Then he gave a small shake of his head. "There is no danger that we know of. I wish to accomplish my mission for the emperor as soon as possible."

When she continued to regard him, he hesitated, looking off in the distance. "My wife expects a child at any time. We've lost two children at birth."

Scribonia smiled kindly. "I see. Then I will pray for your wife's well-being, Captain Laurentius, and for a healthy child."

"Thank you." He thought a moment. "I wish to ask forgiveness for my attitude when I arrived at the villa, Lady Scribonia. I was under the impression that I would find a different situation."

"You are forgiven. I can imagine what you expected, given the gossip at court."

He gave her a wry smile but was silent.

As they rode, Claudia considered the captain's abrupt question back at the villa as to whether she was a virgin. She realized it meant in some way that she had never been with a man. What would she be doing with a man if she had been with one? How did that mean she could bear children? She glanced at her grandmother, fearful of asking the wrong question and bearing her grandmother's anger. Yet, if the emperor arranged a marriage for her in two years, there were

28

things she needed to know. Why had her mother or grandmother never talked to her about this? Claudia gathered her courage, and blurted out her question.

Scribonia frowned. "Your mother has not spoken to you of this? She promised me!"

Claudia hung her head. "No, Grandmother."

Scribonia regarded Claudia for a moment. "Well, you should be told what you need to know before marriage, for your own protection. There are men at the court who would find a young virgin worthy of more than a passing interest."

Claudia leaned forward expectantly to listen.

5

When grandmother finished, many things became clear. Her mother had given birth to her, but there had been no brothers or sisters. Why not? There must be some way a woman could prevent children if she chose. Claudia decided she would never have children. They either died or were wrenched away. Would that be her own fate—married off to a man old enough to be her father, just to get rid of her? The emperor had taken responsibility for her, but what did he have in mind? She put her fearful thoughts away from her and as she watched the scenery go by, she contemplated the amazing and somewhat frightening things grandmother had just told her.

The fifth day they passed outlying villages, and when they stopped midday to rest and refresh themselves, Claudia could see the walls of the city of Rome gleaming in the distance.

"Why did the emperor send for me when he hated my mother so?"

"I don't believe he means you harm, child. He would not have gone to the trouble to bring you all the way to Rome."

"Can you come to the palace with me, Grandmother?"

"The emperor ordered me to return to my own villa and that is what I must do."

"Will you be able to visit me?"

"That is up to Tiberius. It is possible."

Claudia studied her hands, resting in her lap. The scene with the soldiers dragging her mother away from her down the hall haunted her. "What do you think has happened to, to . . ." She could not finish the sentence for the tears that suddenly pooled in her eyes.

Claudia could see that her grandmother was close to tears herself.

"She was near death when we left, child. I don't know. At least she has Medina and Cato. They will see to her when the time comes."

"I miss her, Grandmother. Why would they not let me say goodbye to her?"

"The hatred and anger of Tiberius. He would strike back at her any way he could."

"Because of things my mother did?"

Scribonia stiffened. "There are certain matters best left alone, Claudia. Do not mention your mother in the palace. You could incur the wrath of Tiberius against yourself. He is being benevolent toward you now because of your grandfather. Don't create problems."

Claudia nodded and wiped the tears with the corner of her shawl. Medina and Cato would take care of her mother—her grandmother said so. Claudia sat up a little straighter. She would show Tiberius that she could behave like the granddaughter of an emperor.

❧

As they entered the city itself, its sheer size overwhelmed her. Everywhere people seemed to be hurrying. They passed other carpentums like theirs being driven through the streets as well as litters, carried by slaves. She saw Asian faces with almond-shaped eyes and men and women with dark skin from the African continent as well as Roman citizens going about their business. Everyone seemed in a hurry.

Her grandmother pointed out marble buildings that Augustus had built when he was emperor. "We are approaching the Palatine where the palace is situated."

"I am frightened, Grandmother. Please do not let me go to the emperor alone."

"You must be brave, Claudia."

Claudia balled her fists. "I hate him for what he did to my mother."

Scribonia took her by the shoulders and gripped them tightly. "Do not be foolish enough to vent your feelings to the emperor. He has the right of *paterfamilias*, supreme master over your life. The gods have brought you here for a reason. You must pray, seek your destiny, and they will protect you. You must obey Tiberius at all costs."

Claudia hung her head. She had seldom been the recipient of her grandmother's anger.

"Yes, Grandmother. I will do as you say."

Scribonia sat back in the coach. "When you are settled, I will come to see you."

"Will Medina come to Rome?"

"I have found Medina to be extremely resourceful over the years. There will be a way."

The coach came to an abrupt halt. The captain barked orders to his men.

Claudia looked out at a flight of stone steps leading up to the most beautiful building she had ever seen. The door of the coach opened and the captain gestured toward the entrance of the building.

"The palace of the emperor. Please alight and follow me. Servants will take care of your possessions."

Claudia clutched Felix. "Even my dog?"

The captain suppressed a smile. "It will be taken to your new quarters. You will see it again there. You may not enter the presence of the emperor with an animal."

A large Nubian slave approached the coach and, after a few words from the captain, nodded and reached for the dog as other slaves gathered her belongings. Her grandmother pointed out her own possessions, to be left with the coach.

They followed Captain Laurentius into the entrance hall, and Claudia looked around her with wonder at the beautiful mosaic floor and the statues placed in alcoves. They passed into a large courtyard with a glistening pool in the center. The captain led them toward another archway into a small waiting room.

A figure came to the doorway. "Captain Laurentius. You have returned with your charges."

The captain saluted, striking his heart with his fist in respect. "I have. As ordered, I have brought the Lady Scribonia and Claudia Procula, the granddaughter of Emperor Augustus."

He turned to the women. "This is Lucius Aelius Sejanus, prefect of the Praetorian Guard and advisor to the emperor."

Scribonia acknowledged Sejanus with a nod, and Claudia caught something in her grandmother's face that troubled her. Claudia bowed her head in respect, and when she looked up again, the man was regarding her thoughtfully.

"So you are Julia's daughter. You will find the palace a far cry from Reggio."

The tone of his voice made Claudia wonder what he meant and his perusal of her made her uncomfortable. She suppressed a shudder. Something told her to be on her guard.

Sejanus waved them toward the door, indicating they were to enter the reception room where Tiberius waited.

❧

Claudia's heart pounded as she approached the man her mother feared so much—the man who had given the order to separate her from her mother. The emperor was heavily built with broad shoulders and appeared to be of average height. His hair hung down his neck, and the eyes that regarded her were unusually large. His expression seemed neither gruff nor pleasant.

He watched them approach and held up a hand for them to stop. After studying Claudia intently for a moment, he beckoned her to come closer.

Glancing over at the captain, he nodded his head. "You have made good time, and brought your charges safely. You are dismissed."

"Majesty." The captain saluted and left the room. Claudia sensed he was eagerly heading home to his pregnant wife. She hoped he would be in time.

The emperor turned his attention to Scribonia. "We meet again. What has she learned in your care?"

Her grandmother lifted her chin slightly and looked directly at the emperor. "She reads and writes Latin, and is capable of simple mathematics. She embroiders well, and has helped with the weaving of cloth under our slave, Medina."

Tiberius looked thoughtful. "I can see Augustus was wise in allowing you to remain in Reggio."

As Claudia listened, it occurred to her that truly it had been her grandmother who taught her the things she knew. Her mother had been kind, occasionally loving, but occupied more with herself.

Sejanus regarded Claudia. "She is tall and well proportioned. Pleasing to the eye. If you adopt her as you stated, my lord, she will be a worthy match for the man of your choice."

Claudia bristled. Must they speak of her as if she were not there? Her grandmother gave her a warning glance.

Scribonia spoke up, her voice quiet and carefully respectful. "The child was concerned as to your purpose for bringing her here, Majesty, as was I."

"She is the granddaughter of Augustus and therefore it was not expedient to let her languish in Reggio. I'm gratified to learn she has not followed the path of her mother."

Claudia struggled to hold back angry tears. "My mother loved me and was kind to me. I was not even allowed to say goodbye to her."

Her outburst seemed to amuse Tiberius, but then his face hardened. "You have spirit. That is good, but your life is in my hands and I shall do as I promised your grandfather before his death. You shall be instructed in matters of the court and a suitable husband will be found for you. There shall be no more outbursts."

As his eyes pierced hers, Claudia heard the edge in his tone and realized her error. This was not a man to anger.

He turned to her grandmother. "You are free to return to your family villa."

Scribonia bowed her head in submission, then turned and briefly put a comforting hand on Claudia's shoulder before leaving the room.

Tiberius clapped his hands and a servant appeared. "Milo, take the girl to her quarters and assign a slave girl to her."

The servant bowed low, and Claudia, after a last anguished look at her grandmother's receding figure, walked slowly after him.

She looked up at the beautiful frescos painted on the walls they passed and marveled at the variety of mosaic tiles in the floors. She hurried to keep up with Milo wondering at the labyrinth of corridors they followed.

She faced a new life. What would the days ahead hold? Then, remembering Felix, her heart quickened. Would she really see her dog again? She hurried after the servant.

6

Milo stopped and opened an ornate golden door, sweeping his hand for her to precede him into the room. "Your quarters, Dominilla."

Dominilla. Young mistress, as Medina called her. She entered the room and immediately a small furry head appeared over the edge of her basket. With a glad cry, Claudia ran to sweep her little dog into her arms. Felix wiggled with happiness and licked her face over and over, making small whimpers. "Oh Felix, they have let me keep you."

"The room is agreeable, Dominilla?"

She looked around at the walls, painted with more frescos, birds, and flowers. There was a sleeping couch, an ornate polished wooden chest for her clothing, a cupboard, a small table with an olive oil pottery lamp by the couch, and in front of the window, a small desk and chair. Walking over to look out the window, she observed green plants, a small, tinkling fountain, and an area of soil with flowers. A place to take Felix when the need arose.

"It is a beautiful room. I didn't expect anything like this."

Just then a slender young woman entered and bowed to Claudia. She appeared only a little older than Claudia, with ebony hair cut to her shoulders. She regarded Claudia with expressive dark eyes.

"This is Hotep. She is to be your personal slave, Dominilla. She will see to your needs and acquaint you with life in the palace."

Hotep's smile was tentative and Claudia bravely smiled back.

"Thank you, Milo."

He turned to Hotep. "Have her ready this evening. She will be dining with the emperor and his guests." In a moment he was gone and the door closed behind him.

Claudia's thoughts raced. She'd never had a slave of her own. How was she to begin? She hesitated. "What does Hotep mean? It is a beautiful name."

"It means peace, Dominilla, and a safe place."

Hotep was aptly named, for that was the one thing Claudia needed above all others.

"Let me prepare your bath, Dominilla. You have been traveling long and you must be tired. After the bath, will you desire rest? It will prepare you for the evening ahead."

What could prepare her for the evening ahead? She must appear to be submissive to the man she hated.

Hotep opened a drawer and pulled out a small linen undergarment, a soft white linen stola, a silver belt, silver sandals, and a scarf of soft, fine blue linen.

Claudia ran her hands over the finely woven garment, so soft to the touch.

Then Hotep opened the cupboard and produced Claudia's small wooden chest.

"Oh, it's safe." With a sigh of relief, Claudia opened it, and Hotep came closer to look at the contents: a rag doll, a feather, a leather ball, and small wooden blocks with letters on the sides.

The chain and ring slipped outside of Claudia's tunic.

Hotep's eyes grew wide when she saw them. "This is very beautiful."

"It was a gift . . . from my mother." She unclasped the chain and reluctantly placed it in the chest, under the doll. It would be safer there.

Hotep opened a panel in the wall to reveal a room with a mosaic tile bath and white, thick linen by the steaming water, then helped her out of her travel garments.

As she luxuriated in the warm bath, Claudia realized that the emperor had provided all this for her comfort. She was to become his ward and he would arrange a marriage for her. She tried to feel grateful, but sorrow filled her heart. Could she ever forgive him for what he had done?

After a brief time of rest, she rose to prepare for dinner. When she was dressed to Hotep's satisfaction, she sat at a dressing table in the same room. Hotep not only arranged her hair so it beautifully framed her face, but added a small tiara.

"You are beautiful. The emperor shall be pleased."

Embarrassed, Claudia changed the subject. "When did you become a slave, Hotep?"

The girl seemed startled by the question. Perhaps no one ever asked. She closed her eyes a moment before answering. "I was taken from my parents in Egypt when I was eight. My mother and brothers were somewhere on the ship, but I never saw them again. I think my father is dead."

Claudia looked toward the window, the pain still so fresh. "I was taken from my mother too. She was dying."

"But you are not a slave."

"No, but my life will be controlled by the emperor. He will marry me off to the man he chooses to favor and I will have no say."

"Ah."

Claudia turned and regarded her servant earnestly. "I have never had a friend, Hotep, and I am in need of one."

"I belong to you, Dominilla, but if it is your wish, I shall be your friend." She sighed. "One needs friends in this palace of shadows."

Someone knocked at the door and Hotep hurried to open it. Claudia expected Milo to be waiting to take her to the emperor's dining room. Felix leaped from his bed, barking furiously and snarling at the intruder. It was Sejanus.

Felix had never attacked anyone before. The eyes of the prefect flashed with anger. He kicked out with his foot, but Felix was too quick. He jumped out of his way.

"Take this animal away, now!"

Hotep grabbed the dog and retreated to the back of the room, trying her best to still the barking.

Sejanus took Claudia's arm, none too gently, pulling her into the hall and firmly closing the door.

Claudia's heart pounded. The last thing she wanted to do was anger Sejanus.

7

He stalked down the hall and she had to hurry to keep up with him. Finally he stopped and studied her. He was a formidable figure due to his height and build. He looked almost regal in his formal white toga with a border of purple denoting his high rank.

"Quite a transformation," he finally said. "Not a child, a woman. The emperor will be pleased."

"It does not matter if I please him." In spite of her resolve to hold her tongue, the words from her heart slipped out.

Sejanus stopped suddenly and she quailed inside at the anger in his face.

"Beware of what you say, Claudia Procula. The walls have ears for treasonous words. Do not presume to speak your mind when you feel like it. It is dangerous."

His eyes glittered and bore into hers, causing her to shudder. She had spoken foolishly. "I—I'm sorry, my lord. The emperor made me leave my home and my mother—and she is dying. I don't understand how the emperor could do such a thing."

He stepped back, judging the sincerity of her words. "The emperor can do what he pleases and he does not have to give a reason. You will be forgiven this time, for you are no doubt weary from your travels. Be grateful you are here. The emperor has chosen to be kind to you as the granddaughter of Augustus."

"I thought my grandfather didn't know I existed."

"He had eyes and ears everywhere, as does Tiberius. He knew when you were born. It was Julia he was angry with."

They continued walking the long hall. "Did he know who my father was?"

He halted his steps again. "Why do you ask?"

"There was one my mother spoke of occasionally, but he was sent away. The African coast I think."

"Sent away?" He paused a moment. "Ah, Gracchus. He was fortunate only to be exiled these many years. The others were forced to commit suicide." At her quick intake of breath, he laughed. "Have you been told he is your father?"

She lowered her eyes. "I suspected, because of some things my mother said, but I don't know."

"Waste no more time on that foolish imagination of yours. Gracchus is dead."

Claudia felt like someone had suddenly punched her in the stomach. "He is dead?"

"The emperor received word that the noble centurion has died. A disease of some kind. Come, we are almost there."

As Claudia entered with Sejanus, she was aware of eyes suddenly turned on her.

Six people, as well as the emperor, were arranged around the huge dining table set with graceful glassware. Claudia was led to a covered chair near Tiberius. The women did not recline as did the men. Tiberius waved a hand in the air magnanimously.

"Ah, my esteemed guests, here is Claudia, the granddaughter of Augustus. Since she has no living male relative, I have claimed paterfamilias over her. She will be as my own daughter."

She wanted to run but remembered her grandmother's words to act like the granddaughter of an emperor. She smiled shyly at the guests and sank down on her chair.

"She is lovely."

"Julia's child . . ."

She felt the men's open appraisal and glanced around at the women. They smiled graciously, but their eyes were more guarded.

Fighting the anger that rose up once more, she vowed that while she had no choice over her life now, one day she would be free and live far from the emperor.

Tiberius introduced his guests—Apicata, the wife of Sejanus; Levilla, the emperor's widowed daughter-in-law; and two senators and their wives. She couldn't remember all their names so merely nodded her head in acknowledgment. There was one empty chair and she realized that they were waiting for one more female guest.

Suddenly a woman swept into the room, elegantly dressed, her chin uplifted, her manner arrogant. She was slender and had kept herself well, but her face betrayed her age. Deep lines had formed on either side of her mouth. It was evident she smiled little. She was an old woman, but somehow important, for Tiberius merely growled, "You are late, Livia."

Claudia's eyes widened. This was the stepmother who had made her mother's life miserable as a child.

"Nonsense, Tiberius," Livia murmured. "An empress is never late."

He did not respond but glared at her and nodded toward Claudia. "Your charge, madam."

Bearing the perusal of the empress with patience, Claudia waited for her response. The empress gave a slight shrug and turned her attention to another guest.

Claudia shrank inside. What was ahead for her in this place?

The emperor murmured to his steward, Milo, and servants appeared quickly to remove the sandals of the guests. Then they passed around basins of water and linen cloths so the guests could wash their hands.

A stream of servants came with huge platters of food—succulent pork cooked with grape leaves, black olives in a relish sauce, stuffed pigeon, artichoke hearts and fresh asparagus steamed with carrots, chopped walnuts and fennel, platters of various goat cheeses, and small loaves of white bread, crisp on the outside and soft inside.

Claudia had never seen so much food. Watching and listening had gained Claudia much information growing up. Now she let her eyes rest on the other guests. Levilla seemed nervous and from time to time would glance across the table at Apicata when she thought no one was looking. Sejanus watched Levilla covertly under his bushy brows.

When the table had been cleared of all the main dishes and wiped carefully with a cloth, water and towels were again passed to the guests to cleanse their fingers from the main meal.

Then there was a lengthy silence while Tiberius made the accepted offerings of wine, salt, and meal to the *Lares*, the gods that watched over the household.

Tiberius deferred to the gods out of custom, but there was no reverence in his face. When he had finished, the servants came again, this time with platters of sliced pears in a honey sauce and bowls of fresh cherries and apricots.

Full of rich food, Claudia tried to hide a yawn as she felt the weariness of her journey. Tiberius had obviously been observing her, for with a wave of his hand, he excused her.

Hotep appeared at her elbow and said quietly, "Let me lead you to your room, Dominilla."

The Empress looked across the table. "You are to come to my quarters after the midday meal, Claudia. We will discuss your education."

"Yes, your Majesty." She bowed her head to Tiberius and acknowledged the other guests before following Hotep. She glanced back at Sejanus, but he was not looking at Claudia.

His eyes were on Hotep, and his mouth was curved in a slight smile.

8

Claudia wearily followed her maidservant through the maze of halls and was glad to reach her room. After they entered, Hotep bolted the door, almost fiercely.

"Are you afraid of something, Hotep?"

"I am always afraid, but there is one I fear most."

"Sejanus?"

Her maid looked startled. "How did you know?"

"I saw the way he was looking at you."

"He takes those he chooses and they fear to say anything. He has great authority with the emperor. You do not need to fear for no one would touch the emperor's ward."

"Oh, Hotep, how can I protect you?"

The girl smiled sadly. "The other servants watch out for me, Dominilla, but Sejanus is careful. He waits like a spider to strike when a girl is alone. There are dark places in the palace. Two of the maidservants have disappeared since I've been here."

Claudia was horrified. What could she do? Perhaps there was a way she could speak to the empress tomorrow.

She awoke the next morning to sun pouring in the window. It took a moment to remember where she was. She saw Hotep waiting patiently with a tray. The aroma of fresh bread wafted toward her. One cup on the tray held *mulsa*, a drink of water with fermented honey in it, and another held a small cup of diluted wine to dip her bread in. To Claudia's delight, there was also a fresh pear.

Claudia thanked her but said nothing of her thoughts about Hotep going by herself from her room to the kitchen.

The girl must have read her thoughts, for she murmured, "He is not here in the early morning."

After Claudia was dressed for the day, with a belt under her growing bosom for support, they took Felix to the garden. Claudia asked Hotep to tell her about Egypt.

"We had a farm, near the great river, the Nile. My two brothers and I used to cut papyrus from the marshes. My father sold it to be made into parchment. We also grew wheat and barley and had fig trees. We had two cows. My father was better off than many in Egypt. He had to give a large portion of the harvest to Pharaoh's men, but we were happy. One night Roman soldiers came from the river. They took all our food, and then took us captive. I heard my mother screaming and then she also was led away. I never saw my family again."

"Oh Hotep, I'm so sorry."

She smiled. "The gods have protected me. I am fortunate to work in the palace. That is not the fate of some of the other slave girls."

"I am glad you are here." Claudia looked at the sky. "It is nearly time for the noon meal, then I must go to the Empress."

❧

"Wait in my room, Hotep, and take care of Felix."

"Yes, Dominilla."

Once again Claudia followed Milo through the palace and found herself before another ornately carved door, covered with gold leaf. Milo knocked and was told to enter. He waved Claudia in, bowed to the empress, and retreated.

The empress sat in a large impressive chair as her two maidservants hovered nearby.

"Come closer, Claudia. Let me have a look at you."

She did as she was asked and stood quietly in front of the empress.

"You are tall for your age. When is your birthday?" She spoke in Latin, a test.

"May, my lady."

Livia smiled. "Ah, after the goddess of spring. Your Latin is good. Who was your teacher?"

"My grandmother, Scribonia."

The empress frowned. "Ah yes, Scribonia. Augustus divorced her."

"The day my mother was born, my lady." She stopped short of saying *to marry you.*

"You speak your mind. I would caution you not to be impertinent to me."

Claudia kept her face bland. "I was only stating what I know. I did not wish to offend."

The empress sighed. "You have courage. It may stand you in good stead, dwelling in this place." She leaned forward in the chair. "Have you ever been to the baths?"

Claudia chided herself for her quick tongue. She must be more cautious. "No, my lady, we, uh, remained in the villa."

"Well, then it will be my pleasure to introduce you. No Roman matron would go a day without attending the bath. We learn there of what is happening in Rome."

Claudia realized it was in her best interests to be submissive. She had a feeling the empress had much to teach her.

Livia quizzed her in Latin a little further, then discussed weaving and needlework.

"Do you sing? Play the lute?"

"I play a little, but have only sung to myself."

"We will obtain an instrument and you can demonstrate your skills. You will have a husband to entertain one day."

"Yes, my lady." Claudia did not look forward to playing before the empress.

"Come to my quarters after your morning meal, Claudia, and we will proceed to the baths." With a wave of her hand, Claudia was dismissed. Hotep was waiting.

"Have you been here all this time?"

"No, Dominilla, I took Felix out to the garden and waited in your room. It seemed that it was time to come for you, so I came."

Claudia looked up and down the hall. "You didn't encounter anyone on the way, did you?"

Hotep shook her head and smiled her gentle smile. "No, Dominilla, no one."

9

Whenever she encountered Sejanus, Claudia had a sense of darkness. Felix was a comfort but no real protection against the evil that stalked the halls of the palace. Claudia tried to protect Hotep by forbidding her to go about the palace in the late afternoon or evening.

Hotep often told her things she heard from other servants, how Sejanus filled the ears of Tiberius with thoughts of many plots against him. Those of noble rank fawned over the prefect, considering him the power behind the throne.

"He appears to be devoted to the emperor, for once, when they were traveling, part of the grotto where they were eating collapsed. Several men and servants died, but Sejanus protected the emperor with his body and saved his life. The emperor trusts him completely."

Claudia listened quietly. "But others do not?"

"No, Dominilla, those who oppose him fear his power growing and now the emperor is talking about leaving Rome . . ."

"Leaving Rome? When?" Would Sejanus be in charge of her? That was a thought that caused her heart to race.

"No one knows, but they feel he is grooming Sejanus to run the empire in his place. There is talk about the Isle of Capri where the emperor has a palace."

As Tiberius invoked the blessings of the gods and they began their meal, Claudia had a strange feeling of uneasiness. Something was wrong but she didn't know what it was. She had a strong urge to return to her room but wondered how she could do that gracefully. Was something wrong? She began to rub her head and cover her eyes with her hand. Perhaps she could feign a headache.

Tiberius was the first one to notice and she realized he watched her more than she imagined. "Are you ill?"

"No, Majesty, only a small headache."

His large, luminous eyes focused on Claudia. Finally he nodded. "Milo, escort my ward to her room."

The servant bowed and helped Claudia up as another servant quickly slipped her sandals on her feet. When she entered her room, Hotep was nowhere to be found.

She took an oil lamp and hurried down the dark hall toward the kitchen. Suddenly, in the shadows she heard voices, a girl, weeping, and the harsh voice of a man. Then there was the sound of fabric tearing.

Claudia knew the girl was Hotep and with a jolt of fear, she realized who the man was.

Choking down her fear, she gathered her courage and called out, "Hotep, are you there? I have been looking everywhere for you."

In the shadows, the man turned and his eyes blazed for a moment in the light of the lamp. When he realized who it was, he stepped back quickly, letting go of Hotep.

His voice was low and smooth. "I heard your maid's cries, Dominilla. It seems she fell and hurt herself. It delayed me from joining you at dinner. You are finished then?"

The lie was blatant and anger boiled up in her heart as she faced him, yet something told her to be wary of what she said. He was a powerful force in the palace. She hoped he would not see the fear in her face as she struggled to remain calm.

49

"No, my lord, I had a headache and the emperor excused me to rest. Hotep was not in my room to attend me. How fortunate of you to be near to help her." She kept her voice innocent and soothing.

He gave a slight bow of his head. "It was my pleasure, Dominilla. Please excuse me as I myself am late joining the emperor for dinner."

Her heart pounding, she watched him swiftly walk away. When he was out of sight, Hotep fell at her feet. "Have mercy on me, Dominilla. I only went to the kitchen to get some food for Felix. I disobeyed you. Do not have me beaten."

Claudia lifted the girl to her feet. "Hotep, I'm not going to beat you. I'm only glad I was here in time. The gods must favor you, for I felt strongly during dinner to return to my room and then searched for you. Did he hurt you?"

"Not in the way he wished to. You were very brave, Dominilla. We are fortunate you are the emperor's ward."

On the way back to Claudia's room, Hotep told her of others in the castle who had crossed Sejanus and disappeared.

Claudia was now more fearful than ever. That night she had a dream and saw the face of Sejanus, twisted with hate and anger, his hands reaching for her throat. She tried to scream, but no sound came. She woke suddenly, drenched in perspiration. What kind of a place had she come to?

10

Julia was dead. Tiberius stood on his balcony, watching the morning haze lift off the city. He held the scroll brought by a courier the night before. Surprisingly his vengeance brought him no pleasure. He'd learned she was dying when he gave the order for her seclusion—and starvation. As he considered the woman who had been his wife, the anger rose again. She was no noble Roman matron, blatantly dishonoring their marriage. Humiliated, he'd angrily left Rome for Rhodes, leaving her father to serve the divorce papers. With her condemnation by the Senate, Augustus did the only thing he could do to save her life. Under sentence from the Roman Senate, he'd banished her to Pandetaria. Why had Augustus relented and let her leave that barren island where she should have remained and allowed her to go to Reggio? She only continued her debaucheries, and now there was the child. Augustus knew about the girl, but did nothing. Tiberius pressed his lips together. Augustus was a foolish old man who, in spite of Julia's sins, grieved for his daughter until he died. Tiberius shook his head in disgust.

He considered Sempronius Gracchus, one of Julia's more persistent lovers. The fool had the audacity to try to usurp the throne for Antonius, even requesting a divorce from Tiberius in Julia's name. Too bad Antonius committed suicide before the soldiers could arrest him for treason. As for Gracchus, Augustus merely banished him to the African coast. Tiberius smiled with pleasure. As emperor, he meted out his own justice, and Gracchus was dead.

As he gazed out across Rome, another name came to mind unbidden. Vipsania. Just thinking of her renewed the pain. He loved her still—though ordered by Augustus to divorce his pregnant wife to marry the emperor's prostitute of a daughter. It was as though his heart had been ripped from his body. Vipsania bore a son, Drusus. He should have been heir to the throne, but he was dead of a mysterious illness. He felt the anger rise up again. He never believed that. If he ever found who was responsible—he clenched one fist.

Loneliness crept over his heart like a shadow. He'd never wanted the regency. Sejanus handled so many details for him. Perhaps he could make him a co-regent and leave Rome once and for all for his castle in Capri. The thought pursued him daily. Sejanus on many occasions had insinuated that there were plots against the emperor's life, and fear had become a dark companion. He rubbed his chin with one thumb. When his prefect brought him names of men he insisted were plotting against his life, he'd dealt with them swiftly, despite their cries of innocence. Their families had been banished from Rome and their worldly goods confiscated by Sejanus.

Tiberius ignored a faint fluttering of regret. Some of these men were of good standing, even senators. He turned his attention to the scroll again. So the old slave, Cato, was dead. No matter. However, there was Scribonia's slave, Medina, who asked to be returned to her mistress.

He tapped the scroll against his hand. He'd dealt the girl enough heartache. He would not be the one to bear the news of Julia's death to young Claudia. Someone else would have that duty.

He turned from the balcony and went to the door. The soldier on guard outside saluted.

"Majesty?"

"Bring me the Lady Scribonia."

Scribonia knew she had little to fear for her upkeep. She was of the praetorian class and the family holdings would insure her being able to live out her last days in comfort. At eighty, she was ready to spend her days in quiet retirement. She thought of her granddaughter and sighed. Claudia was now the emperor's responsibility.

This morning, she walked in her garden, shivering slightly in the cool air and feeling every bit her age. Her handmaid, Cassia, hurried toward her.

"You have received a summons, Domina, from the emperor."

A summons? *Why would the emperor send for me? A problem with Claudia?* Then she knew. Julia. Her heart jolted in her chest. Though the anguish nearly overcame her, she braced her shoulders and, with great effort, gathered her emotions in a tight rein. He would not have the satisfaction of seeing her pain.

Cassia slipped a stola of muted blue over her mistress's shoulders and then a woolen shawl around her shoulders for warmth. Scribonia added a pair of pearl earrings and a silver pendant. With a heavy heart, she went down to the entrance of the villa where the coach waited.

When she arrived at the palace, she was led to an atrium where a fountain seemed to play a melancholy sound as she waited.

When Tiberius entered, she bowed her head. "You sent for me, Majesty?"

He handed her the scroll in silence.

She scanned the contents and the anguish of leaving her daughter alone in Reggio rose again in her heart. She wanted to fling the document in his face. Did he feel any remorse for what he'd put them through? Keeping her face bland, she fought for control. Julia was in the hands of the gods now. Cato was dead. It was too much for his heart. Gathering her thoughts carefully, she focused on the one thing that needed to be done. She looked up at Tiberius.

"Majesty, Medina and I have been together many years. It would be good to have someone familiar in my old age." She could not help Julia, but she could protect Medina.

He considered the request a moment. "I will see what can be done."

"Thank you, Majesty." She waited again.

He took back the scroll. "It is a sorry task. You will inform your granddaughter."

"I will tell her." She bowed her head and followed the steward down the halls she had once walked as Empress of Rome.

She waved the steward away and stood for a moment, deciding just how she would phrase her words. In her eighty years she had seen much death. Unbidden tears welled up behind her eyes and she willed them away. Finally, she drew herself up and, gathering control once again, knocked.

11

Hotep opened the door and Claudia looked up from the chair by the window where she was working on an embroidery.

"Grandmother!" She hurried across the room and threw her arms around Scribonia's neck. "You came to see me."

Her grandmother not only allowed the embrace, she even returned it briefly. When they parted, there were tears in her grandmother's eyes. Claudia stepped back, puzzled. She gently escorted her grandmother to a chair where the older woman sank down heavily.

Claudia indicated her maidservant with one hand. "Grandmother, this is Hotep. It means peace in Egyptian."

Hotep bowed her head. "It is a pleasure to serve the dominilla, my lady."

Her grandmother nodded in acknowledgment.

Claudia, sensing a purpose in her grandmother's visit, looked at her face. "You didn't just come to see me did you?"

"No, child, though I would have come eventually. Tiberius sent for me. He received a courier from Reggio last night." Her grandmother said quickly, "Your mother is dead."

The overwhelming pain struck like a dagger in Claudia's heart and large tears welled up in her eyes, spilling down her cheeks. "I knew it would happen soon, but I haven't wanted to think about her dying all alone."

"Medina and Cato were there, even if they could not enter the room. We can only pray that she died quickly."

Claudia nodded, and then in the haze of her emotions, she realized her grandmother might need something to eat or drink. She had traveled across the city to carry out this abominable errand for Tiberius.

"Hotep, please bring some refreshments."

The girl bowed her head and hurried out the door. Claudia looked after her, knowing Hotep no longer needed to fear running into the prefect again in the dark hallways. She'd told the empress about the incident but not the perpetrator. Livia told Tiberius and word went out through the palace that Claudia *and* her maidservant were under his protection. The warning no doubt reached the ears of Sejanus.

Claudia wiped her eyes with a corner of her stola. "Oh Grandmother, I miss her." Both women were silent a moment, sharing their mutual sorrow. Then Claudia looked up. "Medina and Cato? What will become of them now?"

Scribonia hesitated. "Cato had a weak heart. He is dead also."

Claudia gasped. Dear old Cato. She thought of the many times she'd watched him lovingly plant flowers in their garden.

Her grandmother spoke again. "Medina wishes to return to me. I have petitioned Tiberius to let her do so. Now tell me what you have been doing since I left you here."

Claudia wrenched her mind from thoughts of her mother and dutifully told her grandmother about the dinner with Tiberius, meeting with the empress, and going to the Roman baths.

"Livia was hard on your mother. Does she treat you well?"

"Yes, she's been kind to me."

Scribonia nodded. "Are you allowed out of the palace for any other reason?"

"I may go to the marketplace with Hotep, but I must have a bodyguard."

"That is good. It could be dangerous for two young women alone."

Hotep returned with the wine and some fruit and cheese. As Scribonia sipped the diluted wine, she studied the maidservant over the rim of her cup. When she had finished the wine in silence, she put down the cup and slowly rose from the chair.

"I must return to my villa now. I have matters to attend to there," Scribonia said.

Claudia followed her to the door. "Shall Hotep guide you?"

Scribonia raised her eyebrows. "I knew the way around the palace before she was born, child. I can find my own way out."

Claudia put a hand on her arm. "Grandmother?"

"Yes?"

"She liked to . . . laugh, didn't she?"

Her grandmother covered Claudia's hand with her own. "Yes, your mother liked to laugh." Then she turned and hurried down the hall.

Claudia watched her go and put a hand on her heart, as if by pressing very hard, she could stop the ache inside.

12

It was a beautiful day, and after returning from the baths with Livia, Claudia hurried to change her clothing for the outing in the marketplace. She could hardly contain her excitement.

As she and her handmaid neared the entrance to the palace, the large Nubian, who had taken possession of her dog when she arrived, stepped out from an alcove where he had obviously been waiting, along with Milo. The Nubian, Horatio, could not speak. His tongue had been cut out years before. Milo motioned him to accompany them and the women followed.

At the bottom of the hill, Milo turned onto the Via Sacra, the main thoroughfare in Rome. The streets seemed to radiate from the Forum like spokes on a wheel. On the *Vicus iugarius* were the stalls of the spice merchants, filling the air with the fragrances of cinnamon, cumin, mint, dry mustard, and peppers from the Orient. On the *argiletum*, they browsed in bookshops, and Claudia looked longingly at the shops of the shoe merchants.

To the south of the Forum, Milo led them to the *velabrum*, the general market, and then the *forum boariumi* and the *forum cuppedinis*, the markets for luxury goods. Stalls seemed to overflow with silk fabrics and purple cloth from the dye merchants of Philippi.

"If you wish to purchase fabric, I am authorized to allow you to choose, Dominilla."

Claudia's eyes widened. She and Hotep examined several rolls of cloth, and finally she chose a soft, finely woven cloth of deep violet with gold filament woven along the border. The merchant, delighted with his sale, quickly wrapped it up for them in a linen cloth. Milo gave the package to the Nubian to carry and paid the merchant after a lively haggle over the price.

Carts were everywhere and Claudia turned to the steward. "Where does this all come from?"

"The carts bring goods to the markets from the barges that come up the Tiber from Ostia, our port city. The emperor is building a forum there and also a new harbor."

Claudia nodded. Perhaps one day she would see Ostia.

There were such exciting things to see and she wanted to see everything at once.

As they walked, Claudia stopped to watch stonemasons working on a new building. It fascinated her to see how carefully they positioned the huge marble stones with hardly a space between them.

Milo patiently kept up with them, but soon Claudia realized that he was tiring and it was late afternoon. Milo bought them some sweetbreads to tide them over until they reached the palace. She could hardly wait to go again.

At the baths the next morning there was subdued gossip. Each woman seemed to be looking over her shoulder to see who was listening. Statues of Sejanus were being put up around the city along with those of Tiberius, and the senators' wives were uneasy. Their husbands walked a fine line between loyalty to the emperor and staying in the good graces of the prefect. It was dangerous to one's health to criticize Sejanus. His tentacles reached as far as those of Tiberius, and as long as the emperor called him "My Sejanus," it was necessary to curry his favor. It would appear Tiberius was grooming Sejanus for something. Adding to the tension was talk of the census.

On the way back from the baths, Claudia asked the empress about the census.

Livia sighed. "The outcome of the census could change their status. Every male Roman citizen must register not only himself but his entire family, slaves, and his wealth. If he omits any of it or does not give a correct accounting, all he has can be confiscated and he himself can be sold into slavery."

Claudia's eyes widened. "How does the census change one's status?"

The empress looked around to see if anyone was listening. "The censors can look into a man's private life and decide whether he moves up or down on the social ladder."

"His private life?"

Livia waved a hand impatiently. "Has he turned a blind eye to his wife's adulteries, committed perjury, not fathered any children, or failed to cultivate his land properly."

Claudia frowned. "And do they look at the adulteries of the man?"

Livia stopped and gave Claudia a stern look. "You are an outspoken young woman for your age—as was your mother."

At the mention of her mother, Claudia stiffened, remembering what her mother told her of growing up under her stepmother's hand. She bit her tongue. She was not foolish enough to alienate the empress.

When Claudia returned to her room, she was greeted by silence. Felix's bed was empty.

They called and searched the rooms but the little dog was gone. Claudia felt panic rise. "Let us go to the kitchen and see if the servants have seen him."

The cook looked at their anxious faces and began to wring her hands. "It was the prefect, my lady. He brought the dog here and told Milo to get rid of it."

Claudia, nearly shaking with anger, took a step toward the cook. "What has he done with my dog?"

Other servants entered the kitchen, their faces pale. The cook looked around and finally, her eyes filled with fear, said, "My lady, Milo could not bring himself to hurt Felix. He disobeyed the prefect and took him to his son. He has a young granddaughter. The little dog will have a good home. Please, my lady, if the prefect finds Milo didn't obey him, we will all be punished."

Claudia bowed her head. If she had a sword at that moment she would have run the prefect through. She gathered herself together. These good people had taken a great chance and she must acknowledge that.

"In the midst of a terrible injustice you have done me a great kindness. I won't put you in jeopardy. It shall comfort me that his life was spared. I shall remember you with gratitude."

The relief in the room was palpable.

Hotep put an arm around her mistress and led her back to her room where Claudia collapsed in frustration and tears. She hated the palace, hated Tiberius, but most of all, she hated Sejanus.

On her fourteenth birthday, Claudia fought down the despair that threatened to engulf her. Her mother was dead and her precious Felix had been stolen away from her. She stared out the window, wishing there were some way she could leave this place of sorrow and go far away.

The empress kept Claudia's mind busy with practice on her lute, writing poetry in Latin, and instructing her on how to handle servants. Claudia went faithfully to the baths with Livia each morning, but day after day she faced loneliness. She had been able to lavish affection on her dog, who loved her in return, but now she was lonely. Tiberius was her guardian, but she had little contact with him. She didn't mind, for she had no feelings for him as a parent. She missed her grandmother and thought often of her mother. Julia had entertained them with her sense of humor and wit many times at the evening meal. And she had shown Claudia affection. Hotep was company, and nearer her age, but she was not family. The people she grew up with were her family, including Cato and Medina.

It was a beautiful spring day and Claudia sat on a stone bench, listening to the birds calling to one another. She looked up as Hotep approached.

"You are sad, Dominilla?" Hotep's large dark eyes were filled with sympathy.

"I miss my home and family." Claudia spoke almost in a whisper. "Everything I loved is gone. Why did he have to get rid of my dog?"

Hotep sat down on the bench next to her. "You crossed the prefect, Dominilla. He would not let that go unpunished." She put a gentle hand on Claudia's arm. "Perhaps your grandmother will be able to come for your birthday."

"I don't know. I've no word from her. She has come so seldom this last year."

They returned to the room and waited for a slave from the kitchen to bring their lunch. Most meals were eaten in her room, but at least she had Hotep for company.

The empress was indisposed again and Claudia felt restless. Perhaps Milo would make arrangements for them to go into the city again. Surely she could buy something on her special day. As the morning drew on, there was a knock on the door and Hotep, expecting their noon meal, hurried to open the door. Claudia's grandmother stood in the corridor.

Claudia sprang from her chair and rushed to the door with tears of joy. "You remembered. Oh Grandmother, you remembered my birthday." Knowing her grandmother's reserve, she stopped and stood smiling. "It is so good to see you."

"I wouldn't miss your birthday, child. As a matter of fact, I have a surprise for you."

Two other women appeared and Claudia found herself staring into a familiar face—Medina. She threw herself into the arms of her old nurse. "Oh Medina, you're here."

Finally Claudia stepped back and allowed the two older women and the servant from the kitchen to enter her quarters. The servant put the lunch tray on the table and bowed herself out, closing the door behind her.

The cheese was fresh and they dipped their chunks of bread in a relish made from olives, vinegar, coriander seeds, cumin, fennel, and mint. Claudia savored every bite. She smiled at Medina, remembering when they made the relish together.

"How did you get here?"

Scribonia interrupted. "Tiberius arranged for her to travel with a senator and his wife returning to Rome."

Medina turned to Claudia. "I rode in a coach, Dominilla, as you did."

"I'm sure Grandmother is glad to have you back, aren't you?"

Scribonia huffed. "Of course—I sent for her, didn't I?"

Claudia suppressed a smile. "How are you feeling, Grandmother?"

"I am feeling my age. Too many aches and pains, but I am not ready for the gods to call me yet."

Her grandmother's candidness was one of the things she loved about her.

Her grandmother eyed her sternly. "How are you getting along with Livia?"

"The empress is kind to me."

Scribonia nodded. "She has done many good things for the poor of Rome. They speak well of her."

The compliment seemed grudgingly given, but Claudia only nodded.

When they had finished their refreshment, Claudia suggested a walk in the extensive garden. They strolled for a while and then sat by the fountain.

Scribonia looked around. "Where is your small dog?"

Claudia hesitated and looked past her grandmother to Hotep. How much did she dare say? "He, uh, became ill, Grandmother. I lost him." Well, part of it was the truth.

"I'm sorry, child. I know he meant a great deal to you."

"Yes." She didn't want to dwell on Felix.

Scribonia seemed restless, and as the shadows began to creep up the walls of the garden, she rose to go home. Claudia put her hand out and Scribonia covered it between her own. Then Claudia embraced Medina a last time. It had been a wonderful birthday present.

After they had gone, Claudia found herself thinking of Medina and was reminded of her mother. She opened the small chest with her special treasures, fingering the ring her mother had given her. Her grandmother said it belonged to the man who was her father, but since it appeared that all of her mother's suitors were dead, the question of who he was would remain forever unanswered. She sat looking at the silver ring, turning it this way and that in the light as the emerald stones sparkled. Finally, she put it back in the chest. It was as close as she would ever be to the shadowy figure in her mind of the man who was her father.

13

At the end of Claudia's fifteenth year, word came that Tiberius and Sejanus were once again away from the palace on imperial business. Tiberius seldom went anywhere without Sejanus at his side. He spent less and less time in Rome. Everywhere, next to the statues of Tiberius, were statues of Sejanus. Some even prayed to Sejanus and celebrated his birthday. His favor was courted by senators and those of the praetorian rank.

Sejanus made the most of his place of favor, making changes. The Praetorian Guard, once just a small bodyguard for the emperor, was being built into a formidable force, and if the emperor was aware, he did not reveal it. Sejanus wanted the Praetorian Guard to be a powerful and influential branch of the government. Servants who listened quietly in the background at meals with Sejanus said he spoke to the emperor of having the guard oversee public security, civil administration, and even handle political intercession. The health of the emperor was not good and he agreed to any suggestion within reason from his prefect.

Claudia knew that since Sejanus was the second most powerful man in the entire empire, he would also influence the emperor in regard to her marriage. There was no doubt that whatever her future held, the choice would rest, not in the hands of the emperor, but in the man she hated more than the emperor.

Most young Roman women of high standing were married by the time they were fifteen, and Claudia grew restless. On one hand she longed to be out of the palace with a home of her own, but on the other hand, she dreaded being told she was going to marry someone years older than herself for political reasons. She thought of her mother's marriages and how she was used as a political pawn by Augustus. Would she end up like her mother? Claudia made offerings to Venus, praying with all her might for a good husband who would at least be kind to her.

Her grandmother brought Medina to visit as often as possible. Sometimes Claudia and Hotep met them in the marketplace. The mute slave, Horatio, silently watched, his dark eyes taking in everything around them.

With the freedom of a small allowance, Claudia could now shop for things that brought her pleasure. Sometimes she bought sweet rolls from the street of the bakers, sometimes a new pair of sandals.

Claudia now met the empress at the baths instead of accompanying her. Livia was in ill health and many days could not leave her quarters. Claudia didn't mind the absence of the empress, for when her grandmother and Medina came to the baths, the atmosphere was not strained.

Tiberius, already known to be moody, was becoming more withdrawn and had been threatening more often to leave Rome for his palace on Capri.

The standing of Sejanus with the emperor was solidified, for Tiberius had no successor. He had little contact with his nephews. His two sons were dead and here was Sejanus, a man he saw every day, supremely efficient, trustworthy, and an able administrator.

Claudia prayed to the gods for the health of Tiberius, for the thought of Sejanus succeeding him filled her with dread. The prefect had not bothered Hotep again, but what would happen if the protection of the emperor's presence was withdrawn? The times when Claudia joined the emperor for an evening meal, Sejanus watched her from under those bushy brows. To her shock and surprise, he divorced the gentle Apicata and was petitioning the emperor to marry Levilla. Claudia felt badly for Apicata and the children, but there was nothing she could do.

The palace gossip held that Sejanus and Levilla were having an affair, but the emperor could not know or he would have acted against Sejanus. If the prefect married the widow of the emperor's son, Drusus, it would solidify his position with the emperor even more. Everyone in Rome believed the implications that he would become the emperor's successor. For his own reasons, the emperor had denied the marriage request, but Sejanus was a man who bided his time. Sooner or later Claudia felt the emperor would give in and let them marry.

Soon after her sixteenth birthday, her third year in the palace, Claudia was surprised by a summons to have dinner with the emperor on what was becoming one of his rare stays in the palace. The palace was full of intrigue and those who had enjoyed favor one day found themselves in disgrace or worse the next. She dressed carefully in a soft white linen tunic with a silver belt around her chest, silver sandals, and some small pearl earrings.

Her heart pounded as she entered the dining room.

"Ah, Claudia. It is good of you to join us."

As Tiberius welcomed her, his face seemed melancholy in spite of the smile he wore. He watched silently while a slave removed her sandals and handed her the warm wet cloth to wash her hands.

"It is kind of you to have me join you, Majesty. I trust your last trip was successful?"

"It was."

She felt the emperor had something on his mind but was forced to wait patiently through the meal for him to unburden himself. They dined on cucumbers and cabbage in a sauce, fresh bread, a selection of cheeses, and succulent roast duck. The wine was heavily diluted as most Romans preferred it.

To her relief, Sejanus was conspicuously missing, and she wondered if he was off on business for the emperor. Levilla had little to say, and the empress came late as usual, leaning on the arm of her handmaiden. She greeted Claudia and bowed her head to the emperor, then ate her meal in silence. She appeared to be watching Tiberius covertly as she ate. It only added to Claudia's feeling of dread, and while she strove to remain calm, her heart beat erratically.

Tiberius turned to her. "You are in good health, Claudia?"

"Yes, Majesty."

"And how have you occupied yourself?"

She felt he knew everything she did already, for it was said he had eyes and ears everywhere, but she politely told him what she felt he wanted to hear.

"I thank you for the allowance. I have enjoyed the marketplace. I read and work on my loom and embroidery from time to time."

"You are proficient at this?"

"Yes, my lord."

There were long silences in between, and Claudia struggled to keep her impatience under control.

Just as they were finishing dessert, a mixture of plums and cherries served with cream, as if at a signal from the emperor, Levilla and the empress excused themselves.

Tiberius watched them go, his eyes narrowing, then turned to her. "My mother has brought it to my attention that you are of marriageable age and I am remiss in selecting a proper husband for you." He looked down at his hands, and Claudia noted that they were soft, effeminate. Then he continued. "I have sought the counsel of my prefect and he has made a suggestion. There is someone he has known for some time—a man who fought in the campaigns of Germanicus and distinguished himself. He is on his way to Rome. You will be apprised when he arrives and will be introduced. I also wish to meet him before making my final decision."

Claudia's heart sank. A man suggested by Sejanus? How old was he and what would he look like? She lowered her eyes lest the emperor see the turmoil in them. Instead, she murmured, "I'm sure you will make the right choice for me, my lord."

Tiberius put a hand on her shoulder, causing her to suddenly look up.

"Your submission and obedience are noted, Claudia Procula. Make yourself ready, for he arrives in two days' time."

"Shall I know his name, my lord?"

"Ah yes, a noble praetorian family, descended from Gaius Pontius, a fine general. His name is Lucius Pontius Pilate."

14

Claudia returned to her room anxious to share the news with Hotep. In the three years together, they had become close. They talked long hours into the night and Hotep shared all the news that was whispered by the staff of the palace. Claudia always marveled at the vast network among the slaves of Rome—little happened in any household that wasn't soon known across the city.

"Your dinner with the emperor went well?"

"The prefect has picked out a husband for me," she answered petulantly. "The emperor wished to let me know." She waved a hand. "I don't know what he looks like—tall, fat, bald, over forty?" She remembered some of the young brides at the baths talking about their husbands—men that had been chosen by their fathers to seal an agreement or combine two important families. The young women emphasized how well their fathers had chosen for them, but the reality was what they didn't say. Claudia wondered what it had been like to share the wedding couch with a man the age of their fathers. The wife would be expected to produce children as soon as possible, especially a son, to carry on the family name. She shuddered. Was that to be her fate?

Hotep broke into her thoughts. "But Dominilla, that is good news. Do you not wish to be married? You are sixteen. Many of the young noblewomen are married by now."

Claudia sank down in a chair. "I don't know if it is good or bad.

The meal was gloomy, Hotep. The empress and Levilla hardly spoke a word to each other or to me. They ate and ran. I think Levilla is angry with the emperor for not allowing her to marry Sejanus."

Hotep shook her head slowly. "I do not know why any woman would like to marry that man."

"I agree. Levilla is an unhappy woman. Why would he divorce Apicata, who was so nice, to marry her, unless . . ."

Claudia sat thinking of the rumors she'd heard through the staff. It was whispered that Levilla was responsible for the death of her husband. Why would they think that had Tiberius known, it would be the end of Sejanus. If Drusus succeeded his father, Levilla would have been empress of Rome. Why would she do anything to change that? She was sure it had to do with Sejanus.

Claudia contemplated what she'd seen. Now that Apicata was no longer with them at the emperor's dinners, Levilla looked longingly at Sejanus. Life in the palace was full of intrigue.

She sighed as Hotep helped her undress. "Sejanus has chosen a husband for me and the emperor said he would make a decision. No doubt he will go along with this man the prefect recommends. So this Lucius Pontius Pilate will be my husband."

Hotep unwound the silver strands of Claudia's hair and began to take down the curls, brushing her hair until it gleamed softly, cascading down her shoulders.

"You will be a beautiful bride, Dominilla. Your husband will be pleased with you."

Claudia stifled a wave of resentment. But would *she* be pleased with her husband?

❧

The two days passed more quickly than Claudia desired, and she longed to talk with her grandmother. That very afternoon, to her surprise and relief, a slave knocked on her door with a wax stylus containing a message from her grandmother, written in Latin:

Word has come that Sejanus returns to the city with a member of the amici Caesaris, *friends of Caesar. His name is Lucius Pontius Pilate. Sejanus has chosen him for you. I believe you will be pleasantly surprised. Take heart.*

The seal from Scribonia's ring was pressed into the wax.

When the summons came to join the emperor for dinner and meet a guest, Claudia dressed with care, but her mind turned with all the possibilities of the evening. Her tunic was a soft white. She wore a lavender scarf with gold threads woven throughout. A gold belt took up the length of her garment. She slipped her feet into gold jeweled sandals while Hotep swept her hair up in curls, held by two gold hairpins. A long curl fell to one shoulder.

She examined herself in the polished brass mirror. How different she looked from the child who had come so fearfully to the palace three years before. The face of a woman stared back at her.

As Hotep walked with her to the palace dining room, Claudia felt her anxiety settle like a heavy weight in her chest. She pondered her grandmother's words, but still, nothing could change the outcome of this evening. Claudia walked as if to her execution.

As she entered the dining room, conversation stopped and all eyes were suddenly turned to settle on her. The empress looked pale and unwell. Levilla sat stonily on her dining chair across from Sejanus. Claudia slowly allowed her gaze to rest on the stranger reclining next to Sejanus. Expecting a middle-aged man with gray hair and a paunch, she was surprised. He looked to be in his late thirties and his angular face with deep blue eyes was indeed handsome.

The man's body was long and muscular. With a start, she suddenly realized he was enjoying her perusal.

Sejanus indicated his friend. "My lady Claudia, may I present an honored soldier of Rome, Lucius Pontius Pilate. Lucius, this is the emperor's ward."

"I am most happy to meet you, my lady."

A small lightning bolt flashed in Claudia's heart at the intensity of his gaze. "Have you been in Rome long?" she inquired, searching for topics to ease her discomfort as she sank gracefully onto her chair.

"Only one day, my lady. Had I known what pleasure would be afforded me at the table of my emperor, I would have come sooner."

The dark eyes of Sejanus gleamed under his heavy brows. "Then you can see that I did not exaggerate, my friend."

Lucius nodded to the prefect. "No indeed." He turned his dark eyes once again on Claudia. "Word of your beauty has preceded you, my lady."

Sejanus was talking to him about her beauty? She would never understand what went on in the prefect's mind. She glanced at the emperor and could see that Tiberius was indeed pleased with his prefect's choice.

Claudia scarcely paid attention to what she ate. She could only look across the table at Lucius. Warmth spread up from her feet and she felt sure her face was as red as the wine.

Finally, after signaling for their attention, Tiberius stood and spoke. "Since the death of Claudia's mother, I followed the wishes of her grandfather, Caesar Augustus, and took upon myself the responsibility of raising her in the palace and in time arranging a marriage for her. I am pleased to accept the recommendation of my prefect, Sejanus, whom I have found to be a trustworthy counsel. Lucius Pontius Pilate has shown himself a warrior for the empire and has agreed to this marriage. I am giving my approval. The wedding will take place when the augurs have been consulted and a date favored by the gods chosen."

It was a long speech for Tiberius. Claudia had not been asked for her consent to the marriage. Holding the right of paterfamilias over her, Tiberius had the right to choose her husband. She would obediently follow his wishes, for no Roman woman of good family would think of doing otherwise.

When they all stood, Lucius spoke to the emperor, striking his heart with his fist in respect, then turned to Claudia. "I wonder if you would stroll with me in the garden. I believe we have much to say to each other."

Tiberius indicated his consent with a wave of his hand, and the newly betrothed couple strolled through an archway and entered the garden.

Lucius walked with an easy grace and she felt a magnetism emanating from him. The gods had been kind to her and she was still in awe of her good fortune.

Lucius spoke first. "When I agreed to marry the ward of Tiberius at the instigation of Sejanus, I was only being obedient to my superior. He knew I'd mentioned seeking a wife. He spoke well of you and told me how beautiful you were, but I put his flattery down to his powers of persuasion." He stopped and turned her to face him. "I was not prepared for your appearance. When you entered, it was as if the goddess Venus entered the room. When I realized that you were my intended, words failed me."

She smiled. "You have perhaps found your words, my lord?"

"Indeed. But I wish to know more about you. Sejanus has told me only that you were brought to the palace when you were thirteen? Tell me about your life before that."

She told him of her childhood, living with her mother and grandmother. Of learning to weave from her grandmother, cooking with Medina, and of Cato and the garden as the soft darkness settled about them.

"I hated to leave my mother in such a way, but I had no choice. Even though my grandmother told me Mater was dying, she should have had her family with her when the gods took her. Even now, I still think of my mother and that dark day and the sadness remains." He was a friend of Sejanus, so she did not mention her dog.

74

His head was bent and he listened quietly, without comment. She found it comforting. As she spoke, an involuntary tear slipped down her cheek and his strong, warm hand covered hers.

She looked up at him and felt she could talk with him about anything. It was something she hadn't known with anyone else, even her grandmother or Hotep.

His deep voice was soft. "I do not know how it is for you, but the moment you entered the room, I was captivated."

Her heart quickened with a steady beat. "It is the same for me," she whispered. "I didn't realize how such feelings could come so suddenly. I am glad it was you that Sejanus chose for me." Then she added quickly, "With the emperor's consent, of course."

They smiled at each other in the light of the torches placed around the garden, the silence only broken by the splashing of the nearby fountain.

Noticing that she was shivering involuntarily in the night air, he rose. "I must take you back inside. You are cold."

He walked her to her quarters, and she looked up at him, studying his face as if to memorize it.

"I have business to take care of for the prefect, but I shall see you again when our betrothal is announced by the emperor."

She opened the door, and as he turned and walked back down the corridor, she watched him with pride and something more. "Good night, my Lucius," she whispered.

15

Word of the betrothal spread throughout the city, and Claudia appeared on the steps of the palace holding hands with Lucius, as was customary, making the union official. Tiberius appeared with them, signifying his approval of the match. Sejanus stood by his emperor, beaming benevolently like a proud father.

After searching for a date that would bode well for the couple, the wedding was set for the latter part of the month of Juno, named after the principal goddess of the Roman Pantheon and the goddess of marriage and well-being for women. It was the month Claudia was hoping for. It signified a good beginning for their marriage.

When Sejanus and the emperor left to discuss matters of state, Claudia returned to the garden with Lucius.

"Where is your home, Lucius?"

"I have a family villa in Ponti in the mountains of Samnium, a half day's ride from the city. My mother died five years ago, so you will be free to direct the slaves. My staff has been instructed to obey your orders."

"I will be happy anywhere you are, Lucius. Forgive me if I say, I will be especially happy to leave the palace."

He studied her face a moment. "You have not been happy here?"

She considered her words. "The emperor has been good to me, but more and more there is word of his leaving for Capri permanently. I will be more comfortable in a villa of my own." She dared not say more, lest it get back to Sejanus.

"I may not be able to be with you a great deal, my Claudia. I believe Sejanus has an assignment for me, but he has not indicated what that shall be."

Fear suddenly constricted her heart. "Can I not go with you, wherever you are assigned?"

His eyes widened in surprise. "Most Roman women prefer to remain in the city if their husbands are in the army and assigned to a distant outpost."

"I don't care. I want to go with you if it is at all possible. Please, Lucius." She looked up at him, feeling the tears behind her eyes and hating the pleading sound of her voice. She could not tell him she wanted to be as far from Rome, the emperor, and Sejanus as she could get.

He reached up and brushed a tear from her cheek with his thumb. "I too desire you with me. Let us discover my assignment and discuss it then."

She nodded. Then another thought occurred to her. "I would like to bring my servant, Hotep. She has been mine since I came to the palace and I depend on her." How could she say they had become friends and she feared for the girl if left behind?

"If that is your wish, she may come with you. Who shall be your bridesmaid?"

She shook her head slowly. "I have no one here in the palace."

He rubbed his chin with one hand and his brows were knit together in thought. "The prefect has a young daughter, Junilla, who is eight or nine years old, I believe. Perhaps she could attend you. I believe that would also please the prefect."

Claudia had met Junilla once and found her to be a sweet girl, taking much after her mother.

"If the prefect allows her, I would not mind Junilla." She would have liked Hotep, but it was not proper for a slave to be part of a wedding ceremony.

She and Lucius agreed that her clothing and personal property would be sent with Hotep to the Villa Ponti the morning of their wedding.

He ran a finger down her cheek and his eyes left no doubt of his feelings. "With great anticipation I look forward to our wedding."

She felt the warmth rise in her body and spread to her face. "I also look forward to our wedding, Lucius." Her eyes met his unflinchingly.

He took her hand and held it a long moment and then reluctantly took his leave of her.

She thought the month of Juno would never arrive. Since she had no home to be married in, Tiberius chose the temple of Jupiter. The high priest there would officiate.

To her delight, her grandmother sent word that she would dress Claudia on her wedding day—usually a mother's task.

Before her grandmother arrived, Claudia ate what little breakfast she could manage. Anticipation and excitement had dimmed her appetite. She looked down at the engagement ring on her left hand that Lucius had given her—a single jewel that caught the light and sparkled. He'd given her the ring and then held her a long moment, and she felt his heart beating against hers. With great restraint he had put her from him and once again, touching her cheek, bid her goodbye until the wedding.

There was a knock on the door and her grandmother entered, followed by a very shy Junilla. Sejanus had been pleased at the request for his daughter as a bridesmaid and made sure she was brought to the palace at once.

Junilla stared at Claudia. "You look so pretty." She perched on a chair to watch the proceedings, her eyes alight with anticipation.

Hotep had anointed Claudia's body with oil and perfume and

slipped the undergarment of soft, sheer cotton over her head before Junilla and Scribonia arrived.

A stola of soft, sheer white wool came next. Scribonia stepped forward and, with a golden belt, tied the "knot of Hercules" in it—the knot only to be untied by Claudia's husband at their wedding couch. Finally a flame-colored veil was settled over her head. Then her feet were slipped into her gold sandals.

Hotep divided Claudia's hair into six locks as was traditional. The locks were coiled and held in position on top of her head with ribbons. A wreath of flowers was placed on top of the veil.

Claudia rose and went to fetch her small box of treasures, which she offered to the statue of Venus in her room, signifying leaving her childhood behind. Her grandmother's eyes widened as Claudia pulled out the ring her mother had given her and had Hotep clasp the chain around her neck. The ring remained unseen inside her stola, and as she faced her grandmother, her chin up in a moment of defiance, Scribonia raised her eyebrows in question.

"Should it not accompany me on my wedding day?"

Her grandmother sighed heavily but said nothing.

The emperor sent two bouquets of white roses and chrysanthemums, a larger one for Claudia and a smaller bouquet for Junilla. She was touched that he would do such a thing—perhaps a suggestion from Livia?

She said a quick goodbye to Hotep, who hurried to a coach that would take her to the Villa Ponti with Claudia's personal things and her loom. The entourage left Claudia's quarters and walked to the entrance of the palace where a carpentum waited to take Claudia, Junilla, and Scribonia to the Temple of Jupiter for the wedding. The manes of the two large horses had been decorated with flowers, and they stomped their feet and snorted as if anxious to be off.

Lucius met them on the steps of the temple in his dress uniform. He too had a garland around his head. Next to him was the emperor, dressed in a white toga with a larger royal purple stripe on the side.

Sejanus, in his full uniform, nodded to his daughter in response to her shy smile. Lucius helped Claudia out of the carriage and took her hand firmly, leading her into the temple, followed by the ten selected men, who, along with Sejanus and the emperor, made up the twelve required witnesses.

As Claudia and Lucius finally stood before the priest, holding hands, she chanted first, "*Quando tu Gaius, ego Gaia*" (When-and-where-you-are Gaius, I then-and-there-am Gaia). Lucius in turn chanted, "*Quando tu Gaia, ego Gaius*" (When-and-where-you-are Gaia, I then-and-there-am Gaius). Then the bride and groom were seated on stools facing the altar. The priest chanted other words of the ceremony and an offering of cake was made to Jupiter. Then the cake was carefully eaten by the bride and groom.

When the ceremony ended and Claudia was pronounced the wife of Lucius Pontius Pilate, they turned to receive the congratulations of the guests. Sejanus and Tiberius had invited the senators and those of the praetorian rank who were in favor at the time, along with their wives.

The banquet was lavish—bowls of pears, quinces, and plums were placed in the center of the banquet table, along with other bowls of almonds, hazelnuts, pistachios, and walnuts. The servants brought in steaming dishes of carrots, asparagus, peas, and cabbage seasoned with garlic. Roasted chicken as well as stuffed pigeons and partridges were served. Platters of various cheeses were offered to the guests along with small loaves of white bread. The olive relish Claudia loved was also in abundance.

Claudia could hardly contain her joy as she and Lucius exchanged glances throughout the banquet. She looked at Sejanus once and was startled to see him watching her. His expression was almost smug.

When it came time to leave the palace for her new home, Claudia and Lucius bid their guests farewell. She turned to Junilla and thanked her for being her bridesmaid. "In a few years you will also be a bride."

Junilla beamed at this and Claudia could see in her the beauty that she would be one day. Scribonia, acting the part of the mother, clasped her hands around Claudia as if to prevent her from leaving. Lucius, following tradition, good-naturedly pulled his bride away. Claudia turned to her grandmother and Scribonia returned the embrace, tears in her eyes as she whispered in her granddaughter's ear, "Be happy, child. May this be the beginning of a better life for you."

Just as Claudia and Lucius approached their coach, Lucius was stopped by Tiberius and called aside. The emperor drew an official document from inside his tunic.

"I have a wedding present for you."

Claudia stood silently, wondering what this could be. The emperor had said nothing of a gift and she had wondered what he would do. She lowered her eyes so as not to appear to be listening, but what she heard caused her to look up suddenly in amazement.

"You are to report to Caesarea as soon as possible to serve as governor of Judea, to assume the office vacated by the previous governor, Valerius Gratus. He has been recalled to Rome."

Claudia stared in amazement. This was an enormous responsibility. Governor of Judea? Claudia's mind raced considering all the implications. How soon would they have to leave for Caesarea?

The face of the emperor was stern. "A ship is waiting to take you to your province. Your bride will join you later in Caesarea."

"My lord, I am grateful for your confidence in me. This is a great honor." He glanced back at Claudia, waiting by the coach in her wedding finery. "I am to leave—now?"

"You have one hour. The ship leaves with the evening tide."

As Lucius turned away from the emperor and Sejanus, facing Claudia, she alone saw the flash of anger in his eyes. She glanced up at Sejanus who stood with his arms folded across his great chest. His eyes glittered with pleasure, but the smile was cold and calculating. He gave a slight tilt of his head and then she understood. This was his doing.

Lucius turned back and bowed to the emperor. "Your will is my command, Majesty, however it is over three hours just to my villa. I would need to gather certain things."

Sejanus stepped forward, dismissing his concern with a wave of his hand. "They have already been sent for. They shall be on the ship when you arrive."

Lucius saluted in obedience to his prefect. "I shall be ready in one hour."

As the guests whispered among themselves at the turn of events, Lucius took Claudia by the hand and led her back into the palace to the garden where they had some privacy.

She turned into his arms, weeping softly. "How could he do this to us? Why did we tarry so long at the banquet, thinking we had all the time in the world?"

"I cannot guess the mind of the emperor, beloved, but I must obey orders. This is a great honor, though I'm not sure I am ready for such a task. Judea is the hotbed of the empire and the Jews are a cantankerous lot to deal with. But if my emperor feels I am up to the governorship of that land, I will do my best."

He tilted her chin up and kissed the tears that ran down her cheeks. Then he gave her a long, lingering kiss that set her heart on fire. She leaned into him with longing.

When he released her, his breath was ragged, but he held himself back. "I desire you with all my being, wife of my heart, but I will not take you in haste as a woman of the streets. You are my wife, but our first night together must not be like that. We will complete the ceremony and come together as one in Caesarea where I will prepare a proper wedding couch for you."

He sat her down on one of the stone benches and spoke earnestly. "You must be brave and listen carefully to my instructions, beloved. Marcus will help you become acquainted with the household. They know now that you will come alone. You may select anything you wish to bring to our new post. I will make arrangements for the next ship to Caesarea and you will be notified when to arrive at the dock."

She nodded through her tears. "I will do what you ask, Lucius, and will pray the days will pass quickly and hasten my journey."

He stood and drew her up against him again. "I know not why this was done in this manner, but we will be together again soon. I shall await your arrival with my whole heart."

He kissed her again and then taking her by the hand, whispered, "Leave this place, now, beloved, and go to the villa. The driver will see you arrive safely. Pray to the gods for me, for I shall need your prayers."

"I will pray every day, my Lucius, and beseech the gods for you."

He led her once more out of the palace to the carpentum, which still stood at the foot of the steps. The emperor was nowhere in sight, nor was his prefect. The other guests had departed and would no doubt spread word of this strange turn of events.

Lucius handed her into the coach and stood watching it move away. Claudia waved out the window until they turned a corner and she could no longer see him. She rode in silence, muffling her sobs into her shawl.

In her heart she raged at Sejanus. This was his doing and she knew it with all of her being. He had finally extracted his full measure of revenge for the incident in the hallway with Hotep.

16

Claudia finally leaned back in the coach, thinking of the time she and her grandmother had ridden to Rome in a similar coach and she had been fearful of what awaited her. The emperor was a strange man, given to moods, and she didn't try to understand him but had finally forgiven him for what he had done in Reggio. She couldn't carry those thoughts any longer without them destroying her. Now those feelings rose up again as she tried to understand what had just happened. She was married, in name only, and her husband, instead of carrying her over the threshold of their home, was boarding a ship that would take him far away from her. It was not how she pictured her wedding night.

Without Lucius, the trip to his villa seemed to take forever. The cobblestones of the road gave the coach small jolts as they traveled. She finally occupied herself watching the countryside.

At last the coach slowed and entered a gravel road that led to a villa sitting among a series of low hills and shaded by a stand of sycamore trees. The villa was large, two stories, but not forbidding. The door of the coach opened and she was helped out by the driver. She looked up and marveled that she was mistress of such a home.

The steps leading up to the entrance were lined with clay pots of flowers, and as she approached the door, it was opened by a man in his fifties, possibly Greek. Next to him, a slender woman about the same age took in the wedding attire and greeted her with a sympathetic smile.

The man stepped forward. "Domina, welcome to Villa Ponti. I am Marcus, the lord's steward. We were told of your arrival. Come, enter your new home."

The older woman stepped forward and bowed her head. "I am Alba. May we bring you some refreshments, Domina?"

Domina. She was no longer the young mistress but a married woman and mistress of this house.

Claudia acknowledged them. "Thank you for making me welcome. It has been a difficult day. I do not need refreshments at this time, I only wish to rest."

Alba glanced at the steward and nodded. "Of course, Domina, come this way."

As Claudia followed the servant down the corridor and up some stairs, she barely noticed the beautiful mosaic in the entrance hall. She would explore the villa later, but for now all she wanted was to be alone and cry out her unhappiness.

In spite of her heartache and tumbling emotions, Claudia looked around her room. Soft linen curtains moved in the breeze at the windows, and the bed was covered with a blue embroidered coverlet. The furniture was old, but the patina was polished. Each piece was beautifully made. Then once again she felt the anguish of Lucius torn away from her so suddenly.

Alba clicked her tongue against her teeth in a sympathetic sound. "I am so sorry, Domina. We all thought it strange, but packed the master's chests for him and sent them to the ship as ordered by the prefect."

They had that much time? "When did you receive word to pack my husband's trunks?"

"Why, yesterday, Domina. We barely had time to get them ready for transport to the ship."

"I see. Thank you, Alba, for your kindness. I would like to be alone now."

Alba hesitated a moment and then nodded to Hotep and left the room. She understood that Claudia's maidservant would attend her.

When the door closed and they were alone, Hotep came forward, her eyes filled with compassion. She put her arms around her mistress, something she would never dare to do with others around. This time she comforted Claudia as a friend.

Claudia wept in her servant's arms, pouring out her misery. "Sejanus ordered the trunks sent yesterday. He knew before the wedding. Oh how I hate that man!"

When she was spent, she slowly recovered herself, stepping back as Hotep handed her a linen cloth to wipe her eyes. She looked at her handmaid and said fiercely, "Sejanus let us stay at the banquet until there was not enough time left and then let Tiberius announce the news. How clever of him. He knew the ship was waiting and said nothing!" She wept again as Hotep carefully untied the knot of Hercules.

Claudia, aware that it should have been Lucius untying the wedding knot, raged inside again. With Hotep's help, she slowly took off her wedding garments and sandals. Then Hotep began to undo the elaborate hairstyle arranged for the wedding and gently brushed Claudia's hair before helping her to bed—the bed that she had expected to share with Lucius. Her mother's ring was placed back in the small chest. Another wave of sorrow overwhelmed her, and as the coverlet was pulled over her, the last Claudia remembered was Hotep settling in a chair nearby, watching over her mistress as she had done so many times before.

Weary in mind and body, Claudia fell into a deep and troubled sleep.

She woke hours later with a start, trying to clear the remnants of a strange dream from her mind. She opened her eyes and Hotep was instantly at her side.

"You are feeling better now, Domina?"

"I had the strangest dream. There was this man and his face was so clear. He wasn't Roman, a foreigner of some kind, and he was looking at me. I cannot forget his eyes, so deep and full of love . . ."

The handmaid's eyes widened. "You dreamt of another man?"

"It was not like that. He was like a holy man of some kind. He wanted something from me, but I don't know what it was."

"That is a strange dream." She helped Claudia from the bed and helped her dress, then arranged Claudia's hair in a simpler style.

"What must they think of me, Hotep. I arrive as the new mistress and then promptly seclude myself in my room!"

"You had a sad ending to your wedding day and were upset. No one feels anything but sympathy for what you have endured."

It seemed impossible that she was married this morning. A dream, and she would find herself back in the palace. As she thought of the wedding, she again felt Lucius's arms around her and his kiss. She longed for him, but he was on his way to Caesarea without her.

"How Sejanus must have enjoyed planning this. I would like to pound him with my fists."

Hotep looked around fearfully. "Domina, you must not speak like this."

"I am not in Rome and I cannot wait to leave here and go far away. I only pray Lucius will send for me soon."

"He will do that, Domina. His eyes look upon you with love. He also wishes to have you with him."

Claudia sighed and looked toward the door. "I suppose I must go and see this villa I'm suddenly mistress of. Oh, Hotep, I'm a married woman yet not a wife!"

When Claudia came down the stairs, she found Alba waiting. Her face showed compassion as she waited for her mistress to descend.

"You had a good rest, Domina?"

"Yes, thank you, Alba. I'm sorry to close myself away so quickly after I arrived."

The servant shook her head slowly. "It is most understandable, Domina. Nothing you could do. The Master is a soldier and he must follow orders. It is strange that he should be ordered away at such a time."

Claudia had opened her mouth to comment on the prefect, but closed it again. She did not need to speak all her thoughts to the servants. "Yes, but we shall be together soon. He will arrange for my passage."

Alba smiled warmly at her mistress. "Come, partake of some lunch and gather strength."

Realizing she was quite hungry, she followed Alba to the dining room and found fruit and warm bread along with some fresh apple cider and cheese.

When she had finished, she turned to Alba. "I would like to see the villa. The prefect has told me to decide what household goods I wish to bring with me."

Marcus entered the room. "I was just going to suggest that, Domina. Please follow me and let me show you your new home."

Alba bowed and returned to the kitchen.

Marcus started in the atrium and this time Claudia looked more closely at the beautiful pattern of mosaic—a golden circle trimmed in blue with a rectangular pattern surrounding it in blue and white. The atrium was lined with mosaics. To one side there was a stone basin and above it an opening in the roof for rainwater to fall into the basin.

They entered the center of the house where a small statue of Venus faced a square pool with a stone bench at one end. In the far corner was a cabinet with another small statue on top. Marcus opened the cabinet to display some vases and bowls for flowers. Claudia was aware of a sense of peacefulness that permeated the villa.

Cabinets were opened one by one to show the new mistress how well stocked they were. The pottery was serviceable but not heavy. One cabinet even had glassware, new to Rome in the last few years.

Just outside the kitchen was a stone oven used for baking the bread for the household. Beyond that was a kitchen garden, a small orchard with various fruit trees. She could hear chickens clucking and under one of the trees there were two goats in a pen. She was pleasantly surprised to see the villa was almost self-contained.

As they returned to the house, Marcus led her upstairs and showed her the guest rooms and even a room for bathing with a small but deep rectangular pool. It was not like the baths in Rome, but she didn't mind at all.

Claudia followed the steward down another set of stairs to a lower level where smaller rooms housed the servants and storage rooms for foods and bedding.

"When you are ready," Marcus said, "it will be my pleasure to show you the orchard."

"You take good care of the villa, Marcus. How long have you been with the family?"

"Since I was fifteen, Domina. Thirty-five years. Alba came a few years earlier. She was his nurse when the master was born. Both his parents died, several years apart, and Lucius became master of the villa. He has entrusted me with all he owns when he is away."

"I believe his trust is well placed, Marcus."

The servant smiled with pleasure. "Thank you, Domina. There is one more thing to see. Come with me."

He led her through the peristyle, the columned hallway surrounding the garden. A fountain splashed with a cheerful sound, and raised terraces contained flower beds. The sides of the garden were planted with evergreens. Hedges of cypress defined different areas. Some of the tree trunks were covered with ivy. She exclaimed with delight over the *ars topiaria*, hedges trimmed into the shapes of animals. Marcus pointed out violets and roses, along with crocus, narcissus, lilies, and some purple iris.

Claudia determined to learn the names of each of the plants. It would help her if she needed to order plants for their home in Caesarea.

For a moment she compared the beautiful garden to the small one in Reggio. A pang of sorrow brushed her heart, and again she willed the sad thoughts away. She'd had enough difficulties for today.

She turned to the steward. "Let us return to the kitchen. I would like to see what herbs and seasonings you have on hand." Thanks to Medina, she was knowledgeable in that area.

17

Claudia woke the second morning to voices in the atrium. One voice she recognized quite clearly. She rose and slipped a garment over her head.

"I am the grandmother of your mistress. I wish to see her immediately!"

There was a knock on the door and Claudia herself opened it.

Alba was clearly upset. "There is someone to see you, Domina. She says—"

"It's all right, Alba. I know who it is. Show my grandmother to my room."

Scribonia strode into the room, her eyes flashing, but Claudia knew her grandmother's anger was not directed at her.

"This is a disgrace. All Rome is talking about your wedding and the emperor sending your husband off to Judea without even completing the final part of the marriage—the offerings to the gods, lighting the fire, the marriage not consummated. What was he thinking? Could he not have waited one day? Our family is humiliated!"

Claudia glanced at the door, but Alba had gone and closed it behind her. "I do not believe this was the doing of Tiberius." She then told her grandmother about the incident in the dark hallway when she had saved Hotep from Sejanus. "He bided his time, Grandmother.

Now I know why he was almost smirking at the banquet. He knew what he'd done."

"But the emperor, surely he would not do this to his own ward?"

"Tiberius was at the banquet, but his mind is often elsewhere. He is fearful these days of many things. The servants say that Sejanus fills his mind with fears of assassination and I'm almost certain he will leave Rome for Capri soon. I'm told he feels safe there."

"He will rule the empire from Capri?" Scribonia finally sat down on a chair. "Then no one in Rome is safe. Sejanus will have a free hand."

Claudia sat down on a chair opposite her grandmother. "I am praying that Lucius will send for me soon. Rome will not be a good place to be."

"He arrests any of our loyal citizens who oppose him on trumped-up charges and they must commit suicide to protect their good name." Scribonia suddenly looked toward Hotep as though she were an enemy who would carry her comments to Sejanus.

Claudia put a hand on her arm. "Do not fear Hotep, Grandmother. She is a trusted servant and friend."

"A friend? She is a slave."

"The only friend I had in the palace all this time."

Scribonia sniffed. "I don't know what the future holds. I would that the gods take me today. I am old and useless. I cannot even help you in this sad time."

It was the first time Claudia had ever heard this strong woman sound so full of despair and it shocked her. "You have been strength for me all my life, Grandmother. I don't know what I would have done without you nearby. You arranged for Medina to come, and you have helped me in every way you could."

Somewhat mollified, Scribonia rose. "I just had to come, child. I was so angry that he would do this to you."

"I'm glad you came."

"Well, while you are here, I will come as often as possible. It is getting more difficult for me to travel, but I will do my best."

Claudia smiled then. "Thank you, Grandmother."

Her grandmother turned again to the wedding. "What will you do when you arrive in Caesarea? Will your husband complete the ceremony? Who will tie the knot of Hercules about you?"

"Lucius has assured me that when I arrive in Caesarea, we will do those things that are needful to appease the gods, and there will be a wedding couch. Now, while you are here, would you like to see the Villa Ponti?"

Claudia was quickly dressed. Scribonia waited impatiently while Hotep did her mistress's hair. Finally, arm in arm, Claudia showed her grandmother the villa.

Scribonia's face showed her approval. "You have done well in marriage, Claudia, and for that I suppose we must somehow thank Sejanus . . . and Tiberius."

"I will feel better when Lucius and I are together again, truly man and wife."

"Yes, I'm sure you will."

Scribonia peered at Claudia intently. "Claudia, do you know that if something happens to Lucius before your marriage is consummated, the villa will go to the nearest male relative? You will be out of a home. I pray the gods that you will be able to join your husband soon. Sejanus might be his mentor, but he has placed you in an awkward position."

"Yes, I know, Grandmother, but there is little I can do until Lucius sends for me. From our last parting I believe he will not rest until he has secured my passage on the first ship heading to Caesarea."

Scribonia smiled then. "I believe you are right. I saw the way he looked at you through the wedding and at the banquet."

The two women were silent for a while, each with their own thoughts. Then Claudia realized Medina had not come.

"You did not bring Medina?"

"She is not well. The physician said to let her rest and gave her some herbs. He felt perhaps she had eaten something that did not agree with her. I will bring her next time."

As the days passed, Claudia spent time with Marcus and Alba looking at the furniture and the linens. Finally, she decided to take only what linens she would immediately need and purchase others in Caesarea. The furniture in the house had been with the family for many years, and she felt strongly it should stay there. She would furnish the villa or residence in Caesarea after she had time to see what she needed there. Marcus seemed relieved that the household furniture wasn't to leave the villa.

"I think it wise to travel as lightly as possible, don't you, Marcus?"

"You are indeed wise, Domina. The furniture would be difficult to ship and you do not know what your needs will be."

A few chests were ready to be packed with what Claudia felt she would use immediately. She was as ready as she could possibly be, pending word from Lucius.

With each passing week her ties to Lucius seemed to dim. Even the wedding seemed like a dream that really hadn't happened. How would she feel when she saw her husband again, a man who was hers in name only? Would he feel the same?

Her mind turned with all the questions and anxieties that would not be laid to rest until she and Lucius became one.

She read, made a few trips into Rome with Hotep and Marcus to make some purchases. She had no desire to gossip with the other Roman matrons at the baths. She walked in the garden and the orchard and waited. It was almost two months before a young man came from a recently arrived merchant ship with a message for her. She thanked him and hurriedly unrolled the scroll.

My dearest wife, I have settled in the winter palace in Caesarea and will remain until you arrive. I have secured passage for you on the ship that has brought you this message. You are to travel to the port of Ostia and load your goods as soon as possible.

The captain of the ship has arranged accommodations for you and your handmaid. I eagerly await your arrival.

> *Your husband,*
> *Lucius Pontius Pilate*

She sat for a moment, reading and rereading the words from Lucius. She had hoped for something more endearing, but then realized it would not be appropriate.

Finally, the young sailor who had waited patiently for Claudia to read the message said, "My lady, we sail from Ostia in five days when our goods are loaded. I am to return in three days to escort you to the ship."

"What is your name?"

"I am called Titus, my lady."

"Thank you, Titus. I will be ready. Notify the captain that I bring only personal items and clothing. He needs to make room for only a couple of chests. I will also bring my maidservant with me. She will attend to my needs on the ship."

"I will tell the captain and return in three days."

Claudia thought quickly. "Wait, I need to have you take a message to my grandmother in Rome." She sent for a stylus and wax tablet and quickly wrote, asking Scribonia to come right away.

When he had gone, Claudia hurried up to her room to show the scroll to Hotep. "At last, we shall leave this wretched city for Judea."

"I am happy for you, Domina." Her words did not match her face.

"Oh, Hotep, is something wrong?"

"I have heard things about Judea. It is so far away. The only ship I have been on was the slave ship and I was very sick."

Claudia raised her eyebrows. "I have never sailed on a ship. We will look upon it as an adventure, Hotep. Who knows what awaits us in Judea?"

"That is true, Domina. We move according to the hands of the gods and we do not have a say in what that will be."

It was late morning the next day when her grandmother's coach entered the grounds and Medina alighted first and then helped her mistress. Claudia hurried to meet them. With a shock, she saw how frail her grandmother had become. It must have cost her a great effort to make this last trip.

As she entered the villa, Scribonia leaned heavily on Medina's arm. When she was settled in a comfortable chair, Alba brought them small cups of apple cider and bread.

Her grandmother turned to the matters at hand. "Lucius has finally sent for you. What have you packed?"

Claudia smiled to herself. Her grandmother was the consummate Roman matron, making sure that all went smoothly. With great effort, her grandmother climbed the stairs to Claudia's room to inspect her progress.

She spent the next hour reviewing what Claudia had packed—clothes, jewelry, household goods, and a few linens. When she was satisfied that Claudia had chosen wisely, she dismissed Medina and Hotep to talk with Alba.

Now, alone with her grandmother, Claudia felt tears welling up in her eyes. "I don't know when we shall return to Rome. When shall I see you again?"

Scribonia, showing more emotion than Claudia had ever seen from this austere woman, embraced her and said softly, "I shall not see you again, granddaughter. I am old and my time to join our ancestors will be soon. I feel it in my bones. I pray you will remember our years to-gether as good ones. I have loved you like no other child in our family, and you have endured much. You are strong and you will be a good helpmate for Lucius. It is good to have a husband who loves you. In public you may be aloof, but alone together, be the strength he needs. He cannot show weakness in his role as governor." She sighed, and her hands dropped to her sides. "I don't believe he was truly prepared.

Even in his thirties, he is young for this responsibility. He will make mistakes, but he will do his best. Support him in every way you can.

"He is influenced by Sejanus in his attitude toward the Jews. You must temper this carefully. If he is high-handed, he will bring much grief on his office as governor. Tiberius is leaving for Capri within the month. I'm glad you will be far away, if only for what will happen when Sejanus has a totally free hand. I am grateful I will not live long enough to see the maelstrom he will create in my beloved Rome."

The import of her grandmother's words struck Claudia like a blow to her heart. Her grandmother would be lost to her and she shuddered to think what would be happening in the city.

Scribonia continued. "I have signed the papers and set Medina free. She knows this, but has chosen to remain with me in my last days. I do not know her plans for after I'm gone—perhaps she will contact you in some way. I do not know if she wishes to travel to Judea."

"She is welcome to come here, Grandmother. From what I know of Marcus and this household, she would be welcome. I can send an allowance for her living expenses."

"That is generous, Claudia. I will speak to her about that and let her know that is one path she can take. You must also speak with the steward of this household and be sure he is agreeable to such a plan."

"I will do that."

Medina and Hotep helped Scribonia down the stairs and into the coach. Claudia held back tears as she took leave of her grandmother for the last time. Marcus and Alba stood in the background watching the scene with somber faces.

With a heavy heart, Claudia watched the coach bearing her grandmother and her old nurse until it was out of sight. She would never see the last person left of her family again.

She didn't feel like talking. Hotep concentrated on repairing one of Claudia's garments. Claudia worked her loom, reminding herself that in a few weeks' time she would see her Lucius again. She deliberately turned her thoughts in a more positive direction.

That night she hardly slept. She remembered his kiss and his eyes when he parted from her. "Lucius," she murmured softly as her eyes finally closed.

※

When Titus returned on the third day, he and Marcus carried her chests down to the open coach secured to carry Claudia and her belongings to Ostia.

Claudia turned to the two servants who had endeavored to make her brief stay at the Villa Ponti as comfortable as they could. "I will remember you to my husband and tell him how kind you have been to me. I don't know when we will return from Judea, but we will be comforted that the villa is in good hands."

She had spoken to Marcus about Medina and he had agreed to her plan. "She will be welcome, Domina, if she chooses to come." His anxious tone caused her to scrutinize him more carefully. Then she dismissed her thoughts. It was probably nothing. He was just being kind and obedient to his mistress.

Marcus and Alba bowed their heads briefly to her and wished her a safe voyage.

As the coach moved away, Claudia looked back at the beautiful villa that was her new home, even if only for a few months. Would they return? And when?

18

As they skirted the city of Rome, Claudia glimpsed the top of the palace on Palatine Hill and thought of her years there. She passed a statue of Tiberius and nearby a newly erected statue of Sejanus. She tightened her lips in disgust. Praying to the man and celebrating his birthday like a holiday! She pressed her lips together. Rome could have him. She couldn't get out of Rome fast enough.

Ostia, approximately thirty kilometers west of Rome, was reached in a little under an hour, but the trip from the villa had taken longer. The driver had pressed his team at a fast clip. Titus rode up with the driver to direct him to the right part of the port and the ship. As the coach rolled through the small city in the late afternoon, Titus turned to the women.

"My lady, have you seen the forum, built by our emperor?" Claudia studied it as they went by. It was truly an impressive building.

The town was alive with activity, carts filled with merchandise and goods from the ships headed for Rome, pulled by teams of oxen. Everywhere there seemed to be people hurrying to and fro. It reminded her of her first glimpse of Rome.

"Titus, what are in the huge pottery jars on those carts?"

"They are amphorae, my lady. Many of them carry wine to the provinces and other ports. The large round pots carry wheat and grain.

They are taking them to Rome. Those carts heading toward the wharf carry salt from the salt-pans east of the city."

As the coach rolled onto the dock and slowed to a stop, Titus turned to her. "If you will wait a moment, my lady, I shall notify the captain that we have arrived and bring help to carry your belongings."

Claudia nodded her agreement and sat, observing the ship that would convey her to Caesarea and Lucius. She suddenly felt the grip of fear as she faced her first sea voyage. She turned to Hotep, who also looked at the ship with fearful eyes.

"It was such a ship that brought my brother and me to Rome. But it had oars, and there were many slaves rowing."

"Courage, Hotep. The voyage should not take more than twenty-one days according to Titus. We will make port stops along the way and be able to leave the ship."

The ship was a large vessel with double sails that seemed adequate for her safety. It had one great sail unfurled from the mast in the center of the ship and a smaller sail at the rear. In the very front of the ship a graceful swan's head had been carved.

She didn't want to travel on a slave ship and was relieved that this would be a sailing ship, carrying only cargo and a few passengers. Titus returned with several strong sailors who unloaded her trunks and carried them to the ship where they would be stored in the hold. Thankfully her grandmother had advised her as to what foods to take and warned her about the lack of privacy.

There was a structure on the deck of the ship that would house the captain and his first mate. Passengers erected tents on the deck of the ship. Looking around, Claudia wondered where they would sleep.

Two soldiers approached the wagon and one offered his hand to help Claudia down. "I am Commander Ignatio and this is Subaltern Gordian. We have been sent by your husband, the governor, to escort you safely to Caesarea and see to your comfort on the ship. The governor is a fortunate man, my lady. He is most anxious for your safe arrival."

"Thank you, Commander. I shall feel less fearful of the voyage knowing I am under your protection."

Claudia and her maid were shown to a tent that had been set up for them. It seemed a flimsy shelter and she silently besought the god of the sea to grant them fair winds.

A large, heavyset man approached her and bowed his head slightly. "I am Captain Vibius, my lady. I see my son Titus has brought you safely to the ship. It is my pleasure to have you on board. You have met the two *beneficiari* sent by the governor." She was surprised and pleased to find that the young man, Titus, was the captain's son.

Noting the looks given she and Hotep by the soldiers and the men working on the ship, she was doubly grateful for the protection of the soldiers and thankful to Lucius for looking out for her.

When the two soldiers had moved away to prepare their bedding on the deck nearby, Claudia entered her tent with Hotep to settle their things. She thought to rest but it was impossible with all the noise of a ship getting ready to sail. Men called to each other and orders were shouted out as salt and other cargo was being loaded on board. The ship creaked and groaned as it rocked back and forth in the incoming tide. If it moved now, she wondered, how would it be when they were out to sea? Already her stomach was doing strange things.

At last, with the high tide, the ropes holding the ship to the dock were loosened and pulled aboard the ship. Captain Vibius came to see that they were settled.

"Captain, what will be our first port?"

"Puteoli, my lady. We will be taking on additional cargo and unloading salt."

She turned to Hotep. "Perhaps we can go ashore."

Hotep nodded. "I will be glad of any time off this ship, Domina. I pray I will be well enough to accompany you."

"You are ill?"

"As the ship moves, my stomach moves also."

The reminder was all it took for Claudia's stomach to rebel. As the ship moved out into the open sea, Claudia and Hotep both found themselves leaning over the rail.

Titus came to the tent and offered a wet cloth he had dipped in a bucket of water. "I also felt the sickness of the sea on my first voyage, my lady. It is best that you and your handmaid eat something. Bread and cheese would help your stomach. Please, my lady, take my word for it and eat what you can."

The thought of food made her feel worse. She forced herself to eat some bread and had to order Hotep to eat some. The ship settled into a steady pace and the sea was calm, and in time her stomach began to right itself. She stood at the rail and breathed in the fresh air with deep breaths. Hotep remained in the tent, curled up on her pallet in a ball of misery.

To her surprise, the gentle movement of the ship had a soothing effect on her sleep, and Claudia woke up early the next morning as they were entering the small port of Puteoli. They could not disembark as the ship stayed only a few hours, unloading salt and then loading other merchandise in large baskets. Hopefully, the next port would afford them some time on land again.

19

The ship continued through the Straits of Messina and entered the port of Valetta on Malta. Claudia was invited to the estate of the island's chief official, Petrunius, and his son, Publius. Struggling to walk on land again, she felt as if she was still on the rolling deck of the ship. She was made welcome and given a comfortable room for the night. The commander and young Gordian went to the barracks to join the few soldiers who were stationed on the island.

Hotep was delighted to be off the ship. She was not happy with their quarters on the deck of the ship, having to sleep in their clothes for lack of privacy.

Thanks to her hosts, Claudia was again able to bathe and put on fresh clothing. Their hosts were most happy to have a beautiful woman join them for the evening meal, and she admitted to herself that it was a pleasurable thing to be the wife of a province governor.

When the ship had taken on fresh water and bread for the crew and unloaded their cargo for Malta, they got under way again the next day with high tide. She dreaded this part of the voyage. The captain told her it was the longest, from Malta to Fair Havens on the island of Crete.

They sailed many days and Claudia spent most of her time out on the deck breathing the sea air. Hotep, between bouts of seasickness, joined her. Ever near and watching over them were the two Roman soldiers charged with their welfare.

The days and hours passed far too slowly for her. She could not work on her embroidery with the gentle rolling of the ship, for she found the one time she tried, her stomach protested. Sometimes she spoke with the captain when he was free, and sometimes with the commander and his subaltern. Today it was the commander. He was telling her he was close to retirement and this would be his last voyage before returning to his villa. He was looking forward to spending more time with his family.

When he excused himself and strolled away, she found herself glancing down at the dark water that rushed by. White spume was thrown up by the prow of the ship as it plowed steadily through the sea. Birds followed the ship for miles, calling to one another and looking for any scraps thrown overboard at the end of a meal. She suspected they were not far from land.

When they reached Fair Havens, Claudia couldn't wait to get off the ship. This time the commander found Claudia and her maid a small inn and arranged for lodging for two nights. The ship unloaded pottery jars of salt and dried fish and took on fruit and building supplies.

Fortunately there was a contingent of Roman soldiers stationed on the island, and Claudia was surprised to see a Roman warship sail into the harbor not too long after they had pulled up to the dock.

The commander noted her puzzlement and explained. "They have been following us since we left Rome. A fully armed Roman war vessel is a strong deterrent to pirates."

Claudia had not paid attention, assuming there were just other ships on the sea routes. Sudden fear gripped her.

"Pirates? Are we in danger, Commander?"

"No, my lady. Pirates will not chance a meeting with our escort ship. Because of the great abundance of merchandise that travels the Mediterranean Sea, the merchant ships were being seized upon. Now we do not travel without the armed Roman galleys."

As he mentioned galleys, Claudia remembered Hotep talking about the slave ships and the condemned men that rowed them. Nearly a hundred, chained to their oars. If a Roman warship went down in battle, the slaves were not released but, in chains, went down with the ships. She gave an involuntary shudder.

Once back on board the ship, Claudia watched their parting from the safety of the harbor in a different light. This time she felt better only when she saw their escort also pull away from the docks.

The last stop before Caesarea was Myra. As they entered the harbor, named Andriske, Claudia saw rolled multicolored carpets, large baskets containing grain, white wool and blue cloth from an Alexandrian ship. All of which would be loaded on board their ship for Caesarea and other ports.

Looking up at the face of the cliffs, she saw what looked like carved temples.

"Are those temples, Titus?"

"They are not temples, my lady, but very ancient tombs."

"They are quite colorful. I've never seen tombs painted yellow, red, and blue."

"It is their custom."

Titus returned to his duties on the ship as they neared the dock and Commander Ignatio came to her side.

"We have a few hours, my lady. Would you like to explore the city?"

Anything to get off the boat again. "Yes, thank you."

Once again, the two women followed their military escort into the town. The young soldier procured a cart for them. The commander pointed out the temple of Artemis, the protective goddess of the town. There were public baths, a theater, and the granary that stored the grain prior to shipping. Claudia purchased some bread, cheese, and apples. One enterprising vendor had a small brazier going and had cooked some fish. She bought enough for herself, Hotep, and their escorts. A merchant near the town well sold small pottery cups to drink from.

They walked slowly back to the ship, enjoying the stroll on a surface that wasn't moving. Claudia had become so used to the movement of the ship that once again she felt the land under her was moving, as if she were still on deck. It was a strange sensation.

As they had entered the open sea and had sailed for a few hours, a sudden squall sent the women to their tent to huddle in what little protection it gave them. The sailors on the ship, some stripped to the waist, went about their duties with little deference to the storm. With the rougher water, Hotep became seasick again and Claudia had to help her handmaid to the rail and back to the tent, supported by the young subaltern who steadied them on the slippery deck.

The storm passed and the air became fresh and sweet again. Claudia breathed it in and looked in the direction they were heading. The captain told her the next port would be Caesarea. She was close. *Oh Lucius, I am almost to you.*

Her thoughts were interrupted by a disturbance on the ship. There were shouts heard from the belly of the ship. The captain left the helm and hurried down belowdecks. Claudia turned to the commander.

"What is happening?"

Young Gordian was sent to investigate and came back quickly, his face anxious.

"Sir, the ship is taking on water. The captain needs every man available belowdecks to bail."

The commander turned to Claudia. "While we are gone, remain in your tent, my lady. It will be best if you are out of the way."

As Claudia huddled with Hotep inside the tent, her heart pounded in fear. Taking on water? Was the ship sinking? The two women clung to each other. The only thing they could do was pray to mighty Neptune, the god of the sea, to spare them.

20

The men of the ship rushed here and there in frantic activity as the captain barked orders. Claudia looked out at the swirling waters. The icy fingers of terror gripped her at the thought of the ship sinking in the cold sea and taking them all down with it. She was so near her destination. Would the ship sink? She turned to her handmaid.

"Hotep, I don't know how to swim."

"Our farm in Egypt was near the Nile. My brother and I swam in the waters many times. I will help you, Domina," she offered bravely.

That wasn't comforting to Claudia. Swimming in the shallows of a river was not the same as swimming for your life in the sea. Was this a cruel trick of the gods to keep her from Lucius again?

The yelling back and forth belowdecks suddenly ceased and she wondered at the calm. What was happening? The captain appeared in the opening to the hold. He looked weary but relieved. He hurried over to their tent.

"There was a separation in the ship's hull between the siding and we have taken care of it. The ship will be fine until we reach Caesarea for repairs." He shook his head. "My ship has seen many journeys, but has always been dependable. My sincere apologies for any distress this has caused you, my lady. We shall arrive safely in Caesarea tomorrow."

"Thank you, Captain, for a safe journey. You have been most kind."

"It is my pleasure."

The commander and subaltern also came back on deck. They were bare-chested and hastily donned the tunics, upper body armor, belts and sandals they had discarded to help bail the ship. The commander seemed to move slowly as he dressed and his face was flushed. The hard work seemed to have taken its toll on the older officer. She observed him with concern.

"Commander Ignatio, is there need to convey the details of this situation to the governor?"

He shrugged his shoulders and spread both hands. "He shall hear about it. Better I give a full report. Though it was not of our doing or under our control, he would be concerned for your safety."

"Then I shall tell him how valiantly you have seen to my welfare."

He smiled at her. "Thank you, madam." Then he turned and walked to the railing, looking out to sea. She watched him and sensed his concern. Would Lucius blame him for the incident?

⁂

They journeyed still another day from Myra to Caesarea. The hours seemed to creep by, and while her anxiety had subsided over the safety of the ship, another took its place. She had not seen Lucius in over two months. She was eager to reach the end of her journey and Lucius, yet she wondered how well she knew this man she had married. How would he greet her?

They sailed along the coast and finally came in sight of the harbor of Caesarea. The captain's son, Titus, who had been a guide to many landmarks along her voyage, pointed out two huge breakwaters that jutted out into the sea.

"They were built by Herod to form a safe winter harbor."

As she observed them, they seemed like two arms reaching out to embrace the ship as it passed through the entrance.

"How long did it take to complete the harbor?" she asked.

"Actually, it was completed fairly quickly for such a project. Around ten years."

She turned and looked to see if he was teasing, but his face was serious. "Ten years is a short time?"

"Yes. For a project as difficult as this one, with nothing but sand to build on, that is a short time."

The commander joined them. Titus, in the middle of identifying the theater and the Hippodrome, stepped aside. The commander waved a hand toward the enormous edifice rising up majestically on the peninsula. It was almost as large as the emperor's palace in Rome.

"That is Herod's castle, the headquarters of the governor, my lady, and your new home."

She would be living in a castle? For a moment a stab of disappointment went through her heart. There would not be much she could do there. She had hoped for a villa of their own. The castle would be run by Herod's staff, not hers.

She longed for a bath, but there was no way to accomplish that before she saw Lucius. He had told her that when she arrived, the last of their wedding ceremony would be completed as it should have been on their wedding day. Claudia wrapped her stola more tightly around herself in the morning chill.

As they approached the dock, a familiar figure waited. Lucius. She had forgotten how handsome and tall he was. Excitement built in her heart as she waved to him from the railing of the ship. He spotted her and waved back.

After the gangplank was lowered, Lucius strode quickly on board, receiving a salute from his commander and the subaltern.

She moved close to him, unsure what to do. He put an arm around her briefly. She realized just in time that a public display of affection would be unsuitable. His manner was subdued, but he smiled down at her, easing her fears. As the captain and the subaltern waited, he released her and ordered his men to bring her trunks to the castle as soon as they were unloaded.

The commander took Lucius aside and related the incident at sea. "I prepared to protect your wife with my life, Excellency. She showed courage under the circumstances."

Lucius put a hand on the older officer's shoulder. "I'm sure of that. We will talk later, but now I wish to get my wife settled in her new quarters."

"Yes, Excellency." The commander and his aide saluted.

Captain Vibius appeared on deck and greeted the governor soberly. "We had a bit of trouble as we left Myra, Excellency. It was unexpected but easily fixed so we were able to bring the ship safely into port. I shall see that the breach is repaired."

Lucius's voice was terse. "Something like this does not happen all of a sudden, Captain. The ship should have been inspected more frequently. You are fortunate my wife has arrived safely." His tone of voice was harsh as he reprimanded the captain for endangering the ship and his wife.

Claudia listened with some trepidation. This was a side of Lucius she had not seen in their short times together. As gentle as he had been with her, she was reminded that he had absolute control over her life. How would he react if one day he was displeased with her? Apprehension crept into her thoughts. She must set her mind to be all that he needed her to be and not give him any reason to take his temper out on her. She turned to this man who was her husband and yet a stranger and forced herself to smile.

Lucius put a firm hand under her elbow and escorted Claudia and Hotep off the ship. A coach waited on the dock. The three of them entered the coach and were taken on the short road around the peninsula to the massive entrance to Herod's palace.

The palace was imposing. "Is it true we will live here, Lucius?" Claudia asked. "Is Herod in residence also?"

"No, we've been given this by Herod as the governor's summer residence. It is ours alone. He is staying in another castle in Judea."

Lucius helped her from the coach and Hotep stepped down, looking apprehensively at the impressive building in front of her.

When they entered the main hall, Claudia got a glimpse of a beautiful courtyard with trees and flowers and a fountain. Lucius turned to Hotep. "Come." He led them up a flight of stone steps to their quarters. He turned to Claudia and tilted her chin up with one finger. "I will give you an hour, beloved." His eyes were full of promise and she could only nod.

He opened a door in one wall to reveal a bathing room with a tile bath sunk into the floor. Claudia was delighted.

He kissed her again. "One hour, beloved." Then he left them.

Claudia was happy to sponge the warm water over her body and be refreshed. The salt air had dried her skin, and when she left the bath, Hotep gently massaged warm oil over her body.

Hotep fixed Claudia's hair as she had done on her wedding day and dressed her again in her wedding attire, the cord of Hercules tied around her waist. Claudia decided that no other jewelry was necessary and quickly rubbed her cheeks with rose petals from a box she'd brought.

Then there was a knock and Lucius stood in the doorway. "Hotep, the staff below is waiting to meet you. They will show you to your quarters. You may leave us now."

"Yes, Dominae." Hotep fled the room. Meeting a strange staff would be hard for her maidservant, but this was not the time to put Lucius off.

He spread a hand, indicating the small hearth prepared for them. "Let us complete the required traditions that were interrupted, beloved."

He offered a small container of fire and another of water to the household gods, and handed Claudia a special torch that he had lit with the fire. She took the torch and stooped down to light the fire in the hearth, making her mistress of the home. There were no guests to toss the torch to, as was the custom, so she carefully laid it by the hearth and said a prayer. Then she turned shyly to Lucius and waited.

He skillfully untied the knot of Hercules and pulled the pins from her hair. Then he entwined his hands in her tumbling hair and kissed her with all the fervor of pent-up passion. Happiness rose up in her heart, casting aside all the qualms she'd harbored on the long journey. She was safe at last in the arms of her husband who loved her, and she responded with all her heart.

"Beloved . . . ," he whispered as he swept her up in his arms and carried her to the wedding couch. There, at last, with gentleness and skill, he made her truly his wife.

21

Claudia awoke and stretched. It took a moment to realize where she was. She looked at the side of the bed, but Lucius was gone. Hotep came to her.

"The master had duties to attend to, Domina. He told me to tell you he will see you at dinner. I have been given instructions as to where the dining hall is."

Her maidservant busied herself putting her mistress's clothes away, and as Claudia sat up, she saw that her trunks had been brought into the room and were open. Had servants brought them into the room while she slept? She blushed at the thought.

Hotep saw her looking at the trunks. "They left them outside the door, Domina, and after they were partly unloaded, I was able to drag them in one at a time."

Relieved, Claudia swung her feet off the bed and was suddenly aware with all her being that she had been loved by her husband. She marveled at the experience.

Walking to the window, she looked out at the harbor and saw the ship she'd come on. From her vantage point it looked so small. Men looked like toy figures hurrying about the docks loading and unloading merchandise. The sun was close to setting and the sky was glorious in shades of orange and gold. She watched the fiery orb slip into the sea and with a sigh turned back to the room.

Hotep gave her a knowing smile. "You are truly married now, Domina."

Claudia nodded happily. She was a Roman matron now with all the privileges. It was what she was brought up to do and she looked forward with anticipation to seeing the rest of the palace.

As she proceeded down the stairs with her maidservant leading the way, she found herself wondering petulantly why Lucius had not come for her himself.

They passed through the massive entry to a large courtyard. The center was planted with trees, palms, and shrubs. The courtyard was surrounded by rooms. From somewhere across the square she could hear men's voices. She followed her maidservant, entering the dining hall almost the same time Lucius did, coming from another direction. His face, which had held a stormy countenance, softened at the sight of her.

"You rested well, my love?" A small, pleased smile lingered around his mouth.

"Yes, Lucius, I rested well." She leaned forward, filled with love for him.

He gently took her arm and led her into the dining room, seating her on a chair next to his couch. Hotep took her place in the shadows as the formerly elusive servants appeared, one to remove her sandals, and others bearing dishes of steamed artichokes, cabbage, and asparagus; fresh white bread; a bowl of quinces; another bowl of cucumbers and beets in garlic sauce, and finally, roast duck.

There were no other guests, but she saw friendly and appreciative looks on the faces of the servants, who furtively appraised her.

Lucius was most attentive during dinner and she happily filled him in on some of the things she had seen on her travels. She made it a point to mention how helpful the commander and subaltern were to her. Also, how the captain and his son, Titus, had seen to her needs and made sure she saw places of interest at each of their ports.

Lucius listened, almost amused, and she realized he was aware of what she was doing.

"Dear Lucius, now it is your turn to tell me what you have been doing in Judea all this time."

He sighed and leaned back. "They are truly an unruly group of people, these Jews. They have strange beliefs in some unseen god. At least ours are visible when we pray, but they have the gall to claim their god created the universe!" He shook his head in disbelief. "Then there are all the laws they must follow given them by their god, through some man called Moses." He waved a hand in anger. "Our Roman laws are not good enough for them."

"But must they not follow the laws of Rome?"

He toyed with a piece of duck and popped it into his mouth. In a moment, his smile was almost wicked. "I intend to show them who rules this forsaken country, and it is not their invisible god."

He said no more and she felt the subject was closed. He must not think she was going to interfere in his decisions as governor. She ate her meal, but her curiosity was piqued. What did he intend to do?

❧

Claudia had lain in her husband's arms throughout the night. She found she liked being married. When she awoke, though, once again Lucius was gone.

Hotep had been given quarters in the castle with the other slaves, with the understanding she would be called when needed by her mistress. She anticipated and watched when Lucius left. She was there for her mistress with warm, wet cloths to wipe the sleep from her face.

The castle was a whirlwind of activity when Claudia came down after a brief breakfast of fruit, bread, and mulsa. She found Lucius, who was coming from the audience hall.

"My lord, what is happening?"

He put a finger under her chin. "Nothing to concern yourself with, beloved, I am just moving the army from Caesarea to Jerusalem to take their winter quarters there. They are taking Caesar's banners. I intend to show the Jews who rules over their land."

"When will they arrive in Jerusalem?"

"Sometime during the night. When the Jews awake, the banners will already be in place."

That didn't seem like an unusual thing to do. With a brief kiss, he was gone and she went to a balcony overlooking the plaza to see the soldiers massing with their banners.

She was proud of Lucius, feeling that he was showing the people that he was in charge and that the emperor was to be revered. She watched the columns as they marched down the road to Jerusalem in perfect formation. Surely the Jews would honor the image of their emperor.

Claudia spent the day getting to know the servants and exploring the castle. With chagrin she noted that there were plenty of linens and she stuffed down a twinge of guilt for bringing some from the Villa Ponti.

That evening at dinner, Lucius seemed preoccupied. A courier had brought him news that a delegation of the Jewish leaders was on their way to Caesarea concerning the banners.

"Why are they coming about the banners, Lucius?"

He waved a hand in anger. "Something about graven images. I can handle a few angry Jews. This territory seems to thrive on complaints. I'll send them on their way in short order."

Claudia listened to his brave words, but sensed an undercurrent of anxiety. Was Lucius afraid of the Jews? She knew he wanted to prove to the emperor and Sejanus that their confidence in him was not misplaced.

She gave him a warm smile. "You will do the right thing, my love, I know it."

He covered her hand with his. "I wish I could be as sure of that."

Claudia began her new responsibilities as mistress of their living quarters and one by one examined every task done by the servants.

When she found a tile floor hastily mopped and still showing dirt, she called the slave back and in no uncertain terms had it mopped until it shone. She praised the servant when the job was done, and she was pleased when Hotep brought word that the servants considered the new mistress strict but fair.

It wasn't until the next day that Lucius found out what he was facing.

Claudia woke that morning to the cries of a great crowd outside the palace. She quickly wrapped her *palla* around her and slipped out to the balcony. She stood in the shadows and looked down at the plaza outside the palace. People were shouting in angry voices and they were shaking their fists at the palace.

Lucius had brought his seat of judgment to the square out on the porch above the steps to the palace.

When her maidservant joined her, she cried, "Hotep! What is going on down there?"

"It is the Jews, Domina, they have come from Jerusalem and are angry about the banners that were set up in their city."

"Quick, help me get dressed and then get me a cloak that I can hide in. I want to see what is happening."

"But Domina, it would not be safe. There are many angry people out there. It could bring you to harm."

"I must see what Lucius is doing."

They hurried back to her chamber and Hotep helped her mistress dress. Then she left the room and returned shortly with a heavy dark cloak, worn by one of the servants in bad weather. It covered Claudia and hid her face. She and Hotep slipped out of the castle and lingered in the shadows of a huge pillar where they could observe the crowd in safety but hear what was going on.

More than twenty of the priests from the Jewish council had come and were presenting Lucius with a petition. An angry horde surged in behind the priests.

One of the priests, who seemed to be the leader, stepped forward to present their petition.

"Excellency, as you can see, this is a serious matter for us. The banners are in conflict with our Mosaic law, which forbids graven images. Some of your soldiers have actually sacrificed in front of these banners. This is idolatry. And it is offensive to our God."

He cited other complaints and then stated that the petition had been signed by every member of the Jewish Sanhedrin.

Her husband looked over the group of priests. "Is your high priest Joseph Caiaphas or Annas with you?"

"No, Excellency. We were sent."

Lucius rubbed his chin with one hand as he listened. He unrolled the scroll again and read it. Finally, he looked straight at the rabbis. "Honored men of the Sanhedrin, give me a night to consult with my council of state. I will answer your petition at this time tomorrow."

The priests consulted with one another and there seemed to be no objection. They nodded their heads.

"In the meantime," said Lucius, rising, "perhaps it would be to your advantage to disperse the crowd gathered outside." He walked away into the palace.

~~~

After dinner, Lucius was astounded that the crowd was still there. Instead of being dispersed by the priests, they were making preparations to spend the night in the square. To make things worse, the numbers were swelling by the hour.

He could not sleep that night, pacing the floor and considering what to do about the banners.

"Beloved, you must get some rest. How can you face those priests tomorrow if you are weary in body?"

He kissed her briefly. "I am going to my room to dress and then to my study. This is a matter that will not be easy to settle."

She watched him go and began to pray to the gods to give him wisdom on the morrow. She put her head back down, but sleep was elusive for her also, and she found herself dreading the next day. Sejanus had passed his hatred of the Jews to Lucius, but Tiberius did not share that hatred. The emperor insisted on giving the Jews freedom in their religion. Her husband walked a very fine line of diplomacy. He must not let his anger or prejudice sway him. She got up and looked out the window of their room toward the sea. A large moon made a sparkling path across the water. Somewhere a bird called to its mate in the night, and she suddenly felt a great longing well up inside, for what she was not sure.

22

The next morning when Hotep arrived at her room, Claudia was already dressed. Her maidservant arranged her mistress's hair as quickly as she could, for Claudia would barely sit still to let her finish. She was anxious to see how this morning would go with the Jewish delegation.

When at last she could look out the window at the square, she was distressed for Lucius, for some of the people who had come with the priests had set up tents. Others had slept on blankets and wrapped themselves in their cloaks against the cold October night. The merchants of the town were moving among the people selling bread, wine, and other food items to the people. One enterprising merchant was hawking hot cider, a deterrent against the cold.

She shook her head. This didn't look good for Lucius. How would he resolve this dilemma?

Lucius strode down the corridor and came to her side. He also watched the disturbing scene below. "No doubt the merchants are doing well, charging double the price for their wares."

He pounded one fist into his palm. "I will not have them think they can pressure me into giving in. If there's one thing I have been told over and over concerning this cantankerous people, it's to be firm. They shall see how firm I can be!"

"What did the council say last night?"

"I upbraided them for not informing me more clearly on this matter of graven images. They told me that there was no precedent for this occasion since it had not occurred before."

She put a hand on his arm. "What will you do now?"

"We have drawn up a reply to the petition. They will not be happy with it. But they must learn they do not rule Rome, and giving in on my part will be seen as weakness. I cannot have a rebellion at this stage of my tenure here."

She reached up and kissed his cheek. "Be strong, my Lucius. I have beseeched the gods for wisdom."

He nodded and went to face the Jewish delegation.

She watched from the shadows again as he took his seat before the large crowd and unrolled a scroll. He handed it to his tribune to read aloud.

"The council has responded with the following statements: First, the ensigns were designed by and belong to the Roman military. They have nothing to do with the Jews. Second, it is not for the Jews to draw religious meaning into Roman customs which do not concern them. Third, Jews are not required to worship the image of Caesar, and Rome leaves Jewish religious practices alone; therefore, tolerance is required on both sides. Fourth, to tamper with these standards would be a direct and unforgivable insult to the emperor. Therefore, we will not concede on this matter."

There was a moment of stunned silence. Then the leading priest spoke angrily. "You tamper with our customs by changing the high priesthood five times!" He turned and spoke briefly with others in his delegation. The crowd behind them began to murmur.

The priest turned and faced Lucius, his chin up in defiance. "This is in direct conflict with our ancient laws. We will remain here in Caesarea and pray. May the Most High God lead you to remove these accursed and abominable banners from the Holy City."

There were shouts of agreement from the crowd, who shook their fists and cried out to the governor.

"You have no respect for our laws!"

"You defile our Holy City with your graven images!"

"No other governor has dared to do such a thing, it is an insult to our God!"

Lucius sat on his judgment seat, and his face was dark with anger. "There is no god but Caesar. It is time you Jews knew that and gave the emperor the respect he is due. I will not remove the banners."

The huge crowd was growing by the minute as other Jews came from surrounding areas to protest. Lucius listened for a few more moments and then rose and deliberately left the square, ignoring them.

He dined with his council instead of Claudia, but she knew the servants would tell Hotep of the conversation.

Hotep joined her in Claudia's quarters with a simple repast of bread and lentil soup.

"What news do you have for me? What does the council say about this?"

Hotep shook her head. "They are congratulating themselves that the matter is over and done with. They feel that by sunset most of the mob will return home. They won't want to spend another night in the cold."

"I hope they are right."

Claudia was puzzled. Why would these people object to an image of the man who ruled over them? She turned to Hotep. "Is there a Jew among our staff who can explain these things to me?"

"I don't know . . . wait. Yes, Domina, there is an old man named Jeremiah. He works in the gardens. I will see if he will talk to you."

Lucius was busy with the council and other matters of government, and it seemed like a good time to meet with this Jewish man. After lunch, at her maid's suggestion, she waited in one of the private alcoves in the center courtyard.

❧

Claudia sat quietly, contemplating what she had seen that day, and almost didn't hear the footsteps until the man was nearly in front of her. She looked up into a weathered face with piercing brown eyes. He was slightly stooped and his gnarled hands still had dirt on them. His bushy eyebrows were knit together as he stood before her.

His face was guarded and his tone almost harsh. "Domina, you wished to see me?"

"Yes, Jeremiah, is it?"

"Yes, Domina." His entire manner spoke of disapproval.

"I wish to know the reason why the Jews are so angry about the banners in Jerusalem. They were only meant to honor the emperor. Is that wrong?"

He studied her a moment, considering her words, and his face softened a bit. "We serve a God, Domina, who forbids graven images. There have been banners in Jerusalem before, but they had no image on them. We respect the emperor as one must respect the ruler of a conquered people. Your husband has created a very bad situation that could lead to bloodshed. Our leaders will not relent and allow the banners to remain."

"Jeremiah, since we are here to govern this region in the emperor's name, we must do what honors the emperor."

"Except to bring a graven image of an idol worshiper into the Holy City."

"We Romans have always worshiped gods that we can see. I do not understand the worship of an invisible god that no one can see."

He looked at her, and while his look was not patronizing, he spoke as one would speak to a child. "Why do you worship gods that are made with your own hands? They cannot speak, nor hear, nor see. They are only images made of stone or wood. You take a tree and use part of the tree to fuel your fire, and then use another part of the same tree to create an image you can bow down to. How can these images your craftsmen have created hear your prayers?"

Before she could consider his question, she suddenly spied Lucius standing across the courtyard watching them. He did not look pleased.

She stood and gathered her palla about her. "We will talk again, Jeremiah. I wish to know more, but this is not the time."

He gave a slight bow. "As you wish, Domina, but the matter of the banners is not finished."

The old man returned to his gardening and Claudia smiled charmingly at her husband.

"You have finished your business? I was looking forward to your company."

"Who was that you were talking to?"

"He is one of the gardeners, my love. I have been inquiring about different plants and flowers that would brighten up this dark palace. Do you not wish me to get acquainted with the staff? I don't know how long we will be here, and it is my task to oversee them."

"So it is." With a smile, he tucked her hand on his arm. "Let us walk in the garden. It has been a trying day."

"Will the crowd disperse?"

"So far they have not. I will see if they are still there tomorrow. The council feels they will get tired of waiting out in the cold."

"I'm sure you are right."

They talked of mundane things, but Claudia saw her husband glance in the direction of the square from time to time. Then his tribune came and whispered something in his ear causing him to smack his palm with his fist. "Give them another day," he growled.

"Yes, Excellency."

When the tribune had gone, Lucius left her to attend to other matters. She wearily climbed the stairs to her chamber. Why was she so tired?

She lay down to rest and was instantly asleep, but the dream she'd had months ago returned. It was the same man she had seen in the other dream—a man with strange, compelling eyes. There was great sorrow on his face and it was bloody. What did he want of her? Why did he haunt her dreams?

23

The next morning Claudia followed a confident Lucius to the balcony. He told her he'd arranged for a group of soldiers to clean up the plaza. As they reached the balcony and looked down, Lucius uttered a curse. The crowd had not only remained, but it had grown even larger.

Just then someone in the crowd spotted them on the balcony and alerted others. All eyes turned their way and the mob rose as one body, shaking their fists and crying out, "Down with the graven images! Remove the idols from our Holy City!"

Lucius jerked Claudia away from the balcony, back into the palace. His face was clouded with anger as he called his tribune. "Do not antagonize the crowd any more than they are already worked up. Station your men in critical places and watch, but be prepared to defend yourselves if the crowd becomes violent."

"Yes, Excellency." The tribune saluted and hurried away.

The clamor of the crowd seemed to go in waves. One moment Claudia heard tumultuous shouting and then silence for hours. She wondered why Lucius couldn't just take the banners down, but she endeavored to be confident in her tone and supportive of her husband as she listened to him think out loud.

"Beloved, if this mob turns to violence I wish you to return to your quarters with Hotep and bolt the door." He gave her a stern look.

"I am aware you have been nearby listening to what is going on. The crowd could overwhelm the palace and there could be bloodshed. I will not have you in danger."

"Of course, Lucius. With all you have on your mind, you must not have the additional worry of my safety."

He seemed pleased with her response. He kissed her and left to once again speak with his council.

She frowned. Was Lucius anticipating danger from the crowd? His words struck fear into her heart. Would the people overcome the guards? She shivered at the thought of what would happen if the soldiers were forced to use their broadswords.

After Lucius left, she was once again compelled to slip out near the balcony, but this time she stayed out of sight in the shadows to observe the crowd.

Some appeared to be praying, others were chanting. Now and then a song in Hebrew would rise and be taken up by the crowd until the notes swelled on the morning air.

She turned to Hotep, who had joined her. "I wish I knew what they were singing."

"Jeremiah told us they sing some of the Psalms—how their God is an ever-present help in their times of trouble."

Jeremiah. Claudia wanted to speak with him again, but she would have to wait until this crisis passed. She could not ask Jeremiah to come to her quarters, nor could she go down to the garden. Lucius would be angry to find her so near the entrance to the palace and vulnerable if the crowd's mood changed.

By the fourth day, the crowd had not moved. A few stragglers had gone, but it represented a small fraction of the huge gathering. When dark clouds appeared on the horizon, Lucius took heart. Perhaps a rainstorm, common in October, would drench the crowd and force them to retreat to their homes.

Beginning with a light spattering of drops, the storm increased in volume, whipping the tents set up in the plaza and drenching those who had no shelter. Then those who had tents opened them to shelter those who didn't, and others just sought what shelter they could find near the plaza. Claudia and Lucius watched from a palace window.

Lucius shook his head in consternation. "What is the matter with those people? Why do they persist in this ridiculous protest? I should have been given a larger force."

"Why were you not?"

He shrugged. "Sejanus said the legions were needed on the frontiers of the empire and what I had was enough to keep peace in Judea."

"But it is not enough?"

"My dear Claudia, Judea is the most rebellious province in the Roman Empire. Did you know that there have been twelve major rebellions in this area since it was conquered?"

She shook her head. "And the emperor does not wish to see another rebellion under your governorship?"

"It would probably be the end of my tenure here. I would be recalled to Rome and only the gods know to what."

The fifth day more problems arose. Many of the Jews had sent for their own provisions and were no longer buying from the local vendors. Harsh words and insults were traded between Jew and Gentile and several small incidents began to occur.

Claudia knew her husband had to somehow find a way to defuse the situation. When she pressed him for his solution, he merely told her the disturbance had to end and went to confer with his counsel. When he came up to their quarters later, he would not tell her what the council had decided, but the servants told her that additional troops were coming from Sebaste.

Early the next morning, Lucius sent for his tribune. He murmured orders, the soldier saluted and quickly left. In a short time, trumpets silenced the crowd. The tribune announced that the governor of Judea would personally reply to their petition within the hour.

The delegation of priests conferred together and nodded to the people. With much murmuring, the crowd settled by their tents and belongings to wait for the governor.

With a lighter heart, Claudia realized Lucius might have found a way out of this dilemma. Hopefully the plaza would be cleared by the end of the day.

Lucius, appearing smug, allowed Claudia to accompany him. She was seated in the shadows on the dais erected above the plaza. Lucius wore his official toga with its wide stripe of royal purple. The trumpets announced his entrance as he strode to the seat of tribunal on the dais next to his purple governor's standard.

The Jews stood expectantly. A fanfare opened the ceremonial. Lucius leaned forward. "I greet you in the name of the Emperor Tiberius Caesar. Do you have any final words before I render a judgment?"

The Jewish leaders came and once again presented their petition to remove the standards from the Holy City.

Lucius listened, his head tilted to one side. "On this matter of graven images, is there or has there been any instance where you have allowed this? You have no images, even of your own prophets or leaders?"

"No, Excellency."

Lucius fired his first salvo. "I've been told that the Jews in Mesopotamia paint pictorial frescoes on the walls of their synagogues, and Jews even in Rome draw and sculpt figures on their burial vaults. How do you explain this discrepancy?"

The leader appeared shocked for a moment, then recovered himself. "These Jews are cousins, but they do not honor our laws. They are committing sacrilege, for their actions conflict with what our God has ordained."

"I've also been informed that Herod placed a golden eagle over the very gate of your temple."

"It was torn down by the people, Excellency."

"I see. Now what about the silver denarii you use that has the image of the emperor on it?"

The rabbis turned and murmured among themselves. Claudia felt Lucius had them there and waited anxiously for how they would respond.

The Jewish leader approached Lucius again. "Excellency, we are required to pay tribute to Rome. As such we use the monetary coin of the Roman Empire. However, those coins are not used in the Temple. We don't feel the coins have any religious significance."

Lucius was becoming impatient. "Then why are you concerned about the standards? We don't expect you to worship our standards any more than you worship our money."

"Your Excellency, our law forbids religious images, especially in the Holy City." Claudia noted his tone was patronizing and glanced at Lucius.

"Enough!" he bellowed at them. "You try my patience. I have heard all I wish to hear. My final judgment is that the ensigns of the emperor will remain in Jerusalem. I shall not insult our emperor by ordering their removal. You will give me your immediate agreement and you and this crowd will leave Caesarea at once."

The Jewish leaders stood in shocked silence. They again conferred and finally, with one voice cried out loudly. "We shall remain here in Caesarea until the idols are removed."

The crowd, watching in comparative silence, now erupted in angry shouts. "Remove the cursed idols! They are an abomination!"

Lucius nodded to his tribune who gave a signal. Suddenly cries of fear gripped the crowd as they were surrounded by hundreds of Roman soldiers.

His jaw was rigid and his fists were clenched as Lucius stared down at the Jewish leaders. "You are convicted of treason and sedition against the Emperor Tiberius Caesar. The penalty for this is death. You have one last warning to leave this plaza in peace. Those who remain after this warning will be killed. I will not tolerate this disturbance any longer, now go!"

The leaders murmured together, then stepped forward and cried, "Kill us if you feel you must, but we will not agree to leave those graven images in our Holy City."

"You want the blood of these people gathered here on your hands?"

Claudia held her breath. Lucius had not been prepared for these obstinate Jews to die for their beliefs. He looked down at the men standing bravely at his feet. He glanced back at Claudia. She was sure he'd only meant to threaten them, not bring them to the point of death. How could he order a needless slaughter?

"You would die over a banner?"

"Yes," answered one of the leaders. "We would die for what we believe."

When he shook his head. Claudia prayed silently that the gods would give him wisdom.

Lucius turned his attention to the crowd. "Women and children may leave in peace, but go now. Any of the men who wish to live may leave now and you will not be penalized. Return to your homes and families."

To Claudia's relief, some of the women and children began to leave the arena. To her dismay, not one man left his place.

Finally, Lucius motioned to his tribune and spoke quickly. The tribune faced the arena and drew his sword. Claudia gasped at the ominous rasping sound of hundreds of Roman broadswords being drawn from their sheaths.

The Jewish leaders flung themselves on the ground and bared their necks. The rest of the Jews, men and women alike, fell to the ground and did the same. They began to sing one of their psalms.

Lucius stood dumbfounded. Claudia knew he couldn't massacre hundreds of Jews in cold blood. Her poor, dear Lucius thought he could frighten them into turning and running back to Jerusalem. Yet as she watched, man after man knelt and bared his neck to die.

She waited in fear, bile rising in her throat. *Oh Lucius. Don't give the order.* Such a slaughter would get back to Rome and how would he explain this to the emperor? She prayed silently for a solution.

Lucius stood stiffly, perspiration breaking out on his forehead. He clenched and unclenched his fists as he stared at the spectacle before him. Claudia held her breath, pleading silently to the gods. *Please, Lucius, don't do this!*

Lucius finally spoke, his voice carrying over the crowd to his men. "Sheath your swords."

He then addressed the crowd. "With clemency in the name of Tiberius Caesar, I bid you rise. My task is to govern with justice. I see that you are truly sincere in this matter, and while I was forced to put this to a drastic test, it is evident that the military standards are truly offensive to your people. You were not just testing my authority."

Claudia breathed a silent sigh of relief.

"You must understand that this is still an insult to Caesar and I cannot answer for any repercussions, but in this instance, I shall not dishonor the emperor. The cohort with the offensive standards will be returned to Caesarea, but I will send a cohort with new banners without the image of the emperor on them. Romans and Jews must be able to live and work together. Go in peace. Return to your homes."

A hushed silence followed as the full import of his words was understood.

The crowd began a mighty roar of approval and cheered the governor. They hugged each other and some danced in their exuberance. Suddenly a great hymn of praise broke forth and the people began to sing as one as they gathered their belongings and jubilantly left the plaza.

Lucius watched them go and Claudia came to stand by his side, murmuring softly so only her husband heard. "Well done, my Lucius, well done. You were magnificent."

He dismissed his troops, leaving the additional soldiers to return to Sebaste. He called his tribune. "Exchange the cohorts and bring the offending banners to Caesarea." He looked around the plaza. "And arrange a detail to clean up this mess."

The head priest who had been helped to his feet, bowed low to the governor. "You are a wise and gracious man, my lord. We are grateful."

In moments the delegation of priests from Jerusalem exited the plaza and hurried back to their city with the good news.

Lucius watched them leave, his face dark as the evening shadows. Claudia grieved for him. In his first major encounter with the Jews, had he lost face?

As they returned to the castle, Claudia glanced back at the nearly empty plaza. "The crowd has almost gone, my lord."

He almost snarled. "They are leaving, but I'm sure it is not the last time something will arise in regard to their abominable religion." He balled his fists. "I would have slaughtered them all, but I cannot justify such an action to the emperor, though I would probably please my mentor. Sejanus hates the Jews as much as I do."

The vehemence of his words shocked her. This cruel streak was one she had not foreseen. Then the words of her grandmother came back to her mind. *He will make many mistakes. He is young for this responsibility. You must be a helpmate to him and be his strength.*

She spoke gently, gauging the reception of her words. "You are wise, my Lucius, to consider all that such an action would bring. I have seen, in my years in the palace, the repercussions of arousing the anger of the emperor."

She bore his scrutiny with calm as he studied her face a moment. "Perhaps I have wed a wise counsel." To her relief she had diffused his anger.

A soldier appeared in the entry and waited patiently until Lucius was aware of his presence. When summoned, he spoke with Lucius and whatever the matter, it appeared urgent.

Her husband, with a brief smile at her, turned to go with the soldier. "I have business to attend to. I will join you at dinner." And he was gone.

Hotep waited in the courtyard for her mistress's command.

Claudia considered a moment and then said, "Send for Jeremiah."

The gardener came at her summons and she joined him in the alcove in the courtyard. So that she would not have to deceive her husband again, she discussed plants that could brighten up the courtyard and those that might grow well indoors. After she was satisfied that he understood her wishes, she inquired on the matter foremost in her mind.

"You are aware of the incident that just occurred here. Tell me of your religion. What do you believe and how did it begin?"

"It would take more time than we have today, my lady, but I will tell you if you truly wish to hear."

"I wish to hear, Jeremiah. Sit down, and tell me what you can today. Start at the beginning."

He knit his heavy brows together but seemed satisfied that she was indeed interested. He sat hesitantly on the end of the bench.

"Long ago, in Ur of the land of Chaldea, there lived a great man called Abram. One day he heard a voice speaking to him. It was the voice of the Most High God who said to him, 'Leave your country and your relatives and your father's family, and go to the land that I will show you. I will make you into a great nation. I will bless you and make you famous, and you will be a blessing to others. I will bless those who bless you and curse those who treat you with contempt. All the families on the earth will be blessed because of you.'"

Claudia was intrigued. "He heard the audible voice of a god?"

Jeremiah shook his head. "No, my lady, he heard the voice of the one and only God." And he continued: "He had a wife, Sarai, and a nephew, Lot, but no children of his own, for his wife was barren. He packed up all that he had in obedience to the call of God and left Ur. Many things happened to Abram and his wife Sarai, but God was with them and changed his name to Abraham, which means 'father of many nations.' Now Abraham reached one hundred years old and his wife Sarai, ninety, but there was no sign of the promised seed. Then God changed Sarai's name to Sarah and said that he would bless her.

Though Abraham and Sarah were past the age of childbearing, our God is a God of miracles, and according to the time set by the Most High, Sarah conceived and bore a son and they named him Isaac."

Claudia interrupted again. "This sounds like a strange tale. Whoever heard of a couple that age bearing a child? That is impossible."

Jeremiah smiled. "With our God, nothing is impossible." Then, "When Isaac was forty, Abraham sent his servant to his kinsman to find a wife for his son. He found Rebekah. Through their son Jacob were born twelve sons, the twelve tribes of Israel: Reuben, Simeon, Levi, Judah, Gad, Asher, Issachar, Zebulun, Joseph, Benjamin, Dan, and Naphtali. One of the younger sons, Joseph, who was born of his favored wife, Rachel, had many dreams—dreams that his brothers would bow down to him one day—and he spoke foolishly. When he came from his father to check on the herds and see his brothers, out of jealousy they sold him to a caravan of Ishmaelite slave traders. Joseph was taken to Egypt and bought by Potiphar, who was the captain of the guard for Pharaoh. He became the steward of his master, over his entire household. He was unjustly thrown into prison and yet the Most High God blessed him even there. He was made a trustee over the prisoners. When two of the prisoners had dreams, Joseph told them the meaning of their dreams. Two years later, Pharaoh had two dreams that disturbed him. When Joseph was called from the prison to interpret Pharaoh's dreams, Pharaoh learned that the Most High God was showing him that Egypt would have seven years of plenty followed by seven years of famine. When Pharaoh saw that the Most High God was with Joseph and that the plan Joseph suggested for Egypt was good, he was put in charge of all Egypt. Only Pharaoh had more power than Joseph.

"The seven good years happened and were used to store up grain to feed the people of Egypt, but as the famine spread, people from other countries came for food. One day Joseph's brothers were sent by their father, Jacob, to buy grain. They did not recognize their brother Joseph, and just like in his dream, they all bowed down to him. Eventually he revealed himself and brought not only his father but his whole family to the land of Goshen in Egypt where they could raise their flocks and herds . . ."

Jeremiah paused. "Perhaps I am going too fast for you?"

Claudia shook her head. "No. I was wondering. Do you feel that your dreams tell you of something that is going to happen, like the Pharaoh's dream?"

"Sometimes they are a portent of something in the future. Are you troubled with dreams, my lady?"

"Only one that has recurred and it troubles me."

"I am no interpreter of dreams, but if the dream comes to you many times, I would seek to find why. Are you willing to tell me your dream?"

She considered his question for a long moment. Perhaps if he could help her, the dream would go away. Finally she told him what she saw in her dream. "I do not know what this man wants from me."

Jeremiah bowed his head and she realized he was praying to his God. After a moment, he lifted his head and his eyes pierced hers. "This is truly a dream that will affect your future and that of your husband. That is what I feel, but I can tell you no more."

The afternoon shadows were claiming the courtyard. "Thank you, Jeremiah. It is getting late. I will hear more of the story another time."

He bowed his head and left.

She stood, watching him walk away, her mind troubled by his comments on the dream. Something was coming that would affect her life and that of Lucius. What could it be? She shivered involuntarily, and wrapped her stola tighter. "Hotep, I must dress for dinner."

Her handmaid had been nearby.

"Were you listening?"

"Yes, Domina, it is a most interesting story. I also would like to hear more."

Lucius was weary when he joined her. She had dressed carefully in one of her soft blue linen togas. He watched her gracefully settle on her chair, and stroking her arm with his thumb, his eyes darkened with desire. "I could almost go without dinner, beloved. Your beauty is intoxicating."

She smiled at him. "Dear husband, your words touch my heart, but I am indeed hungry."

He grinned and the servants came with the cloths for their hands. Their meal was simple—melons cut in slices, cabbage and peas with cardamom, and a common dish of salt fish, eggs, and cheese.

"How soon will the banners be removed, Lucius?"

He lifted one eyebrow. "That has been on your mind, beloved?"

She reached out and put her hand on the side of his face. "Only in that I know that has been an unwelcome incident. Did you not handle it well?"

"I had no choice."

She sensed he did not wish to talk about the Jews tonight. They finished their meal and he tilted her chin up and kissed her. Then he took her by the hand and led her up the stairs.

❦

When she had been in Caesarea two months, to her delight, Claudia realized she was expecting a child. She waited another week just to be sure and then informed Lucius that he would be a father in early summer.

He held her to him. "You have made me a happy man, beloved. You must take extra care of yourself." When he left her, he was smiling and walking with a lighter step.

24

In the early spring, Dimitris, a Greek, and a friend who had served with Lucius in the Roman army, was transferred to Caesarea. Lucius invited him to join them for dinner.

The two men clapped each other on the shoulders despite the fact that Lucius was now a higher rank as governor of Judea.

"So tell me, Dimitris, what is happening in Rome?" Lucius leaned back on his couch and waited.

"It is not good, my friend. Tiberius remains on Capri, with no intention of ever returning to Rome. Sejanus is in full control of the empire and the city. He sends messages to Tiberius and receives them in return, but still, the emperor will not leave Capri."

Claudia felt Dimitris was measuring his words, knowing that Lucius was loyal to Sejanus.

Lucius shook his head slowly and reached for a piece of fruit. "I don't understand the emperor's desire to remain on Capri. It is like a ship without its main sail."

"There are rumors that Tiberius intends to name Sejanus co-regent one day."

Lucius's hand paused in midair. "Co-regent?"

"I believe this is what Sejanus has been working toward."

When Lucius's eyes narrowed at this statement, Dimitris spread his hands. "I am only repeating what is being said in Rome. And why not? He's been running the government for two years now. The people even celebrate his birthday as a national holiday."

Lucius merely nodded, but the fingers of one hand drummed on the table. Claudia said nothing, but was troubled by this news. Sejanus was becoming more and more powerful. How would that affect their tenure here in Judea? There had been no repercussions after the incident with the banners.

Dimitris was feeling expansive and after taking a few bites ventured another piece of information, gauging their reaction.

"Tiberius has also given his consent for Sejanus to wed Levilla."

"What?" breathed Lucius.

Claudia stopped eating to stare at Dimitris.

Finally, Lucius reached for a slice of meat. "I suppose I am not surprised. He has been petitioning Tiberius for some time."

Claudia decided to take the opportunity of news from Rome to inquire about her grandmother. "Have you any word on the Lady Scribonia? I have written her, but not received a response."

Dimitris winced. "Forgive me, Lady Claudia." He reached into a pouch under his cape and drew out a small scroll and handed it to her. "I bring a letter from her. She is not in good health, though my sister says she has been seen at the baths."

Claudia's heart lifted as she quickly unrolled the missive.

My dear Claudia,

Dimitris called on me at Lucius's request and I am sending this with him. I am not well, but the gods have not called me yet. Medina sends her love and wants me to assure you that she will go to the Villa Ponti at my demise and wait there for you to return to Rome. There is much fear in Rome but I can say no more. I am pleased that you are so quickly giving Lucius a child.

A good omen from the gods. I pray all will go well with you and look forward to the birth of a great-grandchild.

Your loving grandmother,
Scribonia

Claudia read the letter again. Her grandmother was not well. At least she was still alive. She would write back and send it with a courier.

The men's conversation seemed murmurings over her head as she pondered other things.

After dinner Dimitris bid her a good evening and the men retired to her husband's study, no doubt to discuss matters that did not concern women.

Claudia went up to her room to share the letter from her grandmother with Hotep. She found her maidservant staring out the window, and she seemed startled when Claudia entered the room.

"Your dinner is over, Domina?"

"Yes. It is difficult for me to sit very long. I have a surprise, a letter from my grandmother. She is not well. Medina assured me again that she will go to the Villa Ponti when my grandmother is gone."

Sadness suddenly overwhelmed Claudia. Her grandmother was probably dying and there was no way she could see her before she died. The thought caused tears to surge to her eyes. She wiped them with one hand.

She seemed to have little strength these days. The babe was taking much of her energy. The early nausea had passed, but now, months later, had returned from time to time and she was uneasy with it.

Hotep helped her undress, brushed her hair, and saw her comfortably in her bed before bidding her mistress good night.

As she lay on her bed, Claudia thought about the incident in the plaza. Lucius had to make some difficult decisions and she admired the clever way he had gotten out of the matter of the banners. It could have been disastrous. She tried to picture the soldiers wielding their broadswords and tearing into the crowd of Jews. It was horrible to contemplate. She was relieved and grateful that Lucius rescinded the order. Sleep came quickly and she didn't know when or if Lucius came to bed.

❦

The next morning as she started to rise to breakfast with Hotep, she realized two things. One, Lucius had spent the night in his own quarters, and two, she felt violently ill.

"Domina!" Hotep saw her face and quickly brought a basin. She was just in time.

Claudia lay back down on her bed as her maidservant carefully wiped her face with a damp cloth. "We must send for the physician."

"Find my husband. He will know what to do."

The maidservant dashed out of the room and in what seemed like moments, Lucius was at her side. "I have sent for the troop physician." He pulled a chair to the side of the bed and took her hand, his face clouded with concern.

The military physician came. His lined face looked weary, but he looked down at Claudia with kindness. "I see you are with child, my lady. When is the child due?"

"In early summer." She told him of the weariness and the nausea that came and went.

"Though this is common in the early months, my lady, some women do suffer longer. You are healthy. Perhaps you should rest more."

Lucius, who stood back when the physician came to Claudia's bedside, now took her hand again. "You will do as the physician asks, beloved?" It was more a statement than a question.

"Yes, Lucius."

He kissed the palm of her hand. "Rest, my love, and conserve your strength." He turned to the doctor. "Will it be safe for her to travel?"

"Excellency, women have been having babies for a long time. She can travel, but preferably not by horseback. Where were you going?"

140

"We move to Jerusalem for the spring. She will travel in the *carpentum*. The Jews celebrate Passover and the city is filled with pilgrims. I felt it best to be there watching over the activities at that time."

"That should not be a problem, Excellency." He turned to Claudia. "In the mornings, eat some bread and drink a little mulsa before you rise. It should help with the nausea." The doctor gave a slight bow to his superior and left the room.

"I have duties to attend to, beloved, but Hotep will take good care of you as she always has. I will try to join you for lunch here in your quarters. It is best you do not come down to the dining room at this time. I will try to come here and join you for the evening meal." He kissed her cheek and left the room.

Hotep pumped the pillows behind her. "We will be more careful, Domina. I will take care of you."

Claudia nodded. "That is well and good for the future, but for now, bring me some bread and mulsa quickly. I want to be able to stand up."

25

With Lucius away from Caesarea visiting another part of Judea to inspect one of the cohorts stationed there, Claudia sent for Jeremiah. In a week they would leave for Jerusalem, and she was anxious to know more about the Jews before she got there.

She carefully made her way downstairs with the help of her maidservant and waited in the alcove in the garden, looking forward to more of this interesting story of the Jews.

When Jeremiah came, at her invitation, he settled himself slowly on the end of the bench.

"Let me see, my lady, where did I leave off?"

"It was the people of Israel settling in the land of Goshen."

"Ah, yes. Well, the people lived in Egypt many years and, with the favor of the Most High God, multiplied into a great nation just as the Most High God had promised Abraham. But there came a day when a king arose in Egypt who knew nothing of Joseph. He felt the people of Israel were too many and feared they would take over his kingdom. He made them slaves and used them to build the great pyramids and cities of Egypt. Nearly four hundred years had passed since the people had come to Egypt, and now they were doing backbreaking work for Pharaoh. They cried out to the Most High God for deliverance for a long time. The Most High heard their cries and sent them one of their own, a man by the name of Moses. He had been born to a Hebrew couple, but Pharaoh had decreed that all male children were to be killed . . ."

Claudia's eyes widened. "All of them? That seems so cruel."

"Cruelty comes in many forms, Domina."

Jeremiah waited, letting his words sink in.

She let the comment pass. "Go on, Jeremiah."

"The parents hid their son for three months, and then one day the mother made a basket and put pitch in all the cracks and crevasses so it would float. It was placed among the reeds on a day when Pharaoh's daughter came down to the river to bathe. The baby's sister, Miriam, hid nearby and watched over her little brother. Just as the family hoped, Pharaoh's daughter came and found the baby. The princess called him Moses, for it meant "drawn from the water." Moses was trained in all the knowledge of Egypt, but his true mother, who had been called to be his nurse, taught him about his people, the Hebrews. One day Moses tried to settle a fight between an Egyptian and a Hebrew and killed the Egyptian. He was forced to flee into the wilderness to hide from Pharaoh's wrath. He married the daughter of a Midianite chieftain and raised two sons. When he was eighty years old, he was herding sheep in the wilderness one day when he saw a burning bush—"

Claudia interrupted. "A prince of Egypt one day and then reduced to being a shepherd in the wilderness? If he was the son of Pharaoh's daughter, would she not protect him?"

"Perhaps she could not, Domina. Our God always has a plan and this was his plan for Moses, for a time. When Moses saw a bush that seemed on fire but did not burn, he turned aside to see what this strange sight was. When he approached, God called to him from the midst of the bush and told him he was to go to Pharaoh and tell him to let his people go. Moses was reluctant to do this. He was old, he did not speak well, and he knew that Pharaoh would not listen. God made his brother, Aaron, his spokesman, and finally Moses obeyed the voice of the Lord and went."

"What happened when he returned to Egypt? Was he not in danger of his life?"

Jeremiah glanced at the shadows that were filling the courtyard. "Perhaps another day, Domina?"

"Yes, another day, Jeremiah. I will think on what you have told me."

After she had slowly returned to her quarters, Claudia burst out. "Some of this is very hard to believe. A fiery bush that does not burn? I wonder if Jeremiah is making this up."

"I believe he is sincere, Domina. It is an unusual story."

Claudia laughed. "Yes, indeed. The Jews are an unusual people. I cannot wait to hear what Pharaoh says when an old man of eighty and his brother come and tell him to let the Hebrews leave the land."

Hotep was somber. "Would it not be the same if a foreigner came to Caesar and asked him to let all the slaves go? He would not do this."

∽

When Lucius had not returned the next day, Claudia sent for Jeremiah again. In the courtyard she would be aware if and when her husband returned.

Jeremiah lowered himself again to the end of the bench and, after clearing his throat, continued the story of his people.

"Pharaoh would not let the people go. He did not arrest Moses, but deemed him a crazy prophet he could dismiss from his presence. When the Pharaoh refused, the Most High God sent ten plagues on Egypt to change Pharaoh's mind."

"Ten plagues?"

"Yes, my lady. First, the rivers were turned to blood; then the land was overrun by frogs, then gnats; a plague of boils on cattle and people alike; a plague of hailstones that killed people and animals; a plague of locusts that came by the millions and ate what crops were left; a plague of severe darkness where a man could not even see his hand in front of his face. Yet, no matter what the plague, Pharaoh would not listen and refused each time to let the people go."

"Your god did this? And in spite of each of these terrible plagues, Pharaoh still refused?"

"Yes. It took one final act for Pharaoh to finally agree to let the Hebrews leave Egypt."

"What more could this god of yours do?"

"A most terrible thing, my lady, the plague of the firstborn. The Most High God called Moses and Aaron and gave them instructions they were to pass on to the people. At twilight they were to kill and roast a lamb or a young goat over the fire and eat it with bitter salad greens and bread made without yeast. Nothing was to remain until morning. They were to eat this meal in haste with their sandals on their feet, fully dressed and walking stick in their hand. They were to take blood from the sacrificial lamb and, with a hyssop branch, smear it on the sides and doorposts of their homes. They were not to go outside that night, as the death angel of the Lord would come and would pass over any home marked with blood and they would be safe. Any home without the sign of the blood would lose the firstborn son in that household, from the son of slaves to the son of Pharaoh. We were told to celebrate this night, the Passover, from generation to generation as a special festival to the Lord."

She leaned forward. "And did the death angel come?"

He nodded solemnly. "Yes, my lady, and there was the terrible sound of weeping and wailing throughout the land as people awoke to death in their homes. Pharaoh, grieving the loss of his own son, the Prince of Egypt, called for Moses and ordered him to leave Egypt with his people."

"How sad, Jeremiah, that the Pharaoh would not listen and allowed such devastation to his own country and people."

"Perhaps, my lady, we also do not always listen to the voice of our God."

"So this is why there is the celebration of Passover in Jerusalem every year?"

"Yes."

"Tell me, Jeremiah, did the people then settle in the land your god promised them?"

He shook his head slowly. "We have been called a stubborn people, my lady. You have seen this over the matter of the standards. When Moses went up on Mt. Sinai to receive the Ten Commandments from the Most High God—"

Claudia interrupted him. "Your god gave you ten commandments? These are the laws for your people?"

"Yes, my lady. They are the basis for our laws, before the entire law was given to the people through Moses."

"What are these commandments?"

Jeremiah paused, considering, then recited from memory, "You shall worship no other God but the Most High; You shall not make for yourself an idol of any kind; Do not misuse the name of the Lord; Remember the Sabbath, to keep it holy; Honor your mother and father; You shall not commit murder; You shall not steal; You shall not commit adultery; You shall not testify falsely against your neighbor; You shall not covet anything of your neighbor's."

She considered them. "They seem like good rules to follow. We as Romans have laws to follow. That is what civilized people do. They obey the laws."

"But you worship many gods, my lady, and there are idols throughout the city."

She still didn't understand. "Why is it wrong for us to worship many gods just because you choose to worship only one?"

"Because the Most High God is the only true God. He created the heavens and the earth."

This was getting out of hand. More and more she felt confused and that Jeremiah's tale was just that, a tale. Yet, why would the Jews be willing to die for a myth? She had to know more.

"Moses brought the Ten Commandments down from the mountain, and . . . ?"

Jeremiah frowned as if he sensed her disbelief. "The people thought he was not coming back after being on the mountain forty days. They rebelled and began to worship a golden calf that Aaron made for them."

She was amazed. "Aaron was the brother of your leader and served your god, yet he made an idol for the people?"

"Yes, my lady, he sinned greatly in this. His life was saved only because he repented and Moses cried out to God for him. Unfortunately there were other sins that angered our God and the people were forced to wander in the wilderness for forty years."

"Instead of the land your god promised them?"

"Until Moses died, and God called Joshua to take up the leadership of the people. Joshua was a mighty warrior and the armies of Israel were victorious in battle and conquered many people. When they had driven out the people God had told them to conquer, they were finally able to settle the land. It was divided up into twelve portions, for the twelve tribes. From this beginning, down through the generations, through the tribe of Judah, we were given David, and his son Solomon, the greatest king that Israel has known."

"I have never heard of Solomon. How was he a great king?"

"God blessed him above all other men and gave him wisdom beyond his years. He ruled much of what is the Roman Empire at this time. He was wealthy beyond anything we could imagine. Kings and queens came from other countries to hear his wisdom. Yet, his son was not wise. After Solomon's death the kingdom was lost to enemies through his descendants who were wicked in the eyes of the Most High God."

Claudia looked down at her hands and tried to comprehend all that Jeremiah was telling her. What a complicated people the Jews were. She might as well hear the rest. "What did they do that was so wicked?"

Jeremiah hesitated. "They worshiped abominable idols and sacrificed their children to the pagan gods of the land, which the Most High never ordained."

Since Claudia's household gods and the Roman gods were all she had ever known, Jeremiah's words disturbed her. "At least we Romans don't sacrifice our children!"

"No my lady, but sometimes they are the victims of their father's sins. Your Roman women starve themselves to death and families are murdered because of the crimes of the father. Good men commit suicide at the hint of a scandal to save their family name. The Most High God never commanded such a thing."

That was true. Some well-to-do families in Rome had suffered death because of the acts of the father. If Lucius was convicted of a crime by Tiberius, would she be willing to starve herself to death? It was a chilling thought.

Jeremiah went on. "My people sinned many times, and the Lord God allowed other people to conquer our land over the centuries."

"Like the Roman armies?"

He looked away from her. Finally, in a low voice he murmured. "Yes, my lady, like the Roman armies."

With a deep sigh, he rose from the bench and without another word, walked away. He had not waited for her to dismiss him, and for a moment she was tempted to reprimand him. Then, turning, she instead looked up into the face of her maidservant and saw there the import of his words.

26

As the coach rolled toward Jerusalem, Claudia had mixed emotions. She was glad to be able to see the city she had heard so much about. She understood only a little more about the Jews. It was the time of Passover and the city would be crowded with pilgrims all flocking to their holy city for one of their most important holy days. She had prayed there would not be any incidents. While Lucius had troops there, she believed they would be outnumbered if there was a riot of any kind. She hoped it would be a peaceful time for both of them. Hotep seemed to enjoy the scenery too, commenting on the beautiful flowers they passed.

Lucius rode on ahead with his troops but ordered a detail to escort her coach into the city. Lucius hadn't told her much about their quarters, and she wondered if at last they would have their own house.

It was the Jewish month of Nisan, and the barley fields were like seas of golden grain. The spring rains caused the countryside to blossom in green foliage, and along the sides of the road, purple pentagonias and blue lupins vied for space on the hillsides along with the orange vetchling that slipped in around the fields. Fortunately, now that the rainy season had ended, the roads were no longer strips of heavy mud.

The steady rocking of the coach didn't help Claudia's stomach, and she was forced to ask the driver to stop several times. Hotep insisted she try to keep her stomach full with bread. Claudia also sipped a little diluted wine. The detachment of soldiers was patient with the stops, knowing they would answer to their prefect if she did not arrive in good order.

While she had seen little of her husband's temper so far, mostly in regard to the incident with the banners, Claudia knew he could be harsh. With sudden realization, she hoped she would never be the recipient of his anger.

Along the road, the coach passed hundreds of pilgrims heading toward Jerusalem. Some carried bundles of clothing and baskets of produce—pomegranates, grapes, figs, and vegetables. Some could afford to ride donkeys and a few rode camels, but most walked. Some of the men had a lamb around their shoulders to present for the sacrifice of Passover. Here and there she passed an ox with its horns painted gold. Garlands of flowers were draped around its neck and over its haunches. She didn't know the significance of this in regard to the Passover ceremonies but enjoyed the sight.

The mass of people gradually moved aside for the Roman soldiers and the coach, and Claudia caught the eyes of some of the people. Some stared openly, others looked away. Some seemed to dismiss her with a glance.

As the coach approached the city itself, Claudia looked out at huge walls that seemed to gleam pure white in the bright sunshine. Streams of travelers entered the gates of the city from as many directions as she could see, and the coach was finally forced to slow down behind the crowd. When the pilgrims heard the shouting of the soldiers and saw the coach, they gradually parted to either side of the road to avoid being trampled by the horses. As the soldiers shouted rudely at the crowd to make way, Claudia shrank back in the coach. This was not going to endear the governor to the Jews.

Once in the city, she was astonished at the size of the magnificent Temple that rose proudly to overlook the city. Its gleaming walls would have enclosed at least ten hippodromes like the one in Caesarea. Gold covered the sides of the walls, and Claudia felt she had never seen anything like it. She recalled the words of Jeremiah and for a moment could imagine a king like Solomon as Jeremiah had described him, ruling over a city like this and worshiping at a temple of this tremendous size.

Hotep's eyes were wide as she also saw the Temple. "Oh, Domina, surely their god must be very great to have such a temple!"

They passed through traditional marketplaces full of ambitious vendors and pilgrims haggling over prices of goods and trying to outshout each other. Slaves and servants were busy buying food and necessary provisions for their households. Farmers laid out their fresh fruits and vegetables, spreading them out on rugs for those passing by to examine. Tables were set up to display various goods and trinkets. The din was enough to make both women cover their ears.

They passed the front of the Antonia fortress and Claudia could see a large number of soldiers milling about. The Antonia was the headquarters of the present cohorts of soldiers. Also it held the Praetorium, the civil headquarters of the governor. She looked intently as they went by, wondering if Lucius was there.

The coach continued across to the newer part of the city on the western side and approached another large fortress, the second palace of Herod. She sighed heavily. Another palace to live in and still no quarters of their own.

When they paused in front of the palace, to her relief, Lucius was there to open the door and help her out.

"My dear wife, you have arrived safely. How are you feeling?"

"I feel like a great cow. I am glad to finally be here, Lucius."

He put an arm around her waist and helped her mount the steps from the courtyard. As she went up the steps a couple of sharp pains in her abdomen caught her, but she did her best to conceal it from Lucius.

From every angle, all she could see were mosaic floors of magnificent colors, marble statues, and fountains. The palace was beautiful and spacious.

They were met by Chuza, the palace steward. He was very tall, slightly stooped, and thin to the point of looking as if a strong wind would blow him away. His hair, peppered with gray, belied a boyish face and eyes that twinkled when he looked at her. He bowed and spread his hand toward the palace. "Welcome, my lady, to Jerusalem."

He led them down the corridors that faintly resembled the palace in Rome and opened the door to a richly furnished room. Herod had spared no expense in the lavish guest rooms of his palace. There was a dining alcove with a table and two chairs surrounded by pots of beautiful flowers that made Claudia want to seek the garden as soon as she was able. A couch with bright silk cushions sat in another alcove by a window. *A wonderful place to work on my embroidery*, Claudia thought to herself. The bed was enormous, with coverings of rich tapestry and silk.

The floors of their room were made of mosaic in shades of soft brown and green, with thick Persian rugs strewn here and there.

Chuza directed the servants to bring in her trunks, then bowed to Lucius, and the servants left the room.

Fortunately she had packed few household goods. Hotep began putting away Claudia's clothes and personal belongings.

Ignoring the handmaid, who tactfully kept her back to them, Lucius took her in his arms and kissed her. "That is a prelude to a later time, beloved," he murmured in her ear. "Rest yourself for a while. We will have our dinner in the dining hall. I have invited some guests to join us. I will make Hotep acquainted with our residence while you sleep."

She stayed in his arms a moment, reluctant to let him go. He gently put her from him and, with another admonition to rest, left the room.

Hotep came and removed Claudia's stola and sandals and tucked her mistress in the great bed under a warm, thick coverlet. Within moments of lying down, Claudia slept.

When she awoke, she was alone. She wrapped her palla around her and moved slowly over to a window. Though they were high up in the palace, Claudia could still hear the faint din from the crowds of people moving through the Kidron Valley to the city gates. From her vantage point she was able to see over the city to the Temple. At least they were not in the heart of the city, the noise of which still echoed in her ears. She glanced a moment at a large knoll outside the city walls. A tall post seemed outlined in the light of the setting sun and she wondered what it was.

She contemplated the stories Jeremiah had told her, and wanted to know more about these strange people who worshiped only one God and were willing to die for him. Was there someone in the palace here in Jerusalem who could enlighten her?

With a shrug, she turned from the window and began to explore their new quarters. She opened a door in the wall and found a small room with a bench over a hole to take care of bodily needs. There was a small statue bending over a basin with a spigot for water, and she marveled at the care with which Herod planned his palace. Water from the sink could be poured down a small opening leading to a cistern.

A large pot sat over a stove that could be fed by small branches, heating the water in the pot. She ran her fingers around the copper pot and marveled. She saw no place to bathe and wondered if there were baths here where she could go with Hotep. They were near the newer part of the city. Perhaps the Jews had public baths like the Romans.

Hotep opened the door and smiled to see her mistress awake. "Are you wishing a bath, Domina?"

"I was looking around but don't see a place here. Are there public baths?"

"Not in the city, but here in the palace, or rather I should say, the tower. There are many towers here, are there not?"

"I don't remember. All I could think of was seeing Lucius."

"Come with me, and I will take you to the bath tower."

Claudia followed her down a corridor and across a stone bridge, and they entered a tiled room with mosaics implanted in the walls in flower patterns. A fountain fed a large stone bowl of water and went out again through a drain. A rectangular bath sat on a dais with marble steps leading up to it. She reached down and tested the water, finding it was nicely warm.

When she turned to Hotep with her eyebrows raised in question, her handmaid showed her the opening on the other side of the bath that held wood and other fuel. The coals were glowing a soft orange. She lost no time in shedding her clothes and was carefully helped into the soothing water by Hotep. She felt so unwieldy. As she soaked, she marveled at the movements of the child. She smiled to herself remembering the night she was curled up to Lucius's back and the baby had kicked, startling him. She'd taken his hand and gently laid it on her abdomen where a small foot moved under his hand. His eyes had widened in astonishment.

The warm water soothed the ache in the small of her back. "I could stay here all evening," she murmured.

Hotep laughed. "I believe your husband expects you at dinner, Domina."

On the way back from the baths, Claudia looked out at the other towers similar to the one they were in and the one that housed their living quarters.

The towers were extremely tall—she guessed around ninety cubits high. The outer stones of the towers were of white marble, each stone nearly twenty cubits long and ten cubits wide, fitted so close together that they looked like one piece of stone. She stood looking at the towers until Hotep urged her back to her quarters to dress.

Her collection of clothing was considered and several togas discarded until finally Claudia chose a red shawl over a soft white toga and her silver sandals and belt. While Hotep was arranging her hair, Claudia looked at her meager collection of jewelry.

"We must go to the marketplace to see if they have a street of goldsmiths. It will never do for the wife of the governor to wear the same few pieces of jewelry over and over."

"Mmmm," murmured Hotep with a silver hairpin in her mouth as she concentrated on a curl.

"Where are we dining? Did Lucius show you where to go?"

Hotep secured the curl with the pin. "It is large enough to have many guests, Domina. I believe the governor could serve half the army in that dining hall."

She looked over at the table and chairs in the alcove. Just this once, couldn't they dine by themselves? She was always meeting this one and that one. All important personages, but she had trouble remembering their names.

Claudia sat contemplating her circumstances. She still did not have a villa of her own. The palace in Caesarea was Herod's and only for their use; now, here in Jerusalem she must live in another of Herod's palaces. Would he join them here? Would she have to be in submission to Herod's wife?

"What staff do I have here, Hotep?"

"There are many servants, Domina, for it is a large castle. You have met the chief steward, Chuza. In the kitchen there are three cooks and several other servants. I am told there is another woman who lives here in the palace at present, but she is not a servant. She is the wife of Chuza."

Dinner was long. She was introduced to a senator, Trajanius Valentius, and another man, Cadmus Vitus. Both men were in Jerusalem on business and brought greetings from the prefect in Rome. They had been discussing matters of government when she arrived. Their eyes showed admiration when she was introduced, though it was obvious that she was in the later stages of carrying a child. Lucius watched them from under heavy brows and did not smile. She moved slowly, lowering herself on the seat next to his couch, and after a servant removed her sandals and brought a basin and linen cloth to wash her hands, the other servants began to serve the meal.

Cucumbers, beets, and lettuce had been chopped together with a dressing, and there were squash and peas in a sauce along with platters of roast duck and grouse. Claudia ate carefully lest her stomach rebel again.

Cadmus spoke. "Have you spoken with the high priest, Caiaphas, yet, Excellency?"

Lucius put his piece of bread down momentarily. "Yes, we have become acquainted. I believe he and I can work together peacefully. He does not wish any problems with Rome or the emperor."

"Ah," ventured Trajanius, "these Jews are a troublesome lot. Word got back to Rome about the incident over the banners. It was agreed that you handled that very well."

Lucius waved a hand. "I wish someone had told me about the graven images in regard to the Jews, but it was settled and our relations are peaceful, at least for the present." Her husband appeared casual, but Claudia saw the familiar tension in his shoulders. He was not relaxed. "I sent a detailed report to the emperor."

Claudia watched and listened. Were these men sent by Tiberius or Sejanus to bring a report back to Rome? She smiled and strove for her husband's sake to present herself well to their guests.

Trajanius turned to her. "Do you find Jerusalem an interesting city, my lady?"

"I believe that 'interesting' is a good word to describe a place of such diversity. The Jews are a strange people."

He nodded. "Will you then remain here for the child?"

Lucius interrupted before she could speak. "I have not decided. The journey here was difficult."

The men made sounds of approval. "In any case, Excellency, congratulations are in order. May the gods grant you a son."

Every man wants a son, Claudia thought to herself. *May the gods favor us.* She smiled charmingly at their guests. "What news do you bring from Rome?"

The two men glanced at each other and Cadmus cleared his throat. "Sejanus rules the city well in the emperor's stead. His orders come from Capri, as you know."

Lucius nodded. "Yes, we were told of the emperor's move to his palace on the island. Evidently he trusts Sejanus implicitly."

The two guests exchanged looks again and Claudia wondered if they were watching their words. Lucius caught her eye and she felt he was wondering the same thing.

"Excellency, you were appointed by the prefect, were you not?" Trajanius inquired.

Lucius responded cautiously. "Yes, with the approval of the emperor."

"You are fortunate," Cadmus answered, his face bland. "Those not in the good graces of our prefect do not fare well."

"I have heard of incidents in Rome. Loyalty is necessary if one is to rule an empire." Lucius reached for a slice of grouse.

Claudia sensed the men wished to talk with Lucius about other matters but were reluctant to speak of them in her presence.

The ache in the small of her back increased. "Would you excuse me, honored sirs? It has been a long day."

She rose slowly, holding on to the back of the chair, and Lucius got up and steadied her with his arm. She nodded to their guests and moved toward the entrance of the dining hall. Lucius quickly joined her.

"Do you feel all right?"

"Yes, Lucius. I am just very tired these days."

"I will see you later this evening." His finger brushed her cheek briefly and then he turned back to his guests.

⁂

Claudia dozed fitfully and awakened later as Lucius slipped in beside her. Seeing she was awake, he slipped an arm behind her and she laid her head on his shoulder.

"Your guests seemed nervous, beloved. Is there something wrong?"

He was silent a moment in the darkness and she felt he was deciding how much to tell her. Finally, he sighed. "All is not well in Rome. Sejanus is on a purge of anyone who does not side with him in loyalty.

Good men are being arrested and executed without a trial. Families live in fear that they will be somehow accused of sedition or treason by Sejanus or one of his spies. The man seeks the power of regency and will stop at nothing to persuade the emperor that he should be allotted this."

She raised her head in the darkness. "Oh Lucius, is there danger for you in this?"

"I don't think so. I was appointed by Sejanus for this governorship, so surely he doesn't see me as an enemy."

"But your communications have been with Tiberius. Surely the emperor is aware of what the prefect is doing."

"He may not be aware, for evidently he believes the reports from Sejanus. My two guests were not spies for Sejanus, they were sent by a friend to warn me, on the pretext of doing business in Jerusalem."

"A friend? Who is that?"

"It is best I not name him."

He yawned and she knew he would rise early the next morning to make sure all was well in the city. After the seven days of Passover, and most of the pilgrims had gone, he assured her they would return to Caesarea.

She settled back on her pillow and in only moments heard her husband's soft snores.

27

A sharp knock sounded on the door of her chamber, and since Hotep was away arranging for their lunch, Claudia opened the door. A woman with gray and white hair swept back from her face and clear gray eyes stood in the doorway. Claudia estimated her to be in her fifties. "I am Joanna, wife of Chuza. My husband has asked me to introduce myself."

Claudia spread one hand, inviting the woman to enter, delighted to have company.

"My husband said that you were inquiring about our people? If I can be of service to you, my lady, I would be happy to tell you what I can."

Claudia indicated a chair and they sat down. The woman was not dressed in Roman fashion but wore simple homespun in both her tunic and shawl. Then Claudia realized the woman had said "our people." Joanna was Jewish.

"How long have you lived in the palace, Joanna?"

"Almost five years, my lady. We have a house where our son and his wife live, but with my husband's duties here, he felt it was better to be in the palace rather than be summoned from our home so many times. We are comfortable, but I hope to return to my own home one day when my husband retires from King Herod's service."

Claudia nodded in sympathy. "I too long for my own villa instead of living in the palace, but like you, it is not possible at this time."

The two women smiled at each other in understanding, and Claudia had the feeling that she and Joanna could be friends.

"Joanna, what do you do to occupy yourself? You don't work in the palace on the staff."

"Oh, I have much to keep me busy. I am a midwife among our people, and there are always babies to bring into the world and women to care for. I am also skilled in the use of herbs and poultices."

Claudia's eyes widened. "Surely the gods have sent you. You can see that I am with child. I don't know what to expect and have some concerns. Perhaps you could enlighten me?"

Joanna had frowned briefly at the mention of Claudia's gods. "I will do my best, my lady. What concerns do you have?"

"The sickness in the morning seemed to pass several months ago, but came back again as I traveled here in the coach. Then, whenever I mount the stairs, sharp pains strike me in my belly and sometimes they bend me over, they are so strong."

Joanna's face changed to concern. "How long have you been having these pains? You are six, seven months along?"

"I think I am nearly eight months."

"Your time is drawing near. I would suggest you do as little climbing of stairs or walking as possible and rest as much as you can."

Fear pierced Claudia's heart. "Is there something wrong? Something you aren't telling me?"

"It could be something, or it could be just your own body reacting to the changes. The next time you have those pains, would you send for me?"

"Of course. And thank you. It is comforting to know someone nearby is skilled in these areas."

"I am happy to be of service, my lady. Now, there is another matter you wanted to know about?"

Glad for the change of topic, Claudia smiled. "Yes. In Caesarea, there was a gardener in the palace who is Jewish who explained some of the history of your people to me and also why you celebrate Passover. He told me about the lamb, the blood, and the death angel that passed over your homes. I would like to know more."

"Since your husband must rule our province, it is good that you are interested in the people he governs."

Hotep returned with their lunch, no doubt expecting to share it with her mistress. But with a stranger in the room, Hotep could not sit at the table with Claudia; instead she served her mistress and the steward's wife at the table and chairs in the alcove. Then she waited silently in the background.

Considering how complicated the Jews were, Claudia searched her mind for what else she wanted to know about them. "Tell me about the women's part in worshiping your particular god."

Joanna nodded slightly, a smile playing about her lips. "While we women cannot recite the Torah or take part in the duties of the Temple, we also worship in the Court of Women. We say the prayers we have been taught from the time we were children. Like Roman matrons, we are keepers of the home. We train our daughters in the duties of running a home, and our boys go to school to learn the Torah. The women of each household pray on the Sabbath and upon rising in the morning."

"Jeremiah told me your nation was taken captive because they sinned against their god. He told me about Moses bringing the law down from Mt. Sinai to the people."

"The Ten Commandments are not the entire law, my lady, but the foundation of our law. In the Torah, the Most High God gave Moses the more detailed law which governs our lives." She paused, considering. "Did Jeremiah explain the Sabbath?"

Claudia thought a moment. "I don't remember that."

"When the Most High created the world and all that is in it, he rested on the seventh day from his work. Therefore he has commanded his people, the Jews, to honor the Sabbath as a day of rest. No work can be done, not even lighting a fire to cook. Many prayers are said, and we go to the synagogue to pray."

"Do the women go into your Temple?"

"Only the men go into the Temple, and only the priests go into the Holy Place. In another room, called the Holy of Holies, stands the ark of the covenant. The high priest is allowed to go into the Holy of Holies only once a year to take the blood of a lamb to atone for the sins of the people. He puts the blood of the sacrifice on the altar."

Claudia frowned. "I am puzzled. Your people look upon us as pagan because we sacrifice to our gods, yet you speak of a blood sacrifice to your god. What is the difference?"

Joanna seemed to be trying to choose her words.

"You may speak freely, Joanna. I only wish to understand your people better."

"Thank you, my lady. What I must say is that we feel we worship the one true God, who created the heavens and the earth and all that is within them. He ordained the sacrifices that our priests perform for the atonement of the sins of the people. We do not have an image we sacrifice to. You worship images of wood and stone and pray to them, images that cannot speak or hear your prayers. We are taught not to worship the works of men's hands."

Claudia sighed. "Jeremiah said as much to me, but I still wonder how you can worship a god you cannot see."

"We do not need to see him to worship him, my lady. In days of old he has spoken to prophets and kings. They have known his voice. He spoke to Moses when he gave him the laws for our people. Gods of wood and stone are only that—wood and stone."

Claudia considered her words and something quickened in her spirit. Would this god of the Hebrews speak to her, a Roman woman?

The women paused as the sound of a large number of pilgrims singing reached their ears.

Claudia rose and walked to the window to look out. "The melody is beautiful. Can you tell me what the words say?"

Joanna came to stand by her side. "It is one of our Songs of Ascents, my lady. They are sung on our holy days as the people ascend up to Jerusalem. They come from the book of Psalms, which are poems and prayers written by King David and others."

Joanna began to sing softly,

"I look up to the mountains—does my help come from there?
My help comes from the LORD, Who made heaven and earth!
He will not let you stumble;
The one who watches over Israel
Never slumbers or sleeps.
The LORD himself watches over you!
The LORD stands beside you as your protective shade.
The sun will not harm you by day, nor the moon by night.
The LORD keeps you from all harm and watches over your life.
The LORD keeps watch over you as you come and go,
Both now and forever."

Claudia marveled. "What beautiful words. There is comfort in your psalms."

"Yes. There are many psalms like that."

Joanna rose slowly. "If you will forgive me, my lady, I must go. There is a young woman who is due to give birth in a few weeks and I promised to come and check on her." She hesitated again and then said, "Do not fear asking questions. You are known among the people as an inquirer. I believe you are set apart for great things, but in a time only the Most Holy One chooses."

Claudia had risen also, and was about to respond when a sharp pain in her back caused her to cry out and suddenly sit down again. Pain radiated through her body.

"My lady, are you ill? Are you in pain?"

Hotep came quickly and she and Joanna helped Claudia into her bed as she moaned.

Just before she lost consciousness, Claudia heard Hotep cry out, "There is blood on the floor!"

The pain was almost more than she could bear. It rolled through her body in waves and she heard a voice in the distance screaming and realized it was her own. Her body felt like it was being pulled apart. Someone lifted her head and murmured that she was to drink something as a cup was held to her lips.

"Domina, please drink this. It will help with the pain."

She swallowed the bitter liquid and moaned again. Then she felt the baby slide from her body and she lay back in exhaustion. Hands pressed firmly on her abdomen.

When Claudia opened her eyes, her whole body ached. She was in bed and Hotep sat by her side, anxiously watching her face. "You are awake, Domina, we thought we had lost you."

Her voice seemed thick and it was difficult to speak. "Lost me?"

"You have been very ill, Domina. The physician was here and did what he could, but you had a great fever. The physician has gone, but he will return later."

Her eyes focused on Joanna, who was standing with her back to Claudia, doing something. When she heard their voices, she turned around, her face was composed but not joyful.

Claudia turned imploring eyes to her handmaid. "My baby?"

Joanna approached and placed a small bundle wrapped in linen in her arms. "You have a son, my lady. Born a little soon, but he lives."

She caught a look between the two women. "What is wrong?" With fear in her heart, she slowly unwrapped the baby, who began to cry.

Joanna stepped closer. "My lady, you must keep the baby warm. He is a little early, but perhaps you misjudged the time he was expected." Again, there was that sorrowful look.

As Claudia unwrapped the baby's legs, she gasped. His right foot was not fully formed. Her son was a cripple.

She touched the deformed foot with her fingers. The baby began

164

to scream and Joanna reached down and helped her wrap him. Then she put the small mouth to Claudia's breast.

"As he nurses, he will draw up your womb. It will be painful, but it is necessary. Just know that it will pass. The herbs I gave you will help with the pain."

Hotep spoke up again. "The physician told the dominae he didn't think he could save you. Much blood was lost. The lady Joanna boiled some special herbs in water and gave it to you to drink."

Claudia looked up at Joanna. "What did you give me?"

"My lady, there are herbs known to those of our people who are healers and midwives that have been passed down through many years. We are fortunate that they worked for you. They cause the womb to pulse when the body is too weak to do this and helps the bleeding to stop."

"I owe you much, Joanna. Does my husband know you did this?"

The older woman shook her head and sighed. "No, my lady, he credits the gods for giving you your life back and has gone to make sacrifices."

Claudia began to weep. She had given birth to the son Lucius wanted and he was flawed. As paterfamilias, head of his household, Lucius had the right to accept the boy, or because of the deformity, he could order her to get rid of him.

"My husband . . . how long was he here?"

"He was at your side for hours. A matter came up that demanded his attention and he had to go. We are to send for him the moment you awoke."

Claudia needed to see Lucius. She must know how he was feeling about their child. She looked toward the door and Hotep, anticipating her need, hurried to the door. "I will tell your husband our Domina is awake and seeking him."

Claudia forced herself to speak. "I am grateful, Joanna. Thank you for all you've done." She looked down at the small, perfect face and grimaced with pain as she watched his small mouth move. She held him to her and marveled. Except for the foot, he was a beautiful child. A fierce anger rose in her. She would not give up her son, even for Lucius. The tears flowed again.

Joanna wiped her face with a damp cloth. "Hush now, my lady. You have given birth and you must regain your strength. The Lord God has given you a son."

"But I don't believe in your god, Joanna."

The woman smiled gently. "He believes in you, my lady."

The door opened and Lucius strode quickly to her bedside and stood looking down as she held her son tightly to her. There were tears in his eyes. He was a Roman soldier through and through, and she knew it was hard for him to show weakness in front of others.

"I thought I lost you as well as our son."

Our son. Would he feel the same when he knew about the foot?

Lucius reached down and gathered the small bundle from her arms. He gazed wonderingly down at this new life, as she thought fathers through the ages must have done.

She watched him with fear, like a shadow, constricting her heart, and spoke haltingly. "He is not perfect, Lucius."

Something in her tone caused him to narrow his eyes. "Not perfect?"

"His right foot, Lucius. Our son has a deformed foot."

He quickly unwrapped the linen from the baby's legs, and he stared at the small deformity for a long moment.

She watched his face and waited, holding her breath. *Give him back to me, please, Lucius. Don't take him away.*

"Oh Lucius, I'm so sorry. I have been searching my mind for anything I might have done to have this happen. Do you think the gods are angry with us for not honoring them properly at our wedding?"

He didn't answer, but slowly wrapped the baby's legs again and then leaned down and placed their son in her arms. "He is our son. The gods have given us this challenge for their own reasons."

She wept with relief. "Oh Lucius, I was afraid . . ."

Hotep returned from the kitchen with a bowl of something hot and a small loaf of fresh bread. She came forward hesitantly. "The lady Joanna sent me for this nourishing chicken soup."

Lucius took the tray and handed it to Joanna, then picked up his small son and handed him to Hotep, who cooed softly and gently rocked him.

Joanna tucked a cloth under Claudia's chin. "The soup is a favorite of our people when we are ill. It will strengthen you." She settled the tray in her lap and began to spoon soup in Claudia's mouth.

Lucius touched his wife's cheek with his finger. "I must go. I will return later to see how the two of you are doing." He leaned down and kissed her and left the room.

Claudia watched him go and dutifully ate the soup. She closed her eyes, weariness overtaking her again.

Joanna resumed feeding Claudia. "You must give your body time to heal, my lady. You must not carry another child for at least a year."

A year? Claudia knew there was only one way she could prevent that. "And you have spoken to my husband of this?"

Joanna nodded.

"What was his response?"

"My lady, he wishes your health above all things."

Claudia turned her face to her pillow and large tears rolled down her cheeks. She and Lucius loved each other. He seldom slept in his own quarters. How would he manage a year of celibacy? Who would he turn to? As she wrestled with her thoughts, a new emotion filled her heart—jealousy.

28

While Lucius had wished to postpone the naming of the child until they returned to Caesarea, it was the custom to have the naming ceremony eight days after the birth. Claudia was not yet well enough to travel and so it was held privately in the castle in Jerusalem. To his surprise and consternation, his wife beseeched him to allow the Greek name, Doros, which meant "gift," as the child's *praenomen*, the given first name. She felt that her surviving the difficult birth was a gift. He reflected on this and while having his wife recover was indeed a gift to him, it was with reluctance that he finally agreed. The boy's *nomen*, his second name and that of his clan, would be Pontius and his *cognomen*, or third name would be Pilatus. Lucius was firm on that, wishing to follow accepted Roman customs. Claudia had looked at him with such love and happiness, he felt justified in deviating from custom on the first name.

Now he looked back on his decision with chagrin. He could imagine the comments of his compatriots when they learned the boy's name. Perhaps he had been hasty. He sighed. There was no changing it now, but he didn't want to be perceived as weak in bowing to the whims of his wife!

There were few Romans in Jerusalem that Lucius wished to invite to the ceremony, and he felt a low profile should be kept of any Roman ceremonies while in Jerusalem, knowing there was still an undercurrent of distrust among the Jews over the banner incident.

The *crepundia*, a necklace of tiny metal trinkets, had been placed around the baby's neck according to Roman custom and the sound they made seemed to amuse him. Lucius provided the *bulla*, an elaborate gold locket that Doros would wear until the day he became a man in the eyes of Rome and received the white toga signifying his Roman citizenship.

Lucius had duly registered the boy's birth according to the decree of Caesar Augustus introduced many years before. Indeed, in less than a year it would be time for the Roman census again when he must register all he owned. So far there had been no negative communication from Tiberius, or Sejanus for that matter, and he could breathe freely for a while.

His thoughts were interrupted by the official Roman scribe, who asked, "The name—Greek, is it not?" His look was almost accusing.

"There is a reason," was all Lucius could mutter and stared him down, daring him to speak of it. The official wisely held his peace.

※

They had remained in Jerusalem while Claudia recovered her strength and the Jewess, Joanna, assured Lucius the baby was strong enough to travel. He reflected on the good fortune of having her there at the time of birth. She had proved herself extremely capable and, according to Hotep, had saved Claudia's life. In his gratitude, he was willing to listen to her advice over that of the physician, who had told him there was nothing he could do. Lucius ground his teeth. The man was obviously incompetent.

Lucius considered his son's deformed foot and remembered the fear in his wife's eyes. He could not deny the child for he would lose the love of his wife, and he loved her to a point that surprised him. He had cared for no one in the rise of his career. Women were only for his pleasure. Then he had seen Claudia and still felt the astonishment that this beautiful woman, the granddaughter of the Emperor Augustus, was his.

When at last he was assured they could leave Jerusalem, he couldn't return to Caesarea fast enough. He had ordered their carpentum lined with cushions. In the care of her handmaids, Claudia and their small son had made the journey back to Caesarea.

His concern for Claudia had been so great, anticipating the possibility of her death, that he was eager to make sure she was cared for in every way.

He brooded over the dinner he had shared with Claudia privately. It was difficult to do often, for there were times when he had guests in the city on business for the emperor and it was expedient to dine with them alone.

As he prepared to dine with some Roman officials, he reflected again on the words of the Jewess and knew she spoke the truth. Claudia must recover and it would take time, time when he must be celibate. Then a nagging shadow touched his mind. She had endured a very difficult time with this birth. Would she be able to bear other children? He had a son and heir, but would the foot hinder the boy in life? As a man, he wanted a son to bear his name. Now he was faced with a dilemma. He had never dishonored their marriage with other women as he knew friends in the military and senate had done, yet facing a year of abstinence, he balked.

After several months in Caesarea, he was restless, and frustrated. His wife's attentions were centered on their son. He had plunged into his work, spending long hours in his study. He needed a project, something to totally occupy his mind. An idea formed.

He'd studied the water supply for Jerusalem and had received reports that the city had a desperate need for additional water. The problem had been greatest when the city was flooded with pilgrims for the various holy days. Four times a year he had to be on alert with his soldiers to oversee the city when the Jews were required to travel there for worship. He felt it was vital to find a way to bring more water into Jerusalem.

The source of water was a long way off. It would take an aqueduct and the skill of a good engineer, but it would also take a great deal of money. He had the idea, but not the funds. How did the emperor expect him to govern this difficult province with so little? He thought a moment and then smiled to himself. There was another source of money and he intended to use it.

With a goal in mind, he made a special trip to Jerusalem and took temporary quarters in the Antonia with his troops. The next day he gave his tribune a message for Caiaphas, the high priest, to come with the other Jewish leaders to the audience hall on a matter of grave importance. He was tempted to add, "at once," but considering what he would be asking, felt compelled to add, "at their convenience."

❧

Lucius poured over a diagram of the city of Jerusalem with his architect and designer. Together they drew the course that the aqueduct must take to supply more water to the city. It would need to be built a distance of forty kilometers, four furlongs, from the hills south of the city. Supplies and materials were estimated, as well as the man-hours to build the aqueduct. Because it was sorely needed, Lucius reasoned to himself that this would give him a more favorable relationship with the Jews.

Two days passed, and just as Lucius was losing patience with the delay of Caiaphas, he was notified that the Jewish leaders had come and were waiting for him. With purpose of mind, Lucius strode into the hall and had chairs brought for their comfort. He knew they could not eat with him in his dining room because of their abominable customs, but he knew they would accept refreshments in the hall, a neutral area. He ordered wine to be brought.

Caiaphas slowly lowered himself on a chair and the other leaders followed suit. The high priest eyed Lucius skeptically, clearly uncomfortable.

Lucius considered his words. "Thank you for coming. There is a matter of grave importance I wish to discuss with you. I have noted that the water supply to Jerusalem is extremely inadequate to supply the needs of the people, especially when the city is crowded on Holy Days. It is my responsibility to make sure these needs are addressed. Therefore I have drawn up plans to build an aqueduct from a considerable distance to supply additional water for the city."

The leaders murmured with Caiaphas a moment, then the high priest turned back to Lucius. "This is a worthy goal, your Excellency. We indeed need the water, but have you sent for us just to notify us of this decision?"

"No, I am going to need your assistance. There is not enough money in the allotment from the emperor for Judea to pay for such an undertaking. I have been informed that you have the funds that would make this possible." He stared steadily at them as they again murmured to one another.

"Excellency, what is this money you are intimating that we have for such a project?"

Lucius sat back, keeping his face bland as he spoke the words. "It is called Corban."

There was a shocked silence and the leaders all began speaking at once.

"Those funds are holy!"

"It is set aside for God."

"This is sacrilege!"

Caiaphas stood angrily and shook his staff at Lucius. "That is impossible. You may not have the use of those funds, they belong to the Temple."

Lucius glared at him. "May I remind you that you hold your office at the direction of the emperor? Your own people need the water. You would deny them this need to preserve those funds? For what? Would not your god approve of this money being spent to help his people?"

Caiaphas waved a hand in exasperation. "Excellency, you must understand. This money is not to be used for this purpose."

Lucius narrowed his eyes. "I behold the fine garments you wear, and the fine houses you live in. You serve as priests but are not lacking in any luxury. I suspect this money is not used for your god's purposes, but for your own."

There was a shocked silence and then the priests began to protest again. Lucius realized he had struck a note of truth. Disgusted with the lot of them, he raised a hand. "Silence! This is not a matter for discussion. I will send my soldiers to receive the funds from you to-morrow. This audience is over." He rose from his seat of judgment and strode from the room.

When the funds had been placed in an account for the project, Lucius, still smoldering at the arrogance of the Jewish leaders, left Jerusalem. His architect and designer had been given his orders to begin hiring the workers for the aqueduct. Lucius noted that while the Jewish leaders were irate over the project, it didn't stop Jewish men from signing up to work on the project in droves. His eyes narrowed and a smirk crossed his face. They needed money to feed their families, and evidently they had no scruples about receiving the Corban money for their pay.

He rode furiously back to Caesarea, and though feeling a pang of regret for the strength of his horse, they were both spent by the time he arrived and turned the animal over to the soldier in charge of the stables. The soldier noted the horse almost foaming at the mouth, and there was a question in his eyes, but he remained silent, saluted his superior, and took charge of the exhausted animal.

❧

Claudia joined Lucius for dinner that evening, leaving the baby in Hotep's care. Her handmaid loved Doros and cared for him as if he were her own.

As her husband sat brooding at dinner, Claudia, watching him, finally spoke. "Is there something troubling you, Lucius? Your mind has been far away all evening."

Looking up, he shrugged. "I did not wish to trouble you. There is a situation with the Jews."

"Another one? What are they upset about this time?" He had always shared with her, and she waited, knowing he would finally unburden himself.

After what seemed like a very long time, he finally told her of the aqueduct and the response of the Jewish leaders.

Instinctively she knew he had once again erred with the Jews, but she would not tell him so. She put a hand gently on his arm. "Do the leaders not wish to help their own people with the water supply?"

"No, that is what I cannot understand. That money is given by the people, and what better use for it than something like this that would benefit all the people? They are like fat rams, these priests, bullying and denying their own people, while they wear fine clothing and live in luxury themselves. I know what the Corban is truly used for."

"Will they not give it to you then?"

"I already ordered my soldiers to take the money. The project has begun."

She felt a jolt of alarm and sought frantically for the right words. "Will the Jews start another riot over this matter?"

He reached for a small cake of dates and took a bite. "I doubt it. They have no choice, and I will not give in to them this time."

Inwardly she trembled at the import of his words. There would be repercussions. She must support her husband, but how could she make him see the grave error he was making?

"I fear for you, Lucius. Will they complain to the emperor?"

"I am not treading on their customs like the banners. I have not broken their laws and I am not using the money for myself. That should satisfy the emperor if there is an inquiry."

An inquiry? Lucius could ill afford an inquiry from the emperor. She prayed silently that there would not be another riot.

Lucius escorted her to her chamber and held her closely for a moment before suddenly releasing her. "Good night, beloved." He strode quickly away toward his own quarters, leaving her standing just inside the door. She stood there feeling bereft and found herself weeping again. Lucius was on edge due to their situation. She knew it was hard on him. She thought of other wives she had met at the baths in Rome who had lost a child but gone on to have another child quickly. In spite of the advice of the doctor and Joanna, she felt well. She must do something, for in his present mood, she feared only trouble. She prayed very hard that the gods would diffuse this situation.

❧

Her prayers to the Roman gods went unanswered as within days hundreds of Jews descended once again on the palace and filled the plaza. They were angry and shouting that the governor must forgo his plans for the aqueduct and return the Corban. Many shook their fists and called Lucius names. Claudia watched from the shadows at a palace window, her heart beating rapidly in fear. The Jewish leaders had instigated this. She knew it. Just like the matter of the banners. What would Lucius do now?

He came out on the steps and addressed them. "People of Jerusalem, this is not a matter to be settled by shouting and name calling. The aqueduct is necessary for the benefit of the city. I have made my decision, and I will not change my mind. You have one hour to clear the plaza and return to your homes or I will take action."

Claudia waited breathlessly as the crowd not only refused to leave but continued their angry taunts and called for the governor to give up this plan and return the money to the Temple.

Lucius gave a signal to his tribune, and suddenly among the crowd, soldiers threw off cloaks that had hidden their uniforms and began to beat the nearest people with staves. Those struck dropped to the ground and were struck again. Many were screaming and trying to get away, but they were surrounded and the soldiers were merciless. In their haste to leave the plaza, some of the Jews trampled their own people. Those who were able broke through the lines of the soldiers and ran from the plaza, until in a short time it was empty except for the dead and dying and those too injured to rise.

Lucius ordered his troops to cease and the main body to return to the barracks. When they had gone, some of the Jews quietly returned to pick up their dead and wounded and carry them away. Claudia could hear the sound of weeping. Then the plaza was empty and an eerie silence settled on the scene. Claudia remained where she was, her heart as heavy as if a millstone had been placed upon it. She had seen the face of her husband as he turned from the plaza in triumph, and it had shocked her. Who was this man she had married? Two large tears made their way in furrows down her cheeks. She wept for the Jews and their families who had suffered, for Lucius, and for a sense of loss she couldn't define.

29

Claudia settled once again in the palace in Jerusalem. Lucius, cautious of the Jews, had brought his family by night. Claudia's first caller was Joanna, who wanted to assure herself that Claudia had recovered from the birth of her son. As they spoke, Claudia sensed tension in the conversation and finally asked, "How do you feel about the aqueduct?"

Joanna sighed. "I was hoping there was some way the matter could have been resolved without the shedding of blood. Your husband prevailed, but at great cost."

"I wish it too, but I did not know what he was going to do until it was too late."

There was another silence.

"Tell me about Corban, Joanna."

"It is a gift to the Temple, to the Most High God, according to our leaders. A family cannot touch the money for an inheritance if it has been gifted to the Temple for Corban."

"What is done with the money after it is donated to the Temple?"

Joanna's brows furrowed. "I do not know, my lady. I assume it is for the upkeep of the Temple."

"It is my understanding that the Temple tax is for that purpose."

"So it is."

"And the priests are supported by the Temple tax?"

Joanna frowned. "I suppose so."

"Then the Corban is not used for the Temple, but as the priests see fit?"

Joanna twisted her hands in her lap, clearly uncomfortable. "I don't know, my lady, perhaps."

"Joanna, my husband felt the aqueduct was necessary due to the water problems when the city is filled with so many people on your holy days."

"That is true, but could he not have found another source for the money? My people are angry and speak against the governor."

"There was no other source. The emperor only allots a certain amount to each province and that would not cover a project this large."

Joanna shook her head. "The people were stirred up by the priests, yet there are men who need to take care of their families and, against the wishes of our leaders, are working on the aqueduct. I do not understand it at all."

Claudia smiled. "Perhaps we can speak of other things. Do you have any other news for me?"

Hotep had been silent during this exchange, but as she served the women fruit and cheese, she blurted out a question.

"My lady, I have heard from the other servants that there is a strange prophet among the people. He calls for people to repent and then he baptizes them with water. Some traveling through the marketplace spoke of him."

Joanna turned and regarded the servant, a little surprised at the interruption. "Yes, I have also heard of him. He is called John the Baptizer and a strange man he is indeed." She turned back to Claudia. "He wears the skins of animals, eats honeycomb, and roasts locusts for food. Our leaders went out to question him and asked him if he was Elijah returned, or the Messiah."

Claudia was intrigued. "And what was his answer?"

"He said he was neither of them, but a voice crying in the wilderness to prepare the way of the Lord. He told them one was coming whose sandals he was not worthy to untie. One who would not baptize with water but with fire."

"What an unusual thing to say. Would it be possible to hear him?"

Hotep protested. "Domina, you cannot go out among the people. It is not safe for you."

Claudia waved a hand. "I am not so foolish as to dress in my finest and appear in my coach. I would dress simply as one of the people and wear a cloak that would hide my face."

Joanna shook her head. "My lady, the prophet is far from Jerusalem. He is baptizing in the Jordan near Jericho, too great a distance for you to try to travel at this time."

Claudia digested this news. "Oh well, perhaps one day he will come closer to Jerusalem."

"He avoids the cities, my lady. He espouses the Essenes, a sect that deprives themselves to draw closer to God. They live in caves in the desert. They are at enmity with our leaders over some of their ways. It is said that the prophet was raised by them. If you truly wish to hear a different teaching, there is another, a rabbi who is traveling the countryside with the message that the kingdom of God is near. It is said he also heals people."

Claudia laughed. "You seem to have no end of strange prophets traveling about. You say this one heals people? In what way?"

"It has been rumored that the blind see again, the lame walk, the deaf hear, and those who are indwelt by evil spirits are set free."

"He sounds like a sorcerer of some kind. Have you seen this for yourself?"

"No, my lady, I have only heard from those who have been where he is teaching and healing. It is rumored that he is headed for Jerusalem. When he arrives, perhaps you can do as you suggested, disguise yourself to hear him. He usually teaches in the Court of the Gentiles at the Temple, according to my sources."

Claudia was elated. "Then let me know when he is here and I will go. Where is he from and what is he called?"

"He is a Nazarene from the hill country, and his name is Jesus."

30

Claudia made plans to go to the Temple to hear the new rabbi. Hotep would go with her and a servant would watch Doros. Their plans were dashed when, instead, Lucius informed her they were returning to Caesarea immediately for a governmental matter.

"If you might be returning to Jerusalem soon, Lucius, would it not be easier for the baby and me to stay here?"

He stopped and regarded her. "You would stay here? There is too much unrest right now over the aqueduct. I want you with me for your safety."

She could think of no reason to delay and hid her disappointment. She watched Lucius and sensed his restlessness. It was time. She would put her plan into place that evening.

Claudia had her maidservant dress her hair specially with silver pins and curls. She rubbed her cheeks to redden them and put a small amount of blue powder she'd obtained in the marketplace in Caesarea on her eyelids. She wore a tunic of finely woven wool that had been dyed a soft violet with a silver belt and slippers. Satisfied that she looked her very best, she joined Lucius for dinner. He had been reading some reports when she entered, and when he looked up and saw her, he put the scrolls down quickly.

"Is it my imagination or do you look especially beautiful tonight?"

She gave him a gentle smile and seated herself gracefully in the chair next to his couch. "I'm glad you approve of my clothing, Lucius."

All through dinner, she flirted, smiled, and in the ways of women, drew him to her. They finished their meal and this time when he escorted her to her chamber, she drew him in and quietly closed the door behind him. Then, putting her arms around his neck, she kissed him.

"Beloved, are you sure . . . ?

She took his hand. "Come, my Lucius, let us be together again."

He pulled the pins out of her hair so it tumbled down her back in disarray. Then he swept her up in his arms and kissed her. "I have missed you."

When Hotep came the next morning with her breakfast, Lucius was gone, but her maidservant looked at the disheveled sheets and smiled knowingly.

Claudia stretched and leaned back against the pillows with a contented sigh. All had gone well. Now she would wait and implore the goddess Venus for another child

In the 112 kilometers from Jerusalem to Caesarea, Claudia thought about the rabbi who healed people. Where did he get his power? Was he a sorcerer, a mystic? Joanna said he served the one true God, the Holy One of Israel. How was this god different from the gods she served? She had made sacrifices to Venus and prayed for another child. The small statue traveled with her. She glanced over at Hotep, who held the sleeping Doros in her arms and rocked him. Then she let her thoughts wander again. She mused over Jeremiah's words. His god spoke to Moses from a burning bush. The thought of hearing the voice of a god was unthinkable. What would she do if the voice of Venus actually spoke to her? She would be faint with fear.

The familiar cries of the seagulls told her they were nearing the sea. There had been such a sense of unrest and animosity in Jerusalem following the incident of the aqueduct, and while Lucius had left the beginning construction in the hands of his architect, she knew he must soon go back to make sure there was no more hostility from the Jews in that matter. He had confessed he feared they would try to sabotage the project in spite of their own people working on it.

She'd continued to dream strange dreams lately. The face of the man with blood came again, and another dream where she was in the sea, and as hard as she tried to swim away she was caught in the current. Lucius tried to save her, but the current pulled them apart, and she could hear him calling her name as he disappeared into the mist. She'd awakened with tears running down her face and had moved closer to Lucius, who slept soundly, unaware of his precarious adventure.

When they were once again settled in the palace by the sea in Caesarea, Lucius immersed himself in matters of the province and also received steady reports on the progress of the aqueduct. There seemed to be no further uprising among the Jews, and he was pleased with himself for putting down the rebellion over the foolish matter of the Corban.

"Let them appreciate the additional water supply and be silent."

Claudia sensed that for once he felt in control of the province he governed.

With Lucius occupied with his water project, Claudia sent for Jeremiah again.

He came slowly, leaning on his staff, and she wondered how much longer he could work in the gardens, bending and stooping. She indicated the bench and he lowered himself with effort.

"Jeremiah, what can you tell me about this rabbi who travels the countryside preaching about the kingdom of God and healing people? Have you heard of him? His name is Jesus."

A scowl darkened his features. "An imposter, my lady. The people are so anxious to have their Messiah come, they will follow anyone who gives them this hope. He's leading fools astray."

She was startled by his vehemence. "But I hear he heals people of illnesses and even blind men have been given their sight. Surely an imposter could not do such things."

"He works his magic with the help of *Shatan*. That is where he gets his power."

She studied his face. "Shatan?"

"The devil, my lady, the Prince of Darkness."

She sighed. This was becoming tiresome. "Have you ever seen him in person, Jeremiah?"

"I do not need to see and hear him to know he is like many false prophets who have come and gone over the years. I would advise you to avoid him, Domina, if you have any thought of seeing him. He will fade away as the rest of them have done and his followers will return to the Most High God and follow again the ways of our people."

She'd learn no more on this Jesus from Jeremiah. "Tell me, why do the Jewish leaders refuse to dine with us in Jerusalem? They will come into the judgment hall with their petitions, but they will not accept an invitation from my husband, their governor, to a meal. Would that not be an easier atmosphere to discuss matters of importance?"

"Forgive me, my lady, but they are forbidden to enter the house of a Gentile or eat with them by our laws of cleanliness."

"You consider us unclean?" She found herself resenting him. How judgmental his people were.

"The foods you eat are unclean to us. Your meats have been used in a sacrifice to your pagan gods and then cooked to serve at your table. We cannot eat foods that have been dedicated to an idol. Also, we do not eat pork, or hares, for they are an unclean food to us."

"I see. And your god forbids these things in the laws he gave Moses?"

"Yes."

She considered his words but another question puzzled her.

"When your Messiah comes, how will you know him? You say the miracles this man Jesus does are by the power of your shatan. What will the true Messiah do that you will recognize him?"

He sat straight and squared his shoulders. "He will come and free our people from the Roman rule. He will come as a conquering king and we will know him then."

She held her peace a moment. "You know, Jeremiah, that for the words you have spoken against Rome, I could have you flogged."

His reaction was instantaneous. "You have asked for truth and I have told you what you wanted to hear, Domina. If you flog me for that, you have the right. We in the palace know you to be unlike your husband. You are of a gentle nature and kind."

She had to smile at his diplomacy. "Go back to your gardens, Jeremiah, and trouble my mind no more this day."

He rose and bowed but not before she saw a slight smile twitch at the corner of his mouth as he left her. She shook her head and called for Hotep, who had been standing nearby in the passageway.

"I am even more determined to hear this Jesus. Perhaps he will be there teaching when we return to Jerusalem."

31

Doros was two and walking precariously with his crippled foot by the time they returned to Jerusalem. Hotep adored him and spent many hours entertaining the little boy.

The Jews were celebrating the Feast of Lights they called Hanukkah. It was one of the festivals that Claudia enjoyed the most. Their candelabras, which she learned were called *menorahs*, were everywhere in the courtyards and windows of homes.

Joanna brought Doros little gifts and told Claudia and Hotep the story of the Maccabees and their victory over the Greeks who had desecrated the Temple.

"We celebrate this miracle every year at Hanukkah and give gifts to our children—one for each day of the festival."

At first Lucius had just frowned at the small gifts Joanna brought to the baby. Then he learned she had been gone from the castle, following the rabbi called Jesus to various places with other women. Chuza did not seem to object, but it infuriated Lucius.

"What man lets his wife travel around the country following some charlatan?"

Claudia remained silent. She knew Chuza looked upon the rabbi with an attitude bordering on reverence and was also a follower.

Today, the sixth day of Hanukkah, Joanna had brought Doros a small top. When Lucius saw it that evening, he grabbed it from the little boy's hand and flung it across the room, crying, "We are not Jews and we do not celebrate their holy days!"

Doros began to cry for his toy. His father turned from him in disgust and left the room.

Over the last year Claudia had observed a change in Lucius's behavior toward the Jews. He was quick to persecute, even those professing innocence of the charges, and had no patience for the high priest or any of their requests. Word of corruption and violence trickled back to her and she began to view this man who was her husband in a different light. Had she been blind to these attributes?

She grieved at his impatience with Doros during what little time he spent with his son, and if Doros cried, Lucius left the room. Time and again Claudia would have to comfort the little boy when he reached his arms out to the receding figure of his father. She had prayed earnestly and sought the help of her gods to no avail.

She had just put Doros down for an afternoon nap when Hotep came hurrying in to her quarters. Claudia felt impatient herself and was about to scold her slave for being gone so long. Before she could upbraid, she realized Hotep's eyes were shining and she was breathless.

"Domina. The rabbi you wanted to hear is teaching in the Temple courtyard. He is like no one I have ever heard before. You must come."

A flicker of hope rose in Claudia's heart. Perhaps she would hear something that would comfort her during this difficult time.

"I cannot go alone. Go and get Hadriana from the kitchen to stay with the baby. You must come with me."

The girl left and hurried back with Hadriana, an older slave who watched Doros whenever Hotep accompanied her mistress. Claudia covered herself with a heavy cloak that hid her face and clothing so she would not be recognized, and slipped out of the palace. They followed the crowds across the city to the Temple, and Claudia almost shook with fear of being recognized as she and Hotep climbed the stairs to the Court of the Women in the Temple courtyard.

She found a shadowed place in the crowded courtyard behind a pillar to watch and listen. The man who was speaking was perhaps in his thirties. His hair curled down over his shoulders and his eyes roved over the crowd as he made each point. It was as if he were speaking to each person individually and yet to all. His voice resonated over the crowd with ease as the people listened respectfully to his teaching. Not even the cry of a baby broke the silence of his listeners.

"You have heard it said, 'You shall love your neighbor and hate your enemy.' But I say to you, love your enemies! Pray for those who persecute you! In that way you will be acting as true children of your Father in heaven. If you love only those who love you, what reward is there for that? Even corrupt tax collectors do that much. If you are kind only to your friends, how are you different from everyone else? Even pagans do that. But you are to be perfect as your Father in heaven is perfect."

Claudia listened in astonishment. How could one be perfect unless they were a god? Only gods were perfect. She looked around at the listening faces. These were to be perfect? She shook her head in consternation.

The rabbi continued, pointing a verbal finger at the Pharisees. "When you give to someone in need, don't do as the hypocrites do—blowing trumpets in the synagogues and streets to call attention to their acts of charity . . ."

There was a ripple of amusement through the crowd. Claudia smiled also. She had observed some of the priests in the marketplace doing just that. This rabbi had the crowd's full attention.

"I tell you the truth, that is all the reward they will ever get. But when you give to someone in need, don't let your left hand know what your right hand is doing. Give your gifts in private, and your Father, who sees everything, will reward you."

Claudia took the words to heart. This rabbi said to love your enemies. She despised some of the things Lucius was doing. Was he her enemy? He ruled over her and had the power of life and death over his family, yet he had treated her well and she knew he loved her. It was Doros that she feared for. Would he grow up like his father? Was Lucius resenting the fact that his son had a deformed foot after all? She brushed the trying thoughts away and concentrated again on what the rabbi was saying.

The rabbi talked about storing up treasures in heaven rather than on earth, and she realized he was talking about eternal life. "Wherever your treasure is," he intoned, "there the desires of your heart shall be."

He went on to teach about money and worry and judging others. Claudia listened and her heart was stirred. His teaching was different from any she had heard. He was not a scribe or a teacher of the Law, yet he taught with the ring of authority.

When he had finished his teaching, people began to bring the sick to him. He laid hands on each of them and they were instantly healed. Claudia nearly gasped out loud.

Hotep had been cautioned not to call her "Domina" in public lest she call attention to them, but Hotep whispered fiercely in her ear, "Is he not wonderful?"

Claudia nodded, unable to speak for what she was seeing.

As the shadows crept up the walls of the Temple, Jesus rose and, with his disciples, walked through the crowd that parted for him and left the courtyard. Claudia, realizing she had been gone too long, hurried with her handmaid through the city toward the palace. In the marketplace she stopped and hastily bought a set of combs for her hair. She must have some excuse for her absence.

When she and Hotep returned to the palace, Claudia faced an irate husband. "Where have you been? No one in the palace has seen you." His eyes blazed with suspicion.

"Dearest, I grieve that you were worried. I wished to go to the marketplace and Hotep accompanied me. Sometimes I feel so confined." She held out the combs, wrapped in a small piece of linen. "Are these not beautiful?"

He sighed. "Yes, they are beautiful, but you must be careful. There are many in the city who chafe at my rule here. They would like nothing better than to find my wife alone in the city." He moved closer and his dark eyes pierced hers. "I could not bear it if anything happened to you." He tipped her chin with one finger. "I will see you at dinner."

When he was gone, she hurried up to her quarters and clasped her small son to her. He was weeping, having awakened without finding her. Hadriana hurried back to the kitchen, her lips tight with disapproval.

Claudia did not go again to hear Jesus before she and Lucius left Jerusalem to return to Caesarea. She gathered reports on the places he spoke—the hills of Galilee, Capernaum, Jericho, Perea, and Samaria. She could only hope that the next time they returned to Jerusalem, Jesus would again come to the Temple. Reports also came to her of the Pharisees and the Sadducees, who dogged his footsteps, asking questions and accusing him of everything from blasphemy to being used by Shatan to work his miracles. This puzzled her. Someone who did the kind of miracles he did could not be evil. She heard of the blind being given their sight and the deaf hearing and those that were lame walking. A thought began to form in the back of her mind as she watched her small son struggle to stand with his deformed foot. She was not Jewish and Jesus was speaking to his own people. Would he be willing to pray for Doros? She dismissed the idea, for if she went with Doros, she would have to not only reveal herself but humble herself before this itinerant rabbi.

Before they returned to Jerusalem in the spring for Passover, the city buzzed with talk of a major miracle Jesus had done. He had actually raised a man from the dead. A friend by the name of Lazarus had been in the tomb four days before Jesus had arrived in Bethany. Word spread through the city of other people, long dead, who had been seen walking about, and those who believed argued with those who were skeptical. Claudia sent for Jeremiah.

He'd barely lowered himself gingerly on the end of the stone bench when she asked, "What is this I hear about the rabbi who has raised a man from the dead?"

Instead of the angry retort she expected from his past reactions to Jesus, Jeremiah had a different look on his face. His eyes glowed with an inner light as he gazed at her. "My lady, I must confess that this Jesus is not what I thought he was. I was there in Bethany when Jesus came. I had come to pay my respects to the sisters of Lazarus. They were grieved that he was too late to heal their brother, but he went to the tomb with them and merely called out, 'Lazarus, come forth.'" Jeremiah's voice broke and there were tears in his eyes. "My lady, Lazarus walked out of that tomb. I knew then that Jesus was who he said he was. All my doubts were erased. He is indeed the Son of God, the Messiah."

Claudia stared at him. Jeremiah was a changed man. Her heart felt heavy in her chest. What hope was there for her? She was Roman and her husband was the governor of Judea. He had persecuted the Jews. This Jesus would not accept her plea for her son.

She thanked Jeremiah and sent him away, then slowly went upstairs to her quarters. Part of her wanted to cry out her frustration, but she did not wish to upset Doros or Hotep. The boy had no playmates, for Lucius would not allow him to associate with other children due to his foot. He began to withdraw into himself. His long periods of quiet concerned her.

She moved to the window and looked out a long time toward Jerusalem. Lucius had not forbidden her to hear Jesus, but she had not told him where she had really gone that day.

"Domina, the rabbi is at the Temple, teaching in the Court of the Gentiles." Hotep's eyes were alight with anticipation.

"I do not wish to anger my husband again."

"He did not know where you were. He has not forbidden you to hear the rabbi."

"No." She thought a moment, then called for a wax tablet and a stylus. "I will send him a message, letting him know where we have gone."

Dear husband, I have gone with Hotep to hear this rabbi who speaks in the Temple courtyard. I have heard many things about him and my curiosity is aroused. Your loving wife, Claudia

Lucius was at the Antonia with his troops, so she left the message with a servant to give him if he returned before she did. She and Hotep hurried through the streets toward the Temple.

If he was teaching in the Court of the Gentiles, perhaps there would be other Gentiles there and she would not be so conspicuous.

Jesus taught for over two hours and Claudia listened to his words eagerly. She sensed a change in her spirit as she listened. His words made sense to her.

"I am the bread of life. He who comes to me shall never hunger, and he who believes in me shall never thirst . . . And this is the will of him who sent me, that everyone who sees the Son and believes in him may have everlasting life, and I will raise him up at the last day."

As he spoke these words, he turned and looked right at Claudia. She felt a shock go through her body. Was he telling her something? His words touched her deeply and a flicker of hope rose in her heart. He said he would not cast out anyone who came to him. He did not say just Jews, he said anyone. That was the message. He was offering her everlasting life if she would believe on him.

Surely if he said that to her, he would in no way cast out her small son who was in need of healing. Dare she hope? Dare she bring Doros to him? Her mind whirled with questions, but she knew she had changed—she believed him. How she could explain this all to Lucius, she didn't know, but Jesus was real. He was not made of stone or wood, he was flesh and blood and he was offering her eternal life.

"I believe in you, Jesus," she whispered softly, unheard by those around her, and yet to her astonishment he turned and again looked right at her. For one brief moment it was as if there were no one in the court but the two of them. Had he heard her whispered cry? He gave her a brief smile and turned back to continue his teaching. Her heart was bursting as she nodded to Hotep and they slipped back through the crowd and hurried back to the palace.

One of the rabbi's followers was standing by the entrance and Claudia whispered, "Hotep, ask him if the Teacher will be here tomorrow." She kept her head down so the man couldn't clearly see her face. When Hotep inquired, the man was busy watching Jesus.

"The Teacher will be here tomorrow as far as I know," the man answered without looking at them.

Claudia's heart lifted. She knew what she must do.

32

Lucius was still at the Antonia when she returned and she breathed a sigh of relief that he didn't know where she had gone. It was a small miracle and she wondered if she should thank the Jewish God. If Lucius didn't know she had gone to hear Jesus, he couldn't forbid her to go again. She hastily retrieved the tablet and the message she had left for him, erasing the words from the soft wax. Then she went to dress for dinner.

Lucius met her in the dining room and she found him in a strange mood. He greeted her and made sure she was comfortably seated before reclining on his couch for the meal.

"You seem troubled," she ventured, hoping he would enlighten her on the cause of his brooding.

He sighed. "You have heard of this Jesus who is traveling around all of Judea doing miracles, or so people have told me."

"Yes, and I have been very curious about him."

He seemed not to hear her. "It was one of my centurions."

"One of your centurions? What happened?"

"I was speaking with him and asked about this teacher at the Temple and if he knew anything about him or if he was dangerous. He told me he'd returned to his villa in Capernaum some months before to visit his family, and a favored servant became greatly ill and was on the verge

193

of death. The man had been his guardian from the time he was a boy. The physicians were not able to do anything for him. In desperation he sought out this Jesus and sent elders of the Jewish community to him. They pleaded with Jesus to come to the centurion's house and heal him."

She listened in amazement. "But your centurion is Roman. Would a Jewish rabbi come to his home to heal a servant?"

Lucius stared at the wine in his glass. "It seems my soldier is what they call a Godfearer—a man who loves the Jewish nation. He'd even built them a synagogue in the city." He snorted. "A Roman soldier who builds Jewish synagogues!"

"But what happened? Did the rabbi come to his house?"

"He was on his way when the centurion sent friends to tell him— and you will not believe this—to tell him that he, a Roman officer, was not worthy to have this itinerant rabbi come under his roof nor was he worthy to come to Jesus and ask for his servant's healing."

Lucius paused, shaking his head slightly, his brows knit together.

She was getting impatient. "Did Jesus heal his servant?"

He looked up at her, his eyes full of bewilderment. "He said he told Jesus to just speak the word and his servant would be healed. Evidently Jesus was impressed with the centurion's faith. The friends returned to his house and the servant was up from his bed, totally healed and serving his master."

"Then the stories I have heard about Jesus are true." Hope rose again in her heart. If Jesus would heal the servant of a Roman soldier, would he not have mercy on their son?

Still, she couldn't gauge what reaction her husband would have if she told him of her plan, and if he forbid her to go, he could discipline her severely in his anger. She must plan carefully.

She reached out and touched his face. "This troubles you, beloved?"

"If I didn't know of his integrity and his reputation as a soldier, I would think the man demented. As he told me the story, I watched his face for some sign of a joke, but the man was sincere. There was something in his manner that caused me to believe him."

Claudia wanted to rejoice. Was her husband softening toward the Jews? She didn't understand all that he was feeling, but there was a change in him, and silently she thanked the Hebrew God. Then a strange thought came to her. Because she believed Jesus and the words he spoke, did that make her a Godfearer also?

"My husband, have you heard any other stories of the miracles this man performs?"

"There are stories everywhere I go. Feeding a mass of people with next to nothing—a few loaves of bread and some fish, blind men given their sight, the deaf having their ears unstopped. He even casts out demons and they obey him. Where does he get this power? Is he a sorcerer?"

She started to say, "The rabbi says," but changed it to, "I have heard many stories also from the servants and from Joanna of miraculous things. They say he gets his power from his God—the God of the Hebrews. He calls this God his father."

Her husband's mood passed and the wonderment was gone. He was the consummate Roman soldier again, scoffing at the idea of a man receiving power from a god.

That night she comforted him as a wife and he held her a long time. He needed her and she was counting on his favor. She would need all her courage for what she had in mind.

33

Claudia prayed for Lucius to be occupied elsewhere the next day. If he was in his study, her plans were to no avail. When he told her he was traveling to inspect the work on the aqueduct, she silently rejoiced, wished him a safe journey, and from a window in the palace watched him ride away with his men.

"Hotep, help me dress, quickly."

Then she waited impatiently while the girl dressed her hair.

Doros was playing with the blocks that had been in her small chest from her own childhood. He loved to stack them and then knock them down again. The little boy's laughter caused her heart to swell with mother love. She would do anything for her son, even risk the wrath of her husband. What if her mission failed and Lucius found out she had taken Doros to the Temple? She shuddered at the thought. Still, he had not forbid her and she could innocently remind him of that fact should the occasion arise.

When she was ready, she gathered her son in her arms and, with Hotep behind her, went to see if Joanna was in her quarters. To her relief, Joanna was there. When Claudia explained what she wanted to do, not only did Joanna agree to go with her, but Chuza would go also, as protection.

"Oh, Chuza, that would be wonderful." That should be in her favor if she had to face Lucius.

The five of them hurried through the streets, and as they approached the Temple, Doros looked up. "Big, big, Mater."

"Yes, Doros, it is very big."

They went up the steps to the Court of the Gentiles, and when she saw the crowd and Jesus speaking, she realized she'd been holding her breath.

One of the listeners told Chuza that the Teacher had been speaking since early morning. He was telling them a parable.

"The kingdom of heaven is like a certain king who arranged a marriage for his son and sent out his servants to call those who were invited to the wedding and they were not willing to come . . ."

Why would someone insult the host and not come to his son's wedding? Claudia mused at this breach of manners. No Roman invited to the wedding of the emperor would dare refuse.

"Again he sent out other servants saying, 'Tell those who are invited, "See, I have prepared my dinner; my oxen and fatted cattle are killed, and all things are ready. Come to the wedding."' But they made light of it and went their ways, one to his farm, and another to his business. And the rest seized his servants, treated them spitefully, and killed them."

Claudia looked at Joanna and shook her head. Joanna smiled. They both knew what would happen to those ungrateful guests if it were the emperor.

"But when the king heard about it, he was furious, and he sent out his armies, destroyed those murderers, and burned up their city."

The crowd murmured among themselves and nodded their heads in agreement. "This was what those men deserved," she heard someone say.

As Jesus went on, Claudia tried to picture Tiberius sending servants out to gather the poor people on the streets and anyone they got hold of, imploring them to come to the emperor's wedding. She couldn't begin to imagine such a scene.

Doros squirmed in her arms and she passed him to Hotep, who had a way of keeping the small boy occupied and distracted.

Jesus continued with his story. "But when the king came in to see the guests, he saw a man there who did not have a wedding garment. So he said to him, 'Friend, how did you come in here without a wedding garment?' The man was speechless. Then the king said to the servants, 'Bind him hand and foot. Take him away and cast him into outer darkness; there will be weeping and gnashing of teeth.' For many are called, but few are chosen."

What did he mean? Claudia listened carefully. Did it mean that this kingdom of God was available to all, but like the first wedding guests some would turn away and refuse? She recalled the previous day when Jesus had looked at her and warmth had filled her being. Was she chosen? She had spoken to him in her heart, but he had turned at that moment and looked at her, and she knew something had changed inside. She felt lighter and full of hope. Unhappy thoughts of the past seemed to slip away to the shadows where they belonged.

Some of the Sadducees, the sect who did not believe in the resurrection of the body as the Pharisees did, had been listening. They murmured among themselves and then one of them, as their spokesman, smirked and posed a question.

"Teacher, Moses said that if a man dies, having no children, his brother shall marry his wife and raise up offspring for his brother. Now there were with us seven brothers. The first died after he had married, and having no offspring, left his wife to his brother. Likewise the second on through the seventh. Last of all the woman died also. Therefore, in the resurrection, whose wife of the seven shall she be, for they all had her to wife?"

Jesus looked at them with an expression akin to pity and shook his head. "You are mistaken and do not know the Scriptures nor the power of God. For in the resurrection they neither marry nor are given in marriage but are as the angels of God in heaven."

The group of Sadducees looked at him and shook their heads,

clearly perplexed. After commenting among themselves again, they turned and strode out of the Temple court.

Claudia and Joanna looked after them and then at each other as Chuza whispered, "He confounds even the leaders and they have no response."

The four continued to listen to the Teacher and marvel at his words. He was telling the crowd that the Son of Man, as he called himself, would judge the nations.

"When the Son of Man comes in his glory, and all the holy angels with him, then he will sit on the throne of his glory. All the nations will be gathered before him."

Jesus went on to talk about sheep and goats and that the sheep would be gathered into the fold and the goats dismissed. She finally understood that the sheep were the believers and the goats were the unbelievers.

Jesus went on. "'Come, you blessed of My Father, and inherit the kingdom prepared for you from the foundation of the world. For I was hungry and you gave me food; I was thirsty and you gave me drink; I was a stranger and you took me in; I was naked and you clothed me; I was sick and you visited me; I was in prison and you came to me.' Then the righteous will answer him, saying, 'Lord, when did we see you hungry and feed you, or thirsty and give you drink? When did we see you a stranger and take you in or naked and clothe you? Or when did we see you sick, or in prison and come to you?' And the King will answer and say to them, 'Assuredly, I say to you, inasmuch as you did it to one of the least of these my brethren, you did it to me.'"

Jesus taught another hour, and then the people surged forward with those who were sick and invalid. His eyes full of compassion, he began to lay hands on them. As Claudia and those with her watched in amazement, each one was healed.

Claudia could not bring herself to expose herself to the crowd. She could not face Lucius if they turned against her. In spite of the story told by the centurion who spoke with Lucius, she was afraid Jesus would dismiss her plea. She gathered her courage and turned to her maidservant. "Hotep, take Doros to Jesus. I cannot. Perhaps if he does not know whose son it is, the Teacher will have mercy."

The maidservant, her eyes wide with apprehension, clutched Doros to her and moved through the crowd until she was facing Jesus. The Teacher smiled at the boy, and Doros, who had been whimpering, suddenly stopped and smiled back. Hotep stood him on the ground so that Jesus could see his crippled foot.

Claudia could not hear what Jesus said to her maidservant, but Hotep turned and looked back at her mistress. A jolt of fear shot through Claudia. Was she yet to have to reveal herself in front of the crowd? Lucius would never forgive her. *Lord, know my heart. I cannot. Please, have mercy on my son.*

Then, to her astonishment, in her mind she clearly heard the words: *You are mine, beloved woman, and one day you will serve me. Do not fear, for I will go ahead of you.*

Then Jesus reached down and put his hand on the little boy's foot. In moments it became straight and normal like his other one.

Tears of joy ran down Claudia's cheeks and she felt as if her heart would burst from her chest. The crowd parted as Doros ran back to her and she swept him up in her arms. She had dressed simply with no adornments and wore the cloak of a servant. Though the heavy shawl slipped for a moment, it still hid most of her face. She anticipated someone recognizing her, but the people had turned back to watch still another miracle as a man bent over for years was healed and jumping joyously in front of Jesus.

Joanna and her husband marveled at the miracle, touching the new foot. Then Chuza, aware of his duties as guardian, glanced around. "Let us go quickly, my lady, while the crowd is distracted. It is best."

They moved quickly out of the Temple, Claudia still holding her son tightly to her. She could hardly see for the tears that streamed down her face. Her mind turned with the enormity of what had been done. What would her husband's response be?

As they neared the palace and slipped in the back entrance, one of the servants told Claudia that the governor had returned and was asking for her.

Joanna, tears in her eyes, put a hand on her arm. "We will pray for you, my lady." Claudia nodded and as Joanna left, turned to her maidservant. "Hotep, what did the Teacher say to you?"

"He asked where the boy's mother was. He knew I was not the mother. I said she does not feel worthy to come and asks that you have mercy on her only son."

Jesus had heard her silent prayer. To the maid, she murmured, "Thank you. Please take Doros to our quarters. I will come later."

Her handmaid took the boy. "How will you tell him, Domina?"

"I don't know, but the Teacher spoke to my heart and said he would go before me. I must trust him for the right words."

Claudia stood in the courtyard and watched her servant carry Doros up the stairs. Then she turned and was startled to find Lucius watching her, his eyes narrowed.

"Where have you been with my son?"

34

She looked up at him and gave him her warmest smile. "Oh Lucius, after you told me about the centurion, I began to wonder about this teacher named Jesus. When I heard he was at the Temple, teaching in the Court of the Gentiles, I went to hear him. I was very careful to disguise myself and went with Hotep and Joanna. Chuza also went along as protection for me—"

"You went to hear that rabble-rouser at the Temple? Did I not warn you to be careful for your safety? How could you do such a thing? I would have forbidden it!"

"Dear Lucius, had you forbidden me, of course I would have obeyed you. I went only in desperation."

He took her arm and led her almost angrily up the stairs to their quarters. "We will discuss this in private without the ears of the servants."

When they reached the room, Hotep did not have to be dismissed. She took one look at the thundercloud on the face of her master and fled. Doros was asleep on his bed, exhausted from the long day at the Temple and what had happened to him.

When the door closed behind Hotep, Lucius turned to Claudia. "I do not want you to go again and fill your head with false hopes. Our son is crippled and you must accept that. I forbid you to go near the Temple again, do you understand me?"

"Yes, Lucius, I understand you, but first, may I show you something?"

She led him into their son's room, went to the bed, and lifted the coverlet from Doros's legs, then waited for the realization to dawn on her husband.

Lucius looked at the foot that had been so deformed and his eyes widened. Very slowly he reached out and touched the foot, now whole and healthy like other one. "By the gods, what happened—how did it—?"

"It wasn't our gods, Lucius, it was the Teacher, Jesus, who healed his foot. He merely laid hands on the deformity and prayed to his God, and the foot became whole. I saw it happen. Doros ran to me, not with the wobble of a crippled boy but like a normal boy. No more will he suffer as he has."

"Pater?" Doros opened his eyes and looked up at his father, his eyes wide with apprehension. Lucius broke. With a sob, he gathered his small son to his chest as tears ran down his cheeks.

Doros looked at his mother, not sure if he should cry also. Claudia saw his hesitation. His father was acting strangely.

Claudia's heart soared as she looked at her husband's face, stark with raw emotion. "It was the story of your centurion that gave me the courage to believe that though I was a Roman, the Teacher's God might have mercy on our son. It was a chance I had to take, even risking your anger."

Doros, joyful at the attention of his father, wiggled out of his father's arms and slipped to the floor, crying, "See me, Pater, see me!" He toddled around on his chubby legs, showing them how he could walk now.

Lucius swallowed and could only smile and nod. "I see, my son." Then he turned to Claudia and took her in his arms. "You are far braver than I, wife of my heart. I must confess that I was jealous. I have been gone so much with my duties as governor, and I thought you were seeing someone else."

She put a hand on his face. "Oh, dear Lucius, there is no one but you. I have been talking with the gardener, Jeremiah, about the plants, and also having him tell me the history of the Jews. Joanna also has enlightened me on some of their customs. Since it is your task to govern the Jews while we are here, I felt it only natural that I, as your wife, should know more about them."

Lucius shook his head and leaned down to kiss her. "I have married a wise woman."

"You are no longer angry with me, my husband?"

He watched Doros walk across the room, pleased with his new foot. "How can I be angry? I am grateful to this God of the Jews for his mercy to us. I will not berate the Teacher again." He looked toward the window. "Few people know of our son's deformed foot. That is why I had you keep him in the palace."

He walked over and put his hand on the head of his son. "We must act as if nothing has happened. I do not want to create problems. Do you understand what I'm saying?"

"But Lucius, this is a wonderful miracle—"

He whirled around, his voice tense. "Claudia, do as I have bid you. I do not want you trailing around after this teacher like the steward's wife."

She fought down the words she wanted to say, and murmured only, "If you wish it, Lucius." Was he forbidding her to hear Jesus again?

The change in her demeanor didn't soften him. "I will make an offering to the gods for this great miracle. I will see you at dinner."

With a last look at his son, and then her face, he strode quickly out of the room.

Claudia stared at the closed door. An offering to the gods? After he knew who had healed his son's crippled foot? She sank down on a chair and put her face in her hands, trying to hold back the tears for the sake of her son.

A small hand patted her knee. "Mater? Are you sad, Mater?"

She forced a smile. "Oh, no, my love, I am very happy. I am happy about your foot."

"I have a good foot, now, Mater."

"Yes, Doros, you have a good foot now."

The door opened again and she looked up suddenly. Had Lucius had a change of heart?

It was Hotep.

"Domina, I saw the dominae leave. Was he not happy about the child's foot?"

"He was very happy, Hotep, but he does not believe in the Teacher as we do. He wants to give thanks to the Roman gods for the miracle. It is hard for him to change."

"Will that not make the God of the Hebrews angry?"

Claudia considered that. "I have to believe he would understand, Hotep. I cannot fight Lucius."

Doros sat down on the floor and studied his new foot. He touched each toe and patted the foot with his hand. "Jesus gave me a new foot. Jesus, Jesus," he sang.

She shook her head in wonder. Doros at least had no doubts as to who healed him.

35

Lucius had always been given to moods and she'd learned to leave him alone until he worked through whatever was bothering him. Sometimes he told her of his problem, but other times he preferred to keep it to himself. She hoped it was not her imagination, but Lucius seemed more moody than ever. There were times he would watch Doros play in the garden, and she sensed his inner turmoil. How did he reconcile his belief in his Roman gods with the miracle of the Jewish God? While she was anxious to talk with him about what she now believed with all her heart, she sensed it would only drive him further into himself.

At least when they went out in the coach, Doros was allowed to go with them instead of being left in their quarters with Hotep. It was obvious Lucius was proud of his son and anxious to show him off now, but if Doros tried to talk about Jesus, he was quickly cut off by his father. The boy was hurt and disappointed and, while silent, watched his father with sad eyes.

Claudia and Hotep prayed to the Lord God in their times alone and slipped out to see Jesus one more time to hear his teaching the week before Passover.

The people were coming into the city in droves as usual for this High Holy Day, and there was more shouting and singing than usual.

Claudia and Hotep took Doros along to watch Jesus enter the Holy City in triumph. He rode on a donkey and the people were spreading their clothes and flowers in his path. As the people proclaimed him a king and shouted their hosannas, Claudia felt the shadow of fear creep across her heart. There was no king but Caesar in the Roman world, and she wondered at this man of God who rode so regally, though it was only upon a donkey. He had the bearing of a king, and when she listened to the words the people were shouting, she feared for him.

Slipping back to the palace with Doros, she asked Chuza and Joanna to keep her informed on what was happening with the Teacher.

She paced the floor of their quarters, trying to understand this feeling of apprehension that gripped her. It was Joanna that brought her the first foreboding news.

"My lady, he has devastated the Temple! He entered and made a whip of cords and chased the money changers out. It was chaos. He overturned their trading tables, opened the cages of doves and let them go, then opened the pens for the lambs. People were picking up money until the Temple police arrived and drove them away. Animals were running everywhere . . ."

Claudia's eyes widened. "This will not set well with the high priest and the other leaders."

"No, it won't. They wanted to arrest him, but the people were cheering him, so they could not without causing a riot."

"Oh, Joanna. I fear he has created danger to himself. To teach is one thing, and heal the sick, but to openly defy the Pharisees is reckless. Did he give a reason for all this?"

Joanna nodded. "He said, 'My house shall be called a house of prayer, but you have made it a den of thieves.'" She went on, "When the chief priests and scribes saw what he was doing and heard the people crying out, 'Hosanna to the Son of David,' they were indignant. When they objected, the Teacher merely said, 'Have you never read, "Out of the mouths of babes and nursing infants, You have perfected praise"'?"

'What a strange thing to say. Did the leaders not arrest him?"

"No, my lady. They were angry, but they stalked away. I think they feared the people. They believe he is the Messiah, the promised king."

Claudia listened and her heart was heavy. If the Jewish leaders did not arrest him, the Roman soldiers no doubt would. Her emotions were in turmoil. To believe in him as the Son of the Living God and to follow his teaching was one thing. To challenge Caesar as a king was another.

Joanna hurried away to her other duties, and Claudia went to the window and stared out at the city a long time.

Hotep brought Doros back from the garden and took him to his small room adjoining their quarters for his nap. They had discovered the room by accident, turning a carved flower attached to the wall. It turned out to be a handle and opened to a lovely sunlit room, perfect for a nursery. Because the thick stone walls muffled any sounds from Claudia's room, Hotep was moved in to share the other room with her small charge.

At their evening meal, Lucius joined her but was obviously angry. He reclined on his couch in a huff and glared at her.

"Your Teacher nearly caused a riot in the city today. You should have seen the grand procession. Fools shouting, 'Hosanna to the king!'" He sneered and flung one hand in the air. "Don't you know he could be accused of treason?"

She faced him calmly. "Joanna told me what happened. The Jewish leaders could have arrested him and they didn't. I don't think he meant any harm."

"No harm? Claudia, he entered the city as though he were a king! My sources say the people view him as the Messiah. If the people proclaim him as such, how do I explain this to the emperor?"

"Were the people not just excited? He has healed so many." She waited for him to realize what she did not say.

His shoulders slumped. "Yes, he healed our son. I have not forgotten." Then he suddenly pounded his fist into his palm. "But I must have order in this city. That is my job. I cannot risk further confrontation with the Jews. Tiberius has ordered me to respect their beliefs."

"You had word from the emperor?"

"After the incident with the banners."

"You never mentioned that."

"I feared a recall to Rome for a while, but nothing further was said, and I'm still here. I didn't want to worry you."

She put a hand on his arm. "Oh, dear Lucius, how you must have worried over that."

He smiled at her then. "Always soothing words from you, beloved. What would I do without you?"

She gave him a saucy look. "I hope you never have to find out."

❦

Doros wanted to see Jesus again, but after the incident in the Temple, Claudia did not feel it was safe for her to go again. Yet her hunger to hear his teaching won out, and while Joanna agreed there was danger, she also wanted to hear him. Chuza was persuaded to go with them as before, but Doros was left at home.

She didn't tell Doros where she was going, only that if he was good and minded Hotep, she would bring him a sweet from the marketplace.

The three stole quietly through the throngs in the city, Claudia's face well-covered by her heavy stola. Chuza led them through some back streets and Claudia prayed for safety and that she would not be recognized.

Jesus had returned to the Temple in the morning and was teaching as usual. As the crowd settled down to listen, Joanna recognized the disciples and some of the other women who followed Jesus. Claudia was introduced to Susanna and a woman called Mary from the city of Magdala, but only as "Procula," Claudia's family name, which she seldom used. For the first time she heard herself referred to as a Godfearer and believer.

The eyes of the two Jewish women held curiosity, but they asked no questions and finally moved on to greet other believers and some of the disciples of Jesus.

Claudia, Joanna, and Chuza slipped into the shadows of a large pillar to listen unobtrusively. As Jesus began to teach, some of the chief priests and elders confronted him.

"By what authority are you doing these things? Who gave you this authority?"

Jesus answered, "I also will ask you one thing, which if you tell me, I likewise will tell you by what authority I do these things: the baptism of John—where was it from? From heaven or from men?"

The leaders reasoned among themselves, their voices low but fierce as they sought an answer. Finally they turned to Jesus. "We do not know."

Jesus sighed. "Neither will I tell you by what authority I do these things."

He spoke to them in parables, and sometimes Claudia had to strive in her mind to understand his point.

Now he was speaking of wicked vinedressers who were to care for a vineyard for a certain landowner. When he sent servants to receive the harvest, his servants were beaten, stoned, and killed. Finally he sent his son, thinking they would respect him, but the wicked vinedressers, knowing this was the heir, killed the son to seize his inheritance. Jesus looked around at the crowd. "When the owner of the vineyard comes, what will he do to those vinedressers?"

One of the priests answered, "He will destroy those wicked men miserably, and lease his vineyard to other vinedressers who will render to him the fruits in their seasons." As the crowd digested those words, Jesus spoke directly to the Jewish leaders. "Have you never read in the Scriptures,

> "'The stone which the builders rejected has become the chief
>   cornerstone.
> This was the Lord's doing, and it is marvelous in our eyes.'?

"Therefore I say to you, the kingdom of God will be taken from you and given to a nation bearing the fruits of it. And whoever falls on this stone will be broken, but on whomever it falls, it will grind him to powder."

Claudia realized that he was speaking directly of the chief priests and Pharisees, and she watched their faces as they listened. One priest's face was almost purple with anger and outrage.

Jesus faced the multitude in the courtyard and also his disciples gathered nearby. "The scribes and the Pharisees sit in Moses' seat. Therefore whatever they tell you to observe, that observe and do, but do not do according to their works; for they say and do not do. For they bind heavy burdens, hard to bear, and lay them on men's shoulders, but they themselves will not move them with one of their fingers. But all their works they do to be seen of men. They make their phylacteries broad and enlarge the borders of their garments. They love the best places at feasts, the best seats in the synagogue, greetings in the marketplaces, and to be called by men, 'Rabbi, Rabbi.' But you, do not be called 'Rabbi,' for One is your Teacher, the Christ, and you are all brethren. Do not call anyone on earth your father; for One is your Father, he who is in heaven. And do not be called teachers; for One is your Teacher, the Christ. But he who is greatest among you shall be your servant, and whoever exalts himself will be humbled, and he who humbles himself will be exalted. But woe to you, scribes and Pharisees, hypocrites! For you shut up the kingdom of heaven against men; for you neither go in yourselves, nor do you allow those who are entering to go in . . ."

As Jesus went on, berating the scribes and Pharisees, Claudia looked around, expecting the Temple police to appear at any moment to arrest the Teacher for his vehement scolding of the leaders. The disciples also looked uncomfortable and surreptitiously glanced around. She reasoned that they were thinking the same thing she was.

"Joanna," she whispered. "How can he get away with such words?"

"They fear the people," Joanna whispered back.

When Jesus finished his rant against the scribes and Pharisees, they turned and plowed back through the crowd, their eyes flashing against anyone in their way and their jaws clenched in anger.

Oh, dear Lord, please be careful, she pleaded in her mind. She turned to Chuza and whispered again, "What will they do? He has greatly angered them."

Chuza shook his head and answered softly, "He speaks the truth, but they do not wish to hear. They will retaliate, but I fear it will not be when he is in front of the crowds."

The three slipped out of the Temple area again, and Claudia kept her head down to keep from being recognized. Only when they had reached the courtyard of the castle did she sigh with relief. She was doubly relieved to learn that Lucius was at the Antonia and had not yet returned.

In the quiet of her quarters, with Doros down in the garden with Hotep, Claudia knelt and prayed fervently for the safety of the Teacher. "Please protect him, Most Sovereign God." She prayed for Lucius, for understanding and enlightenment. She sensed the turmoil in her husband. On the one hand, he could not help but acknowledge his son's miracle, but on the other hand, his mind was that of a soldier, hardened by years in the army. Above all, there was the need to keep peace in the city he ruled, and he was ruthless in accomplishing what was needed. She had heard stories that caused her no end of grief in her spirit. She could not breech that barrier no matter how many times she tried. Once or twice she had gone too far and earned a quick rebuke. He loved her but never forgot that he was the governor and the paterfamilias of his household with absolute rule over her and their son.

❧ 36 ❧

S he had lain in Lucius's arms the night before, soothing his concern as only a wife can do. At times she thought of him as a little boy who had taken on a task too great for him. She knew he was doing his best, but the responsibility was taking a toll on him. His hair was beginning to show signs of gray and the worry lines in his forehead became grooves that were permanent now.

When she at last fell asleep, the dream came to her again. Once more she saw the face of the man covered in blood from a crown of thorns on his head. It was running down his face and his eyes were sad. There was no fear in the face, only great sorrow. Angry voices shouted in the background and with a shock of recognition, Claudia realized who the man was. It was the Teacher, Jesus. Her heart pounded as she suddenly sat up in bed and reached for Lucius, but he had gone. Many times he was summoned for one reason or another in the early hours of the morning. Could they not let the man have a night's sleep?

She came down to breakfast and found Lucius with his friend Trajanius. She was apprehensive. Trajanius did not travel all the way to Judea just for a visit. He always brought news for Lucius. Her husband's face was thoughtful. She joined them and looked from one to another. "What news is there from Rome?"

"Livia Drusilla, the mother of the emperor, is dead, my lady."

"Livia? Was it illness or . . . ?"

Trajanius nodded. "She was eighty-six and has been ill for the past year." His tone was disdainful now. "The emperor did not see the need to visit her nor did he personally attend to the laying out of her body. There was a public funeral, but no matters of importance."

Claudia was horrified. "But she was his mother. Did he not seek to honor her?"

"Tiberius forbade deifying her and conducted business as usual. The senate, however, because of her good works among the women of the country, voted to build an arch in her name. An unusual and unprecedented move, if I may say so."

"Where was she buried?" This from Lucius.

"In the mausoleum of Augustus, Excellency."

Lucius nodded. "And how are things in Rome?"

"Tiberius remains in Capri. The winds of change blow over the city, and Sejanus, with all the honors Tiberius has heaped on him, is rumored to be in line for the consulship, the highest magistracy in Rome. There is no reason not to give it to him, considering he rules in the place of our absent emperor."

Lucius had listened thoughtfully, but now spoke what was truly on his mind. "And is there word of Judea?"

Claudia, picking up a cup of mulsa, paused, her hand in midair.

"My sources in the senate have not mentioned any unfavorable news. I believe you are secure in your position here, at least for now. As long as Sejanus is in charge of Rome, you have no reason for concern. Also, as long as there are no riots among the Jews or circumstances like the issue over the banners, Tiberius will not concern himself with matters of the far provinces. He seems content to remain in seclusion in Capri."

Lucius digested that news, chin in hand, and Claudia inwardly sighed with relief.

Trajanius turned to Lucius. "It is rumored that you and Herod had a falling out. What happened?"

Lucius shrugged and glanced at Claudia. Puzzled, she waited for his explanation.

They had seen little of Herod other than one banquet they had attended. She found Herod overbearing and his eyes, rheumy with drink, had ogled her body shamelessly when Lucius was looking the other way. She had endeavored to hide her disgust and be pleasant to Herod's wife, Herodias. Later she learned Lucius had been aware of Herod's attention to her and couldn't wait to leave the palace as soon as the appropriate opportunity presented itself. They had to be civil to the man, since they were living in one of his palaces.

Then Joanna had told her of the beheading of the Baptizer by Herod on a whim of his stepdaughter, Salome, who had performed the dance of the seven veils so seductively that Herod, inflamed with lust in his drunken state, offered her anything she asked for. At her mother's instigation, the girl had boldly asked for the head of the Baptizer whom Herod had imprisoned. He had no choice but to order the deed carried out. Claudia shuddered, hearing of the incident. Joanna told her that even the Teacher, Jesus, wept at the news.

She prompted Lucius. "What incident with Herod?"

"It was a matter of shields again. The golden shields I set up in my headquarters. While they didn't have the image of Caesar on them, only a bare inscription of dedication to Tiberius, the Jews, with the help of Herod, formally protested to the emperor. I received a very terse reply from the emperor to transfer the shields to a temple in Caesarea and that I was to uphold all the religious and political customs of his Jewish subjects!"

"You never mentioned this."

He glanced at his friend and, with a touch of irritation, murmured, "It is not necessary to inform you of all that goes on in Judea, my dear."

She felt the rebuke like a slap in the face but swallowed her first impulse to respond and, instead, inclined her head toward him. "Of course, Lucius, there are many matters of government that I'm sure do not concern me."

She had showed herself a submissive wife and not embarrassed her husband in front of his friend but knew now that there were things going on in her husband's realm that he did not wish to share with her.

"So you and Herod have not spoken because of the shields?" Trajanius said.

"That was five months ago. It will pass. I intend to invite Herod to a banquet and mend our relationship. He will be in Jerusalem for the Passover as usual."

Claudia sensed they wished to talk more, without her presence. At the end of the meal, Lucius stood, as did Trajanius, and politely waited for her to excuse herself. She nodded to Trajanius, who bowed his head in return.

Doros was awake when she came into his room and Hotep was dressing him for the day in a small tunic. She held out her arms and he went into them. "Pray, Mater?" he asked.

"Yes, Doros. We will pray." She had begun with Hotep after the healing of Doros's foot to pray daily to the Most High God. She had cautioned Doros not to talk about their prayers to his father. "Pater is very busy and Jesus is not his friend yet, as he is ours."

The three of them knelt by the side of her son's bed and prayed earnestly for Lucius, for wisdom and protection, and that he would see Jesus for who he truly was, the Son of the Living God.

❧

She didn't see Lucius until the next evening. He'd slept in the small austere quarters he'd used after Claudia had given birth and had been gone all day on affairs of the province. He finally joined her for dinner, but was subdued. He picked up a slice of melon and stared at it absentmindedly.

"Your thoughts are deep, my husband. Is it the news Trajanius brought you last night?"

With Trajanius gone as of this morning, perhaps Lucius would feel free to talk to her.

He took a bite of the melon and then looked up at her. "I was grateful for the news that I am not under discussion by the senate or Tiberius. Sejanus convinced the emperor to appoint me, and other than the letter from the emperor over the shields, it seems I am doing well in their eyes. Trajanius did caution me to keep a low profile and allow no more incidents that would cause the Jews to riot. It could end in my recall to Rome."

"Dear husband, you have governed to the very best of your ability, and I'm sure that Sejanus and the emperor know that."

"I have not been recalled, so that is my assumption. Still, these Jews are an unruly people. I thought the aqueduct would please them, bringing needed water into the city. What do they do? They riot because I used the Corban money to build it." He sneered. "They were only angry because I know what they use the money for—themselves."

"Your son asks for you. He misses you."

His countenance lightened. "I need to spend more time with the boy." He took her hand. "I am not ungrateful for the healing of his foot, beloved, I just do not understand it. How can a man touch another and they are instantly healed?"

Claudia considered her words. It was an opening with Lucius to talk of her faith, but she needed to tread carefully. "Those who listen to him feel he is more than a man. He is not arrogant, nor does he advertise himself. His words are compassionate and teach us better ways to treat our fellow man. His only harsh words seem to be for the Jewish leaders, the scribes and Pharisees who mock and question him. He calls them 'white-washed tombs, full of dead men's bones.' They follow the letter of the law, but not the intent."

Lucius laughed out loud. "Now if I called them that, they would certainly see to my demise as governor."

"Dear husband, only a god could do what Jesus does. He is not a sorcerer or a magician. His eyes are full of compassion for the sick and the lost."

"Is it true that he fed several thousand people on a hillside with only two salted fish and a few loaves of bread?"

She was taken back. "Joanna told me about that. She was there, as were two other women, Mary from Magdala and another follower called Susanna. You have heard the story also?"

He leaned back. "My centurion is full of stories about this Jesus and what he has done. I admit some skepticism. It seems a very large tale."

"He is a good man, Lucius, a man sent from God."

He became uncomfortable with the turn of the conversation. "Well, he has many followers. I just don't want to have to deal with a Jewish rebellion on my hands."

"He does not speak in those terms to incite people. He is a teacher of the law."

"So you say, my dear." He rose. "Some duties await me to prepare for tomorrow. The Jewish Passover is the time most likely for trouble to come, with the city so crowded. I may rise early. I will go to my own quarters tonight."

She hid her disappointment. He seldom used the room set aside for him in the palace. "Will you come and say good night to Doros?"

He nodded. "Of course. I'll come now before it becomes late and he is asleep."

Doros sat on the floor with his blocks and jumped up when Lucius entered the room.

"Pater!" Doros went across the floor as fast as his legs would carry him.

Lucius picked him up. "You are being a good boy for Hotep?"

"Yes, Pater. I am a good boy."

"And how is your foot?"

Doros glanced at his mother, who gave him a slight warning look. "My foot is good, Pater. I can run and play. I like Jesus. He was kind to me and fixed my foot."

Lucius glanced at Claudia. "Yes, so I have been told." He put Doros down. "Is he telling this to everyone?"

218

"No, my husband, he only feels free to talk about it with us. He has been cautioned not to speak of it outside our family."

"Good. See that he doesn't. I have work to do. Good night, my son. Sleep well."

"Yes, Pater." Doros watched his father leave the room, and when the door closed, he ran to his mother. "Pater came to see me."

"Yes, Doros, your father came to see you. Now it is time for bed." She motioned to Hotep, who took the little boy's hand and led him to his bed.

Claudia suddenly felt weary. The strain of keeping an even balance between her husband and what she believed was taking its toll on her. She had to be careful not to say too much, not to criticize when Lucius made a bad decision, to encourage him. She no longer worshiped the household gods and had the small statue of Venus removed from their room. She longed for another child, but month after month passed by and there had been no pregnancy. She prayed to the Most High God, but her womb was closed.

As Hotep helped her prepare for bed, she couldn't shake the sorrow that seemed to overwhelm her, and the feeling that something was coming that would change her world.

❧

The dream came again, the intensity and vividness of it was overwhelming. There were voices shouting and the face of the Teacher covered in blood and looking at her with such compassion, she wept. It was as if he wanted her to help him and she was helpless. Angry men shook their fists at him and hurled insults. Yet the Teacher stood immobile through it all, silent as one of the stone gods in the patio. She woke up during the night drenched in perspiration.

Hotep came to her bedside. "Domina, you cried out. Are you all right?"

She rubbed her forehead with one hand. "It was only a dream, Hotep."

"The same dream?"

"Yes, the same dream. Someone is planning to hurt Jesus, I'm sure of it. I cannot help him. In the dream my hands are frozen at my side . . ." She lay back down. "Go back to sleep, Hotep, it was only a dream."

The maidservant left, and Claudia, in spite of the turmoil in her mind, fell into a deep sleep again.

37

The sun rose slowly, pushing the shadows back and spilling over the walls of the sleeping city as Lucius stood at the window of his quarters. Passover began today and there were always incidents. With millions of people crowding Jerusalem, he dreaded the day. He could only hope his soldiers, posted visibly throughout the city, would be a deterrent to lawbreakers.

He looked at the city without seeing it, his mind tossing with questions. He'd lain awake for a long time, thinking of the words of his wife. Who was this Jesus anyway—a rabbi who mesmerized the people with his words, who miraculously healed those who came to him with their ailments? His spies told stories of Jesus even casting out demons. He had been in Judea long enough to learn that the Jewish priests had elaborate exorcism rituals. This man merely commanded demons to leave and they left the body of the possessed. Where did he get his power?

He would have put these incidents down to sorcery or magic of some kind, but there was the witness in his own household. How could he deny the healing of his son? Born with a deformed foot and destined to be a cripple the rest of his life, Doros now walked with two normal feet. What power did this man have? How did Jesus do these things? He rubbed the back of his neck in frustration.

Cautious of any group that would threaten the peace of Judea, Lucius had poured over every report on this rabbi during the last three years. He'd looked diligently for evidence that Jesus was stirring up the people for a rebellion against Rome, but there was no sign of that. Instead there were stories from his own hardened soldiers—of thousands fed with a few fish and loaves of bread, blind men given back their sight. One man had been born blind. He had no eyes! Yet Jesus laid hands on his face and gave him new eyes. By the gods, no human being could do such things!

His reverie was interrupted by an urgent knocking on his door. It was his tribune.

The man saluted. "Excellency, there is a delegation of the Jews outside the gate of the palace. They say they cannot come in because of Passover and defilement."

He sighed. "What do they want this time?"

"They have a prisoner, Excellency. They want you to sentence him."

He strolled through the palace with the tribune. "That I can do." Perhaps it would put these troublesome Jews in good humor and alleviate any trouble.

He stepped outside the palace and faced the priests. "What accusation are you bringing against the prisoner?"

The priests looked at each other. "If he were not a malefactor, we would not have delivered him up to you."

A typical reply he'd dealt with before. "Then take and deal with him according to your law. Why bring him to me?"

"We cannot do it ourselves. We want you to decree the death penalty for him, and we are forbidden to put a man to death."

"Let me see the prisoner."

They brought the man forward, and as Lucius saw who their prisoner was, a jolt went through his body. It was the Teacher, Jesus. Dismayed, Lucius ignored the curses and shouts of the rabble as for the first time he looked into the face of the man who had healed his son.

The rabbi stood silently, almost serenely, and in his eyes Lucius saw only kindness and compassion. In the midst of a storm of protest, he was an island of calm. There was a dignity about him that gave Lucius pause. He had the bearing of a king.

His mind surged again with memories of the stories he'd heard—from the centurion and others. Claudia called him the Son of God. She believed that. He must be a god to cause twisted flesh to right itself—toes to become normal. Claudia had witnessed the miracle, along with Hotep, the steward, Chuza, and his wife, Joanna. A great weight settled on his heart. He sensed something here he was totally unprepared for.

He drew himself up. "I wish a formal charge against this man."

The priests looked at him in disbelief and then at each other. To his chagrin, Lucius realized that to keep the peace he'd usually gone along with their decisions. The rabble shouted in the background as one priest came forward.

"Excellency, it is best you accept our decision in this matter. Too many questions are not necessary."

Lucius forced down a bolt of rage and clenched his fists. How dare they tell him what he should do? He directed his gaze at Jesus again. He had learned to read people well, and it was obvious that the man was innocent of any charges they were bringing against him. He could not take his eyes away from the face before him. His mind raced. He could not hand Jesus over to his enemies. He could not face his wife or his son.

The leading priest spoke up. "We found this man perverting the nation and forbidding to give tribute to Caesar, saying that he himself is Christ, a king."

Lucius turned to Jesus for his reaction to their charges, but the man did not respond to any of them.

Any of the three charges alone would make the prisoner guilty of treason. Yet Lucius suspected all were without foundation. Tiberius dealt harshly with traitors, real or imagined. Many in Rome were victims of the emperor's reprisals. Even the slightest hint of treason sent the emperor into a frenzy of retaliation. Judea was a volatile province. Tiberius would expect him to deal quickly with such a charge.

He nodded to his tribune. "Bring the prisoner into the judgment hall. I wish to question him privately."

The priests hung back as Jesus shuffled forward and was escorted into the Praetorium to come face-to-face with Lucius.

When they were alone, Lucius asked quietly, "Are you the King of the Jews?"

Jesus answered, "It is as you say."

"So you are a king?"

"You say rightly that I am a king. For this cause I was born, and for this cause I have come into the world, that I should bear witness to the truth. Everyone who is of the truth hears my voice."

Lucius sighed heavily. The man talked in riddles. "And what is truth?" He looked into the face of Jesus, his voice low. "You healed my son."

"Yes."

"You knew whose son he was, yet you healed him."

Jesus stood there with no shred of anger or accusation. He was under condemnation by the Sanhedrin, yet it was Lucius who felt he was the condemned man. The Teacher's destiny was surely death if the Jews had their way, and Jesus seemed resigned to the inevitable. Lucius listened to the cries of the rabble outside the palace. "Do you not hear the things they testify against you?"

Jesus did not answer and Lucius shook his head slowly, marveling at the man's composure under the circumstances.

He had no choice but to escort Jesus back outside.

Lucius faced the crowd. "I find no fault in this man." He had rendered his judgment. It should have ended there. He knew he should free Jesus and dismiss the rabble, but they continued to accuse the prisoner.

The lead priest stepped forward, his face twisted with anger. The governor had not gone along with their plan. "He stirs up the people, teaching throughout all Judea, beginning from Galilee to this place."

At the mention of Galilee, Lucius rubbed his chin. "Is this man a Galilean?"

When they nodded yes, Lucius folded his arms. "Take him to Herod. This prisoner is under his jurisdiction."

Totally frustrated, the leaders jerked on the ropes binding Jesus and, muttering, hauled him away to Herod.

When they had gone, Lucius was handed a tablet. It was from his wife and read, "Have nothing to do with that righteous man. I have suffered much in a dream because of him."

He turned and saw Claudia standing in the shadows, watching him. Her face was stark with fear and something else—anguish.

He went to her, seeking to find the right words to comfort her, but all he could say was, "Those fools are mad with jealousy. I can do nothing with them, they are bent on his blood."

"Lucius, what do you mean you can do nothing? You have rendered judgment. He is innocent of their charges."

He sighed. "Yes, I know, but I've sent him to Herod. Perhaps he can persuade them to release the rabbi. He told me once he admired Jesus and wanted to see him. I cannot take a chance on this crowd becoming violent."

He led her to a private area of the patio and sat with her.

"Lucius, you know as well as I do that they have totally ignored their own laws. They took him last night in the Garden of Gethsemane where he had gone with his disciples to sleep. They didn't give him a trial. The Sanhedrin just passed judgment. They found him guilty. No trial date was set or any of the rights of their laws followed. Joanna told me what the Jewish law says and they have ignored it. Everything about this arrest is illegal."

He shook his head. "I don't understand why he does not fight this. It is as if he is resigned to his fate. He doesn't deny the charges—in fact, he says nothing in his defense." Lucius waved a hand. "He says nothing at all."

A servant brought them some refreshments, some cheese and diluted wine, but neither of them were hungry. All they could do now was wait and see what Herod would do.

Claudia rose suddenly. "I cannot understand this, Lucius." And with a sob, hurried upstairs. He started to follow her, but turned to his study instead. He could not let her emotions sway him. His role as governor was at stake here. Yet, he shivered as a sense of impending doom brushed over his soul.

※

Toward midday, the tribune entered Lucius's study where he was going over some scrolls, glancing through them yet not reading them at all.

"They are back, Excellency. His Majesty, King Herod, has returned the prisoner to you."

"And his verdict?"

"He found no cause for the charges against him."

Lucius swore. This was getting complicated. So the old fox could not find him guilty either. Perhaps when this sorry incident was over, he should make an effort to solidify their friendship. With reluctance, he gathered himself and went out to the waiting crowd. Putting on an air of disdain, he addressed the priests.

"You have brought this man to me as one who misleads the people. And indeed, having examined him in your presence, I have found no fault in this man concerning those things of which you accuse him. Neither did Herod, for nothing deserving of death has been done by him." Lucius now rendered the third verdict of "not guilty."

The crowd roared like the beasts of the coliseum in Rome, as though deprived of their prey.

By the gods, they were determined to kill this man! He searched frantically for an answer and an idea came. It could relieve him of this unwanted responsibility. Barabbas. The man had killed two soldiers at the time of his capture and was guilty of other heinous deeds, leading a bunch of hardened criminals, rebels that had plagued Judea for over a year. If Lucius had his way, the man would have been sliced in two when they found him, but his soldiers brought him in for trial. He'd been found guilty and was awaiting execution. Lucius smiled to himself. The man was like a beast, in stark contrast to Jesus.

He had his soldiers bring out Barabbas, who pulled on his chains, sneering at the soldiers and cursing. They jerked him into place near Jesus. Barabbas, his tunic dirty and torn, stood defiantly, surveying the people before him from under heavy brows.

Lucius addressed the crowd whom he suspected had been stirred up by the priests. "You have a custom that I release one prisoner to you at Passover. Which do you want me to release—this murderer who stands before you or Jesus, the Christ?" Pleased with himself and his idea, Lucius was certain the crowd would choose Jesus.

To his shock and dismay, they began to chant, "Barabbas, Barabbas, release Barabbas!"

He had to shout himself over the tumult. "Then what would you have me do with Jesus who is called Christ?"

The crowd shouted back, "Let him be crucified!"

His heart was as a stone within him. He felt helpless and defeated. He'd bluffed over the matter of the shields, but there was now no way out of this. He looked at Jesus, who stood calmly while the deafening noise swirled about him. Lucius felt his face drain of blood as he fought against the fear that rose up within him. Had he condemned a god to die?

He sought frantically for a way to appeal to the angry mob.

There was one more desperate measure that might appeal to the sympathy of the mob. Lucius nodded to his tribune. "Chastise the man." And Jesus was led away by the soldiers.

Lucius drew on all his experience as a soldier to steel himself and not flinch as he listened to each stroke of the whip as the soldiers did their duty. The man cried out in pain but did not beg for mercy. When it was over, Lucius did not look around, for he sensed that his wife was somewhere nearby, watching from the shadows. He would have to face her later. He swore under his breath. Could she not see he was trying to save the man?

When they brought Jesus back out, a crown of thorns had been jammed down on his head and the blood ran down his face. His body was torn and bleeding, yet the eyes that looked into Lucius's still held no accusation. Jesus was resigned to his fate and meeting it with dignity.

"Behold the man," Lucius cried out, "that you may know I have found no fault in him."

The crowd began to cry out again, "Crucify him! Crucify him!"

Disgusted, Lucius flung up a hand and cried out above the uproar, "Take and crucify him yourselves. I find no fault in this man." He knew he was charging them to take the law into their own hands.

The leading priest responded with, "We have a law and by our law he ought to die, for he made himself the Son of God."

Lucius stared at the priest with revulsion. So that was it. There was no treason involved. They wanted him to die because he said he was a god. What if he was who his wife said he was? The Son of God? Fear rose up like bile in his throat. He had done everything he knew to do and to no avail.

Then the leader spoke the words that sealed the matter once and for all.

"If you let this man go, you are not a friend of Caesar. Whoever makes himself a king is an enemy of Caesar."

"You would crucify your king?"

"We have no king but Caesar!" the mob shouted.

His heart sank. If they appealed to Caesar, he would be recalled to Rome and an uncertain future. The emperor was unpredictable and could order his death. Lucius sank down on his seat of judgment and turned to his tribune. "Bring me a bowl of water."

When it was brought, he said loudly, "I am innocent of the blood of this just person. See to it yourselves." He washed his hands before them. "His blood is on your hands."

"Be it on the hands of us and our children," they shouted.

Lucius got up and turned his back on them. He could not look at the man he'd allowed to be condemned. Claudia was gone. He walked back into the palace and slowly climbed the stairs to their quarters. Looking down, he met the eyes of Chuza and Joanna standing in the entry and knew they'd heard everything. Tears ran down Joanna's cheeks and she shook her head slowly as they turned and walked away.

38

She heard the door open and close. She'd sent Hotep to the garden with Doros, knowing he would come. She continued to look out the window, hearing him approach behind her. He waited until she spoke.

"There is a hill outside the city, called Golgotha. It is the place of execution. Will they take him there?"

"Yes."

She heard his ragged breathing and turned slowly from the window. His face was drawn and pale—his eyes dark with pain.

"I had no choice."

"You had every choice, Lucius. You are the governor. You made a decision that he was innocent. Why didn't you send them away and free the Teacher?"

"Claudia, you don't understand. They were determined to kill him, no matter what I did. If I'd insisted on freeing him, they would have rioted all the more. The city is filled with millions, here for Passover. I do not have the troops to quell a rebellion of that size. At the first word of trouble, Tiberius would send the army and there would be bloodshed in the streets. Is that what you want? It is this one man's life for an entire city! That is the choice I had to make."

He gripped her shoulders and she did not resist. "They accused me of being no friend of Caesar. Tiberius is a madman, paranoid of treason and assassination . . ."

She looked up at him, feeling the frustration rise. "And who convinced him that he should fear this?"

He released her. "Sejanus persuaded him to go to Capri for safety!"

"So that Sejanus could rule Rome in his stead!"

She startled him with her vehemence and his face became hard. "Beware, woman, of how you speak. Even the walls have ears where Rome is concerned."

She could only shake her head. It was no use trying to reason with him. The deed was done. Their law boasted that no innocent man hung on a Roman cross . . . until now. One innocent man was going to his death, and Lucius had allowed it.

His voice softened. "Claudia, if the Jews send another delegation to Rome, I am finished here. Tiberius ordered me to uphold all the religious and political customs of his Jewish subjects. If I did not, if I thwarted them, what then? With the irrational behavior of the emperor, who knows what fate would await me if I am ordered to return."

Her eyes searched his face and saw his fear. Her grandmother was right. He would make mistakes and need her to be strong for him. She thought of the Teacher's disciples whom Joanna said were in hiding, terrified of arrest themselves. They had scattered in the garden when the Teacher was arrested. Faced with evil, they too had run in fear.

Help me, Lord God, to say the right thing. I am so confused. My husband comes to me for solace and I want to strike him for what he has done.

Just as quickly, the anger lifted. She didn't understand it, but the God she believed in had heard her prayer. She was strengthened.

She put a hand up to his cheek. "If the Teacher did not fight this, there must be a reason, Lucius."

He crushed her in an embrace. "They are jealous of the people who flock after him and listen to his teaching."

She held him, this man who could be so ruthless and cruel at times, now amazingly in anguish over what he had done. "He has given us a wondrous gift, Lucius, a little boy who can walk normally again. For that I will be eternally grateful."

He shook his head. "I told him I knew he had healed my son. All he said was, 'Yes.' Yet he didn't condemn me. There was no anger in his face."

Suddenly a cry went up outside the palace and Claudia pulled away from him and went to look out the window. "It has begun then. They are making him carry the means of his crucifixion."

Lucius came to stand beside her and saw a figure bent over under a heavy crossbeam, struggling to walk through the mob of people. Soldiers went ahead of him and drove people back, snapping their whips.

Claudia stifled a sob with her fist, then turning away from him, rushed to her cupboard and grabbed a heavy cloak. Before he realized what she was doing, she was out and running down the stairs. He followed after her, but he was too late. She disappeared in the sea of shouting rabble.

Thankfully, his tribune stood in the palace entry. He looked toward the entrance and back at his superior. "Excellency?"

"My wife is distraught and doesn't realize the danger. Send two of your most trusted men to find her. Bring her back to the palace. Not a word of this is to leak out. Is that understood?"

The tribune, looking at the thundercloud on the face of his superior, saluted. "Yes, Excellency."

When he had gone, Lucius sought another officer who was standing on the steps of the palace watching the Jews milling in the courtyard. "Who is in charge of the execution detail?"

When he learned the name of the centurion, he nodded and turned away, holding his emotions in check. He called over his shoulder. "Let me know if there is any change in the crowd."

The officer saluted and continued to monitor the crowd.

Lucius went to his study and leaned both hands on the table, his head bowed. By the gods, what further grief must he mete out today? The centurion was the man whose servant had been healed.

39

Claudia pushed her way through the crowd to get to the Via Dolorosa, the main street the criminals were being driven up. When she neared the head of the procession, her eyes widened with shock. That sorry mass of human flesh with blood dripping on the ground and struggling beneath the weight of the heavy wooden cross-beam could not be her Lord. He was hardly recognizable. What had Lucius done to him in the name of trying to save his life? She slipped into a doorway and surveyed the crowd. To her surprise and relief, she spotted Joanna and two of the other women she'd met, Mary of Magdala and Susanna. There was a fourth woman, older and supported by a young man. She seemed bowed with grief. When Jesus neared her, the woman struggled through the crowd and dropped to her knees beside Jesus as he fell again from his pain and burden. With her shawl, she tenderly wiped his face.

One of the Roman soldiers took hold of her arm to jerk her away. She said something to him and he hesitated. Finally the soldier appeared to speak kindly to her and even helped her up as she rose. The woman was reluctantly drawn back into the crowd by Susanna. Claudia watched and wondered what was special about this follower that the soldier would speak kindly to her?

Then she knew. It was his mother. Only a mother could look beyond the bloody form that was her son and tenderly wipe his face. Claudia's heart grieved for her.

Just then Joanna's eyes caught her own. Joanna beckoned to her to join them, and still hiding her face, Claudia slipped out of the doorway and made her way through the crowd to them. When she reached the group, Joanna turned to the older woman and the young man who supported her and gestured toward Claudia.

"She is a Godfearer and a believer. Jesus healed her son." She wisely did not mention Claudia's name. Joanna then swept a hand toward the two other people. "This is Mary, the mother of Jesus, and one of the disciples, John." Mary and John nodded, but their eyes were riveted on the event taking place before their eyes.

The group moved with the crowd and reached the foot of Golgotha. Claudia stopped, surveying the gruesome scene. "Joanna, I can't."

"It's all right. I understand. It is enough that you came. The disciples are hiding in an upper room, and after this travesty is over, I will join them. We don't know what to do, but we can at least comfort one another."

"I am so sorry. Lucius did try to save him. The priests would have none of it. They want him dead."

Joanna studied her face briefly. "I must go. Mary needs me." She turned and moved through the crowd to stand with the others.

Did Joanna believe her? She clutched her heart in grief. The sounds of the hammer nailing the spikes through the Lord's hands seemed deafening. As she tried to decide what to do, she was aware of someone on either side of her. Roman soldiers. They had thrown dark cloaks over their uniforms to try and blend in with the crowd.

"My lady," one whispered. "The governor is concerned for your safety and has asked us to find you. Please, for all our sakes, do not cause a commotion. Come with us."

She looked into the young soldier's face and saw his concern. He was right. There was nothing she could do, and if she resisted, she would call attention to them. "I will return. Just walk behind me."

Keeping her head down, she moved through the crowd, but no one noticed, so intent were they on the spectacle before them. The two soldiers followed discreetly.

When they reached the palace, the soldiers bowed their heads briefly and turned back to the crowd.

Lucius stood in the middle of the entry, his face torn between worry and anger.

"Did I not have enough to contend with today without your foolish actions? The mob is wild with the thirst for blood. Had they recognized you, do you know what could have happened?"

Her shoulders drooped. "I acted rashly, my husband. I'm sorry."

Only because she knew him did she see the slightest change in his countenance. Relief that she was safe.

"Return to our quarters and remain there. This will not happen again."

"Yes, Lucius." With head down, she obeyed.

❧

Hotep returned to the room with Doros. The little boy had no idea what was happening and seemed puzzled by the sad faces of his mother and nurse. He placed a small wagon, his favorite toy, in Claudia's lap and looked up at her hopefully.

She gathered him gently to her and kissed the top of his head. Her eyes sought Hotep's and the maidservant shook her head. What could either of them say about the events that had unfolded this day?

Hotep went to put Doros down for his nap, and Claudia went back to the window where she could see three crosses on the hill. She could barely make out the figures on them. Two men had been crucified with Jesus. She wondered who they were. Anger rose up inside her. One of them should have been Barabbas!

The roar of the crowd in the city quieted down. People seemed to be waiting. Those who had cried out hosannas in his name had turned on him, and now waited for his last breath. When they had sick and lame to heal, where would they turn now? They had murdered the healer.

She sank down to her knees by her bed, weary in body and spirit. How could she still bear to have Lucius touch her after this? How could she forgive him for such a terrible deed?

She could only pray, for Joanna and Chuza, for the disciples and the mother of Jesus, for his family that must be in terrible anguish.

When at last she had emptied her heart and prayed as fervently as she was able, she lay down on her bed and fell into an exhausted sleep.

She was suddenly awakened by the shaking of the bed. Objects in the room fell onto the floor and broke. The door to Doros's room opened and Hotep, holding the terrified child, staggered into the room. She put Doros on the bed and the three of them clung to each other as the room rocked.

"What is happening, Domina?" Hotep wept in terror. Outside the window, the sky was dark and threatening. After a long moment, the shaking stopped. Claudia climbed off the bed and stood cautiously, holding her small son who was whimpering and clinging to her.

"I am afraid, Mater."

"You must be strong, my son. This will pass. We need you to be our big boy."

He sniffed. "I will try, Mater."

She went to the window and looked out. The darkness was heavy, but she could hear people running to and fro and calling out to each other. How had Jerusalem fared? Was there much damage? She knew Lucius would be with his men, doing whatever was needed to bring order to the chaos.

The young officer who had come to her in the crowd looked in on them and, assured that they were all right, went back to report to the governor. At least Lucius had done that much.

It was late in the evening when Lucius returned to their room. Hotep and Doros were asleep in the boy's room. Lucius was dirty and exhausted. Stubble covered his chin. He sank onto a chair and pulled off his sandals. "There is much destruction in the city. We have been pulling people out of the rubble. Many have died and there were bodies to bury. There was a little boy, the age of our son . . ." He put his face in his hands.

She went to him then, compassion stirring in her heart, forcing out the anger. He needed her now and she must be what he needed.

She helped him off with his uniform, then brought a bowl of water from the large jar in the bathing room and began to wipe his face.

He looked up at her, his dark eyes pooled with the sorrow he bore. "Do you know when the earthquake started?"

She shook her head. "I was asleep, my husband. The shaking of the bed woke me."

"Toward midafternoon the clouds began to roll in. Do you know what his last words were?"

She knew then he was speaking about the Teacher. "No."

"The centurion told me. The man said, 'Father, forgive them, for they know not what they do." He shook his head slowly as though trying to comprehend the magnitude of what he'd learned. "The earthquake began the moment he died." He looked at her with fear. "I was told that the curtain in the Temple was torn in two. Do you know how thick that is?"

She dropped the cloth. "Oh, Lucius, don't you know now that he was who he said he was? Surely the Most High God was angered at the death of his Son."

His eyes widened in fear. "Then I am cursed of men, for I have put to death God's Son."

She led him to the bed and covered him, then slipped in next to him, warming his body with her own. She held him through the night, praying, as he alternately shivered and cried out in his sleep.

40

Lucius left the room in the early hours after gazing down at his wife, sleeping soundly. She had brought him comfort in his darkest hour and he was filled with love for her. As to the events of the previous day, he would have to live with that—if he could. There was no undoing the horrible deed he had allowed. Now he must move on and do his job. Whether Tiberius would call him back to Rome over this, he knew not.

He stared down at the long letter he had just written to the emperor, laying out all the facts of the case and giving the reasons behind his decision. He reminded the emperor, as tactfully as he knew, that he had been admonished to uphold the Jewish laws and customs, and since this was a matter of their law, he had allowed the death penalty rather than deal with another riot. He rolled up the scroll and sealed it, pressing his signet ring into the warm wax.

Calling for his tribune, he sent the message by courier. Now he could only wait for the answer from Rome.

The city seemed quiet, but the quiet could be deceptive. There were areas to inspect for damage that would take several days.

As he went out on the steps to wait for his horse to be brought out, a delegation of the chief priests and Pharisees came hurrying toward him.

"Excellency, we must speak with you."

If it was up to him at the moment, he would have slaughtered the lot of them, so great was his revulsion. He forced himself to answer them. "What is it you want this time?"

"Excellency, that deceiver told his disciples that after three days he would rise from the dead. Therefore we request that the tomb be made secure until the third day, lest his disciples come by night and steal him away, and say to the people, 'He has risen from the dead.' So the last deception will be worse than the first."

Was he hearing correctly? Lucius's laughter spilled out as he looked from one self-righteous face to another. These fools wanted him to send a detail to guard a dead man? The very idea was preposterous. What would these Jews come up with next? He regained his composure, shaking his head. Well, what harm could it do if it was a means of keeping the peace.

"Very well, you have a watch, now leave me. Make the tomb as secure as you can." He almost sneered at them. Puffed-up hypocrites! Turning to his tribune, he murmured, "See to it."

The tribune called some of the waiting soldiers over and chose ten men, directing them to follow the Jewish leaders to the tomb and stand watch through the night. Some of the men grumbled at the unusual request, but they were trained men and did as they were told.

Lucius watched them go, and as a slight breeze ruffled his cloak, he wondered at the contrast between the darkness the day before and this day. Something troubled him, but he didn't know what it was. His horse was led out, and dismissing the strange premonition, he mounted and rode out with his men toward the aqueduct.

❧

Hotep swept up pieces of broken pottery and put Claudia's room back in order. Lucius had ordered the repairs of the water pipe in the bathing room and the cistern checked, but it would have to wait until someone was free to repair it, due to the damage in the city.

When the first day of the Jewish week dawned, no more Passover lambs could be sacrificed and roasted. The smell of roast lamb still permeated the city from the many ovens set up at various strategic points. Because lamb was plentiful during this season, there was even lamb on their dinner table. Claudia felt strange about eating it, because of Passover and the fact that she wasn't Jewish, but Lucius assured her that there were many lambs not used for sacrifice left over.

It was early evening two days later when there was a soft knock on the door, and Hotep opened it to see Joanna standing with the glory of the sun shining from her eyes.

"I had to come and tell you."

"What has happened?" Claudia ushered the beaming woman into the room and indicated a chair, but Joanna seemed too excited to sit.

"My lady, the Lord has risen."

"Risen? What do you mean?"

"We have seen Jesus. He came into the upper room where we were praying and stood among us."

"You saw his ghost?"

"No, it was not his ghost. It was the Lord himself. He actually ate with us and showed us the nail prints in his hands and feet. He tried to tell us so many times that he would rise on the third day, but it was hidden from us. We didn't understand. We thought him dead, but he left the tomb where he'd been laid. Peter and John went to the tomb and saw the burial garments, lying there as though he had just slipped out of them."

Finally Joanna sank onto the chair. "After the Lord was crucified, we were bereft. We thought he was dead. He was taken down from the cross and one of the members of the Sanhedrin who is a believer, Nicodemus, asked for his body. He and another member of the Sanhedrin, Joseph of Arimethea, took the Lord's body to a nearby tomb. We followed, not knowing what to do. The two priests anointed the body with myrrh and aloes as is our custom and wrapped it in burial cloths. When they had finished, we waited until they had gone and then marked the place of the tomb. We wanted to return in the morning when the Sabbath was over to make sure the body of our Lord was prepared properly."

Claudia interrupted. "But you said the men prepared the body."

"Yes, my lady, but it is the women who usually do this and we needed to be sure all was done that was to be done."

Claudia nodded and indicated Joanna was to go on.

"We purchased spices in the marketplace early in the morning before daylight and made our way to the tomb. There were three of us, including Mary from Magdala. Since the stone was so great, we discussed among ourselves who could roll it away for us. We had heard that your husband had authorized a watch of soldiers to guard the tomb, and we were hoping some of them were there and would move the stone for us. When we got there, the soldiers were gone. It appeared they'd left in haste, for some of their belongings were scattered on the ground. We were wondering what to do when we realized the stone had already been rolled away. We feared the worst and cautiously entered the tomb."

Joanna stopped and her face lit up again. "There was this wondrous being in the tomb, I'm sure it was an angel. The light from his body illuminated the entire tomb and was almost blinding. The angel said, 'Do not be afraid, for I know that you seek Jesus who was crucified. He is not here; for he is risen, as he said. Come, see the place where the Lord lay, and go quickly and tell his disciples that he is risen from the dead, and indeed he is going before you into Galilee; there you will see him. Behold, I have told you.'"

"You saw an angel?" Hotep could not keep silent at Joanna's words.

Joanna nodded. "Yes. I believe that's what he was."

Claudia's brow wrinkled. "This was the very thing the Jews thought would happen. My husband told me they asked for a watch. They were afraid the disciples would steal the Lord's body and claim he had risen from the dead."

"But he did, my lady. No one stole the body. The graveclothes were still lying on the slab as though the body had just slipped out of them, and the head cloth was folded in its place. With soldiers guarding the tomb, how could the disciples move that great stone without making noise and drawing the attention of the soldiers?"

Claudia wanted to believe her. "That is true. Since I heard that all the disciples ran away when Jesus was arrested, it would have been a reckless move on their part. They would have been arrested by the guards."

Joanna went on, "And here is an even more wondrous part. I went with Susanna to tell the disciples what we'd seen, for we knew where they were hiding. Mary Magdalene stayed behind. She was so devoted to the Lord. She was weeping and wanted to remain there alone.

"We were doing our best to convince Peter and the other disciples of what we'd seen and they would have none of it. Then, suddenly, Mary burst into the room crying, 'I've seen him! I've seen the Lord!' She had actually seen him in his resurrected body and he'd spoken to her. She was nearly beside herself with joy. Well, I can tell you that Peter and John, as men do, scoffed at our story and wouldn't believe Mary either. They decided to see for themselves and ran to the tomb. Of course they found it just as we had told them. They went back to the upper room to talk to the other disciples and believers, and suddenly the Lord himself appeared in the middle of the room!"

"Are you sure he was not a ghost?"

"Yes. He spoke with us and actually asked for some food, and ate it in front of us. No ghost can do that."

Joy rose like the dawn in Claudia's heart. The Lord was not dead after all. In spite of what her husband and the Jewish elders thought they had done to him, he had risen and was alive. She reached out and clasped Joanna's hands in her own. "What will the believers do now?"

"We are to wait. The Lord said to wait until we receive power from on high."

"Power from on high? What does that mean?"

"I don't know, my lady, but we will wait in the upper room until we know."

"The believers and the disciples will need food then." Claudia turned to Hotep. "Tell the cook I need baskets of food prepared to send with the Lady Joanna." She turned back to Joanna. "How many are there?"

"Over one hundred."

Claudia raised her eyebrows but instructed Hotep to prepare for one hundred—bread, wine, fruit, and cheeses. She dared not send meat, for the Jews were careful not to eat the meat from the Gentile markets, lest it had been offered to an idol.

"Would they be afraid if I went there?"

Joanna nodded. "It is too soon. Your husband ordered his crucifixion. I believe you would be regarded as a spy in their midst. Give them a little time. There are many groups meeting in homes throughout the city. Perhaps in time, a small group of believers . . ."

Claudia's face fell. "I am ordered by my husband to remain in the castle until we return to Caesarea. I can no longer go about the city."

Joanna patted her hand. "Then I will start a group in my quarters. Chuza has already mentioned doing that. We will have to be discreet, but you are welcome to join us when you are here in Jerusalem, and you would not have to leave the palace. No one would suspect the staff meeting with us in Herod's very palace. I will let you know when we begin."

The women embraced and Joanna left. Claudia turned to Hotep, who had been listening.

Hotep looked anxiously at her mistress. "Might I go also, Domina?"

"Of course. We will both go."

"What about your son?"

"He shall go with us. I want him to learn at an early age about our Lord. He will be ready for a tutor in a couple of years, and if there is any way to do so, I intend to make sure the man is a believer."

"What is a believer, Mater?"

The women turned to see Doros standing in the doorway of his room, rubbing his eyes. How long had he been there? "Did you hear what Joanna said, Doros?"

"Jesus is dead, but he came alive. How did he get dead, Mater?"

"Don't worry about that, my son. Jesus is alive. He is not dead."

He came over to her and climbed up on her lap. "I am glad. I like Jesus. Can I see him?"

Claudia glanced at Hotep. "Not right now, my love. He had to go on a journey. When he gets back, perhaps you can see him."

"All right." He slipped off her lap and went to play with his small wagon.

How quickly children could be distracted, Claudia reasoned. With a sigh of relief, she watched Hotep lead Doros back to his bed, then she began to undress for bed herself.

Sleep would not come. As she lay there, her mind turned with possibilities. Would she be able to see Jesus herself? Would he appear to her? She dismissed that thought. She was a believer, but she was not one of his close disciples, and she could not go to the upper room as the others did. Even so, she would look forward to meeting with other believers in the palace. They were scheduled to leave in a few weeks for Caesarea for the late spring and summer, and she was reluctant to leave Jerusalem with all that was happening. Perhaps she could find believers in Caesarea.

Finally, after praying for Lucius, she stared at the ceiling. Would there be a way to share this news with her husband? And if she did, what would be his reaction? In his present emotional state, would he believe her?

∽ 41 ∾

Claudia sought an opportunity to speak with Lucius about Jesus, but there never seemed to be a time when he wasn't preoccupied. At first he was depressed, expecting a summons from Tiberius to answer for the things that had happened, but it didn't come. The weeks and months passed and the year ended. Lucius seemed more ruthless than ever, as if to prove to the Jews that he was not a weakling who could be manipulated by their leaders. Claudia lived her faith quietly, for Lucius would not allow her to talk about Jesus to him. Doros had been cautioned not to speak of Jesus around his father just yet, for she knew the incident still bothered him. If he became angry, he could take him away and find a tutor who would exorcise any of Claudia's influence as a believer.

Claudia enjoyed the celebration of Hanukkah and met with a group of believers. She had finally been accepted into Chuza's group, but not without much anxiety on their part.

When they found out who she was, their smiles had turned to anger.

Claudia faced them calmly. "I am not responsible for the actions of my husband. I love our Lord and am grateful for his mercy in healing my son." She beckoned to Hotep, who came hesitantly, holding the hand of Doros. "My son was born with a crippled foot. In Roman society that is a curse. Jesus had no hesitation, and he knew whose son he was. I only ask that you let me learn more of our Savior so my son will grow up to love him also."

After she had spoken, one of the Jewish men stood and faced the group. "If our Lord had compassion on her son, so must we also have compassion on one who seeks the truth." He then turned to Claudia. "Welcome, in the name of the risen Lord."

Relief flooded her being. "Thank you."

Chuza cautioned them, "She comes with great risk. Let us be sure that no word leaves this room of her presence here."

They all nodded and faces that had been anxious now greeted her with smiles.

One by one, members of the group spoke and told their stories. One young man sat listening and brooding at the side of the room. He didn't speak until most were getting ready to leave. As Claudia prepared to leave with Hotep holding the now sleeping Doros, he challenged her.

"Jesus was innocent of any crime, yet the governor sentenced him to death. What kind of a man does that?"

Claudia sighed. "A man who, in his own mind, had no choice. He could not have another riot. He would have been recalled, and who knows what kind of man Tiberius would send in his place?"

Joanna faced the young man. "I have traveled with Jesus. He told us several times he would be killed and would rise on the third day. We didn't listen. We didn't want to believe, yet all came to pass as the Lord told us. The Most High God merely used our governor to accomplish his will."

The young man was startled at her words. Conflicting emotions crossed his face. Finally, he shook his head and went out the door.

Claudia had been careful to attend the meetings only when Lucius was away. She didn't want to take a chance on his forbidding her to go or to take Doros. Lucius was short-tempered these days. He had not heard from the emperor, but messages took time to reach the outer provinces. They both knew there was turmoil in Rome as Sejanus tightened his hold on the city and paved the way for his being named co-regent with Tiberius.

When Lucius returned, he was silent at dinner, and while the pigeons stuffed with nuts were succulent and tender, he toyed with his food.

"Something troubles you, my husband?"

"I am expecting a courier from Rome. There are strange rumors floating about."

She'd had a sense of apprehension for several days but thought it was guilt because she'd been attending the meetings without her husband's knowledge.

"When will the courier arrive?"

"Any day now."

"And you are fearful of the news he will bring."

He frowned. "I'm not sure how I feel. Waiting to find out if I have been recalled is never far from my mind."

"Is it the death of Jesus that troubles you?"

"He was innocent. How could I put to death the man who healed my son?"

He finally looked up at her and she saw the ragged pain in his eyes. He had been torturing himself. Was now the time?

She began hesitantly, "Dear husband. I have news that you may not receive or believe, but it might put your conscience to rest."

He put a small chunk of bread down, his eyes fixed on her face. "What news?"

She took a deep breath and sent up a silent prayer for guidance. "When Jesus was traveling around, toward the end of his ministry, he told his disciples several times that he would be taken by the Jewish elders and killed. They didn't want to believe him. They didn't want anything to happen to him. Joanna told me that he also told his disciples that on the third day after his death he would rise from the dead and be alive again."

He shook his head. "You have been listening to foolish tales. No man rises from the dead after the death he suffered. I know about the empty tomb, Claudia. The disciples stole the body right from under the noses of the soldiers."

Claudia suppressed a smile, thinking of the argument Joanna had used to convince her. She would use the same argument now with her practical husband.

"Dear Lucius. I know that you keep a finger on all that goes on in Judea and you insist on the facts when you are making a decision. Let me share what I have learned. First, there were ten soldiers. What is the penalty for going to sleep on their watch?"

"Death. No soldier sleeps on duty," he growled.

"Then the soldiers would not go to sleep. The stone was large—so large I hear it took several men just to roll it into place. Would it not have made a noise if the disciples tried to move the stone out of the way?"

"Yes." His eyes narrowed. "Where are you going with this, woman?"

"Just this. The disciples ran away when Jesus was arrested in the garden. They were in hiding, fearing arrest themselves. Would they have gone to the garden and boldly moved the stone with ten soldiers nearby? Would they have unwrapped the graveclothes from the body and left them behind as they carried the Lord's body away?"

She had his full attention. "The graveclothes were lying in place in the tomb as if the body had just slipped out of them. The head cloth was neatly folded and lying by itself. Would the disciples take time to do this under the circumstances?"

He rubbed his chin. "You present a good argument, beloved. Caiaphas besought me to ignore the penalty for the guards. He said they had been bewitched." He gave her an indulgent smile. "So what then has been done with this rabbi?"

"He is risen, Lucius, and has been seen by all of his disciples, including Joanna." She couldn't keep the excitement out of her voice. "Lucius, he ate with them, and showed them the nail prints in his hands and feet. He is alive. You may have ordered his death, but he ordered his life."

"You want to believe these stories because of what he did for our son."

"No, Lucius, I want to believe because in my heart I know it is true. When he walked in Judea and taught the people, he raised three people from the dead, remember? You told me about it yourself. A man named

Lazarus, a widow's son, and a little girl. He just spoke the words and life came back into their bodies. The man Lazarus was raised before dozens of witnesses. Could not a man, who called himself the Son of God, have the power to take up his life again?"

"Woman, you would almost persuade me . . ."

A servant interrupted them. "Excellency, there is a courier waiting to speak with you."

Lucius's softened mood changed instantly. "Send him in."

The soldier saluted Lucius. "Excellency, I bring disturbing news from Rome."

"Speak on. I have sensed something is not right."

"Sejanus is dead."

Lucius nearly rose from his couch. "Dead? How?"

"Sejanus was expecting to be named co-regent with the emperor. He was summoned to the senate meeting by the emperor in a letter, supposedly to confer on him the tribunician powers. As he entered the hall, the senators all cheered, and then settled down to listen to the letter from the emperor. Meanwhile, Naevius Sutorius Macro, whom we learned later had already been chosen by the emperor to replace Sejanus, quietly replaced the soldiers loyal to Sejanus with members of the Praetorian Guard, including myself, who were loyal to Tiberius. We waited until the letter was read. The emperor rambled, stating he was near the point of death and stepping down as consul, which forced Sejanus to do the same. Tiberius then conferred an honorary priest-hood on Caligula, which rekindled support for the popular house of Germanicus. Then Tiberius suddenly accused Sejanus of treason! He was immediately arrested and led in chains from the hall."

Claudia glanced at her husband, whose face registered not only shock, but dismay. His worst fears had come true. Is this what Tiberius had in store for her husband? A knot formed in her chest and she felt she could hardly breathe.

"Then what happened?" Lucius strove to maintain his composure.

"The senate condemned him to death and he was strangled. When they threw his body down the Gemonian stairs, the people fell on the body and tore it to pieces."

Claudia shuddered. When she lived in Rome, she had seen the bodies that had been thrown down these steps that led from the Capitoline Hill to the Roman Forum. Bodies of the dishonorable and outcast were left to rot at the foot of these steps for days.

Lucius shook his head. "I never imagined such a fate for Sejanus."

"That is not all, Excellency. The city was in an uproar. Mobs rioted and anyone they could link to the prefect's reign of terror was hunted down and killed. Dozens of men were crucified. It took us days to quell the mob and bring order."

Claudia could no longer keep silent, shivering at the bloodbath that must have ensued. "What of his family?"

The soldier continued, adding to her horror. "His sons were strangled and his former wife, Apicata, committed suicide, but not before she wrote a letter to Tiberius claiming Levilla had poisoned the emperor's son, Drusus, at Sejanus's instigation. Levilla's own mother, Antonia, was so angry she had her starved to death. The slaves in Levilla's household confessed to administering the poison at her request and they were put to death."

Claudia clasped her hands in her lap to maintain composure herself. "You said the sons of Sejanus were dead. What of his daughter, Junilla? She would be about thirteen now. Was she spared?"

The man could not look into her eyes. He hesitated and then looked to Lucius for direction.

"Answer the question or she will give me no rest."

"She was strangled also, my lady."

"But she was unmarried as yet, a virgin."

"Yes, my lady, and there is no precedent for putting to death a virgin. It seems that one of the—ah—guards took care of that matter before her death."

"You mean he . . . ?" Claudia felt as if she was going to be sick.

"Yes, my lady." He shook his head slowly and turned to Lucius.

"There is more I was sent to tell you, Excellency. Tiberius has plunged into a series of trials and is relentlessly pursuing anyone who can in any way be tied to the schemes of Sejanus. Or . . . ," and he paused meaningfully, "or courted his friendship."

Claudia, already distraught, gasped and put a hand on the arm of her husband, whose jaw was clenched at the news. "You were appointed by Tiberius, but it was at the suggestion of Sejanus."

Lucius leaned back, his face resigned. "Then I am in danger from the emperor also." He remained silent for a long moment and finally rose. "Thank you. Now refresh yourself and partake of a meal. Then my servants will show you to your quarters."

The man stood and saluted. "Thank you, Excellency. I must admit I am hungry. It has been a long journey, but it was urgent you receive this news. Your friend Trajanius made arrangements with Macro for me to come to you with all haste."

Lucius took Claudia's elbow as they climbed the stairs and the air was heavy with portent. She was heartsick and anxious. What did this mean for them? Would soldiers arrive one day with orders for her husband's arrest?

Lucius looked toward the room of his small son and slowly pushed open the door. Hotep rose from tucking Doros in his bed and bowed her head as she stepped back respectfully. He walked over and picked up the small wagon that was Doros's favorite toy, and put it down beside him.

"Pater?" Doros looked up, his face a combination of delight and concern. "Are you well, Pater?"

"I am well. Sleep now, my son." He reached down and touched Doros's face.

The little boy smiled happily, enjoying the rare attention from his father.

Lucius looked down at his son for a moment and then turned and slowly left the room.

As Claudia watched him, she wondered what Lucius was thinking. Had not the sons of Sejanus been little boys like Doros once? Apicata had nurtured them and, when they were small, tucked them in their beds. How devastated she must have been to learn they were both murdered because of their father. Then, suddenly Claudia saw again in her mind the mother of Jesus, wiping his face with a cloth as he struggled under the burden of the heavy beam in the street. He may have been God's Son, but she had given birth to him and raised him. Pain struck like a heavy blow to her heart. What awaited Doros if they were recalled to Rome? She drew herself up and, with a mother's resolve, vowed to protect her son with her life.

When the door between the two rooms was closed, Claudia and Lucius were alone. He sat down heavily in a chair and put his head in his hands. She knelt at his feet, her hands on his knees.

"Do not despair, my love, I will pray that the Most High God have mercy and spare you from the emperor's wrath. You have been far away for so long that perhaps the emperor will not connect you with Sejanus. You have had nothing to do with his actions these past five years. Whatever happens, we will face it together."

He looked down at her, tears in his eyes, and reached out a hand. He cupped her chin. "You are always my comfort, beloved. There is nothing we can do but wait."

"You have done well, Lucius, just continue to govern the best way you know."

He stood up and gently drew her to himself. "Whatever happens, you have been the light of my life, beloved. I do not fear for myself, but for you and my son. If I am recalled to Rome, I will send you and Doros to the Villa Ponti, and if that is still too close to Rome, our family has a villa in Vienne. It is seldom used but is adequate. It could be far enough away to protect you from Tiberius."

"I am his ward, the granddaughter of Augustus. Surely he would not harm me."

He took her by the shoulders. "That is not something you can count on. Look at what happened to the family of Sejanus."

"You have not committed treason, Lucius. You have not done the things Sejanus has done with an eye on taking the throne from Tiberius."

"No, but I could lose my position as governor. My lands and possessions could be taken away. Who knows what Tiberius will do?"

She shivered against him. "Hold me, Lucius. I need you so."

With his arms tight around her, he leaned down and kissed her slowly. "And I am in need of you, beloved."

42

Claudia went to the garden and sank down on a stone bench to think. She wrapped her shawl closer around her shoulders. The sun shone, but the air was cool still. As she watched butterflies sailing from flower to flower, their golden wings fluttering in the slight breeze, she remembered wanting to catch one as a child in Reggio. Their old gardener, Cato, had told her solemnly that if she touched the wings, the beautiful creatures would not be able to fly again. What freedom they had to fly where they wished.

She wondered if she would take Doros to the Villa Ponti or the villa in Vienne. Did Tiberius know about the villa in Vienne? Lucius said it was held in the name of his cousin in Rome, and few people knew about it. If Lucius was recalled to Rome, that is where she would go, before Tiberius knew she was gone.

Claudia turned just then and saw Lucius standing at the entrance to the garden. She rose and went to him, her eyebrows raised in question.

"I must see to a problem at the Antonia with the auxiliary troops. There is an uproar—probably over their pay again." He shook his head angrily. "That is the problem of having native troops. Throwing Syrians, Samaritans, Idumeans, and Nubians together like a pot of stew and expecting them to all get along. A more unruly and undisciplined group I've not known in all my years in the army. I may not be back until late this evening."

She watched him walk away, the burden of his governorship bowing his shoulders.

They returned to Caesarea for the late spring and summer. While Claudia would miss Jerusalem and the band of believers that seemed to be growing every day, she loved the sound and smell of the sea. At night she could lie in bed and hear the waves crashing against the breakwater. In Jerusalem she was confined to the palace because of the unruly element of the city, but in Caesarea she was free to attend the marketplace and accompany Lucius to various events.

In Caesarea she and Lucius attended the theater. The histrions, as the actors were called, made Lucius laugh, if only for an evening, and took his mind off the worries of his office.

The chariot races were a favorite of her husband. She loved to see the horses with their manes flying and their hoofs churning up the soft earth of the arena. Doros would clap his hands in delight.

He was nearly four and Claudia was teaching him to read Latin. She showed him the letters of the alphabet on a wax tablet and had him trace the letters with his finger as she had been taught by her grandmother years before. Soon he was carefully making the letters himself with a stylus. She had only a few years until he was seven, when he would go to a regular teacher and Claudia's influence on him would be diminished. She prayed every day for the right teacher for him. One that would not lead him back to the Roman gods, but who knew the true God.

Lucius seemed to tolerate her faith as long as it did not interfere with what he had to do. Sometimes he listened to her as she shared and sometimes she sensed it was a time to be quiet and just lend him her strength. Her faith in the Lord was a constant source of joy to her, and she felt peace settle over her spirit when she prayed.

Yet while Claudia grew in her faith, to her dismay, Lucius seemed to revert to crueler measures to keep the peace at all costs. Isolated when in Jerusalem, she heard stories in bits and pieces, whispered by the palace staff.

The Jews still rankled over the matter of using the Corban for the aqueduct, but other than the usual small crimes of a city, Jerusalem was peaceful. Like a sleeping giant, the huge city sprawled over the hills, awakening on high holidays when the masses poured into the Holy City. During those days, every soldier was on high alert.

❧

Lucius rode ahead of the carpentum bearing his family and Hotep. He sensed a lifting in his spirit as he put Jerusalem and the troublesome Jews behind him and returned to Caesarea. The garrison there held soldiers more disciplined than the ones in Judea, and he could relax his hold a little, trusting the officers he'd put in charge.

As he rode, he had time to think and his mind turned to the religion his wife had embraced. She was discreet, sharing some of the information about this strange rabbi, Jesus. He still scoffed at the idea that Jesus had risen from the dead, yet she told him there were dozens of witnesses to the fact.

The one who puzzled him most was one of the Teacher's disciples by the name of Peter. The man was an ignorant fisherman, unlearned and crude, but after a strange incident having to do with what they called the Holy Spirit, the man had preached with courage of conviction, and over three thousand people had gone to be baptized and follow the teachings of Jesus. The city had literally buzzed with this amazing performance.

Lucius knew the leaders were watching Peter, and he sensed, to his amusement, their total frustration. They thought by killing Jesus that they had ended this teaching for good.

Instead, the disciples spread the teaching even farther. His soldiers were told to be on the alert for any sign of a rebellion or insurrection, but so far these believers seemed content to meet with each other in various homes to sing their hymns and share stories.

His brow furrowed. What was there about this dead rabbi who inspired such loyalty and belief? More and more stories came to him about those who had seen this risen Jesus. Chuza the steward seemed like a levelheaded man, thorough in his duties, yet he too was a believer in Jesus, his wife, Joanna, one of the rabbi's followers. All over Rome and the provinces there were statues of the Roman gods, so people could see whom they were worshiping. How could one worship an invisible God?

"You are deep in thought, Excellency." His tribune had ridden up to join him.

Lucius glanced at him. "The events of the last few months puzzle me. Have you heard rumors of that Jewish rabbi who was crucified being alive?"

The tribune shrugged. "Perhaps he wasn't completely dead, Excellency. He might have revived in the tomb."

"Impossible. I ascertained his death before releasing him to Joseph of Arimethea, a leader in the Sanhedrin. I was assured by my centurion that Jesus died before the sword was even thrust into his side."

The tribune nodded, thoughtful.

"So you think this Jesus is alive?"

"I have no proof, Excellency, other than the account of witnesses who swear they saw him."

Lucius shook his head. "These are difficult times, Tribune. I'm not sure I understand them myself. The Jews are a strange people with strange beliefs. I'm always glad to return to Caesarea."

The tribune was dismissed and rode on. Lucius turned back to ride alongside the coach. Doros put a hand outside the window and waved at him. On impulse, Lucius had the coach stop.

He lifted Doros in front of him on the horse. The little boy was apprehensive at first, but safe in his father's arms, he beamed. As the horse jogged along slowly, Doros fell asleep against him. Lucius looked down at the boy's tousled hair and was filled with pride in his son. He and Claudia had hoped for another child, but so far there had been no indication of a pregnancy. She had gone through a dangerous birth with Doros. He had almost lost her. Was she now unable to conceive again? He had made offerings to Juno, the goddess of the well-being of women, on Claudia's behalf, but to no avail. At least he had a son to carry on the family name and for that he was grateful. He rode back to the coach and gently lifted the sleeping child down to his mother's arms. He tipped two fingers to his forehead, then rode back to the head of the detail.

Claudia watched him ride away, still tall and handsome. It appeared he would be left as governor of Judea, but for how long? Would they ever return to the Villa Ponti? Would she ever be mistress of her own home? And Medina. Had the old servant gone there after the death of her grandmother? She leaned back against the seat of the coach, holding Doros against her, and gazed out the window of the coach at the countryside. Lucius had not heard from the emperor in Jerusalem, but what awaited them in Caesarea?

43

In the tenth year of her husband's reign as governor of Judea, Jerusalem was at peace, the emperor had not recalled him to Rome, and Lucius, with misplaced smugness, noted his term as governor had been one of the longest of the Roman rule. Claudia, however, sensed that they were foolish to assume they would be in this position for an interminable length of time. She had observed the blunders of her husband on many occasions and his roughshod rule over the Jews. With certainty she felt their time was drawing to a close. Sooner or later her husband would incur the wrath of Rome. She just didn't know what the final event would be and prayed earnestly for Lucius, for wisdom and peace in Judea.

Hotep responded to a knock on the door and admitted Doros's tutor, Florian. Chuza had found him, a freedman and a former scholar in Greece, well versed in language and art.

Claudia presented him to Lucius, emphasizing his skills as a teacher, which duly impressed her husband. He was distracted by many things these days and readily agreed to acquiring Florian as his son's tutor.

"A good morning, Lady Claudia." Florian inclined his head in respect. "Is my young charge ready for the day?"

Doros, now dressed, emerged from his room. "I am ready, Teacher."

With another slight bow to Claudia, Florian smiled at his pupil and they left the room.

"What will the boy learn today, Domina?" Hotep asked.

"Doros is very quick of mind. They have progressed to Greek poetry." Fortunately Lucius did not inquire as to their time spent on the gods of Rome.

❧

Lucius was having problems with Samaria. It was situated in the northern part of his province and populated by what the Jews considered half-breeds—Jews that had long ago intermarried with the pagans of the land. There were many religious differences between the two, and he kept a wary eye on them.

His advisors told him that the Samaritans only recognized the first five books of Moses as their true Scripture, ignoring any other Hebrew books written, including the Psalms. They had built a temple on their own holy mountain, Mt. Gerizim, but it had been destroyed and not rebuilt in over a century. Mt. Gerizim, however, was still their holy mountain and they celebrated their own Passover there.

Now a man had risen up claiming to be the long-awaited Messiah. Lucius had learned the man was quoting from the Scriptures a passage that said, "The Lord your God will raise up for you a prophet like me from your midst, from your brethren; him you shall heed."

Lucius saw it as a disaster in the making. The Samaritans were accepting this man as the prophet Moses had predicted. Reports poured into Caesarea of mass movements of men following this prophet. He promised to unearth sacred vessels from the ark of the covenant, which he claimed Moses had hidden in a cave on the mountain.

As Lucius consulted his council, he learned that huge gatherings of Samaritans had hailed the man as their deliverer, who would rebuild the temple on Mt. Gerizim. Lucius knew that he did not need a mass gathering of men following a false prophet. His sources revealed that Moses had never even been in the vicinity of Gerizim and thus could not have hidden anything. Evidently this was not considered by the adoring Samaritans who were blindly following this charlatan.

A date had been set for the Samaritans to assemble at the village of Tirathana, near the base of Gerizim. Lucius learned the prophet had sent out a call to arms. Gerizim straddled a major highway in Palestine, the route from Jerusalem to Galilee, and an armed mass of men could do anything. He had to take action and now.

Choosing two detachments of heavily armed infantry and half of his cavalry, Lucius led them toward Samaria. He also called in his auxiliaries from Jerusalem, knowing the motley mix of men from other lands included Samaritans. Perhaps, he reasoned, they would cause the armed mob to balk at fighting their own people.

As he rode toward the area with his troops, Lucius realized this was the first time he had faced a possible armed resistance in his entire ten years as prefect of Judea. He had dealt with angry multitudes, but never one that was armed.

He thought of appealing to his superior, Lucius Vitellius, the newly appointed governor of Syria. With clever negotiations Vitellius had settled other matters without a drop of Roman blood. What vexed Lucius was that the assistant to Vitellius in the negotiations was none other than Herod Antipas, who had been brought into the matter since he could speak Aramaic. Not wishing to show any weakness, Lucius reasoned he could handle the situation in Samaria himself.

Riding hard, he arrived with his troops the day before the projected gathering on Mt. Gerizim. His herald blew the trumpet to get the attention of the mob. Then Lucius shouted to them, "If you are on a religious pilgrimage, you need no weapons. Lay down your arms at once."

He was greeted by jeers and angry shouts. Did the crowd believe they needed to defend themselves from the Roman troops?

He shouted again. "You will come to no harm if you lay down your weapons. You are in danger of committing treason and gathering an illegal army."

The false prophet shouted to the people, "Our army will be victorious! Drive these Roman pagans off our holy mountain!"

The Roman troops were surprised at the sudden ferocity of the attack. Lucius had expected no resistance to his order. There was suddenly a clash of swords and cries of pain as the Samaritans attacked his soldiers. Caught off guard, Lucius ordered his men to fight and he himself wielded his Roman broadsword. He then signaled to his cavalry and infantry to move in quickly. After an intense battle and many casualties on both sides, the Roman soldiers were victorious. The remaining Samaritans were chased down, and though some got away, many were captured.

Lucius declared martial law and set up a tribunal. Justice was meted out swiftly with death by sword to the ringleaders and the false prophet. The uprising was over.

As he observed the sentences being carried out by his men, Lucius could not help but compare this prophet and his followers to the followers of Claudia's Jesus. There had been no armed rebellion or threat to Rome, only the jealousy of the Jewish priests.

As he rode with his remaining troops back to Caesarea, Lucius felt triumphant. He had faced an armed rebellion and ended the revolt. As he rode, he mentally composed a letter to Tiberius, detailing the conflict and how the conflict had been handled. He was sure the emperor would agree that he'd done the only thing possible in the light of the Samaritan's attack on his men.

The letter was sent and Lucius looked forward to dinner with his wife and son and a recount of his actions in the matter.

44

As Claudia listened to her husband recount the scene leading up to the battle and the ensuing fight, her heart thudded in her chest. Lucius could have been killed.

"I'm sure you did what you had to do, Lucius. Wouldn't the emperor agree with how you handled this rebellion?"

"He should. I didn't ask for a fight and told them if they laid down their arms, no harm would come to them. They wouldn't listen, and since they attacked first, we had no choice but to engage in battle."

"Were there many soldiers, Pater?" Doros was captivated by the tale of the battle and proud of his father for being victorious over the enemy.

"Yes, my son, there were many soldiers. As a matter of fact, we were outnumbered, but my troops were better trained in battle. I hope the Samaritans will eventually appreciate being saved from that false prophet who deceived them."

Claudia let relief sweep over her spirit. It was over and Lucius was alive. A letter had been sent to the emperor.

Claudia had grown in her faith and it was what sustained her in times of difficulty. Doros, because Jesus healed his foot, had believed in him from a small boy. At his mother's word of caution, he no longer brought up the subject in front of his father.

Claudia had Hotep add an extra blanket on the bed as the coldness of the castle by the seashore in winter chilled her bones.

One month later, while having dinner with Claudia and Doros, Lucius was informed that a special envoy by the name of Marcellus was waiting to speak with him. He carried a message from the governor of Syria.

Lucius rose and told the servant he would meet the man in his study. He bent down to touch Claudia's face. "I have been attempting to arrange a meeting, a state visit. Perhaps this is his reply. See to the boy, I'll be up later."

She took Doros by the hand and together they went up the stairs. Doros, at nine, had balked months before at having a nurse. "I'm not a baby, Mater. I do not need a nurse. I can sleep by myself."

Hotep was moved back to the servant's quarters in the castle, coming to Claudia's room in the morning to tend to her mistress.

Claudia made arrangements for another set of rooms nearby for Doros to share with a young male slave, Otho. Lucius felt it was time his son had his own servant. It had been difficult to let go, for Doros seemed to be growing up so very fast before her eyes.

When she had bid Doros good night and left him in the care of Otho, she turned to her own quarters where Hotep was waiting.

"Domina, the palace is whispering about this courier who has arrived. He is no ordinary courier. Very pompous, a senator perhaps?"

"I don't know, Hotep. My husband wanted a meeting with the governor of Syria and perhaps that is what this is all about." She bid Hotep good night and wandering around the room, absent-mindedly picked up the copper mirror and studied her image in it. She was a Roman matron, with a child, and nearly twenty-seven. The years had taken their toll on her; the worry over the various incidents in Jerusalem and how Lucius had handled them. Then there was the rebellion in Samaria. Some days she felt older than her years, though she had kept her figure and had the love of her husband. At this time she could only be grateful for that.

When Hotep had bid her good night and gone, she wandered over to the window and listened to the sounds of the waves hitting the breakwater. The steady crash and swish as each wave broke seemed timeless to her. She leaned toward the window, inhaling the pungent sea air.

She was still at the window when she heard the door open and close softly. Turning with a smile to greet her husband, one look at his face caused her heart to turn to stone. His face was pale and he appeared stricken. He moved as if in a daze, and when she reached him she saw he was near collapse.

"Lucius, what has happened?"

"I'm being recalled to Rome. The council of Samaria has formally accused me of a needless massacre of their countrymen on Mt. Gerizim in my province. They stated that the assembly intended no rebellion against Rome, they were merely there as refugees from my violence. Furthermore, the council has affirmed their allegiance to the emperor."

"What? But that is untrue, Lucius. That is not what happened."

He shook his head, "No, it isn't, but I must account for the incident before the emperor. Vitellius is my superior, he could have heard my case and judged it, but for some reason he's passed the matter on to Tiberius. I must defend myself against a delegation of Samaritans who will travel to Rome as *accusatores*."

Claudia felt a chill go down her spine. This is what she had dreaded for a long time and it had finally come.

Lucius went on, "The courier, Marcellus, is none other than my replacement. He will serve as acting governor during my absence." He gave a harsh laugh. "I am to spend the next week acquainting him with the functions of my office. Vitellius himself will arrive in late December to assist him in his new duties."

"How much time did they give you?"

He rubbed the back of his neck with one hand. "It is winter, and there are no ships traveling to Rome. We will have to travel overland through Antioch. I've been given three months to make the journey."

Now he stood suddenly and his eyes flashed with anger. "He had the nerve to state that he hoped I would not delay my journey and that a guard will not prove necessary! What does he think I'm going to do?"

Tears formed in Claudia's eyes and she struggled to hold them back. "Are you under arrest?"

His shoulders slumped again. "No, but I might as well be. It is the end of my tour here, Claudia. I know I shall not be returned as governor. I only hope I can convince the court of Tiberius of the truth in the Samaritan matter."

"Is Marcellus still in the palace?"

"Yes, I provided rooms for him and his aides. Tomorrow I will start briefing him on my duties as governor."

"Do you know what prompted this?" They sat on a small couch in the alcove where she had led him.

"The Samaritan Council was outraged at the executions that took place after the rebellion was over." He waved a hand and spat sarcastically, "The fools are probably grieving over their great prophet who was going to lead them to victory over the Roman Empire."

Claudia understood the Samaritan Council to be similar to the Jewish Sanhedrin, the ruling body of the Jews. As such, they held absolute sway over their people. They also had the authority to challenge Lucius over this matter.

"Did Marcellus tell you this?"

He shook his head as he began to remove his uniform. "My tribune—he knew one of Vitellius's aides. They had served together at one time. He managed to gather some information for me. I don't know how he did it, but he knew of some matters before I did. It seems that Herod was bragging to Vitellius that I did not understand the Jews like he did. The aide also divulged the information that Tiberius had asked Vitellius to keep a watch on my activities in Judea."

So Tiberius had not forgotten about Lucius. Had there been spies, swiftly bringing the emperor news of all that went on in Judea? Claudia was not surprised. She had thought the emperor out of touch, living on Capri, but she should have known better. Her grandfather,

Augustus, was the same. Little went on in his vast empire that he did not know about, from the highest magistrate to the poorest peasant.

When Lucius had undressed and stretched out wearily on their bed, she put an arm across his chest and he covered it with his hand. "When we reach the road to Rome, I want you and Doros to go to the Villa Ponti. The worst that should happen is that my rank will be stripped and I will be released from the emperor's service."

She was sure he could feel her heart beating erratically as she leaned her head on his shoulder. "That is the worst, truly, Lucius?"

"I have done nothing worthy of death, beloved. Of that I am sure. I believe I can successfully defend my case before the emperor." He was silent for a moment, then swore softly. "Strange, what the Jews have been threatening to do for years has been accomplished by their hated rivals."

His hand tightened on her arm. "There are things I must take care of before I turn the governorship over to Marcellus. Tomorrow morning, early, I want you to go to my study and remove any letters of communication that Marcellus should not see. My aide, Vitus, will help you. I spoke with him tonight. He knows what needs to be destroyed. I will distract the new governor for the morning and my tribune will see that the aides remain with us."

"I will do whatever you tell me to do."

"When you have done that, have the servants pack whatever gifts we have been given over the years and anything else that is transportable that you wish to keep. I will arrange for several carpentums for transport. We will need to send to Jerusalem to have the servants pack what we have left there. We will leave from here in a week's time."

"Joanna will help me. I will send her word of what to pack. Sleep now, my Lucius. We will go through this together and that is the most important thing. I will do what you have requested in the morning."

He murmured something and then she heard soft snores as the weariness of the day claimed him. She lay awake for a long time, her mind turning with all that was ahead of them and what she must do first.

❧ 45 ❧

Claudia and Lucius were up before dawn. She dressed quickly, and Lucius went to his private quarters to dress and take care of some scrolls he kept there. Slipping quietly down the stairs, Claudia went to her husband's study wondering what to look for, only to find Vitus already sorting through her husband's desk and shelves for incriminating documents. From the looks of things, he had been there all night.

"I have put the papers that the Dominae requested in that basket, Domina." He indicated a large woven basket with two handles.

Claudia set about straightening the study so it did not look ransacked.

Hotep hurried in and, seeing her mistress at work, clicked her tongue in admonition. "That is servant's work, Domina. Rest yourself while I finish for you." She led Claudia to a nearby chair.

"Vitus, Hotep, how will we dispose of these documents?" Claudia was terrified of Marcellus coming upon them and discovering what they were doing.

Hotep produced a large linen sheet she brought with her and, crumpling it up, placed it in a heap over the contents of the basket. Vitus lifted the basket and gave her a knowing smile. "I will be glad to take the laundry to the appropriate place, Domina."

Claudia smiled back and silently applauded their ingenuity. "I'm going with you, Vitus."

The three conspirators made sure the study looked undisturbed and went down the dim corridor to the kitchen. They were nearly to their destination when a voice behind her spoke suddenly.

"You are up early, Lady Claudia."

Her heart quickened. It was the new governor, Marcellus.

"You are up early also, sir."

"I thought I would view the garden. It is my custom to stroll there in the morning before breakfast."

She inclined her head politely. "Do not let me detain you then."

Vitus stood holding the basket, and Claudia turned to him with what she hoped was a casual dismissal. "I will need the laundry back by this afternoon, Vitus, make sure the servants are diligent."

Vitus nodded submissively. "We shall be diligent, Domina." He hurried away with the basket.

When Marcellus didn't give a second glance to the departing servant, Claudia stopped holding her breath and gave him a patient smile. "My husband informed me last night of our impending journey. I have much to do to prepare my household and pack our things."

He appeared uncomfortable. "Ah, yes, I would imagine you do. Forgive me for delaying you." He continued on toward the garden. When he'd gone, she walked quickly to the kitchen. In a separate room where the servants had a fire going, Vitus was feeding scrolls into the flames as fast as he could.

"That was close, Vitus. I was afraid he would look into the basket."

He smiled. "No man wants to examine the dirty laundry, Domina."

"Thank you, Vitus, for your loyalty to my husband, and to me. He could not do without you. What will you do now that we are leaving?" She knew he was a freedman, not bound to Lucius.

He tossed another small bundle of scrolls into the flames. "Ah, but Domina, I am coming with you."

She resisted the urge to hug him. Maintaining her dignity, she nodded. "Thank you, Vitus, you are needed."

Claudia and Hotep returned to her quarters. "Bring me a tablet and stylus, Hotep. I must send a message to the Lady Joanna."

Since it was winter, she would need her heavy woolen palla and her traveling shoes with cork soles. The winters in Judea were not without snow and frequently there was heavy frost. Claudia shuddered at the prospect of attempting the roads at this time of year with several heavy wagons.

A courier was dispatched to Jerusalem to deliver the letter outlining what she needed and telling Joanna farewell, as well as her greetings and farewell to the believers there in the castle.

Looking up at the sunlight streaming in the window, she thought of the first time she heard of the rabbi who healed, the first time she heard him speak, and the transforming moment when with only a gentle touch, a malformed foot had morphed into a normal, healthy one. That she was a Roman made no difference to Jesus.

Doros had wavered in his childlike faith when he learned of how Jesus had died. In time Claudia patiently helped him to see God's eternal plan, lest her son hate his father for what he had done. It was her day-to-day faith and the knowledge that Jesus was alive again that restored the faith of her son.

She still felt a constriction in her heart as she remembered the day the Lord was put on trial. The roar of the crowd still rang in her ears as they called for his blood—the same crowd that had hailed him as the Messiah only a few days before. Had he disappointed them that he didn't wield a sword and lead them against Rome? They wanted a conquering king, and he came as a servant, giving his life for them all. He'd defied death and returned, victorious in his risen body. Even now, as she thought of her Lord, joy filled her heart. No matter what happened in Rome, even if she should die with Lucius, she had the hope that all the believers clung to—the hope of heaven and the presence of their Lord. That hope and the strength of his presence would sustain her on the long journey to Rome and whatever awaited them there. She did not fear for herself, but with the love of a mother, she feared for her young son. Then she bowed her head and asked for forgiveness for not trusting. Mary's son, Jesus, was not spared and Claudia could only place Doros in the hands of her Lord . . . and let go.

46

Lucius laid out a map and showed Claudia their journey would take them through Asia Minor and Greece.

"The Anatolian Plateau could pose difficulty. If the rains are heavy, we may have to travel through mud." Then he pointed out the Cilician Gates mountain pass. "If there is snow there, we could be delayed for days until it clears."

"Can we not wait somewhere until the weather is safer?" She had visions of being stranded in her coach in a freezing snowstorm.

He shook his head. "The letter from Vitellius will be in the hands of the emperor before the end of the year, a mere forty days with the speed of our couriers. We have no choice but to try to reach Rome as soon as possible."

"I'm sure you are right, Lucius. How far exactly must we journey to reach Rome?"

He rolled up the map. "Almost three thousand kilometers."

She caught her breath. "Then I will pray for a safe and speedy journey."

Claudia found Marcellus as Hotep described, pompous and impatient. His attitude dismissed her husband from his post as one would

272

brush away a worrisome child. How Lucius had held his temper she wondered, but she knew he was doing his best to appear efficient and capable in the eyes of one who thought him the opposite.

❧

When the day of departure came, Lucius was more than ready to leave the whole of Judea behind. Let Marcellus deal with Caiaphas and the Sanhedrin and the self-righteous priests with their air of superiority.

Claudia made sure Doros was dressed warmly. Her young son was nearly dancing with excitement.

Hotep gave him some small tasks to occupy his time. A nine-year-old had no idea of the dangers they faced and the weather they would have to travel through.

Lucius had a *diploma*, his official letter of introduction giving him exemption from the usual customs, road taxes, tolls, and duties. It also assured them lodging at the mansios situated every forty kilometers and fresh horses at the mansios between the lodges. A detachment of soldiers would also ride with them as an escort.

The journey to Antioch was made in record time with the weather reasonably mild. The Taurus mountain range proved more difficult and they wrapped themselves in layers against the cold as they battled sleet and snow before reaching Tarsus.

Doros was tired of looking at the scenery or doing his studies, so Claudia tried to remember some of the stories she had heard Jesus tell and shared them with her son.

The storms came down upon their entourage, and Claudia was grateful for her husband's foresight. Knowing what they would be facing in terms of weather, Lucius had ordered the usual canvas covers of the coaches replaced with strong wooden ones. The carpenters worked day and night to finish the covers in time.

When Lucius learned that the pass at the Cilician Gates was closed due to heavy snow, they waited in Tarsus for it to clear. Then mile after mile, they struggled through the pass until they reached the summit and began their descent.

The route, used by the Roman imperial post, led them across Asia Minor, to Philippi, and then west through Greece to the Adriatic Sea. Finally, they traveled up the peninsula on the last leg of their journey to Rome.

As they neared Rome, Claudia noted a change in her husband's demeanor. A haunted look in his eyes and the slump of his shoulders denoted his fear of what he faced at the court of Tiberius. He had been so sure of his innocence and had prepared his case in detail, yet there was about him a sense of impending doom.

When she broached the subject of the trial, he would stare off into space and slowly shake his head. "I fear all is lost," he murmured at one time, sending a jolt of fear into her heart. Was he contemplating suicide?

One evening he sat down with her alone and finally shared his thoughts. "You must know, beloved, that if I am found guilty of dereliction of duty or worse, I could not only lose my life but my entire estate could be confiscated. I've told you of the villa in Vienne and you would be safe there with the boy. There is another path," and now he hesitated, not wanting to look at her.

"I know what you are thinking, Lucius. Taking your own life will not solve the problem. Would you leave me and your son in such a way?"

"Claudia, I do not know what I am facing in Rome. If I commit suicide, under Roman law you may inherit my estate without disgrace. You and Doros would be assured a home."

She clung to him. "I will go where I need to go and protect our son, but do not leave us in such a way. My God is able to protect you."

"He is your god, Claudia. I am the one who put the Son of God to death in the cruelest manner Rome has devised. What mercy should he show me for such an act? Perhaps this is the justice of your god, my life for the life of his son."

"Oh Lucius, he is not a vengeful God. He is a God of forgiveness.

Jesus spoke of this many times. The death of Jesus was part of a greater plan. You have been forgiven for your part, for without knowing it, you helped God fulfill his plan."

"What kind of a god allows his son to die like that?"

"A God who loves us deeply, and made a way for us to be forgiven and be with him in heaven one day. All who put their trust in the name of Jesus are forgiven of their sins. You have only to ask."

He pulled away from her and stood up. "You would almost persuade me, but I cannot reconcile what I know with what you are telling me."

Her voice was soft, pleading. "Every time I see the foot of our son, I am reminded of his mercy and forgiveness."

When he looked at her, his eyes were glazed with inner pain, and struggling with his torment, he went out into the night.

Claudia could only drop to her knees and pray with all her heart.

Lucius returned later that night, and with a sob she flew into his arms. He held her tightly, kissing her eyelids and then her lips. With his fingers he brushed the tears away. "Do not fear, wife of my heart."

"You've reached a decision." It was not a question.

"Yes, beloved. I do not know how I would have lasted in Judea these last ten years without you. For your sake and the sake of my son, I'll present my case and trust the mercy of the emperor. My villa is on our way. I will leave you and Doros there. If I win my case, there is hope of another assignment. If I lose all, and live, we will go to Vienne. If you and Doros must travel to Vienne alone, Vitus will see you safely there in my place."

She slumped against him. There was still hope. "It will be good to have a home of our own finally."

The mansio provided breakfast of warm rolls of white bread, pears and sliced apples, goat cheese and warm apple cider. Then, with Lucius riding ahead with his men, they rolled on toward the mountainous region of Sanmarim, and the Villa Ponti.

47

The villa hadn't seemed to change in the ten years they had been in Judea. Waiting on the steps were Marcus, Rufina, and to Claudia's joy and surprise, Medina!

Lucius, who had allowed Doros to ride with him the last few kilometers, let the boy slip down and then gave his horse to one of his soldiers. He helped Claudia out of the coach. Florian and Vitus stretched their legs after descending from the second coach.

Doros studied the house and, having grown up in a palace, frowned. "It isn't very big is it, Mater?"

She laughed. "It is big enough for us, Doros. And it is our own home."

Marcus bowed to Lucius. "Welcome home, Excellency. It has been a long time."

"It is good to see you again, Marcos." He looked around. "And where is Alba?"

Marcus hung his head. "She was very ill, Dominae. She died two weeks ago" He turned to Medina. "She is the one who nursed Alba in her last days."

Lucius nodded to the older woman. "I have heard of you from my wife. I'm grateful for your kindness. Alba was my nurse as a boy."

Claudia moved forward and embraced the former servant. "Oh

Medina, it is so good to see you." Her voice caught in her throat. "Tell me about my grandmother."

"Before she died, she asked me to send her love to you and was sorry not to be able to see her great-grandson."

Claudia took a deep breath and let it out again. "I had hoped there was some way to see her in these intervening years, but she told me when I left not to hope for that. We were too far away."

The coaches were unloaded and driven to a clearing near the stable. Lucius thanked his men for their service, saluting each one individually and dismissed them to return to the garrison in Rome.

Claudia, suddenly feeling the exhaustion of the long journey, went up to the master suite with Hotep. As her maidservant prepared a bath, she sat down by a window that looked out over the orchard. Seeing the three figures, one tall, one slightly stooped, and a boy strolling among the trees, she felt at peace. It would be a good place for Doros to grow up.

They rested two days, but the third morning Claudia found Lucius gathering his trial documents as Vitus packed them in a pouch. It was 243 kilometers to Rome, a journey of three and a half days. Even then, Lucius and Vitus would have to ride hard to make it in that time. Lucius was fond of his horse and Claudia knew he could only demand so much of the animal in a day.

Vitus tactfully left the office and Lucius gathered her to his heart. "I've implored the gods for my favor, but Tiberius is unpredictable. I only hope I can prove that I did what any other prefect would have done in my place."

"May the lies the Samaritan Council are telling be made known. You did what you had to do."

"I have convinced you, beloved, but I pray the emperor sees it as you do."

She felt the rapid beating of his heart and looking up into his face, saw his fear and uncertainty. "I will pray to the God I believe in for your safety also, my love."

With an effort, he put her from him and picked up the pouch. "I must go. Vitus is bringing the horses around."

Doros, seeing him leaving the villa, ran and was caught in his father's arms.

"You must take care of your mother while I am gone, my son. She will need you."

He patted the boy's shoulder and with a last look at Claudia, mounted his horse.

Claudia held back her tears as she watched them ride away.

In the late afternoon at the beginning of the second week, the sound of hoofbeats on the road to the villa brought Claudia hurrying out to see Lucius and Vitus dismounting. He looked tired but elated and she ran into his arms.

"Your hearing before the emperor must have gone well."

"There was no hearing. Come inside and I will tell you about it."
He gave the reins of his horse to Vitus, who led the horses to the stable.

Lucius led Claudia to his office and closed the door. Thankfully, at the moment, Doros was in the orchard with Marcus and his tutor.

Claudia turned to her husband in astonishment. "What did you mean, no trial?"

"On the way to Rome I learned that the emperor was staying in a villa at Misenum on the Bay of Naples. We rode there instead and I presented myself to the prefect, Naevius Sutorius Macro, and asked for an audience with the emperor. I was told the emperor had just died."

"Oh, Lucius! He's dead?"

"His nephew, Gaius, has been proclaimed emperor. He will be a popular emperor since he is of the line of Germanicus." Lucius frowned. "A strange young man, tall and slender, but eyes that seem almost . . . vacant."

"What about the hearing then?"

"Macro told me that more than likely there would not be a hearing now, but he would speak with Caligula after he's confirmed by the senate. I told him where we were and then went in to pay my respects to Tiberius as he was being prepared for a state funeral. As soon as I could, I rode back here."

He leaned down and kissed her, and with a lighter step, went upstairs to bathe and dress.

Later, in the peace of the garden, Rome seemed far away. Yet Claudia knew they were within easy reach of the emperor. Lucius had a reprieve, but for how long? Her future and that of her husband hinged on word from Macro, and the clemency of a new emperor.

48

Three weeks had passed since arriving at the villa. Lucius was in his office, going over the scrolls he'd prepared for his audience with Tiberius. With each passing day, their hope grew that the matter would be dismissed or ignored.

Doros loved to walk in the orchard with Marcus when he could escape Florian and his lessons. It warmed her heart that Lucius was at last proud of his son, who seemed to be growing taller by the hour.

Claudia's heart was joyful at being mistress of her own home at last, and the love between she and Lucius seemed to grow even more. Now she also had Medina, who to Claudia's delight had also become a believer.

Caligula, or Gaius as he preferred to be called, lost no time in endearing himself to the Romans. He named the month of September after his father, Germanicus, and burned documents publicly that pertained to former legal suits. Of great interest to Lucius was Caligula's recalling of many who had been exiled from Rome and dismissing indictments against those awaiting trial for offenses against Tiberius. Lucius felt good about the chances of his own case being dismissed.

Claudia and Lucius were invited to a lavish banquet for prominent equestrian families by the young emperor and traveled to Rome to attend.

Claudia dressed in her finest with her golden pendant with the ruby and gold earrings. She looked every inch the granddaughter of an emperor. Lucius told her later he'd thought her the most beautiful woman at the banquet.

Caligula acknowledged Lucius, and mentioned that he would like to speak to him about Judea sometime. His eyes had roved over Claudia in a way that made her uneasy. At one point he brushed her arm with his hand and smiled, his eyes filled with desire. Claudia ignored the subtle invitation and kept her voice and manner polite but distant. He turned away abruptly, joining another group. She was more than ready to leave and return to their villa.

Two months passed and there was no more word from the emperor. It was a warm afternoon in June when Claudia sat in the garden with Lucius. He spoke again of his father who was so often gone with the military and his mother more concerned with Roman society than with her son. From the time he was young he had striven to please his father and entered the Roman army as soon as he was old enough. He'd faced hours of backbreaking marches, gradually moving up in the ranks. He'd distinguished himself in the campaigns and yearned for a higher rank. One auspicious day, Sejanus, an old friend, and then prefect of Rome, sent for him.

"That Sejanus had suggested me as a husband for the emperor's ward was almost unbelievable," he told her, brushing a leaf from her hair as they walked in the orchard. "I was lost the moment I saw you. Any other woman I'd known before paled in your beauty. I felt the gods had favored me beyond belief to give you to me for my wife."

"I thought you extremely handsome and was relieved that the man chosen for me was not old and bald!"

They laughed together. Love in an arranged marriage in Roman society was rare.

Today their time was interrupted by Vitus, who hurried toward them. "There is a messenger from the emperor. He says it is urgent."

Claudia's heart pounded in her chest. They hurried to the atrium to meet the soldier who had obviously ridden hard from Rome. He saluted and handed Lucius a scroll. He unrolled it and began to read aloud:

"Lucius Pontius Pilate is hereby ordered to present himself to the Emperor, his Imperial Majesty, Gaius Caesar, at once to answer certain charges against him by the Council of Samaria."

The *accusatores* had arrived.

Claudia suppressed a cry. His eyes sought hers and she saw the fear.

He rolled up the scroll. "So it has come. The emperor has summoned me." He turned to the messenger. "Be refreshed and then return to Rome and tell the emperor I am on my way."

The soldier saluted and Claudia called Medina, who led the messenger toward the kitchen.

Lucius took Claudia by the hand into his office and closed the door, then gathered her in his arms. She looked up at him. "I hoped, Lucius, I hoped and prayed that you would not be called to Rome by the emperor, at least not for a trial."

He held her against him. "I shall need your prayers, to the God of the Hebrews, if that comforts you, for the audience with the emperor. He is young and perhaps will continue to be lenient in his first year of rule." Shaking his head, he murmured, "I do not see how I am being called into question for doing my duty. Any other prefect would have acted as I did to put down an insurrection, and an armed one at that."

"I shall pray every day that you are gone, my love."

He released her and she hurried to the kitchen to tell Medina to prepare food for the men's journey. Lucius called the waiting Vitus and they began to gather his papers and put them in packets.

Claudia went to find her son. Doros listened solemnly as his father explained he had to make a journey to Rome. The boy squared his shoulders. "I will look after Mater in your absence, Pater."

Lucius put a hand on the boy's shoulder. "I will count on that, Doros."

The horses were brought and the staff of the villa came out to see them off. Lucius thought to go alone, but Vitus insisted that he was needed and wouldn't be put off.

Claudia, standing bravely, would not show her emotions in front of the staff. She waved and returned to the villa. With the distance, it might be at least ten days before she could hope to see Lucius, or hear the outcome of the hearing.

That night, Claudia gathered together the small group of believers in her household, and they earnestly prayed for her husband's journey and the outcome that could change their lives.

49

Each day Claudia looked in the direction of Rome, wondering what was happening and feeling helpless. Their future was in the hands of a young emperor.

On the ninth day, near sunset, Claudia heard the sound of hoofbeats. She hurried to the entry as the riders pulled up in front of the villa. It was Lucius and Vitus. As Lucius dismounted, she put a fist to her mouth. His face was pale and his eyes had a haunted look.

Lucius slowly followed her into the villa. When he finally spoke to her, his voice was low and broken. "All is lost."

"Tell me what happened."

"The hearing was a travesty. Vitellius had notes on every infraction, every riot. It was as if he'd had someone following me every single day of my tenure in Judea taking notes."

She entered his office with him and closed the door. "Your defense was well prepared, was it not?"

"I laid out the truth that countered their lies and had my tribune from Judea speak as a witness in my defense."

He sat down wearily. "However, Thallus, who led the prosecution, suggested that death, not exile, was not too great a punishment for my shameful abuse of public trust in a province of imperial Rome."

She clasped her hands to her heart. "He was calling for your execution? Oh Lucius . . ."

"I told the emperor I was not on trial for treatment of the unruly Jews, that no prefect has governed that territory without trouble. I told him the province needed more garrisons and is vastly misunderstood by Rome. The delegation from Samaria must admit that they have their own confrontations with the Jews—there is no love lost between the two. Finally I rested my case, having presented a clear report of the actual happening at Mt. Gerizim."

"And Caligula's judgment? You are here so it could not have been death."

"He taunted me, with pleasure, with the prospect of death and what it could entail. I was expecting the soldiers to arrest me at any moment. I thought that I would never see you again. Then he smiled and it chilled my heart."

"And . . ."

"And in his clemency, his gracious charity in the early days of his reign, as he put it, he would be lenient. He sentenced me merely to the loss of my rank, position, my entire estate, and banishment from Rome. I have three weeks from the day of sentencing to leave. He suggested Gaul."

"Oh Lucius!" She put her arms around him and wept on his shoulder. He held her and she felt his chest rise and fall with his own emotions.

They remained that way for a long time, and finally she pulled away and looked him in the face. "I told you we would face this together. We have almost ten days before the soldiers come to take the villa. Caligula does not know about the house in Vienne. We will start packing at once."

As she started toward the door, she turned back. "You kept the wagons just in case, didn't you?"

"Yes. I thought it best to be prepared, if not for both of us, at least for you and Doros."

She nodded. He left her and climbed the stairs to his room, and Vitus, always waiting to be of service, watched him pass and climb the stairs.

That night after dinner, she and Lucius lay in each other's arms, listening to the frogs in the garden and the hooting of the owl that lived above the stable. They had taken a walk in the orchard in the early evening, and Claudia had looked at the trees that would be ready for harvest by spring without them, bearing fruit for another household.

❧

In the morning the villa was in a flurry of activity as they hurriedly packed the wagons. Claudia considered what to take and what to leave behind. They would need to travel rapidly with as little as possible.

Lucius called the staff together and told them what was happening. Marcus was a freedman and, in his advanced age, chose to go to his daughter and son-in-law. Out of loyalty to the Pontius family, he'd remained until Lucius had returned.

Medina had been involved with believers in Rome and had friends there. She too didn't want to travel so far away. Claudia understood. Medina would send them news of what was happening in Rome. Claudia sent her off with Marcus, who would take her to the city on his way to his daughter's. Lucius provided a cart and a mule for the journey. He also gave Marcus the goats.

With a last embrace of her old nurse, Claudia tearfully said goodbye. "Give my greetings to the believers, Medina. May our Lord watch over you and protect you until the day we meet again in his kingdom."

"May he watch over you also, Domina, and see you safely on your journey."

Claudia watched the two old people ride away in the cart, and her heart was heavy. "Oh Lord, take them safely to their destinations."

Vitus and Hotep would go with them to Vienne. Rufina begged to remain near Rome, and Claudia suspected a man was involved.

She was sent to the household of a neighbor. Florian left to seek new employment in Rome.

Doros was sad, but Claudia suggested that he might attend grammar school with other boys. He'd had few companions his age and he seemed happier at the idea.

He took the news of his father's exile well and Claudia vowed to keep up her courage in front of the boy. He would never wear the Roman toga, nor be declared a citizen of Rome, and that grieved her husband.

Lucius and Vitus bound one wagon to another and hitched the four mules to each of the front wagons. The horses were tied on the rear. Vitus would drive one set of wagons and Lucius would drive the other. Claudia, Hotep, and Doros would ride in the smaller coach. The larger coach was loaded with necessary household items—linens, some dishes, sheets and bedding, and cookware. Marcus had sold several valuable vases and smaller items in the marketplace. Lucius would need all the money they could get for their journey. Claudia carefully packed her jewelry in a pouch to keep it in the coach with her to be sold later if needed. She brought her simplest tunics, and Lucius dressed as a common citizen, leaving his uniform behind. There would be no need for it since he had been stripped of his rank.

Pieces of furniture that had seen three generations in the villa had to be left behind. Lucius said little, but the tight set of his jaw said much to Claudia. She remembered how she felt leaving Reggio and grieved for her husband.

When at last they were ready to leave, Lucius took one last look around his family home. He would not ride as prefect of Judea but as a common citizen of Rome, banished forever from the city where he'd come so long ago to better himself.

Claudia refused to look back. She would be strong for her family. She didn't know what the future held, but she placed it in the hands of the Most High God. Knowing others far away were praying for her, she set her face toward Vienne.

50

They traveled more than twelve hundred kilometers in two weeks. Lucius pushed the mules as hard as they could go, averaging almost eighty-one kilometers a day. He needed to be far from Rome, across the border before the end of the three-week grace period Caligula had given him.

They avoided the large cities and bought what food they needed in small markets along the way. Lucius would have liked to remove the ornate carvings on the coaches that called attention to them, but there was no time nor funds to pay a workman to do it. Once, when someone inquired about the coaches, Lucius told them he was delivering them to a Roman senator.

They stayed at the cheapest mansios and Claudia covered the bed she and Hotep shared with a large sheet, shaking it well each morning. Doros shared a room with his father and Vitus. After forcing down the coarse, dark bread and the well-diluted wine offered by the innkeepers, they were glad to be on their way in the mornings.

They passed Venice and finally crossed into Gaul. A friend of Caligula's, Valerius Asiaticus, was consul of Vienne and Lucius felt he would no doubt report their arrival to the emperor.

After a few inquiries, they found the road to the villa. "It has been fifteen years since I've been here," Lucius told her that morning. "My second cousin, Gaius Pontius, lived there, but at present he's a consul in Rome. We conferred briefly after the trial and he gave me a document entitling us to dwell in the house."

They passed through rich pastureland dotted with flocks of sheep and fields of waving wheat. Vineyards were plentiful and it seemed a bountiful land to be exiled to. Lucius had commented on the vineyards that morning. "It is said that the wine from Vienne can cost up to a thousand *sesterces* for one amphora. It is highly prized by the Roman gentry."

She tucked her arm in his. "I shall look forward to tasting it, my love."

After a few inquiries, they finally came to the small villa tucked among a copse of sycamore trees. It looked ill cared for and unoccupied. As each of them got down from the wagons, Claudia's heart sank. She and Lucius approached the entrance and Vitus pushed open the door. A mouse scurried across the floor and dust was everywhere. There were dirty dishes in the small kitchen area. At least some furniture had been left.

Hotep was surveying the mess with a shocked expression on her face and followed Claudia upstairs. To their relief, there were beds in the three bedrooms.

Satisfied that the house could be livable with a good cleaning, she turned to her handmaid. "You cannot do this alone, Hotep, I will help you."

Hotep shook her head. "This is not work for you, Domina. Perhaps in the town we can find another servant to help?"

"That is a possibility, but for now, if we wish to sleep in this place tonight, we must set to work."

"I will clean. You can make the beds, Domina, and direct the unloading of the wagons. We need to know where to put those things."

Claudia resisted a smile at the directions of her servant, but nodded her head.

The men went to unhitch the mules and horses and see if there was any hay in the stable.

Doros helped his father and Vitus unload the wagons, and Claudia decided to put things in the main room until the house was cleaned. Hotep began scrubbing the kitchen. At least they'd brought soap.

⚬⚬⚬

Vitus went to town and secured the help of two local women who soon had the villa spotless. They had been told that the master of the house had retired from the army and come to Vienne for his health.

There were many Roman exiles in Vienne and people did not ask questions. It was better not to know too much.

Vitus had packed tools and set to work trimming dead branches in the orchard for the fireplace and the kitchen. He and Lucius went to Vienne and sold the ornate wagons and six of the mules. They kept one flat wagon and the last two mules for hauling feed.

Claudia discovered the kitchen garden. A melon and squash had come up by themselves, and she saw the evidence of carrots, garlic, cucumbers, and beans. She and Hotep worked to weed and water it to see what else might come up.

Coming upon his wife on her knees working in the garden, Lucius angrily raised her up. "You are not a servant. This is not work you should be doing."

She looked up at him, sensing more his frustration with their circumstances than anger. "I must do my part, beloved. We must make the money you got for the mules and wagons go as far as possible."

He hung his head. "What have I bought us to, Claudia? The granddaughter of an emperor, raised in the palace of Rome, now reduced to working in her own garden in a wretched villa?"

"We do what we must, Lucius. You had no idea the emperor would rule against you. I am thankful he spared your life. We are together, Lucius, and that is all that matters."

"That is all? What lies ahead for us? The army has been my whole life . . . but now there is no pension. How can I support my family? How will we live?"

"I have jewelry I can sell, and I am skilled at embroidery. I will sell my things in the marketplace. We have Vitus and Hotep to help us, and Doros can go to the local grammar school and get to know other boys his age in the area. We will be all right."

He looked down at her and his eyes were filled with a sadness she had not noticed before. "You will support the family with your jewels and embroidery?"

Why had she not thought before she spoke? Lucius was a proud man. He would never stand for using money from his wife to manage their household.

"Surely there is an opening for someone as knowledgeable as you are in one of the government offices."

"Yes, perhaps." He turned away and left the room. She knew he would walk in the fields where he could think most clearly.

The weeks went by, but there was no work. He was only one of many exiles seeking employment. Some, in desperation, had committed suicide in the hopes that their families could return to Rome unscathed by their scandal. He told Claudia he had met ex-senators and men of praetorian rank like himself, now struggling to live.

A cloud of depression settled on his shoulders, and she watched him with growing anxiety. Even Doros received absentminded responses. One night Lucius fingered the bulla around the boy's neck. It would have been put aside in the ceremony to make Doros a citizen of Rome. It served only as a reminder that he would never be able to parade his son to the Forum ceremony.

They had found a grammar school taught by a former slave, and Doros excelled in literature, Latin, and poetry. The company of other boys his age was exhilarating to him.

Claudia went into the city with Hotep and sold a few pieces of her gold jewelry. The merchant's eyes glittered as he noted the quality. He tried to offer a low price, but Claudia was able to bargain for a price both she and the merchant could live with.

Lucius worked the orchard and the land around the villa. The fruit was ripening and Claudia saw it as the providence of her God, but Lucius felt he had brought his family to a poor existence.

Time and again, Lucius sought work in one of the government offices to no avail. He would return to the villa discouraged, wanting only to sit on a bench and stare out at the fields.

When she tried to encourage him, he flung at her, "What is our life, Claudia? My house and lands are gone and we live only at the discretion of my cousin. You and Doros could go to Rome to your grandmother's villa. You have family there and could return to society."

Fear stabbed at her heart. "What are you saying, Lucius? Do not do what I think you are considering. You would break my heart and the heart of your son. That is not the life I want. I am content here. Do you not remember I grew up in a small villa like this in Reggio? I don't care for all the pomp of Roman society. Please, beloved, there is another way. You will find work, I know you will."

He did not answer. He only drew her head down and kissed her tenderly, as he did when he left on a journey or went out into the fields. She watched him go, silent tears running down her cheeks, her anguish too great to even pray.

51

The wind caused the leaves on a sycamore tree outside the window to slap against the house. The rain had been falling all day in a steady cadence. As Claudia worked on her embroidery, she watched Doros by the fire, studying his assignment from school. Vitus brought in wood to keep the fire going. Lucius was in his study with the door closed. She sighed as she pulled the thread tighter. He spent too much time alone, and no matter how hard she tried to distract him, his depression grew. Vitus found work in the orchard of a nearby villa and gave all he earned to Lucius. His loyalty to Lucius was deep. Claudia wondered what they would do without his help.

One of the sources of his deep pain surfaced one day when Lucius told her of something else Caligula had said. "He accused me of killing a man who called himself the Son of God and wanted to know how I could willfully murder a man considered a prophet by the Jews. He asked me how it feels to put to death a god. The way he said it made me realize I had lost the trial. The emperor had ignored all our testimony. I can still see Caligula's face. It was pure evil staring at me."

Lucius turned a tortured face to her. "It was only a moment, but enough to convince me that Caligula borders on madness." He shook his head sadly. "Are we safe even here?"

She had done everything she knew to reassure him. "You did not put him to death, Lucius, the Jewish leaders did. They gave you no choice. They wanted his death."

She put her arms around his shoulders. "Oh my dear husband, Jesus had to die for all of us. He was the Passover Lamb that was sent for the sins of all of us. He made atonement for us for all time. You must understand. You were part of the plan. He died for you. You are forgiven."

He reached up and touched her hand. "I do not feel forgiven. I should have done more to save him."

"You tried four times to save his life, beloved, and they would have none of it. Didn't they cry, 'His blood be on our heads and on our children'?"

"I washed my hands of it." He examined his hands. "But the blood is still there."

Claudia recoiled. Was he going mad? Could she not convince him?

She took another direction. "Come, dearest, let us retire for the night. You are weary."

"Yes, I am weary. Weary of many things," he said tonelessly as she took his arm and led him out of the study.

To her surprise, Lucius made love to her after many weeks of abstinence. She held him and willed him to come back to her, to be the man she had married, a man who could be ruthless and selfish, but infinitely patient with her and a loving husband.

"The rain is a comforting sound, don't you think?" she asked as she lay with her arm across his chest and her head on his shoulder.

"Yes, a comforting sound." He was silent and then, "I have been blessed with such a wife. You have courage and strength. Something I seem to have lost along the way. I who strove for prestige, a leader of troops and governor of a Roman province, now reduced to the status of a farmer. I was ambitious, but where has it gotten me? A life in exile, far from the country I served. It is a bleak ending to my career."

The fear rose again, filling her being so she could hardly breathe. She forced it down. "But you did all those things. More than some men do in a lifetime. We have a good home here, Lucius, and Doros is doing well in his school. He is intelligent and one day will make us both proud."

"What if my cousin wishes to return? Where would we go? And what advancement will Doros know? He attends school with the sons of senators and magistrates. He will never wear the toga of the praetorian class and be recognized as a citizen of Rome. Not here in Vienne. He must be able to return to Italy and your family if he has any hope of a life."

"We cannot do that, Lucius, at least not now. If another emperor takes the throne, we may be able to petition to return. Perhaps even have your lands restored."

"And when will that be? Caligula reigns supreme, the idol of the people. It could be years, and then it will be too late."

She put a hand on his cheek and kissed him. "We are together, my Lucius, and that is all that matters to me." As she moved her hand, it was wet. Was he weeping? She put her arm back across his chest and held him until they both fell asleep.

Perhaps it was the silence of the end of the rain that woke her. She rolled over to Lucius, but his side of the bed was empty. He often rose early and walked in the fields, but something nagged at her mind and she went to put on her warm linen robe. She went downstairs and looked around. Lucius was not in the house, so she sat down in a chair by the fire and began to pray. She beseeched the Lord to heal her husband of this frightful mood, to help him understand the forgiveness that Jesus could extend to him. She was lost in prayer and startled when the door burst open suddenly. It wasn't her husband, it was Vitus, and with tears running down his cheeks, he held the lifeless body of Lucius in his arms.

52

Lucius! No!" She ran across the room as Vitus gently laid Lucius on a couch. Her husband's face was pale in death, and she knelt, weeping, to cradle his head in her arms.

"I found him at the edge of the field, my lady. There doesn't seem to be a wound anywhere."

"Then how did he die?"

"He has carried great sorrow for a long time, my lady. Either he took poison, or his heart just could not bear the burden any longer."

She looked up through her tears. "Lucius would not leave us like that. He would not take poison."

"If he thought you could return to Rome?"

"But I thought—I hoped—we could be happy here. It was not the Villa Ponti, but we could have had a decent life. Why would he do this to me?"

Vitus put a gentle hand on her shoulder. "A man must work, Domina. His self-worth demands it. He had everything taken away from him."

She rocked back and forth, wrapping her arms around herself. "I needed him. I needed him," she moaned over and over.

Suddenly there was a sound on the stairs and Claudia looked up into the face of her son. His eyes were wide with fright as he stared at the body of his father.

Claudia sat observing the small urn that held the ashes of her husband. Doros had endeavored to be strong for her, but he was only a boy. She had withdrawn him from the school, since she needed to reserve any funds from the sale of her jewelry to return to Rome.

Picking up the scroll that had finally come in response to her query, she read that her grandmother's son-in-law, Paulinus Aemilius Lepidus, learning of her need, had agreed to take them into her grandmother's villa.

Vitus and Hotep packed only what was necessary, for they had only one wagon now. It was late summer. At least they would not have to travel in bad weather.

"It is time, my lady." Vitus stood in the doorway.

Hotep came down the stairs with the last small trunk of personal things and handed it to Vitus.

Claudia went out to the wagon and carefully placed Lucius's urn in the small trunk. Doros sat silently in the wagon—he had not smiled since his father's death, and spoke little. When the women were aboard, Vitus clicked his tongue at the mules.

Claudia brought the money she'd saved from selling pieces of her jewelry, carrying it in a pouch under her clothing, and prayed for the Lord to watch over their long journey back to Rome.

When at last the city came in sight, Claudia was fearful of what awaited her there. Would the emperor order her to leave? The sentence had been against Lucius, but there were rumors of strange behavior on the part of the emperor after he recovered from a nearly fatal illness. He was not the benevolent young man the people had hailed less than a year before.

When Vitus finally pulled into the courtyard of her grandmother's villa, Claudia looked up at the huge two-story building and wondered who would come out to greet them.

A servant appeared and eyed their clothing. "The servant's entrance is around the back," he said finally.

Vitus helped Claudia down and she drew herself up before the servant. "I am Claudia Procula, granddaughter of the Lady Scribonia."

The servant, realizing his error, bid her wait and hurried into the villa.

In moments a tall, heavyset man wearing the purple-striped toga of the praetorian rank, came out to meet her.

"Welcome, Lady Claudia. I am Paulinus Aemilius Lepidus, husband of your aunt Cornelia. Come in." He glanced back at the wagon and noted her simple dress. "This is all you have?"

"It is, my lord. We left Rome with little after the emperor's edict and now that my husband is dead, I return with little. This was the only transportation available to us, and my husband's servant has watched over us and brought us safely here. I am in debt to you for your gracious hospitality in our circumstances."

Doros climbed down from the wagon and came to stand beside his mother.

"This is our son, Doros. He has been a great help to me in our distress."

The man's face softened. "These are dark days, Lady Claudia. Many are in your circumstances. You and your son are family and welcome to whatever we can do for you."

"I shall look forward to meeting Cornelia."

He sighed. "Unfortunately, she died two years ago."

She put a gentle hand on his arm. "I am so sorry to hear that."

"It is as the gods will."

Her personal things were taken to her grandmother's old quarters. Doros was led to a smaller room near Claudia's to refresh himself.

Now she stood on the steps of the villa facing Vitus. "You are leaving us?"

"I promised your husband that I would look after you if something happened to him. You will be safe here, my lady."

"Where will you go?"

"I wish to seek out my own relatives if any of them are still alive."

"Then you have my blessing on your quest, Vitus, and thank you for all you've done."

She gave him the wagon and mules and watched him drive away with mixed emotions. Now it was only she and Doros, and Hotep. As she climbed the stairs, she contemplated what to do with Hotep—her maidservant, yes, but a loyal friend. Vitus, a freedman, had stayed out of loyalty. Hotep had no choice. Feeling suddenly bereft, Claudia made her way to her quarters, once again in a home that was not her own.

She sat at dinner with her host, refreshed and dressed as a Roman matron again. She turned to him. "Tell me, Paulinus, what is the latest news of Rome? I have been away so long."

He glanced around. "Many things are happening, Lady Claudia. We revere our emperor, yet there are strange changes. We walk carefully these days."

His words were guarded and Claudia caught the warning in his tone.

"Will my presence here cause difficulties for you?"

"I don't believe so. Friends in the palace keep me informed. However, what I hear causes me to be wary."

She found herself wondering how long she would be able to impose on his friendship and hospitality.

53

To her relief, two years passed without incident. She was grateful for the kindness of her host. He seemed to enjoy having a woman in the villa again, adding her touch with flowers and conversation at dinner. Paulinus provided a small allowance for her needs and for Doros's school.

Hotep found a small group of believers who met in a home, and the two women and Doros slipped out when they could to join them and share their love of the Lord. Doros was able to tell them about his crippled foot, and how Jesus had healed him. Claudia enjoyed the hymns they sang from the Psalms of David and felt her faith growing day by day. The sorrow that had made her heart feel like stone began to lift and she praised her God for his mercy.

One morning as Claudia walked in the garden, her thoughts were broken by someone calling her name. She turned to see Paulinus, hurrying across the garden, his face pale.

"I have dire news. The emperor is dead, slain by one of his own guards. His uncle, Claudius, was found and declared emperor by the Praetorian Guard who dared the senate to oppose them!" He shook his head. "What will Rome be subjected to now?"

Caligula was dead! Hope rose in her heart. Did she dare petition the new emperor to restore her husband's estate to her? Would he consider the fact that Doros was the great-grandson of an emperor and be lenient?

Paulinus went on, "Of course Caligula was totally mad, his debaucheries a disgrace to the throne, but Claudius?" He sank down on a stone bench and put his face in his hands.

After a battle between the armies loyal to the senate and the several thousand armed men of the Praetorian Guard, the senate surrendered. All of Rome watched with apprehension as Claudius was crowned emperor. The new emperor's reputation was that of an idiot, shunned by family and kept in seclusion due to the fact that he limped, stuttered, and at times drooled.

In spite of the rumors, as the months progressed, the populace of Rome found Claudius to be an able ruler. Seeking to cement his ties to the military that had placed him on the throne, Claudius planned a major military expedition into Britain. Because of his preoccupation with this campaign, he appeared oblivious to the actions of his second wife, Valeria Messalina.

An astute player of politics, Valeria used her physical charms as a weapon, destroying lovers when she had no more use for them. Jealous for her son, Britannicus, now the heir apparent, she sought to eliminate any contenders for the throne. As rumors spread, Claudia realized it was only a matter of time until Valeria learned of Doros, the great-grandson of Caesar Augustus. Would Valeria consider her son a threat? Must they flee again? Where would they go?

Paulinus had introduced her to several eligible men of position and was speaking generously of a particular senator when Claudia interrupted him. She knew she must stop hiding her faith from her cousin, even if he would withdraw his protection.

"Forgive me, dear cousin, I must speak. I am forever indebted to you for your shelter these past two years. But I cannot marry a man devoted to the gods of Rome. When my son's deformed foot was healed by him, I became not only a Godfearer but a follower of the Jewish healer, Jesus."

"You have not spoken of this before. Jesus is dead, by order of your husband. How can one follow a dead prophet? I see no reason to rebuff a suitor over another god."

"The man I marry must believe as I do, Paulinus."

His eyes flashed with anger. "You repudiate the gods of Rome? Trouble is brewing and you shall bring it down on my house!"

She bowed her head. "I do not wish to put you in any danger. You have shown us kindness in every way."

At her submissive manner, Paulinus calmed down. He waved a hand impatiently. "I suppose you will believe as you must, but these are difficult times. If your son comes to the attention of Valeria, we are all in danger."

"I must leave as soon as possible. I only wait for word from friends." She leaned forward, her eyes beseeching him. "I cannot take Hotep. I will give her a document of freedom. Would you allow her to remain here? I don't want to endanger her life as well."

He considered the request a moment. "I will help her. I am sorry you must leave, but it is the safest way for us all."

She rose and, thanking him again for his kindness, bid him good night. She hurried to her quarters to see if Hotep had returned and was relieved to find her handmaid waiting.

"Domina, I have news. You and Doros are to be taken to the catacombs where you will be safe. The Roman soldiers believe dead spirits are present there and will not enter. You must go tonight. Someone will meet you and your son outside the back gate when the moon is high." She pointed to a large cloth bag. "I have packed for you both, only what you can carry."

Relief flooded Claudia. "Oh Hotep, thank you. Paulinus has agreed to allow you to remain here. I am setting you free, so the future will

be your choice. You have been a faithful friend and I will miss you."
She handed Hotep her document of freedom.

Hotep embraced her mistress and they clung to each other for a long moment, tears running down their cheeks.

Finally Hotep stepped back. "I was so afraid. I didn't know what to do."

"Goodbye, dear friend. Your service over the years has blessed me. I wish you well."

"May our Lord watch over you and your son," Hotep murmured, and with her freedom in hand, she fled from the room.

⁂

Claudia gathered her remaining jewelry and put the pouch into the traveling bag. Then she and Doros slipped out to the garden and waited. Paulinus would be able to say she had run away and he didn't know where she was. She hoped it would protect him.

There was a soft knock on the gate and Claudia cautiously opened it. A man stood on the step. "I am to take you to the safe place." He was tall and well built. He had a beard but didn't look Jewish. His dark eyes surveyed her and she was startled by the feeling his eyes evoked in her. Still, she had to be cautious.

"What is your name?"

His deep voice was almost soothing. "It is best you do not know."

She hesitated still. "What is the secret word?"

"*Ichthus*, the fish."

Claudia and Doros followed their guide through the maze of streets, both wearing dark cloaks that hid their faces. They walked a long time before rounding a deserted building and entering a hidden opening in the granite cliffs. Claudia felt chills run down her back as they passed indentations in the rock where skeletons lay amidst decaying burial wrappings. The air was stale and she pulled her shawl over her nose. They wound their way through a series of tunnels and came to a cavernous room where people were gathered in various groups.

Small cooking fires burned. She turned to thank her guide, but he was nowhere in sight.

She looked around, wondering what to do next, when a familiar voice spoke her name. It was Medina!

Overcome at finding a beloved friend in this strange place, Claudia fell into her arms. When she regained control, she stepped back. "How is it you are in this place, Medina?"

"I am a courier, my lady. I help bring those seeking refuge from Roman persecution to this place of safety, just as Quintas has done."

His name was Quintas.

Medina put her arm around Doros. "Come to my fire and warm yourselves. I have food."

She shared cheese, a small loaf of dark bread, and some apple cider from her meager supply.

Claudia looked around as she and Doros ate. "How long do people live here?"

"Only as long as is necessary. When we can, we get them out of the city and on to other countries or safer areas." Medina looked around and whispered. "It is best we find a way to smuggle you out of the city. Valeria is looking for you. For your own sake, I will simply call you Claudia. It is safer for others not to know who you are. There have been betrayals, mostly for money."

"The man, Quintas, is he trustworthy?"

Medina smiled sadly. "He was a Roman magistrate and was away on business when Caligula had his family murdered. The wife of Quintas rebuffed Caligula's amorous overtures."

Cold chills went over Claudia's body. She remembered the banquet and Caligula's subtle invitation and perusal of her. Could that be why . . . ? She shook the thoughts away. It was too late to even think of those things.

Medina went on, "Quintas is a believer and was found at his villa in great anguish. Knowing the soldiers would return to look for him, two of our brothers brought him here to save his life."

Claudia's heart went out to him. How would she feel if she came home one day and found Doros murdered? It was enough that Lucius was dead, possibly by his own hand.

Claudia and Doros rested three days as Medina sought for a way to smuggle them out of Rome. Soldiers were everywhere, looking for a woman and a boy of about eleven years old.

"Mater, will we have to stay here forever?"

She smiled. "No, my son, not forever. Medina will find a way to help us."

She and Doros gathered with the other believers, some of whom were Jews, who brought Scriptures from the Pentateuch. She listened to the comforting words of the Most High God and the songs of David from the psalms. Peace settled on her spirit and she knew she was in the hands of the One she could trust with all her heart.

From time to time she would look up and see Quintas watching her. Something in her heart wanted to soothe the sadness she saw in his face.

As she sat working on her embroidery, he came and sat down on the carpet beside her. "Why are you hiding from the empress? There are rumors of a great search in the city."

The directness of his question startled her. "My son is in danger."

"Your son?"

She looked into blue eyes the color of cobalt. "He is the great-grandson of Caesar Augustus."

His eyes widened a moment and he nodded slowly. "That would be enough for Valeria."

She felt directness was in order on her part. "I am sorry about your family. How many children did you have?"

The pain crossed his face and she saw him clench his fists. "Two girls and a boy. He had just been given his toga and been declared a citizen of Rome. I hoped he would follow me into government service."

They spoke of their mutual heartaches and loss. When he learned her husband's name, he frowned. "The man who killed the Christ."

She felt renewed pain and anger at the assumption. What did this man know of her husband and what he went through? "It was not possible to save him. The Jewish leaders would have found another way to get rid of him."

"But he was the Messiah, the chosen one."

"The people wanted a conquering king. One who would free them from our Roman oppression. What they did not recognize was that he came as a suffering Messiah. His death bought our freedom, not from the Roman Empire but from our own sin. My husband was a part of the plan of the Most High God, even though he did not know it."

He studied her face and she became uncomfortable. Why did she feel so unsettled when he looked at her?

"I had never thought of it that way," he said at last. He rubbed his beard with his hand.

"Did he not rise from the dead as he had raised others?" she countered, pressing her point.

"So he did. The grave could not hold him. I heard him speak to the crowds once. I came as a scoffer, ready to discredit him as a charlatan, but his words pierced my heart and would not let me go. I became a believer. My wife eventually believed also."

"Then you will join her one day in the kingdom, Quintas."

It was the first time she had used his name.

He rose and stood looking down at her. "This is no place for a boy to grow up. We need to get you out of Rome. I have an idea. Perhaps Medina can help us."

Before she could ask him what it was, he was striding away, looking for Medina.

※

The next day Medina came to Claudia with a bundle under her arm. It turned out to be peasant clothing for Claudia and Doros to wear. When Doros opened his garments, he stepped back. "These are girl's clothes, Medina. I cannot wear these."

Medina tipped his chin with one finger. "My Doros, the soldiers are looking for a boy and his mother. You would be stopped immediately before you got out of the city. To save your life and that of your mother, you must dress as a girl. Quintas came up with this idea. You will leave the city with a man who is dressed as a farmer. He has an old ox cart, pulled by a mule. The soldiers aren't looking for a poor family."

Doros nodded reluctantly. "If it is the only way—"

Claudia put on the frayed garments while Doros, still mumbling, put on his tunic and headscarf along with the bracelets.

Medina smiled mischievously. "I hope you like pigs."

Doros stared at her. "Why?"

"Because you will ride with a small pig in the back of the cart."

He looked at Medina, lifting his chin. "I like pigs," he answered bravely.

Medina embraced Claudia, tears in her eyes.

Claudia held her tightly. "You have been like a mother to me. I will always miss you."

When they were ready, Medina led them toward another exit where a cart and mule waited. The driver was Quintas.

54

Quintas didn't speak. He drove the cart hunched like an old man, but she was sure he was alert for any sign of danger. Her heart pounded in fear as they passed groups of Roman soldiers, but no one looked their way. The marketplace was busy still in the late afternoon, and the cart moved along steadily but slowly, lest they call attention to themselves. Other travelers and farmers joined them heading out of the city. Claudia's traveling bag was used as a pillow by Doros, who clutched his pig tightly. The bag held only food for their journey and some simple clean garments—nothing unusual if the soldiers looked through it.

Soldiers were stopping carriages looking for a woman of upper class. Claudia prayed silently and blessed Quintas for his ingenuity. They passed through the city without being stopped.

The countryside was in bloom and she breathed in the air scented by flowers along the side of the road. Birds sang in the trees and she heard the buzzing of bees over the wheat fields.

"Where are we going?"

"Ephesus. It is the farthest point on the Royal Road from Rome, but it is almost thirteen hundred kilometers. Are you up to such a journey?"

"I will do what I have to for my son's sake."

She turned to look down at Doros and smiled indulgently. Only a boy could sleep innocently at a time like this.

Quintas inclined his head toward the back of the cart. "How is your son?"

"He sleeps, the pig also."

Quintas chuckled and then grew somber. "My son was almost his age."

"How long has it been?"

"Almost two years. I considered revenge and friends had to forcibly remove me from my villa. We made it to the nearby forest just before the soldiers came looking for me. I got drunk for the first six months. I was a believer, but angry with God." He shook his head. "Caligula was insane. I'm surprised he wasn't assassinated sooner than he was. I'm glad he's gone, but it cannot bring back my family."

"What made the change? You said you were angry—"

"I met Medina one day in the marketplace. She told me to come with her. How she knew me, I don't know. Why I followed her, I also don't know. She brought me to the catacombs and introduced me to other fugitives from Caligula. When I heard their stories, I realized others had also suffered, and I had nowhere else to go. Caligula had seized my estate and holdings. I'd been a magistrate and now a fugitive. I grew a beard since Roman upper class are clean shaven, and started helping bring others who were in danger to safety—as I brought you."

"I too am grateful for Medina." She told him about Reggio and her mother and grandmother. She told about cooking with Medina in their small kitchen. As she shared about leaving her mother, she felt sad, but realized that the pain was gone."

"How did you like living in the palace with Tiberius?"

"I seldom saw him. I was terrified of Sejanus." She told him about his attack on Hotep and the vengeful orders for Lucius on their wedding day.

He raised his eyebrows. "So you didn't see your husband again for two months from the day you were married?"

She glanced sideways at him, but he looked straight ahead, a smile twitching his lips.

"It made our reunion all the sweeter."

The miles rolled on as they shared stories about their lives. Doros woke up. "Mater, I am hungry. Do we have anything to eat?"

Quintas pulled the cart to the side of the road and they got out, stretching their legs. Claudia found fresh bread, cheese, and fresh pears wrapped in linen that Medina had packed for them. Quintas produced a goatskin bag of water mixed with wine. When they were refreshed, they started on the road again.

"Where shall we sleep tonight?" The voice from the back of the cart held a plaintive note.

"I'm not sure, Doros." She turned to Quintas, a question in her eyes.

"The highway is patrolled by Roman soldiers, but it is best we not sleep out in the open unless we can find a large party traveling together for protection. Perhaps a mansio if we can find one that charges little."

"Do you have any money, Quintas?"

"Some coins, perhaps not enough to reach Ephesus. I will try to find work along the way."

"I brought some of my jewelry, but I don't know how to sell it in the marketplace without calling attention to myself. What should I do?"

He rubbed his chin. "There is a town coming up. Let me try."

When they reached the town, he pulled the cart to one side and looked around the marketplace. Seeing a merchant who sold jewelry, he took a ring from her and bade them wait in the shadows with the cart.

He walked up to the merchant and held out the ring. The merchant's eyes lit up greedily at the sight of the jewelry. Claudia had told Quintas what she paid for it in Caesarea, so he bargained with the merchant until in exasperation the merchant agreed to a price. It wasn't what the ring was worth, but it was enough.

He got in the cart and gave the money to her. "This will fill our stomachs for a while."

As they ate a simple meal, Quintas unrolled a map of the Royal

Road to show Doros. He pointed to the towns and cities they would encounter on the way. Doros, hungry for the attention of a man, took in every word.

Claudia also took in every word, for she loved the sound of his deep voice, and when he spoke, something resonated in her that had been dormant a long time. She felt her heart quicken when he looked at her but despaired of his finding her attractive. She had not bathed in days and had no fine clothes. Her hair was simply bound by a cloth.

The innkeeper, assuming they were a married couple, gave them a single room. As she stood looking at the one bed, Quintas smiled. "Doros, we shall make our beds on the floor so your mother will sleep well."

Doros yawned. There was no other choice, and exhausted, all three slept soundly.

Quintas was able to sell more jewelry with two other merchants in separate towns without suspicion. He got enough to pay for food and lodging for several nights. They also sold the pig, to the dismay of Doros, who had gotten attached to the animal.

Once Quintas got a job with a farmer on their way and they stopped three days while he helped harvest grapes. They were given a room in the farmer's house to stay briefly, and Quintas graciously slept on a mat on the floor, giving Claudia and Doros the bed. As he stretched out to sleep, Claudia glanced at his lean body and thought of Lucius. She missed his touch and lovemaking. It had been a long time and she felt the stirrings of dormant feelings. Was she falling in love with Quintas? Her thoughts kept her awake for an hour or so, listening to the man's soft snores, and finally putting her heart and her future in the hands of her Lord, she fell asleep.

She was able to heat water in a large iron pot over a fire and brought a basin to their room. Doros had a bath and put on clean clothes. She heated water for herself, dressed, and bound up her hair. She washed their dirty clothes and spread them out in the sun on bushes to dry.

The farmer was kind and gave them food for their journey—grapes, bread, and goat cheese. Quintas refilled the goatskin bag, and bidding the farmer farewell with their thanks, they once more headed toward Ephesus.

Over the next few days they passed detachments of Roman soldiers, but the soldiers paid little attention to a poor family plodding slowly along the side of the road in a cart.

It took them over two weeks to reach their destination, and Claudia and Doros were awed by the size of the city. They marveled at the beautiful buildings and temples. Their small cart was almost lost in the mass of people and animals traveling about the city. Quintas pulled out a smaller scroll he had put in his waistband and studied the directions to a settlement of believers who would give them shelter.

He drove through the *Agora*, the marketplace, where they bought food for themselves and the mule who had plodded along faithfully but was obviously weary.

Quintas eyed the mule. "When we find the believers, we will sell the cart and mule."

They wound through several streets, and Quintas was forced to make a few inquiries, but they found the street they were looking for and a large villa set back from the road.

He jumped down from the cart and knocked on the door. When a man answered, he told them they were refugees from Rome and had been given this address as a place to go.

The man glanced at Claudia and Doros and then back at Quintas. "This is your wife?"

"No, I was her escort to help get her and her son out of the city. Their lives were at stake. We have traveled two weeks to get here. Can you take us in?"

"And is there something you can tell me that vouches for who you are?" It was not said unkindly.

Quintas smiled. "Ichthus, the fish."

The man smiled. "Welcome. Please come in."

Claudia gratefully stepped down from the cart and, with Doros at her side, entered the house with Quintas.

❧

After being introduced to the host, Elijah, and his wife, Zeanna, they met two other families and two women who cooked and took care of the house. They were all family here, Elijah told them, and each did a share of work. No one had slaves.

Claudia had come a long way from being the pampered wife of the governor of a province of Rome. Yet, she felt a happiness she hadn't imagined.

After a simple meal of broiled fish, salad, and warm bread, Elijah asked them to tell their stories as an encouragement to the others. No one kept secrets here and a nod from Quintas told her it was safe to share.

Claudia told them who she was and why they had to flee Rome. When she mentioned her husband, there were some raised eyebrows, but she told them how Lucius had tried to save him and reminded them of the Lord's resurrection. Lucius had only been an unwitting part of what they ultimately realized was God's plan. When Doros shared about his foot, they praised God for his mercy.

Quintas in turn told about hearing Jesus speak, becoming a believer along with his wife, and then losing his family and becoming a fugitive himself.

Elijah observed Claudia. "Was it not difficult to travel together for such a long period of time?"

Quintas knew what he was asking. "The lady Claudia is a virtuous woman to be treated with respect. My mission was to see her and her son to safety."

Elijah nodded and Claudia felt the group accepted Quintas's words.

After the meal, the group gathered to pray. Rebecca, whose husband had been killed and their property seized, produced a lyre and sang some of the psalms. Her words were full of longing and her soft voice brought tears to Claudia's eyes. When Claudia finally looked across the circle at Quintas, he was looking at her, and in his face she saw that same longing. She lowered her eyes, her heart beating a little faster.

As the meeting went on, her son's eyes began to droop and soon he was asleep with his head on Claudia's lap.

Elijah took one of the olive oil lamps and motioned for them to follow him. He showed Claudia to a room she would share with Doros. Quintas, who had carried the sleeping Doros, laid him down and turned to Claudia. "He will sleep. Come, walk with me for a few moments."

She hesitated, but Doros was sleeping soundly, so she nodded and they left the room. Elijah showed Quintas his room down the hall and lit a lamp on a pedestal in the hall before saying good night.

She walked with Quintas in the small garden in the center of the villa and stood looking up at a sky full of stars. He was quiet, as though something was on his heart. She broke the silence.

"You have cared for us on this long journey. You have been patient with my son. For that I am grateful. I can tell that he admires you."

"He is a fine young man. You can be proud of him."

"I am most grateful he shares my faith."

He turned and gazed down at her. "What will you do now?"

She sighed. "If they will allow Doros and me to stay here, I will help in any way I can. I have nowhere else to go."

"Have you thought of marrying again?"

The question startled her. What was he saying? "Only if God wills it and the man of his choice comes into my life." Then she blurted, "What will you do in Ephesus?"

He didn't hesitate. "I must find work and a place to live. I am considering marrying again."

It struck a blow to her heart, but she kept her composure. "I wish you well in your endeavors then."

His eyes were dark pools in the dim light, but she sensed he was smiling. "Come, it is late and you and your son need your rest after a long journey."

He took her to her door and left her there as she puzzled over his words.

The next morning at breakfast, Quintas was missing. Elijah told her he'd left early. Would she ever see him again? She tried to be strong for Doros, who was also disappointed not to see Quintas. She must consider his future, yet her heart felt suddenly bereft.

It was three days before, to her surprise, Quintas returned to the villa. She was so overjoyed to see him, she couldn't help the happiness that spilled from her eyes.

When they were alone in the garden again, she asked, "Where did you go? I thought you had left us."

"I was looking for work. I found a job in one of the government buildings that pays an adequate wage. My experience stood me well. I start in two days."

"I'm glad for you, Quintas. Doros will be sorry he missed you. He has started school."

"And did you miss me, Claudia?"

She hung her head, her voice almost a whisper. "Yes, Quintas."

"The Lord has brought us together," he said softly, "under circumstances we may not have chosen. Yet, as we have traveled together, I have seen what a woman of courage and strength you are. I thought that after my wife was killed, I would never look at another woman, but there is something between us. I know you feel it too."

She looked up earnestly into his face. "I have grieved for my husband a long time. I do not know how it happened, but my heart quickens when you are near."

"Your son needs a father, and I desire a wife."

She glanced up quickly. "Just a wife? Someone to cook and clean for you?"

He tipped her chin with his finger. "No, my beautiful Claudia, not just any wife will do. I have someone very special in mind. Someone who has stolen my heart."

As she grasped his meaning, joy filled her heart. She leaned toward him and he kissed her forehead gently. "Let that be a promise." He studied he face. "I have little to offer you, worthy of your status."

"Neither of us have any status, Quintas. Not any longer. I am just a widow who has fallen on hard times, but I would not trade where I am now for all the prestige I had before."

"I needed to find work to be able to support a family, and that I have done. Will you become my wife, Claudia?"

"I have waited this long for you to come into my life, Quintas. I will be your wife."

He drew her into his arms and kissed her again, sealing their promise to each other.

Epilogue

Claudia hummed as she placed the twigs one by one into the bottom of the small clay stove. Her kitchen was small, but Quintas had built her some shelves to store their meager supplies. When she went to the marketplace, she shopped carefully, looking for the best bargains. Thanks to Medina's help years before, she was creative with her herbs and spices, but it was no small task to keep her husband and son well fed.

She mused on how much Quintas had become a father to Doros. Because Lucius had been distant, Doros reveled in the camaraderie with his stepfather. She looked over at the shadow on the wall marking the time of day and knew Doros would be home from school soon. No longer a small boy, he seemed to be growing taller as each month went by. He would never celebrate his majority in the forum as did the sons of other wealthy Romans, but that didn't matter anymore. He was only the son of a government worker and was known as Doros, son of Quintas, at his school. With all they had been through, he understood well the need to keep his true identity secret. The wife of Emperor Claudius, Valeria Messalina, was still a distant threat. Rumors and word of multiple murders and suicides in Rome were rampant. No one appeared safe from the tentacles of her desire to rid Rome of all contenders to the throne, save her own son.

Claudia was grateful to God that she and Doros had been spirited out of Rome when they were. Had she remained with Paulinus, she and her son would have been captured and killed.

She had word through the believer's grapevine that Paulinus still resided in his villa, though she was sure the soldiers had indeed come. He must have convinced them that she had run away and was probably hiding out somewhere in the city. To Claudia's relief, the soldiers had not arrested him.

Medina sent word a year later that Hotep had returned to Egypt, traveling with other former Egyptian slaves who had come to know the Christ. They would take the word and the news of the kingdom to Egypt.

Her thoughts turned to Vitus. A man who had been so loyal to her husband and had made it possible for her to reach Rome safely. She prayed that all was well with him.

Just then there was the sound of the door opening and Doros burst into the small house. Full of exuberance and a quick mind, he would choose a worthy occupation in time, perhaps in the government buildings where Quintas worked.

"Mater, the teacher praised my work today. I was able to recite all of our assigned lines from the great poet, Homer."

"I am proud of you, my son, and I will let you tell Quintas yourself."

He beamed and looked in her kitchen for the apple she usually saved for him.

"We will eat our meal as soon as Quintas gets home, so only the apple, Doros."

"Yes, Mater."

Claudia was sad that Doros would only be able to attend school a very short time longer, for it took much of their income to pay the teacher. Perhaps Quintas would have some suggestions tonight. They must talk about it.

A short time later, Quintas returned. He looked tired but always had a smile and a kiss for her. Tonight he kissed her, but seemed distracted. He put a hand on Doro's shoulder and listened as Doros shared his praise from the teacher.

Finally, with a glance at Claudia, he sighed. "Doros, you will not be able to return to school."

The boy looked up at him with wide eyes, "Why? Am I not doing well?"

"You are doing very well. We are very proud of you, but there are rumors through my sources that the soldiers of Valeria are coming even this far, seeking you and your mother. We must be very cautious. No one here knows who you are, other than my son, but we must not take any chances."

Doros face fell, but he gave Quintas a brave smile. "I will not go then."

Claudia put a hand on her husband's arm. "Do you think she can still find us?"

"I don't think so, dear one, but we must not take a chance. Perhaps we should have changed his name when he started at that school."

"But Quintas, he is known there as your son. I'm sure there are many boys named Doros in the Roman Empire, and it is a Greek name."

He put his arms around her and held her close. "I would not lose someone so dear to me again. When you go to the marketplace, cover your face as some of the women do. Do not do anything that would call attention to you."

"We will pray, Quintas, and the God we serve will protect us. I know he will. Has he not seen us to safety thus far?"

"That is true, and we must be grateful. We can only trust—there is nothing more we can do."

The three of them sat down to their dinner. Claudia had obtained a good piece of fish and some cheese. She had ground the meal that morning for the coarse bread that was a staple of their meals now. With diluted wine, they felt they had a fine meal.

When Doros had gone to his bed in a small alcove and they knew he was asleep, Claudia took her husband's hand and drew him down on their small couch. He sat with his elbows on his knees, listening.

"It is perhaps a good thing that Doros cannot continue school, though it grieves me. He loves to learn." Claudia looked down at their entwined hands. "There may be another need for those funds."

Quintas straightened up. "What need is this?"

She looked up into his eyes and smiled. "It is for our child when he or she is born around seven months from now."

He stared at her and then caught her in his arms. "You are sure?"

"Yes, my Quintas, I am sure."

His smile seemed to go clear across his face. "Oh, beloved, you have made me a man even happier than I have been all these months." He paused. "Have you told Doros yet?"

"No, foolish man, would I not tell his father first?"

"We will tell him in the morning."

They prayed together, thanking the Lord for this blessing, and then he drew her again to himself. His kiss sent a warmth through her.

<hr>

"I shall have a brother or sister?" Doros crowed. He hugged his mother and beamed at Quintas.

Claudia had wondered how Doros would accept the news and she breathed a sigh of relief.

Quintas left the house and promised to see if he could find an apprentice job at the government buildings for Doros.

Claudia studied Homer with Doros and marveled at his ability to memorize the lines so quickly. She prayed that Quintas could find something to keep Doros occupied. She needed to go into the marketplace and debated about taking Doros, then thought better of it.

"You must remain here, my son. The soldiers are looking for a noblewoman and her son, not a poor village woman. It is best we are not seen together. Stay here and lock the door."

As she hurried into the marketplace, she kept her head down and her palla wrapped around her head and shoulders, obscuring her face. To the observer, she was only a poor village wife, purchasing a few items for her family's dinner.

She found some day-old vegetables the vendor was willing to part with cheaply and some fruit for Doros. Then she saw a small plucked quail that looked as if it had been there awhile. Knowing that she could make it into a soup, she bargained for it and triumphantly added it to her basket.

As she walked down the narrow street toward her home, Claudia had a strange sense of apprehension. *Lord, what is wrong?* She entered the house and was met by silence. Doros was gone. Her heart pounded as she rushed over to a neighbor's house. Galla, a heavyset Greek woman, had befriended her, and as they got to know each other, Galla quietly revealed she was also a Christian.

"Galla, Doros is gone. Have you seen him?"

A subdued Doros appeared from the other room. Relief flooded her being as she embraced her son. "Doros, why are you here? I told you to stay at home."

Tears filled his eyes as he looked up at her. "I was staying home, Mater, but then the Lord spoke to me and told me to go to Galla's house."

"The Lord spoke to you?"

"It was in my head, but it was so strong, I went."

Galla, who had been standing by, shook her head in amazement. "The soldiers were on the street, going from door to door, asking questions. When they came here, I told them he was my son, Nikos, and his father was Greek." She shrugged. "May the Lord forgive a small untruth."

"What did the soldiers say?"

"They turned away and went on down the street. They did not even stop at your house, though the door was in plain sight."

"Praise his name, Galla, Surely he has protected us once again."

"Mater, can we go home now?"

321

Galla spoke up. "We have had a close call, but let us rejoice. I have some fresh baklava. Let me send some home with you for your dinner."

Her son's eyes lit up. It was his favorite dessert, but Claudia seldom had the money to buy the ingredients.

When Quintas returned that night, Claudia told him what had happened. "Do you think they will return?"

"I don't know. If they remain in the city, we may have to go to the safe house again. I cannot take a chance on losing you or Doros. Galla was very brave and I am grateful to her for her quick thinking. We must pray and seek the Lord as to what we must do. We must not go ahead of his will for us."

Claudia, Quintas, and Doros prayed fervently and Claudia felt strongly they should stay where they were. Quintas felt the same and promised to keep his eyes and ears open to any news of Valeria.

Two nights later, he came home and his eyes were shining. "Claudia, the soldiers are withdrawing from the city. The attachment sent by Valeria is gone. Valeria is dead,"

"She is dead? What happened?"

"She was caught up in her own web of intrigue and murder. She divorced the emperor and secretly married Gaius Silius, the consul elect. The emperor recognized it as an attempt to take the throne and had her killed, along with Silius."

"So she met the same end she meted out to others."

"Yes, my love, but the most important thing is that we are safe. There will be no more soldiers hunting you and Doros down."

Safe. Claudia could hardly conceive of the magnitude of that word. She would not have to fear being recognized in the marketplace by a Roman soldier. They could live their lives in the open. The woman who had known wealth, prestige, danger, and ultimately sorrow as the wife of Lucius Pontius Pilate, was now the wife of Quintas, a contented woman with a husband who loved her. That other world seemed only like a dream that had passed away, leaving only its memory. She was safe at last.

Author's Note

How do you weave a story around a person who is only mentioned in one paragraph in the Gospels? There is also a Claudia mentioned in 2 Timothy. Is this the same Claudia? This is where research comes in. I had to determine Claudia's background.

Claudia is believed to be the daughter of Julia, who was the only daughter of Caesar Augustus. Julia's mother, Scribonia, was divorced by Augustus when Julia was born because he wanted to marry another woman. He takes Julia away from Scribonia to be brought up in the palace. Julia was married at fourteen to a cousin, and widowed at the ripe old age of sixteen. As she is recovering from that, her father marries her to Agrippa, who is forty-one. They have five children before he dies. While she is still in mourning from that marriage, her father marries her to Tiberius, who is being groomed as his successor to the throne. One problem: Tiberius is happily married to Vipsania, who is expecting their first child. He is forced to divorce Vipsania and marry the emperor's daughter, who by now is rebelling and generally living a wild lifestyle. Tiberius and Julia hate each other. They have one child who dies. Then, due to her growing reputation and his embarrassment, Tiberius leaves for Rhodes while Julia's father, Augustus, serves her with the divorce papers. The senate, ready to condemn Julia to death, allows her father to save her life by banishing her from Rome.

After years of separation, Scribonia is finally given permission to join her daughter in exile. Julia, not about to give up her suitors, gives birth to Claudia illegitimately and refuses to reveal the father . . .

Well, I could go on, but do you see a story here? So much intrigue and changing of partners, it read like Hollywood.

Due to what she has experienced, Claudia becomes a strong woman, one who must temper the personality of Pontius Pilate as he makes blunder after blunder as governor of Judea.

Much speculation exists about whether Pilate became a believer. There is an Orthodox church named for him, so I would like to believe that he finally realized who Jesus was and that he was forgiven. How Pilate died is also speculation. Some say he committed suicide, some say he died in exile of natural causes. No two accounts were consistent. Some historians didn't even mention Claudia, and the timelines I looked at did not always agree.

At least that left things open for some poetic license and freedom to write my own story. Was it true? Is that the way it happened? No one knows but our Lord.

Acknowledgments

I would like to thank my editor, Lonnie Hull Dupont, at Revell, for her encouragement and for giving me the opportunity to write for a great publishing house; my agent, Joyce Hart of Hartline Literary Agency, for believing in me for so many years and for her encouragement; Barb Barnes, editor, who made sure my timelines, maps, and locations were right on; Lindsay Davis, marketing manager, and Jennifer Nutter, marketing assistant, for a job well done; Michele Misiak, for her expertise as marketing manager in previous books and early work on *Claudia*; and Cheryl Van Andel, senior art director, for her exquisite taste in cover design. I'd also like to thank the members of the San Diego Christian Writer's Guild critique group at the home of Martha Gorris and the online critique group for their insights and suggestions in so many chapters in the writing of this story. I would especially like to thank my friend Dr. Vicki Hesterman for helping me pare down the final manuscript when I got carried away with the Roman Empire and the history of this fascinating woman who appears so briefly in the Scriptures. Her expertise in the field of journalism and editing was invaluable.

I thank my daughter, Karen Eubanks, for her encouragement and insights as the story progressed. Also, I thank my Spiritual Life Book Club ladies for their prayers and encouragement through the years.

I would like to thank the people who tirelessly input information on the internet for seekers like me; for the authors of other books on Claudia, for their wonderful and unique stories; and lastly, I thank the Holy Spirit, for giving me inspiration when I wasn't sure which direction to go when I came to an impasse.

Kudos to my patient husband, Frank, who entertains himself while I spend hours on my computer!

Lastly, I am grateful to the Lord, who has allowed me the amazing privilege of sharing my stories at this time of my life.

Diana Wallis Taylor is an award-winning author, poet, and songwriter. *Journey to the Well* debuted in 2009, as did her Christian romance, *Smoke Before the Wind*. Her collection of poetry, *Wings of the Wind*, came out in 2007. A former teacher, she retired in 1990 as director of conference services for a private college. After their marriage in 1990, she and her husband moved to northern California where she fulfilled a dream of owning a bookshop/coffeehouse for writers' groups and poetry readings and was able to devote more time to her writing.

The Taylors have six grown children between them and ten grandchildren. They now live in the San Diego area, where between writing projects Diana participates in Christian Women's Fellowship, serves on the board of the San Diego Christian Writers Guild, and is active in the music ministry of her church. She enjoys teaching poetry and writing workshops, and sharing her heart with women of all ages.

Visit Diana's website at www.dianawallistaylor.com.

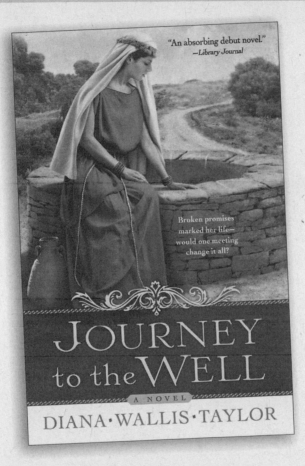

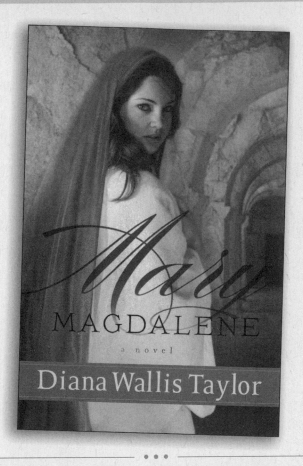